# WALKER

## *In the Company of Snipers*

### Book 21

# IRISH WINTERS

WINDY DAYS
PRESS

# COPYRIGHT

**Walker; In the Company of Snipers, Book 21**

Copyright ©2020 by Irish Winters
All rights reserved

First Edition

This is a work of fiction. Names, characters, dialogues, places, and incidents either are the product of the author's imagination or are used fictitiously. Any resemblance to actual events, locales, or persons, living or dead, is entirely coincidental. The publisher does not have any control over and does not assume responsibility for author or third-party websites or their content.

No part of this book may be reproduced, scanned, or distributed in any printed or electronic form without permission. Please do not participate in or encourage piracy of copyrighted materials in violation of the author's rights. Purchase only authorized editions.

Cover design: Kelli Ann Morgan, Inspire Creative Services
Cover image: Paul Henry Serres Photography, www.paulhenryserres.com
Interior book design: Bob Houston eBook Formatting
Editor: Linda Clarkson, Black Opal Editing and Proofreading

ISBN Paperback: 978-1-7348097-6-3
ISBN eBook: 978-1-7348097-7-0
Library of Congress Control Number: 2020913407

# In the Company of Snipers

You can find Irish Winters

On Facebook:
https://www.facebook.com/author.irishwinters

On Twitter: https://twitter.com/irishwinters1

For news on upcoming releases, sign up for Irish Winters' Newsletter at IrishWinters.com.

For more information about all my books, visit IrishWinters.com.

# IN THE COMPANY OF SNIPERS

This series revolves around former Marine scout sniper, Alex Stewart, and his covert surveillance company, The TEAM, home-based out of Alexandria, Virginia. An obsessive patriot and workaholic, he created the company to give former military snipers like him, a chance at returning to civilian life with a decent job, security, and a future.

This is not a serial with each book ending at a cliffhanger. *In the Company of Snipers* is a collection of passionate love stories involving strong women and men who are tough enough to take on the world alone. Each is a stand-alone read, complete in itself.

Spoiler alert: Every story contains adult scenes including sexual situations (some explicit), language, and violence. I don't write sweet romance, so be forewarned.

Book 1, *ALEX*, reveals how The TEAM came to be, as well as how Alex met Kelsey, how they fell in love and fought all odds to stay together. Each of the following books is a complete romance in itself, where, in the course of an active TEAM operation, one agent comes face to face with his or her demons. The men and women I write about are all patriots and warriors, dealing with what they've lived through or mistakes they've made.

It's my hope that you will come to realize along with my heroes...

*Love changes everything.*

# Chapter One

The instant he stepped onto the lonesome beach, Walker dropped to his knees, emotionally spent, but damned thankful to be out of the ocean and back in the land of the free. That honored moniker might not apply to him any longer, since he wasn't exactly free. But this country was still the land of his birth, and to the day he died, he'd be proud to be an American. Still was. Every other time he'd arrived in the States, he'd thanked his lucky stars. Why should this time be any different? No other country on Earth had what America had. Liberty. The pursuit of individual happiness. Inalienable rights. The Constitution he'd fought and damned near died several times for.

Weary to his bones, he peeled his diving mask off. The ten ton gear bag on his shoulder hit the beach next. He leaned forward, pressed his dry, cracked lips to the damp, fragrant sands of freedom, and whispered the word that was more precious than most: "Home."

He held that position on this lonely stretch of beach in the Florida Keys, his eyes closed and his forehead resting on the spot he'd kissed, a silent homage to the Spirit of Liberty and the men and women who'd died for her. Ah, the sweet, sweet smell of US soil. Nothing like it in the world. Dog-tired, he succumbed to the tender emotion of being alive and free. A tear wound its way out of his eye and disappeared into the same sand.

God, he loved America. Too bad she didn't love him back.

With that depressing reminder of who he was, Walker rolled to his butt, and contemplated spending the night where he'd landed. Why not? The beach looked deserted, and by hell, he'd earned a reprieve. But that wasn't the way this world worked. Only a fool would sleep in the open, and Walker wasn't that kind of stupid. A lone man was an easy target for riffraff, drunks, seagulls, and the occasional alligator these islands were known for. Besides, the last forty-eight hours had been hell, and he was spent at every level. He needed a decent meal, then two days of sleep.

Reaching into the large, sodden, yet waterproof bag at his side, he tore into one of the smaller black plastic bags inside and lifted two protein bars and a bottled water up and out. He hated the bars. They were dry, tasteless, and stuck between his teeth, but he was shaking so hard from his long hours of exertion, there was no choice. His blood sugar had to be flatlined; the jitters had already begun. His gut needed something in it right damned now.

Tired to his core, he stuffed one bar after the other into his mouth, between gulps of just enough water to keep the dense, highly-nutritional mass moving. After the last gulp and swallow, he followed the routine with a couple mints from the tin he'd kept with the bars. At last, the sharp taste of *curiously strong* cinnamon burst over his tongue. Its powerful, vaporous scent hit his airways. Sometimes the littlest things in life made all the other crap bearable, if not worthwhile. Like these little sugar nuggets. They were made in America, too. He popped a couple more to get the taste of the sea and those bars out of his mouth.

Night was coming on fast. Sunlight had faded over the turquoise ocean, turning it gray, and each wave was now tipped with orange-ish pink foam, as if kissing the sun goodbye.

It'd been two damned long days of hard swimming. Thankfully, he'd made it. This hundred-mile swim had begun north of Havana, Cuba. Unseen, he'd prepared as much as he could for his journey to Florida. But the ocean had grown more dangerous since the last time he'd made this swim. Walker hadn't expected the hundred-mile channel between here and there to be rife with so many swarms of poisonous box jellyfish, Mother Earth's signal that her oceans had become polluted and too warm. The pesky, curious, cold-blooded whitetip sharks were another unexpected surprise. Damned things would as soon bite a man's foot off, as nibble or taste his phalanges. Walker would know. His dive fins now had deep, serrated toothmarks from those few encounters.

He'd been lucky he hadn't set off a feeding frenzy.

Saltwater was the only constant in this long-distance swim. It never changed, and, as usual, it had seeped into his tightly fitting mask, under his wetsuit, too. Not only was he dead-assed tired, but his skin was dry and burned from too long, too personal contact with the corrosive powers of ocean water. He needed a bar of soap and plenty of clear, running water. A shower'd be nice. Top that off with a thick coat of petroleum jelly he meant to slather everywhere—if he could find a jar.

But first...

Walker stashed his empty wrappers and bottle back into his bag, then kicked out of his fins and pulled off his dive boots. Into his waterproof rucksack they went, on top of his garbage, his prized modified, bolt-action SOCOM MK-13 rifle, two pistols, his knife, and what was left of his ammo. And, oh yeah, he'd almost forgotten that hypo of Special K from his last close escape. That he kept in a tiny sealed pocket in his bag. One could never be too careful.

He'd packaged everything separately in zippered waterproof pouches designed specifically for underwater black ops. Explosives. Blow-out kits. Just enough protein bars to get by. Bottled water. Important stuff like that. Made expressly for SEALs, the bags could handle almost everything. Best of all, they kept every drop of saltwater out.

Unzipping his suit from neck to hip, he peeled it slowly and methodically over and off his shoulders, then pulled both arms free of their skin-tight sleeves, and folded the suit over his legs. Undressing always hurt in intimate, excruciating ways. Though he knew better, it always felt as if the suit took every last body hair and the topmost layers of epidermis with it. To work, neoprene had to lie flat against a man's body. And Walker's suit was the best. It had almost become part of him. Hence the pain of separation.

He had no SCUBA gear, comm link, or rebreather. This swim had been entirely unscripted, and he'd been unprepared when it began. But that was what guys on the run did. They improvised.

Climbing to his feet, he stepped out of his suit, then rolled the top and bottoms together, avoiding getting more sand in them. Methodically, he stowed the suit with the rest of his gear. At last down to his swim trunks, he unzipped another waterproof bag, pulled out one more bottled water, and rinsed his mask. The mask went alone into a dry, soft cloth bag to protect its lens, then back into yet another protective bag. SEALs always took care of their gear. Even former SEALs.

He'd no sooner zipped his bag, when the tiny hairs on the back of his neck prickled to attention. This beach was too open. He wasn't alone. Time to go.

"You're dripping on my sand," a lazy feminine voice drawled from somewhere within the shaded trees ahead.

His head snapped on target. There she was. A lone woman. Behind that screen of tall beach grass. Leaned back in an Adirondack chair beneath a gnarly eucalyptus, itself shaded by the lofty pine on its westward side. Which explained why he hadn't spotted her until now. But where had she come from? Had she been there all along? Why was she here?

There weren't any other lights on this tiny island. Yet she wore dark glasses. Day tripper maybe? Or someone sent to take him in? Damn it. She'd been there the whole time, watching him come ashore and undress. Hell, watching everything. His demeanor. His current lack of weaponry. Hell, even where he'd stowed his knife. At least he hadn't peed on the beach.

Walker cocked his head, striving to see the stranger better in the diminishing light of day. Her two long, bare legs were crossed, hardly visible from where he stood. One white woven sandal slapped the heel of an extended foot, taunting him. Daring him. But those legs…

She had to be in a swimsuit to be showing that much leg. Walker licked his chapped lips, pissed that his mind had already gone—there. Up those legs. Between those legs.

Hopefully, wishfully, to sweet, sweet heaven. It'd been a long time since he'd been with a real woman. The last one, a wannabe USN wife, a frog hog whose name he refused to remember, didn't count. Barflies were the same the world over. Shallow. Selfish. Nameless. Users, like him.

But this mystery gal had attitude. "Your sand? I don't see any No Trespassing signs."

Slap, slap, slap went that lazy sandal. "Well, bless my heart, you're a nosy son of a bitch, aren't you?" She stabbed those dark glasses up higher on her nose. "Like I said, my sand. You're on it. You got a name?"

*Yeah, one you'll never know.* He noticed she'd used her middle finger salute when she'd repositioned her sunglasses. And that sweet *bless my heart* line? It might sound endearing, but that finger was the old 'fuck you' salute if he'd ever seen one.

Instead of bowing to her demand, he offered his SEAL handle. "Hotrod. You?"

The evening had grown darker, the last of the day's sunlight fading the western sky from sultry Piña Colada oranges and pinks to purpling grays and ash. Midnight shadows scuttled across the tiny island, like crabs searching for safe places to hide, where gulls couldn't get them.

Of all the places in all the Keys to come ashore...

Reminded him of Bogart's famous line: *"Of all the gin joints in all the towns in all the world...."*

It was time to leave, even if it meant sloshing back into the surf, disappearing again, this time without wearing his wetsuit or mask. That was what he did best. Do without. Run for his life. Stick to the backroads, swamps, and alleys. Walker had places to be, other places to visit where no one knew his face or thought they knew the details of his alleged crimes. Armchair quarterbacks all of them. Bastards. Braggarts and opinionated has-beens.

And yet…

This was no ordinary woman sparring with him. Lifting his bag, he shouldered it, and like the SEAL he was and would forever be, Walker Judge walked straight into trouble.

# Chapter Two

"Damn," Persia hissed under her breath. "This guy's got balls."

Definitely not her type, though. He wasn't dark-haired nor slim nor debonair like the fictitious James Bond. More muscled than lean. But unshaven. She liked her men clean, no scruff.

When this guy had first come ashore, she'd thought his hair was dark brown, but now that it had dried, it was sandy brown and too short. Military short. Overall, the guy was basically nondescript. Plain. The kind of man women looked through when they passed on the street.

Except for that tightly muscled body. Like an idiot, her heart pounded a zippy salsa beat watching the way his hips rolled with every step he took toward her. The guy had nerve. Her breath hitched. He wasn't walking as much as stalking. There was danger in every step that brought him closer. Lethality vibrated between them. She could sense it, like a repressed bow wave, it surged ahead of him. Should she run?

Her instincts screamed, *Yes! He's dangerous. Run, run. Run! Before it's too late!*

She bantered back, *Never. You know better. Send me to hell, and I'll come up swinging. I don't back down, and I don't back up.*

*But, but, but…*

*But nothing. I'm staying. This is my beach. Get a grip.*

As she talked to herself, Persia's fingers curled over the ends of her armrests. Whoever he was, this guy was no wimp. He was packing, and she didn't mean handguns, although the bag he'd slung over his shoulder looked heavy enough to hold more than a change of clothes and dive gear. There were weapons in there. She could smell them.

Every last inch of her visitor was washboard hard and solid. A scant dusting of hairs darkened his bare chest, and the rare blond or golden ones glistened in the last rays of sunlight through the trees. *But I'll bet he's dark blond where it counts. Hmmm…*

She'd already seen enough of him, aka the magnificent, carved rectus abdominus muscles that comprised his unusual eight-pack instead of a measly six. That alone had started her drooling. More impressive were the finely-crafted external obliques, the much-touted V ordinary men never acquired throughout their sedentary, fast-food, drive-through lives. She licked her lips. The level of hard core-muscles rippling in her direction meant this guy either spent endless vain hours in a gym—which she doubted—or he was disciplined as hell. Focused.

There were no islands south of hers and no boats on the horizon that she could see. This guy had obviously just swum from Cuba. Which meant he was either an Olympic swimmer, an idiot, or an operator, as in Army Ranger, Air Force Special Warfare Pararescue, or SEAL. There were few men who could've accomplished a long-distance swim like that. Fewer who would've survived the rough, shark-infested ocean.

"Who the hell are you?" she asked again, her instincts on high alert even as she maintained her cool, calm, I'm-the-bitch-of-this-beach demeanor. Cue the sandal slap. He was the trespasser, not her.

"Already told you, ma'am. Hotrod."

*Ma'am, huh? Definitely former military.* "That's just a handle. Really."

"You first."

She gave him her chin. "Agent Persia Coltrane. I'd say it was nice to meet you, but I'm not nice." *Take warning, tough guy. I might look like a harmless runaway housewife, but I can take you down, and if you make me do that, I'll make you suffer.*

He looked to his left, then right, scanning the beach. Was he searching for something or someone? Seemed like it.

"Yes, I'm alone," she said before he asked. He didn't need to know she carried. Her tiny bikini was misleading. Let him think what he wanted and let that be her surprise. If he made one wrong move, she'd whip that loaded .380 auto out of the mesh holster tucked at her side, so fast he'd never see it coming.

"Hotrod's good enough for now," he murmured, his sharp eyes scrolling up her legs to her belly and on up to her breasts.

"Up here, asshole," she ordered, removing her glasses. "I have eyes, too."

"I can see that." He gave her a curt affirmative nod of his head, which wasn't square nor much larger than hers. Which was unfortunate. True alpha males, the kind she preferred, had bigger, wider skulls than women. Of course, sometimes, that also made them bigger assholes. But more often than not, it made them cavemen in the bedroom.

Persia set her glasses in the bottle holder carved into her chair's armrest. She had no illusions about who she was. The men in her life had to be stronger than she was, for her to like them, and so far, she hadn't met any who were. Not even her new boss. He was tough all right, but he was too damned old.

She let a breath go on a disappointed sigh, not sure what she'd expected from this chance encounter. But this guy wasn't it. Even as ripped as he was, Hotrod was nothing special. To prove her point, she spread her knees and let her sandals hit the ground at the upright legs of the chair.

As expected, his eyes lowered straight to the juncture of her thighs. See? How utterly, predictably boring. She was wrong. He wasn't spec ops. If anything, he belonged in a nice clean gym, not out risking his life. He wasn't the same caliber as her, and he'd probably never seen the ugly side of life, not like she had. Want to bet he lived in his parents' basement with a boatload of athletic gear they'd paid for? That his mommy still did his laundry? Yeah. This guy was just plain ordinary from head to toe. Or. Din. Ary.

"Why the fuck are you here?" snapped out of her. She had better things to do than waste time on a one-night stand. They weren't her specialty, and she hadn't come this far south looking for a hookup. This was her beach, her vacation, and her time away from the messed-up world. She'd come here to recharge, not deal with beach trash. Hotrod needed to buzz off.

He rolled his shoulders, which were… *Nice.*

"A warm shower'd be good," he said quietly, even as he cast a gaze down the beach again. "Don't suppose there's one handy? I can pay."

"I don't need your money," she said dismissively. "There's a hose outside my front door. It's cold but you can rinse off there. Then leave."

His head bobbed like the meek man he was. "Thanks, ma'am. That'll work."

*You're damned right it will.* "Okay then." She cupped her kneecaps and tried to hoist herself out of that chair. Unfortunately, Adirondack chairs turned her into an idiot every time she struggled out of their deep, angled posterior, especially after she'd been drinking. Why she'd ever bought the thing, she'd never know. Except she had. It was the chair's bright, vivid purple color she liked instead of the overdone, boring, tropical hues this state was known for. Who needed more turquoise, pinks, baby blues, or creamy yellows? Not. Her.

She'd no more than huffed at the spectacle she was making of herself, when Hotrod stepped up and offered his hand. *See? Mama's boy.*

Persia grabbed hold anyway, amazed at the callused roughness she found there. She'd expected baby soft. Wasn't what she got.

By then he also had hold of her elbow, and she was caught. "You okay?" he asked gruffly, looking down at her.

Her breath caught at the sudden hit of cinnamon in the air. "Why wouldn't I be?" She needed him to back off, but he'd pulled her to her feet so quickly, her other palm hit the middle of his chest. *Oh. My. Hell.*

Women had cleavage between their breasts. It, breasts, and nipples had been created in part for the primitive, animalistic purpose of making men look. Of driving them out of their minds with lust until they did what men did best. Fuck. That was their primary mission, their one good reason for breathing.

And Hotrod was looking. He couldn't seem to take his eyes off her breasts, but then neither could Persia take her eyes off his chest. There was a veritable slice between his breathtaking pectorals. A narrow grand canyon of sinew between two sets of finely-packed, rock-solid muscle. And they were warm. So warm. And solid.

A woman had needs, damn it. Could she help it if she might possibly be drooling at the snug way her thumb had just slid inside that warm, male crevice where it landed? Hotrod wasn't just built. He was carved out of deliciously living granite that pulsed and thrummed under her touch.

Was he as turned on as she was? The edge of her thumb slid deeper between those two slabs of muscle, as if it had found its place in the grand scope of things. Like it wanted to stay there. Which put her fluttering fingertips over his nipple, as if they'd found their new favorite toy.

"Don't worry, ma'am. I've gotcha," he said, his voice husky and heavy with desire.

He most certainly did have her. Fighting to catch her balance—and her breath—Persia looked him square in the eye. His blue eyes were as pure and breathtaking as the Key West ocean before an afternoon rain. She'd pegged him wrong. This guy wasn't short, and he wasn't ordinary, not the way he'd stepped up and taken charge. He had her beat by a good six inches, up close. Maybe more. And he had her hand.

The man she'd thought forgettable was anything but. Close-up, Hotrod was lethally raw and wickedly potent. His masculinity whipped out and wrapped her in their own private bubble. She really was caught.

Her nostrils flared at the luscious scents of wind, sand, and sea, combined with the distinctly male musk coming off him. And cinnamon. She couldn't breathe. Didn't dare swallow.

But she could step back, damn it!

Flustered like she'd never been before in her life, Persia retreated until her calves bumped the front of her chair. Out of breath at this overwhelming, incredible first contact, she reached down with her free hand and grabbed her towel with its hidden weapon.

"My bungalow's behind us. In the... trees," she told him, pissed that a breathy hesitance had replaced her usual, domineering snark. "You'll see the… the garden hose attached to the post just outside the door. It has a nozzle to control the flow, and all you have to d-d-do is..."

And she was stuttering!

Struggling to gather her wits, Persia jerked her hand back. "It's actually an outdoor shower with a four-by-four tiled floor. There's a bench alongside to set your stuff on, and I'll…" *I'll be damned. I've turned into a silly, chatty, feminine idiot, who... Is. Not. Me!* "And I'll get a towel while you shower," she bit out, in case he thought she was weakening. Which she was not. "Leave it on the b-b-bench when you l-l-leave." Why couldn't she talk straight?

"Yes, ma'am."

Hotrod was so damned polite, she had a feeling he might salute any second now. Her lips were dry, so… she licked the bottom one. Then bit it. Held her lip between her teeth, overcome by—something.

Of course, he noticed her mouth. Men liked any female orifice. He was suddenly a jungle cat with big, black, glowing eyes. Alert. Poised. Ready to strike. And… And… She wanted to do erotic, carnal things to him. With him. He needed to squirm, and she needed to be the dominant one making him squirm.

Logic evaporated. Persia didn't waste time thinking twice, just slammed into that rugged, sexy mouth, needing whatever was simmering between Hotrod the liar and her to boil the hell over. To consume her and him. To get it over and done.

Just that fast, he was a match to her gasoline. His heavy bag hit the ground with a thud. His warm, capable hands smoothed down her back and cupped her mostly bare ass. Bikinis weren't made to cover much. This one surely didn't.

Their mouths crashed together, all lips and teeth, growls and tongues. Their bodies followed suit. Breasts to chest. Hip to hip and thigh to thigh. One of her knees landed between his thighs. The rousing sensation of his hair-roughened skin against her bare skin excited the hell out of Persia. It'd been so long. She wanted this stranger more than she'd ever wanted a man before. And that had been damned few times.

Lust roared like an out of control forest fire between them. It licked up her spine, and Persia couldn't get her fingers on his head and into his hair fast enough. Delightful. Simply, decadently delightful, holding this man's skull. Threading through waves of burnished gold. Mapping the curve of his head and his strong neck. Cupping his scruffy jaw, she held him still.

And he let her. Breathing was hard. But then Hotrod cupped both hands under her jaw, took possession of her mouth, and...

His breath became her air. Her lifeline.

*Dayum.* The man could kiss. His tongue was sweet and slick, demanding, tasting of cinnamon and male passion, determination mingled with brimstone and heat. And she was lost in a maelstrom of willing, dancing flames. The oncoming darkness swirled around them.

When she opened her eyes, Persia found herself standing under that silly outdoor showerhead. With a snap of his wrist, Hotrod cranked the handle and…

*Br-r-r-r.* Cold water doused over her head and over him. Not that it slowed her down or cooled her off. Not. At. All. If anything, it cranked her libido higher. He still wore his swim trunks, but that feral, needy glare in his eyes when they skated over her semi-nakedness, was her undoing.

And God created fire. Burning, aching flames in her gut that Hotrod seemed to know precisely how to cajole into a roaring inferno.

With one quick snap of his fingertips, the tie to her flimsy top was undone. It fell to the tiled floor between them. Likewise, her skimpy bottoms went next, a soggy number eight on the tile. Persia stood there stark naked, completely exposed where anyone could see her. While he was still semi-dressed. The inherent naughtiness of her being nude out in the open, when he wasn't, turned her body to liquid flame. What a rush. Erotic anticipation zipped up the insides of her legs.

As if he knew precisely what she needed, he sank to his knees and…

*Oh, yes, yes, yes, please.*

He caught her breast in one big, warm palm, the other with his mouth, suckling that sensitive mound of needy flesh like a master. Licking it. Nibbling it. Scraping his teeth over the hardened tip, enough that she wanted more. He rolled her other nipple between his fingers. Pinching with just the right amount of pressure and squeeze and…

"Pleasssse," she hissed. The tips of her nipples were hard as diamonds. If he kept suckling, licking, and pinching, she'd combust right here, right now.

"Inside. Sh-shower. Soap," she informed him before she lost all control. Not like she had much left. Not with the steady buzz in her blood. But behind the closed doors of her tidy, clean bungalow, even if they landed on her kitchen floor instead of in her shower stall, was still safer than continuing this craziness outside.

His palm slipped down her belly even as his tongue swirled crazy circles around her nipple inside his mouth, and…

Two wonderful male fingers breached her core, as if he owned her. Which he did at the moment. Persia couldn't think. Didn't dare. She could hardly breathe, but she needed this, and whoever this guy really was, she needed him. Just for tonight. Then he could leave, and she'd never think of him again. Okay, that made her a one-night-stand. Well, so what? She had needs, damn it!

Between the chilly water sluicing over her bare skin, and the roaring, out of control fire he'd started with those gently probing fingers and his skilled mouth…

Between the stars twinkling down on her, and the fact that she was about to have consensual sex in the open where anyone with a decent pair of binoculars—or eyes—could see…

The heat in her blood turned into a thrilling zip ride of pleasure. She couldn't believe how quickly he'd taken her to the edge. Didn't dare speak it, afraid if she thought too hard, she'd kill the sizzle racing up her core. All she could do was stare wide-eyed at this stranger as a monster shockwave hit her. "I'm… I'm…"

"Come for me, princess," Hotrod murmured tenderly, his blue eyes now midnight dark, his lips curled into a proud, ragged, manly smile. His voice had gone masculine deep, so low, it rumbled over her like a security blanket. A strong male security blanket.

Before she let go, she pulled back far enough to be sure what she was doing, what she was seeing. Still holding his head, she looked straight into the brooding face of loneliness. Need. Hunger.

How perfect. She wasn't the only desperate one here. Man, he was good. So were his fingers. But that glimmer in his eyes was pure det cord, and she was Semtex. Her breath caught. Her heart stopped. Lightning struck down deep and low and hot in her belly. Like a freight train, it exploded, an uncorked bottle of champagne. She closed her eyes, savoring the release of a lifetime. What a rush!

"This! Yessss, thisssss," she hissed, like he didn't already know what he was doing to her. Biting her tongue to keep from screaming like a wanton alley cat, she pulled him to her face and ground into his forehead, "M-more, Hotrod. Dammit, more."

Kisses. All she had to give him were kisses, so she peppered his handsome, rugged face with her lips and mouth and breath. But she also needed something to hold onto. Her legs had turned to jelly. Her palms skated down his neck, over his collar bones, to his solid shoulders.

"Wrap your legs around me, sugar." The man never even grunted when he palmed her ass and lifted off his knees with her in his arms. "Is your door locked?"

"N-no," she murmured, weak as a lamb, and as foolish as she'd ever been. She'd never come so quickly nor flown so high. Which was either a testament to his skill as a lover, or her total departure from reality. That had to be it. Her last missions into Brazil had both been brutally difficult. She was suffering a psychotic break. That was all. No doubt post-traumatic stress, too. Nothing serious. Nothing a few months of therapy and enough whiskey couldn't cure.

Slanting his body sideways, Hotrod leaned against her door. Somehow, he held onto her while he turned the knob, then shouldered her door open, and maneuvered her through so as not to bump her head. He kicked the door shut, then locked it. Good man. Really good, good man.

Persia laid her head on his shoulder. Except for the dim light from her bedroom nightlight, her entire house was dark. Hotrod seemed able to see in the dark.

Still thrumming from her fantastic, once in a lifetime orgasm, she focused on the odd sensation of being held like a child in this strong, hard male hands. Hotrod was one sexy, muscular beast, and that eight-pack wasn't spray paint. Her fingers told her so, but what's more… He wasn't as slim as she'd thought at first glance. Neither was he nothing special. Grand, sprang to mind. Grand and slippery, hard as steel, and ready for action.

She opened her mouth to tell him—something—but found herself tossed onto the middle of her bed, surrounded by her pillows. Persia flattened her palms to her chest to keep her breasts from bouncing. They were big enough and had plenty of bounce in them, but she found it embarrassing, breasts being mostly fat and all. If anything, her full figure had held her back in college and during her career. Too many men equated full figures with opportunity—for them. Not her. She'd worked damned hard to be who she was today.

But if Hotrod liked them…

Her palms hit the mattress as she let him look.

He came to a full, abrupt stop at her bedside. He was still in his swim trunks while she lay exposed and mussed and completely on display. At his disposal. Those beautiful blues skated over every inch of her bare skin. From head to toes and in between, his sharp gaze lingered. His tongue ran a quick, sensual lap over his lips when his eyes landed on her breasts.

*What have I done? I don't know this guy. At all. He could be Jack the Ripper!*

He must have seen the worry in her eyes. She'd no more than doubted her sanity, when his knees hit the mattress. Not breaking eye contact, he climbed up her legs, pushing her gently over as he dominated the whole damned room. She didn't know whether to purr or scream. This was her place, not his. She was the dominant, not him. There wasn't enough air in this room!

"You're safe with me, princess," he reassured quietly, his forearms now alongside her head, and that rugged, ripped, to-die-for body poised directly over hers. Perfectly aligned. Like an addled-brained idiot, her knees had automatically opened wide for him, and there he was. Pressed hard and ready against her core. Waiting on her. Melting her with those gentle blue eyes. Asking permission…

"I'd never do anything to hurt or scare you. I'm not one of those guys."

"Well, yeah, I'm… I'm not one of those women," she groused, not ready to admit it was highly possible she'd made a huge mistake by throwing herself at him. Not that she'd ever confess to that, because oh, yes, oh yes. She certainly *was* one of those stupid, needy women.

What on earth did she really know about this guy? Even Hotrod wasn't his real name. And okaaaaaaay... So what if he was the hottest male she'd ever—ever—laid eyes on? So what if he was kind and gentlemanly, that he seemed to like her? And okay, yes. He smelled really, really good, and she was fairly sure he liked what he could see of her. Which was everything. Was that all this was about? A good fuck and goodbye?

"I mean it, sugar," he growled, his voice a ragged whisper that caressed her skin like sweet Georgia honey on bee stings. "Just say the word and I'll leave. But just so you know, I put your weapon on your nightstand. If you want, I'll secure it in your drawer. But if you'd feel more comfortable holding it—"

"My piece!" she all but screeched. No FBI agent ever lost track of her service weapon. Not like she was with the Bureau anymore. She wasn't. But what would Alex Stewart say? He'd fire her!

Frantic now, Persia's head snapped to her left and—oh, good. Thank God. There it was, right where Hotrod said. Still in its holster. On her nightstand.

She had to know. "Did it get wet when we… I mean, in the shower?"

"No, ma'am. It must've fallen out of your, umm, suit, when I dropped my bag." The twinkle in his eye told her he knew there was no way that handgun had been hidden in her bikini bottoms. She'd had a good hold on it before she'd kissed him. But then… she hadn't.

Persia vaguely remembered two thumps before he'd stepped into that shower. But the smile that cracked his lips now was so damned sweet and tender, she wanted to cry. He'd taken care of her. She swallowed hard. Gulped was more like it. That explained why she hadn't missed her pistol until now. She'd been so intent on how he'd made her feel. So focused on all the wrong things. On him. On what he was doing to her.

"I… I don't usually do stupid stuff like this," she murmured, swallowing again before she apologized. Silly women always did that. They apologized for the weather, come sunshine or rain, as if everything was their fault. Not her. Only now…

She'd just committed the worst mortal sin in spec ops history. She'd lost track of her weapon. This was all her fault. She should've told Hotrod to take a shower and a hike. To drop dead. Anything but let him inside her life and handle her like a pro.

"No worries. It happens," he said quietly.

See? He'd done it again. He'd given her a way out.

"Not to me, it doesn't. Where's yours, huh? Have you ever lost track of your weapons? Even for one second?" She knew damned well he hadn't, because his bag was sitting on the floor in her bedroom, wasn't it? True, she hadn't seen a weapon in his hands, but she honestly couldn't remember him hauling that bag inside along with her horny, naked ass, either.

"What makes you think I have any?" he asked, his lying eyes sincere and sweet and so damned believable.

"Because that bag of yours is not standard issue Walmart," she snapped. "You're an operator like me, aren't you?"

The strangest thing was happening. She was lying flat on her back in her bed, but falling into those handsome eyes.

They were more tender than she deserved, and she couldn't catch herself. Didn't know why she should even try. He seemed so honest. Which was her undoing. Hotrod was the epitome of a strong, silent male. Ever standing guard. Ever faithful. Ever… everything.

Instead of answering, his mouth descended over hers with slick, wet heat that lit her internal fuse again. The one that led from her lips to her core, both as willing as the other. Just that fast. She growled, needing him deep inside. *All the way, honey. Here. Now!*

# Chapter Three

With his forearms alongside Persia's head, Hotrod pumped into her. The light from some outside source filtered through the window above her bed. His swim trunks were now on the floor, and he was on his way to being a happy man. At least, on his way to being happier. That swim had done him in. His energy flagged. So had everything else.

As stern and unyielding as this woman had seemed at first, she was everything but that now. Persia got him on some intrinsic level he'd never experienced before. Maybe her losing track of that handgun had something to do with what was happening now. She obviously understood him. That was why she'd challenged him about his gear. They were cut from the same cloth, both working for Uncle Sam. Both career operators in their own ways. It was as if their souls had recognized each other at first sight. The only problem was she didn't have to leave, but Walker did. And he would. As soon as the time was right.

Her hips bumped up off the bed into his, drawing his mind back to the enticing task at hand. Oh, yeah. He definitely intended to make her scream again. And smile. The exotic woman beneath him was utterly beautiful when she smiled. But those deep-brown almond eyes fringed with thick black lashes, and the rich, warm caramel of her skin? The way she blinked and her breath hitched when he'd first touched her?

The tip of her delicious tongue when she'd moistened those rose-red lips? Downright intoxicating. Alluring.

One of her parents or grandparents must've hailed from some Mideastern country he couldn't name with complete confidence. Iraq maybe? Iran? Saudi Arabia? India? Not like her ethnicity mattered. He'd met many exotic beauties during his travels across the world, but he'd never loved one. Not like this. If this were love. Which it wasn't. Couldn't be. Not this soon and not this fast. Hell, he didn't even really know her. That had always been his problem. He gave his heart away too quickly. Not this time.

At the end of the day, love didn't matter anyway, because convicted Navy SEALs didn't have time to get that kind of lucky. As he'd already learned the hard way, they had to keep one step ahead of the hounds snapping at their heels. He'd just fled a firefight on a tiny sandbar that the last hurricane had choked up east of northern Brazil. Like Cuba, he'd swum away from that one, too. Then, he'd wandered the eastern coast of South America, traveling north from town to town. Keeping to the shadows and shallows. Stealing a fishing boat or canoe here and there.

Like a moron, he'd always left a few American twenties to pay for his thefts. The way he saw it, they weren't really thefts, more like long-term borrows. But the poor fisherman left without anything to fish in at the start of their day, were better off come sunset. Hotrod made sure they had enough American dollars to live on for months, maybe years. He knew the cost of poverty, and many of the people he'd encountered had been unbearably kind, despite their lack of reais and centavos. American dollars would make them rich—for a little while.

Persia's naked body writhed beneath him. Her hips lifted and she ground herself into him, inciting his need to mark her. To possess her. She was a beauty like no other, a sinuous combination of dark and milk chocolates. Her hair, once loosely braided behind her back, had come undone. It lay like a shimmering ebony fan on her cream-colored pillow. It was as if her entire bungalow had been decorated to enhance her exquisite beauty. The whole place was working together, pulling him in like a moth to her sensual flame.

Yet Walker held back from sucking raspberries up her neck. She didn't need his brand or his mark. She wasn't a cow, not this smart, savvy, willing woman coming undone again in his hands. He dipped down and took her open mouth just as she'd stiffened her legs straight and hard. She was so responsive and wet. For him.

And yet, damn. His body struggled. Getting nowhere fast, while, with a hiss and a growl, she exploded in his arms again. That should have made him crow. The aftershocks rippling through her should've made him damned proud he was a man.

Instead, a tear glimmered at the corner of his eye, reminding him that he was nothing in this great land of liberty. The rush of his much anticipated, but not going to happen release, died in the awfulness of that bitter truth. How embarrassing, to be able to get it up, only to lose it the moment she needed it most.

What was worse, he'd been so caught up in her fierce possession of his body, that he'd neglected to use protection. Not like she was going to need it. Still, he was the gentleman here. He should've taken better care of this passionate woman. It was time to leave. Before he couldn't.

"Hey," Persia asked huskily, her dark eyes bright and her slender fingers combing over his hard Navy head. "I thought we were in this together, honey. Where'd you go?"

Affection warmed her words and he liked that she called him honey. Walker wished he could say he was right there with her, but he wasn't, and she was smart. She already knew.

"I'm still here," he growled, poking her with his one and only pointer before it completely deflated. "Can't you feel me inside you?"

That earned him the rarest, sweetest smile. Persia, at least, was satisfied. That was what he'd wanted most, to keep that lazy smile on her lush lips and the sparkle in her eyes.

"Before we go any further, I sure as hell hope you're on the pill or something." Because for damned sure there were no condoms in his bag.

"Implant," she breathed. "No worries. It's good for three years. I'm safe. Are you?"

"Yes, ma'am," he replied honestly. It had been a long time since he'd thought about sex or intimacy. He was so damned safe, pathetically safe, especially after his ex's very public exposé about their love life on every damned, sensation-seeking late-night propaganda show in America. A guy didn't stand a chance once a station turned their character assassination machines on.

She cupped his cheeks, both palms warm and gentle. Almost caring. And he was lost inside those pretty melted chocolate eyes. Everything about this woman drew him like a magnet. Her lovely, elegant brows arched with genuine concern. Her thick butterfly-wing lashes. Those lush, wet lips. Like a sweet, intoxicating vintage wine. A woman shouldn't taste so rare nor so fine. But she did.

To conceal what was left of his heart and his manhood, Hotrod closed the distance between Persia and himself. Since he'd lost his drive, he took her mouth, savoring every nip and nibble of what he'd soon have to live without. That was the problem with chance encounters in the big wide world of runaway convicts. A guy never knew what he'd find or who he'd have to leave behind.

She eased away from him, sinking her head farther into her pillow, her hands again on his head, her thumbs on his cheekbones. "But you didn't" —her hips arched into him— "you know. Come."

He gave her that. "Guess you wore me out, princess."

"More like swimming from Cuba wore you out. That's what you just did, right?"

"Yes," he admitted quietly. She didn't need to know why.

"That's what? A good hundred miles? How fast did you swim that, Hotrod?"

And now they were on a pseudo-first-name basis. *Hotrod and Princess.* Somehow that just made everything—sadder.

He scratched the back of his head. Every inch of his skin itched, and it would for days. That was what happened to idiots who spent too much time in saltwater. "Just under forty-eight hours. Next time, I'll do better."

"Next time? You have got to be kidding. Forty-eight hours? With no one on your six? No relief boat following along in case you ran into trouble? How'd you eat or drink or… or sleep? How'd you manage out there all alone?"

He shrugged, loving the glint of worry in her eyes. Persia might sound and act tough, but there was a nurturing side to her as well. "Swim a little. Roll over and rest on my back when necessary. Puppy paddle when I could. Snag a protein bar or bottled water once in a while. No big deal."

"No big deal, my ass. Weren't you worried? What if you hadn't made it? What would you have done then?"

That earned her another shrug, but telling her he would've drowned didn't seem like the smart thing to say after they'd just made love.

"I'm serious. I'm surprised you can keep on going after that swim. Aren't you exhausted? Can I get you something to drink or eat?"

Grinning, he cocked his head playfully at her.

"No, no, no, not me, you crazy man," she said pointedly. Lovingly. Was that affection in her voice he wondered as her fingers smoothed back over his head and into his hair. "I meant how about a hot-turkey sandwich? I've got gravy and leftovers from the breast I roasted yesterday. Or breakfast. I've got wine and whiskey, too. Name your poison."

"Breast?" he asked. Of course, that was the only word he'd heard. He let his gaze shift from her pretty face to those succulent pillows mashed against his chest. And suddenly, he was hungry again. Starved. But not for turkey. "Later, princess. I'm working here," he whispered as he tipped his face between those breasts and breathed. Just breathed in her feminine bouquet.

A hard man had to take whatever comfort he found along the way. Only this wasn't just comfort. This woman's plush, warm body truly was heaven.

# Chapter Four

Persia didn't want to feel anything for this man. This was a one-night stand. Nothing more. Her life was too busy for dating, too unpredictable to get tied down, even with some military guy who obviously knew what working for Uncle Sam entailed. As in no life of your own, possibly no future with anyone but your handler. Definitely no cutesy four-bedroom house with two and a half kids, a poodle, and a family van, in quaint little Somewhere Suburbia.

She couldn't deny that this tough guy had awakened something in the softer side of her, though. He seemed so—lost. Or hurt or damaged or… something. There were shadows lurking in those brooding blue eyes. Exhaustion bracketed them. She recognized the lingering ghosts of one too many operations gone wrong. Or just one too many operations.

Uncle Sam seemed to forget that his best-in-the-world armed-forces consisted of flesh-and-blood men and women. He just kept ordering deployments, undercover operations, all while expecting more, more, more. Too often, he expected more done with a helluva lot less to do it with. Which explained the current suicide epidemic among the military, emergency responders, police… hell, anyone who had to deal with man's inhumanity to man. Nurses and doctors, too. Ambulance drivers. Dispatch operators. They'd all seen and done too much. They suffered in ways most US citizens would never understand, not until they needed a first-on the-scene hero.

But that didn't mean she and Hotrod couldn't explore a few moments of private normalcy. That was all this chance encounter was about. A break. Downtime. An interlude of quiet relaxation in each other's arms.

Gently, she eased his head up from between her breasts. "Hey, did you fall asleep on me?"

He blinked down at her. No smile. No pithy comeback. Just a glazed stare. He'd fallen asleep all right. This guy was running on empty, but those eyes. Even in the dim glow of her outdoor security light coming through her window, Persia could see enough. Hotrod was like her. He kept his guard up. He didn't let anyone in.

"I knew it. You were asleep, weren't you?"

"No. Just…" He sucked in a deep breath. "Okay, yeah. I might've dozed off, but I'm ready for more. Are you?"

"Shower?" she asked coyly, wishing he'd let her inside the force field that surrounded him. "I mean, after swimming through all that salt water, I know you need a shower with real soap and…" *And tender loving care…* In case he might decline, she tempted him with, "I might even join you."

He lifted up on his hands and knees. "Let's get this party started."

And it was a party. She'd no more than bolted off the bed and ran for the bathroom, when he was on his feet, running after her. She'd made it to her ivory-tiled shower stall when he snapped her ass with the hand towel from the counter.

"Ouch!" she squealed, rubbing her backside, but secretly loving Hotrod's playful side. "If you keep that up, I'm going to have to—"

*Ooomph.* He had her back against the cold tile wall, her hair fisted in his hand, and making love to her mouth while he palmed the faucet on and—

"Br-r-r-r! That's c-c-cold!" she giggled around his prehensile lips. The beginnings of his beard brushed whisker burns over her mouth and chin. Persia took this amazing man's head between her palms. Breathing his breaths. Sharing his space. Loving the way his harder body scrubbed over her breasts and belly.

His knee shifted between her legs. He ducked, and instantly, the ice water steaming over her taut nipples didn't seem so cold anymore. He had her now, and it was divine, his mouth opened wide, swallowing her breast, the tip of his tongue flicking her nipple. Driving her crazy. Urgent messages jolted like shocks between her breasts and her core.

Tipping her head to the tiles behind her, she basked in the skilled hands of a man who knew what he was doing. Instinctively, one knee cocked. His hand slipped under that knee, and with one smooth tug, she was off her feet, her body angled into the tiled corner, and both her legs around his waist.

Like before, he was ready for action, the tip of him positioned at her starting line, the pulse in his neck beating "yes, yes, yes." But there he stopped. The poor guy's knees were bent and his feet were spread to support her weight. He'd hunched down to her level, yet he tipped back enough to peer at her. "I see you, princess," he murmured, his voice a husky mix of whiskey and smoke. "You think you've got it in you for one more time?"

That shouldn't have made her smile, but a giggle bubbled up from her heart at his inadvertent insinuation. Persia reached between their bodies and took him in hand. "Not yet, Hotrod, but I'm ready to get it back in me if you are."

And he was big. Hard and dripping wet and perfect.

One thrust. One whispered, "Yesssss…." And he was right where she needed him. Sheathed deep inside her clenching body. To the hilt. The dance started then, a steady rhythm that seduced and inspired. And it was happening again. With each push of his hips into her, her needy body responded in kind, until they were slamming together. Gasping for more. Clawing each other.

Sparks flew. His fingernails dug into the cheeks of her ass. She intertwined her fingers around his neck. Holding him while he held her. He angled his head, licking her lips as he took her mouth. Drops of water drizzled between them, creating tiny streams that pooled in her eyes.

"Look down, princess. See what we're doing," he murmured into her mouth.

Persia bowed her head next to his to see. Him, all male, driving into her, all female. They were Adam and Eve, and this was paradise. With just that one hurried glimpse of their joined bodies, white-hot lightning speared her.

"Gah! Yesssss!" she hissed. Damn. He'd done that on purpose. He'd known precisely what she'd needed to hit her mark.

Persia lost track of Hotrod's hands on her backside for a split second. She couldn't breathe. Didn't need to. Her world had exploded into slippery wet fireworks and smoking, falling stars. Drifting sparks that fell over her and into her. She was hanging on for the ride of her life. This! This man! Him! Only him and now and…

Tears ran out the corners of her eyes, mimicking the tears raining down from the shower. Suddenly, the whole world was crying, and she didn't know why. All she could do was breathe and hold onto the only man standing brave and wild in her brand-new world, while she tried not to fall apart.

Lovemaking this perfect had to be the real thing, didn't it? Persia hoped so. Because, like it or not, she felt something for this guy. Her heart had cracked wide open, and a tender wellspring of emotions were crowding out of her like a spring held too long in a Jack-in-the-box. Like a tulip bulb planted under a stone, starved for the sun. The fiercest emotions burst out of her, searching for light and love and quite possibly—for Hotrod.

Yet he still hadn't found his release, and his legs were shaking.

"Honey," she breathed into his neck, her arms still hooked around his shoulders in case he didn't want to look her in the eye. "Are you okay?" Probably not the best thing to ask a man when he was having performance issues. But she cared. He needed three days of solid sleep, not a night of rowdy sex in a shower, where he could slip and fall just because she'd been selfish.

His chin sank to the top of her wet head. "I'm good," he growled into her streaming wet hair.

But Persia heard weary frustration edging his words. She changed the subject. "You, my man, need sustenance, not wild, crazy sex. I prescribe bacon and eggs for breakfast, along with a tall stack of blueberry pancakes, topped off with homemade orange marmalade. I picked the oranges and made it myself."

He huffed. "But I like wild, crazy sex. With you."

He had a way of bringing her back to square one all over again.

When the taut, hard muscles bunched beneath her fingertips relaxed, she slipped down the incredible slide of his muscular body, turned on again by his raw masculinity when that was the last thing he needed. Damn, this guy was Greek-god handsome, just not sculpted in gray, cold marble. There wasn't one part of him that wasn't tanned, bronzed, and tantalizing. Blond highlights glinted at his forehead. He hadn't gotten sunburned from that long swim, and neither did he sport a farmer's tan. There simply wasn't one lily-white patch on him. But all that rugged skin still needed attention. She could see that clearly now. The saltwater he'd swum through had taken its toll.

"Come on. Let's get out of this shower. Then breakfast and back to bed with you, Mister." That she could do.

"Yeah," he growled reluctantly, one hand raking over his head. "Guess that'd be smart."

"Yes," she answered brightly, her eyes tracking the seductive way his bicep bulged when he lifted that arm. The thick veins running up to his armpit. The broad, hair roughened width of his chest. Ropes of veins stretched there as well, all signs that this man was used to carrying heavy loads. "B-b-but first…"

And she was back to stuttering like a little girl who'd never seen a naked man before. Which Persia hadn't, at least not one like Hotrod. "Shampoo and s-s-soap. Lean over. You're taller than me. I can't reach all of you." *And I'm afraid if I touch what I can reach, we'll never get out of this shower.*

He eased to the other side of the stall while he watched her pour a goodly sized dollop of golden shampoo into her palm. Then, leaning into her, Hotrod bent over and let her suds his head. She traded the shampoo for body wash, and damn-n-n-n-n. The slick, wet sensation of her fingers on the hard-as-rock ridges and the squared-off planes of his body set her heart to jackhammering again. Yup. She was in trouble.

Maybe this wasn't such a good idea. He had to know she was turned-on again by the way she kept soaping his muscled, and wow, strong arms. His biceps and elbows came next. His underarms. His ribcage. Then the curve of his waist and the angular jut of his hipbones. By the time she was through scrubbing everything but his manhood, Persia needed a really c-c-cold shower.

Instead, she jerked her head at the spray and told him, "Rinse," before she fell to her knees and worshipped this stranger.

As if he lived to obey, Hotrod stepped under the shower spray, skimming one quick hand over his head, the rest of him naked and wet and so damned edible.

*Oh. Be. Still. My. Foolish. Stupid. Heart.* Persia lifted a hand to her mouth, pretty sure she was drooling, and just as certain she'd sighed out loud at the sight of all this raw masculinity. Nude. In. Her. Shower.

God was great!

When the last soapy suds circled the drain, Hotrod turned to face her. Like some courtly knight of old, he held out a hand, as if she were someone important. Swallowing hard before she fainted, Persia took that gentlemanly hand and stepped gracefully out of the enclosed stall.

Life threw curve balls sometimes. Until recently, she'd been a tough FBI investigator, then just as tough a CIA Officer. She'd brought thugs across the world down, and she'd brought them down hard. Lace and drama had never been her schtick. The baby doll she'd been given as a child had only survived in family photos, and then, without its head. Rifles and pistols, yes. Her favorite color was gunmetal gray, not pink. She drove a mean four-wheeler back on her dad's cotton fields in Mississippi. She'd never once in her life felt graceful nor queenly. Yet Hotrod did that to her. Just by being himself.

Two towels hung over the bar at her left. Only when she stepped out of the shower and into the light, did she see the red chafe marks under his chin and around his neck.

"You're hurt," she whispered, reaching for his shoulder.

"Nah, I'm good."

"No, you're not. Are these abrasions from your scuba gear straps?"

"More like from two days of hard swimming."

"I've got just the thing."

That earned her a wry smile as his gaze slipped down her body to her toes. "Yes, you do, princess, but can I please grab a bite of that breakfast and a quick nap first?"

Hotrod was tired, but still all-male. He also intended to stay awhile longer than she'd expected. Morning was looking up. Her face broke into one of those silly, happy emoticons.

"You bet. Food first, then three days in bed." Persia could have kicked her own ass for what came out of her big mouth. She'd actually batted her lashes when she'd said it, too. What had come over her? She back-pedaled. "But it's entirely up to you what you do with all that free time." *And if you want to jump me, the answer is yes.*

Persia grabbed one of her fluffiest towels, but instead of handing it to him, she eased it over his head and around his shoulders. Drying him off should not have been so erotic, but everywhere that towel touched, her fingers dared to go. First through the short-cropped hair on that handsome head, then down the expanse of his rugged neck. Down his back. Around to his front. His chest boasted crisp hairs that danced their way to his belly to… there.

She patted everything dry as quickly as she could without teasing him. But damn, this man had the build of Hercules. Wide and powerful in all the right places. His thighs. His calves. His arms. Hard as steel. Not bulky, but just right.

"Your lips are going to chap if you keep doing that," he murmured, looking intently down at her now that she'd dropped to her knees at his—knees. Just to dry his legs and feet. Nothing more. Though he was right. She was licking her lips at the squeaky-clean male standing before her. But one taste of this incredible temptation would only add to his frustration.

So, no. Just no. She wouldn't do that to him. He needed time to recuperate, and for someone to take care of him for a change. To feed him, not just hump him like a bunny. In spring. In clover…

Persia jumped to her feet, her heart pounding with all the things she wanted to do with and to this quiet, handsome, gentle man. Like a boss instead of a naked seductress, she pointed to the stool near her sink and ordered, "Sit. I've got just what you need."

"You certainly do," he murmured as his arm snaked around her waist, pulling her back to his mouth. Loving her all over again. One hand slipped up her spine and into her wet hair while he cupped her jaw with the other. With breathy heat and a promise he couldn't quite deliver at the moment, Hotrod anointed her lips, chin, and neck.

There was no resisting this guy, so she let him play. Let his tongue tangle with hers again. They were good together. She liked the way their bodies seemed to recognize each other. The way they slipped together without effort or trying. The way they'd clicked. But for this one brief moment, she knew better than him. Sex was off the table.

"Sit down," she ordered huskily, before she lost what little restraint she had left. "You can have all you want of me, but after breakfast. First..."

She reached past him for the Aloe Vera gel on the shelf behind him. Before he had a chance to tease or tempt her, Persia lathered a goodly amount over his broad shoulders and down his arms.

A sigh breathed out of him.

Shifting from the danger zone between his thighs, she smoothed more across his back and over the top of his very fine backside. Around his ribcage to his abdomen. Talk about muscles. Every inch of this man was a memory in discipline she'd never forget. Her modest-sized bathroom was suddenly stuffy and warm. Make that h-h-hot.

Standing back in front of him, he pulled her between his knees. Then his thighs. Not a good idea. She didn't have to look down to know her breasts were now heavy, her nipples as taut as solitaire diamonds, and mashed against a handsome, manly chest. Besides, if she looked down any farther, she wasn't sure she'd be able to tear her eyeballs off that bad boy once again pressed into her belly.

Hotrod sat there as still as a statue, his blue eyes dark with passion...

That. Was. Not. Helping.

"Tip your head back," she breathed, her entire body thrumming with need. "Please. I can't r-r-reach under your chin." *Because I'd rather take a firm hold of something else.*

It was oddly arousing to command a beast as magnificent as the big guy now seated obediently on her bathroom stool. All Hotrod had to do was lean forward, put one elbow on his knee and a fist to his chin, and he'd be Auguste Rodin's *"Thinker."*

Yet he pulled her close again. "I wish I'd met you years ago," he murmured, the black in his eyes now wide and deep. His fingers tangled into her hair, still dripping water down her back. "You make me forget who I am."

To hell with the aloe.

Persia curled her arms around his head and pressed his face to her breasts where this whole thing began. Kissing the top of his wet head, she breathed in the scent of her shampoo in his hair, wishing she knew his real name. What foods he liked. Where home was and the names of his mom and dad, his sisters and brothers. His favorite color. Which department he'd served with. Important details like that.

Damn, she wanted this man to stay. But like the good aunt that she was to her sister's two boys, she told Hotrod, "It's time for midnight breakfast, then back to bed with you."

"Hmmmmm," he rumbled against her breasts, his scruff inciting tingles over her bare skin. "You might be right."

"I am right," she whispered, wishing he was already rested and raring to go. Like she was. "Bacon and eggs, coming right up."

Those piercing blue eyes stabbed her. "Then sex? Pretty please?" he asked like a naughty little boy she couldn't resist.

"Yes, sex. For as long as you want," she promised. Pressing her lips to the middle of his forehead, she breathed him in. Life wasn't always hard and lonely. Sometimes, it was perfect.

# Chapter Five

He didn't want to leave Persia. Not like this. For the first time in his life, Walker Judge had found something rare and precious—a woman who understood him. Who truly seemed to like him as much as he liked her.

But then he'd failed her when he couldn't perform. Not cool. Not even the slightest bit funny. Mother Nature was a bitch. Yet Persia acted as if sleep and rest could fix that, so he let her think so. Truth was, he was running on fumes, just like she'd said. Two days of relentless swimming had tapped every last bit of his physical reserves and his nerves. The weeks on the run before that swim hadn't been any easier. He needed some serious downtime before he attempted seducing her again. Mostly because, after that lackluster performance, he had to prove himself to her. He was not a wimpy lover. He *could* get it up! Just give him a minute or two. An hour. Maybe three… Or four…

Ha! Who was he kidding? He hadn't seduced anyone. She'd been the aggressor from the start, yet even that was refreshing. Women who knew what they wanted and needed were a real turn-on. And she'd wanted him, straight out of the ocean when his fingers and toes and—that—were still prunes. Which—that—still was. Yeah. He could get it up, but getting it off the launchpad and into orbit wasn't working so well.

Rest. He needed to eat, load up on carbs, and sleep, preferably with her beneath him.

It was oddly comforting watching Persia work on their midnight breakfast in her kitchen. Almost made him feel like half of a whole. Part of a real couple. Like he belonged. Until he took stock of where he was.

Her bungalow was straight out of *Pottery Barn*. Clean. Crisp. Too clean.

Everything, from the comfy white cloth couch covered with red, white, and blue pillows, to the just-as-white pedestal bed, white linen comforter, more white and blue pillows, seemed to be in its proper place. The floor throughout was stained gray hardwood, a driftwood kind of gray. And clean. Not an errant flip-flop in sight. No dust. No knick-knacks. Not so much as a loose magazine.

White painted end-tables and a matching coffee table decorated the main room. A white painted bookshelf covered the entire wall behind her couch, and a navy-blue rocking chair sat at a right angle to that pristine couch. But there wasn't a single personal item anywhere. Not framed pictures of family. Not a swimsuit cover-up tossed carelessly over the rocker. Not even a set of keys, a cell phone, or a phone charger.

Needing to know if she was just OCD, Walker had the urge to check her closets and drawers. The bungalow felt… staged. As if she'd just arrived and didn't expect to stay long. As if this were a façade. A set-up. The kind federal agents used in a sting.

Yet he'd seen her bedroom, and that bed was certainly mussed now. The head as well. Walker let it go. He wouldn't be here long. Why ask questions he didn't want to know the answers to?

"Do you think you can handle this?" she asked, handing him a ten-inch kitchen knife, a cutesy melon baller, and a ripe cantaloupe as big as a small basketball. The tease.

"I prefer peaches to melons," he teased back.

Her lips thinned, but he caught the surreptitious glance down at her chest. "Peaches?"

Hotrod nodded. She most definitely had a luscious pair of cantaloupes, but size wasn't everything. "Yes, firm, fragrant, delicious peaches that fit snug inside my hands. Makes me want to rub them all over my face. Can't do that with melons."

She blushed, and wasn't that a beautiful sight? Already a lovely shade of caramel, her cheeks turned rose, then the prettiest russet red. Better yet, like a shy little girl, she ducked her head into her shoulders. "Okay, then. Peaches, I guess."

He felt the need to expound lest she thought she was in any way inferior, or that he'd meant her breasts weren't what he preferred. They damned well were.

Stiffening his arm, Hotrod held the melon out to her at eye level. "See this fruit? It's round and it's good-sized, but it's also covered with a tasteless rind that's as rough as dirt. It has to be washed, halved, then the guts cleaned before you can eat it. If you want to get fancy, the fruit has to be cut from the rind, then sliced and diced or balled. By the time a guy gets to pop one tasty morsel into his mouth" —he popped his lips— "he's lost his appetite. But peaches…"

Hotrod let his gaze drop to her succulent, tempting— peaches. Lifting up from the breakfast bar, he set the cantaloupe on the counter where it couldn't roll. This next demonstration needed to be up close and personal.

Persia's breath hitched when he rounded the counter and slipped both hands beneath her robe. Gently, he cupped her bare breasts, his thumbs rubbing over her pebbled nipples. "But peaches are something else altogether," he murmured, his voice gone husky and deep.

The delightful globes resting in his palms were warm and lush. "They don't need a rind because they were created perfect." His thumbs tag-teamed her nipples until both were hard and begging for his mouth. "They're soft and sweet and warm, kissed by the sun and ready to melt in my mouth."

"Your mouth?" she asked, her voice trembling. Man, her eyes were melted chocolate, so deep and enticingly dark that he wanted to dive in and never be seen again.

He parted her robe and dipped his nose into her warm, fragrant cleavage. "Oh, yeah," he breathed as he turned his head and drew one succulent nipple between his lips. Hollowing his cheeks, he suckled like a baby pig in heaven. Breast heaven. It didn't—couldn't—get any better than this.

Her arms wrapped around his head, trapping him where he wished he could stay. Hotrod closed his eyes. Melons or peaches, he didn't really care, as long as it got him here. With her. Inside her prickly defenses. Persia was a different kind of woman, hard as nails, yet so damned soft and feminine. He wanted to stay where he was. If only he could.

"Hey," she murmured, her voice raspy in his ear. "Umm, bacon, anyone?"

"Yes, ma'am," he answered, suddenly remorseful. Tipping back on his heels and out of her arms, he drew in a deep breath, covered her peaches, and pasted on a lying, happy face. Life was what it was. The longer he stayed and played with this tempting woman, the harder it'd be to walk away from her. As soon as he ate, he had to go. Or he'd never leave.

Time to clean and quarter that cantaloupe.

Breakfast at midnight was uniquely Persia. She whipped up a batch of blueberry pancakes while the bacon sizzled, then set a pint-sized crock of marmalade on the breakfast bar, along with a plate of sliced cheese, cucumbers, and tomatoes. There was no maple syrup, just another crock of rich, creamy butter. And she ate with relish. Which made him smile. It was easier to enjoy a good meal when the woman with you wasn't dining on salads or yogurt or fussing about calories or her weight. How Persia kept a trim figure, Hotrod didn't care. She enjoyed his company and that was what mattered.

She'd taken the stool beside him and now waggled a slice of crispy peppered bacon under his nose. "Where are you from?"

"Around," he replied, keeping it vague as he speared a small stack of pancakes. But then he added, "I was born in Miami, but I keep a post office box in Texas. That's my official residence." *Used to be San Diego, but that's another story.* "I graduated from the school of hard knocks, but majored in sociology at the University of San Diego." *In between deployments and before murder trials...*

"Navy brat," she murmured, taking a bite off the end of that crispy treat.

Her lips closed over the slice of meat and Hotrod had to close his eyes. Everything this woman did drew him back to sex. Either it was all her, or he was still that horny.

"Just interested in group dynamics. People. What makes them tick. That's why I went into sociology. But how about you? You said you were an agent. I'd guess either CIA or FBI. Truth or dare?"

She snapped at that crispy slice, and he grimaced, painfully aware what those straight, pearly whites could do to a treasured part of his anatomy. If she were ever to get that close.

"You're good," she purred. "I was FBI, but I worked an op for the Agency last year. Not doing that again. Don't like what they expect of their agents. Moved onto something better."

He could've watched her chewing and swallowing all night. "Like what?" he asked, his voice a mere whisper. His eyes on her luscious lips and mouth. The suggestive tease of her tongue on the end of that salty slice of meat.

"Ever hear of a covert surveillance company called The TEAM, out of Alexandria, Virginia? Alex Stewart? He's former USMC and owns that company. It's one of the best on the East Coast, may even be the best in the States. I needed a break, so I quit the federal circuit and signed on with him last month."

Hotrod cocked his head, finally understanding why this bungalow didn't feel lived in. "So you're on vacation? This place isn't yours?"

Snap went another inch of that crispy bacon.

"Oh, it's mine, all right. I bought it on a whim last month, but just arrived yesterday. Needed time to decompress."

"Oh? Why?" They had yet to touch the cantaloupe.

She shrugged. "Can't do the deep, dark infils the Agency wants anymore. Not like I worked for them to begin with. Uh uh. No, sir. I was FBI until my boss loaned me to the CIA, just because I *look* Spanish." She stabbed air quotes around the bacon hanging off her lip and mumbled, "Me. A second-generation Iranian immigrant. I look Spanish. Do you believe that?"

That answered another question. "Your mother?" he guessed.

She nodded. "Yes, Mom was one of the Iranian scientists who handled mustard gas canisters during the Iran-Iraq War back in the '80s. Do you remember that? When Israel caught wind of the attack, they bombed the weapons depot where Mom worked. No gas canisters were damaged, but she took advantage of the chaos to escape. She still won't say how she got out of Iran."

"Because she's protecting her friends."

Persia's head bobbed. "I realize that. Anyway, I'm Iranian on Mom's side, American on Dad's. They still live in Mississippi."

That surprised Hotrod. "Not working for the American government?" Usually the USA grabbed up foreign scientists.

"No. Not for Uncle Sam. Dad had just bought a rundown tobacco plantation before they met. She helped him change it from a derelict dump to one of the county's most productive farms. They grow cotton now. They met at a baseball game, do you believe that? An Iranian scientist falls in love with a cotton farmer over baseball? Sounds like a fairytale, but I swear it's true."

"The American dream," Hotrod whispered.

"I guess." She huffed, blowing a silky ribbon of dark hair out of her eyes. "Anyway... My last job in Brazil damn near killed my heart. Too many kids involved. I hate when children get hurt. Still messes with my head. Makes it hard to remember why I was really there. You know? Part of me turns into a raging beast thinking about it. I wanted to kill anyone who touched them and save every last child. Only I couldn't. I didn't."

Brazil? That cut a little too close to home. Hotrod had just been undercover in the Highlands of Minas Gerais, Brazil, along with his US Army Ranger buddy, Gregor, aka 'Charlie Brown' Jorgensen, Special Agent Julio Juarez, and another damned cocky female, one-time US Army Corporal Duncan. Meg. She'd planned on adopting an entire orphanage of unwanted children the last time Hotrod saw her. She and Juarez were instrumental in ending Orlando Zapata's bloodthirsty reign. They'd done the impossible. Saved a hand full of orphans in the process.

Hotrod had to know. "Where in Brazil?"

"Highlands of Minas Gerais." *Oh, shit.* And then it got worse. "Ever hear of Domingo Zapata? His brother Orlando?"

Hotrod's heart all but stopped at the uncanny coincidence that Persia had been precisely where he'd been only weeks earlier. "I've heard of them. What'd you do? End the sons of bitches?"

He already knew different. She might have ended Domingo, but it was Julio Juarez who'd ended Orlando. Aka Oz, the dirtbag. With a freakin' two-fer. In Hotrod's mind, Julio was a straight-up hero. He'd lined up his shot to blow several diesel gas pumps, but when Orlando stepped in the way, Julio had taken down two birds with one stone, Oz and the pumps. Actually, Julio had taken down every last soldier in Oz's army, plus a couple Russian spies, with the ensuing explosion caused by that single shot. Zapata's gravel pit and gold mine were still burning. Juarez was a god.

"I wish," Persia murmured, her eyes gone flat and her gaze a thousand miles away. "But, no. My mission was only to infiltrate and keep eyes on Domingo. To pass intel back to Washington, DC. Wish I could've killed him, but that honor belongs to my buddy, Julio Juarez. Man, I adore that Mexican stud, but he's married, and he's in love with his wife."

Hotrod stifled another grimace. She knew Julio, too. *Shit.*

"But when he and Meg ended that rat bastard, I had to go back to DC. Domingo thought he was one badassed man, but he was wrong. Julio is. There's nothing stronger than love, and Julio proved it in spades that day."

Hotrod cocked his head, not sure who else Julio loved, other than Meg. That had been obvious since day one. Had he married her then? Was she the wife Persia mentioned? "So Domingo kidnapped Meg?"

Which was Domingo's standard operating procedure. Kidnap a woman, then subject her to all manner of heinous tortures. In the end, they all died the same, with Domingo painting his ugly face with their blood.

"Nah. Meg was hurt, but she didn't need saving. She can take care of herself. But yeah, Julio was there to rescue Dominic. Do you believe Domingo was his father?" Persia flicked her fingertips dismissively. "Least, that rat bastard was the sperm donor."

Hotrod listened more intently. Julio rescued Domingo's kid? Unbelievable. "Really?"

Persia kept talking. "Yeah. Really. You see, Domingo kidnapped Julio's wife and kid, I think his name was Tomas. Poor Julio went out of his ever-loving mind, searching five years for his wife and that little boy. He finally gets them back, but Tomas isn't a baby anymore. He wasn't even the same kid. He was messed up, you know?"

She'd captured one long, silky black tangle with her finger by then, and kept pulling at it, as if she could straighten the curl. "He died after all he suffered in Domingo's bunkers. But once Julio turned up in Brazil to rescue Meg and her orphanage, he ended up fighting tooth and nail to save Domingo's kid from his old man." Again Persia asked, "Do you believe that guy? Saving the son of the creep who'd killed his own boy? Guy's got big, brass cojones."

No. Hotrod couldn't believe the kind of hero Julio was, nor all he'd suffered. "Juarez sounds like a good man, but did he rescue his wife? Or was she…?" He hated to think Domingo had hurt Julio's wife as much as he'd hurt Tomas.

"Nah. Turned out Domingo didn't kidnap Bianca or Tomas like Julio thought. She went willingly, the cow. Guess she was into full body tats, sharpened teeth, and" —Persia shivered—"Who knows what else? She deserted her little son. That I know for damned sure. I was there. I watched how she walked away from Tomas. I heard him screaming and crying for her."

Jesus Christ. Hotrod hadn't known that, either. He couldn't imagine any woman tossing her son to a beast like Domingo. Bile climbed up his throat.

Persia had turned into a flowing fountain of information. "Julio did go after Domingo, and he did save Domingo's little boy, though. Long story, short. Meg shot most all of Domingo's guards, but it was Julio who finished what Meg started. He's the guy who put a bullet in the middle of Domingo's ugly face. Julio, Meg, and Dominic are now living happily-ever-after outside Big Springs, Texas, not far from her parents' ranch. You both live in the same state now. You ought to stop by and introduce yourself next time you're home."

Yeah, not going to happen. Not because Julio didn't deserve the recognition, but because he already knew precisely who Hotrod was. But knowing Julio was finally safe back in America, and that he'd married Meg Duncan? That he'd saved that skinny little Dominic, whom Meg loved so hard? Best news ever.

Only now, Hotrod also knew Persia was a trained undercover specialist, and a damned good operator if she'd been inside Domingo Zapata's lair. She was smart, no doubt smarter than Hotrod. For tonight, that was who he was, but come morning, she would've had time to think. She might've put two and two together by then, and come up with one escaped convict. A murderer.

Instead of talking or asking more questions, he filled his mouth with pancakes slathered in marmalade and murmured, "Mmmm."

Yup. Definitely time to leave.

# Chapter Six

She woke up with a start. Shivering when it wasn't cold or chilly. Alone in her bed.

Wide-eyed, Persia lifted to her elbows. Her gaze shot straight to her nightstand where… *Thank God!* Her handgun was still where Hotrod had left it. Bless his heart. The Smith and Wesson Bodyguard, .380 auto, her favorite personal weapon. Not TEAM issue, true, but bikini bottoms weren't stout enough gun belts for the man-sized SIG Sauer P226 she wore when on active duty. The Bodyguard was easier to hide—or sit on.

Jerking back the light woven bed cover she and Hotrod had slept beneath, the sweet musky scent of his male body lingered. On her sheets. On her fingertips.

Struggling against the silence, she cocked her head, hoping for the slightest indication he might be in the kitchen, maybe the shower. Anywhere within the confines of these four walls. Her nostrils tested the air for the slightest hint of Arabica beans or buttered toast or freshly squeezed juice. He'd make breakfast before he said goodbye, wouldn't he?

Shaken to her core at how foolish she'd been, Persia slid out of bed and put her bare feet to the floor. Damn it. His gear bag was gone.

She grabbed her light, summer robe off the hook near her bedroom door and ran through her home-away-from-home, her heart stuck high in her chest. He wouldn't just leave, would he? He couldn't. Not after the way he'd made sweet, slow love to every inch of her body last night. He'd been so gentle. So tender.

And she'd been so damned stupid! There was no one in her bungalow or on the beach. Or in the kitchen. Or anywhere that she could see. Only sand. Hotrod had really left her.

The old-fashioned ringtone of a rotary phone from forever ago jangled from her cell. That tone was particular to Alex Stewart, her new boss. Him calling meant this two-week vacation between the end of her FBI career and her new life as a security specialist for The TEAM in Alexandra, Virginia, was over before it'd even started. He needed her. She'd have to go.

Persia let the damned thing ring. Hotrod couldn't have just walked away, could he? Her heart refused to believe. He'd seemed so kind and sincere and—broken. They'd shared something last night. Hadn't they? She'd thought so.

The rotary ringtone ceased, only to commence again. *Ring. Ring. Ring.*

She should answer. After all, she was the one who'd sought Stewart. That last undercover gig in Minas Gerais, Brazil, had proven too brutal for her. Then, as if all she'd been through there meant nothing, the Bureau wanted to loan her to the CIA again, for yet another undercover narc operation. One where she would have gone into Iran, the country of her ancestors, as an undercover spy. She would've had to cozy up to the latest ayatollah. Not only no, but hell no. That guy was a pedophile and a liar, not a prophet.

Didn't the CIA have anyone else brave enough or dumb enough to waltz into Iran for them? Persia was beginning to feel expendable, as if dying was the least she could do for her country. She, on the other hand, thought she was a unique asset. Yes, her Middle Eastern looks gave her an inside advantage, but she'd seen enough beheadings in her short career to know that was not how she'd intended to serve.

Persia simply hadn't the nerve or heart to go undercover again, not so soon after what she'd seen in Brazil. In the course of infiltrating Domingo Zapata's lair, she'd done things that still haunted her. Plus, she'd done them alone.

Her mark, Domingo Zapata, the ruthless killer of men, women, and children, could've easily ordered her execution with one snap of his blood-stained, stubby fingers. Instead, she'd stood by while he'd imprisoned innocent women and children in his bunker, all to gain his trust, to become part of his inner circle. Not like she could've stopped him. The monster had guards everywhere, all as ugly and evil as him.

Then along came Special Agent Juarez. While she'd been busy *blending in*, he'd stormed the bunker and ended the son of a bitch, once and for all. The worst part was that he'd had to go into that bunker twice. Two years earlier to save his son. The last time, ironically, to save Zapata's son.

*Ring. Ring. Ring.*

Persia glanced back through her home to her bedroom and the mussed bed, where she was pretty sure she'd slept soundly for the first time in months. Last night. Without a bottle of whiskey. With Hotrod instead. With his strong arms wrapped around her like steel ribbons on a Christmas present. With her head tucked under his chin. With her hands on his chest, her thumb in that narrow canyon between his pecs, and his warm, cinna-minty breath in her face. Listening to the steady, sure beat of his heart.

For the first time in she couldn't remember how long, she hadn't woken up screaming. She hadn't even been drunk when she'd gone to bed, either. Which was annoyingly interesting. Yet the jerk had screwed her, then ditched her. Hotrod hadn't enough class to say goodbye. Just slam, bam, not even thank-you ma'am.

That hurt. Persia swallowed hard, wishing she weren't such an easy lay. But knowing, deep down, if she had another chance to be with Hotrod, she'd do it again. Like that would ever happen.

She swiped a finger under her runny nose, not going to cry over spilled milk, damn it. That rat bastard must've gotten up extra early. It wasn't even five in the morning. It was late spring, nearly summer, but the sun had just broken through the East. What'd he do, swim back to Cuba in the dark?

*The phone just kept ringing!*

Persia marched back to her kitchen counter, where there was no freshly made coffee, warm, buttered toast, or icy cold OJ. Not even a hint that Hotrod had ever been in her home. Man, she was stupid!

Picking her phone off the charger, she snapped at her new boss, "What?"

Alex Stewart snapped right back at her, "When can you get back?"

"I'm on vacation. Two weeks, remember?" she reminded him tersely, her gaze on the breakers pounding her beach and the gulls caught in the breeze overhead. How damned idyllic. Looked like it was shaping up to be another freakin' day in paradise.

"Vacation's canceled. Now, I'll ask again. When can you get here?"

Her eyes watered at the level of snark in his tone. If she'd been in Brazil, if he'd been Zapata, she would've handed that snark right back to him. Domingo would've respected her then.

But Alex wasn't anything like the Zapata brothers. He was decent and fair. Yes, he was OCD about his people, and he had one helluva nasty temper when riled, but she respected him and the work he did. There wasn't another company like his band of former snipers, The TEAM, anywhere in the States. They got things done, and many times, they did it for free— just because they really were the good guys.

She needed a damned break from all the federal alphabet agencies she'd worked for these past few years. Besides, The TEAM had a solid reputation, and oh, yeah, Alex paid one helluva lot more than Uncle Sam.

"I can be on a jet by noon," she replied more calmly. Then she added with a touch of sarcasm, "Unless you need me sooner."

"Be at US Naval Air Station by eight. I'm sending a chopper. Need you now."

She wanted to ask how he could possibly need her, his newest agent, but he'd disconnected the call. He'd hung up. But hey, that was Alex for you. Badassed. Hard-charging. One of those absolute alpha males all the way. Damn him and damn Hotrod What's-His-Name!

Angry and fed up with the world of men—all men!— Persia cocked her arm, meaning to fastball her phone into the wall, or out the door and all the way to Hell! But she saw it then. The tiniest piece of paper. Stuck in the edge of her front door jamb.

All it said was, "Later." Oh, that was real sweet. Downright precious, if you were dumb enough to believe anything the guy who'd run out on you said. Which she wasn't.

"Fuck you," Persia hissed at the only man she'd ever allowed inside her bungalow and her heart. She didn't need Hotrod or anyone else. She had a job to do. Good riddance!

# Chapter Seven

Walker didn't go far, just to the other side of the island, where he could get his head straight and plan his next move. He dropped his tired ass to the beach. The long stretch of Florida Keys lay across the narrow channel in front of him. They were so close, he could make out the cars on Interstate One, the highway that kept the Keys connected to the mainland.

He felt like crap. Sneaking out from under Persia's warm embrace before sunrise, without waking her, had been one of the worst things he'd done to a woman in years. Not because he hadn't wanted to disturb her, but because he'd felt something in her arms last night, something rare and unique that had thrown him off balance.

The sensation of all he'd run from, that he was the biggest loser, lingered still. Like a sucker punch square in his solar plexus. A rogue wave on the ocean. He couldn't shake it—or her. Yeah, he should've stayed, at least left a better note than that scribbled 'Later.' But there'd been no choice. She didn't need his kind of trouble, and he wasn't going to Leavenworth.

But mostly? He couldn't stand to be betrayed by a woman he finally cared about. Persia was no uneducated SEAL wife-wannabe, no flirty bar fly, and no loser. She was smart enough to figure him out. And when she did, she'd be mad as hell that he'd used her like he had. She might even shoot him on sight the next time she saw him, and he wouldn't blame her. He had used her. She'd used him too, but women tended to forget that part of the equation, when a man walked away from them.

Walker rubbed his sternum, not sure why it ached. Maybe the long swim from Cuba to the mainland had been too much, even for a disciplined swimmer like him. Even competitive swimmers tore tendons and muscles during exhausting forty-eight-hour marathons.

Or it could be the bag drag from Cuba to Florida. The weight of Walker's gear had fought him every forward thrust and through every wave. He knew no shark had gotten close enough to have bumped his chest with its sandpaper snout, so the ache wasn't from that. Even if one had, his suit would've prevented any abrasions. No box jellyfish stings, either. He'd checked. Yet the center of his chest throbbed with a hollowness he'd never felt before and couldn't explain.

That ache was all about Persia. They'd connected at some elemental level and leaving her just plain hurt. Yet, it was for the best. He'd been on the run too long, and with every step, every backward glance, he hadn't been able to work out why he'd been targeted, convicted, and condemned. He needed time to think and to plan. To dig into his own case. Jesus, he just needed a quiet place for a change. This last year had been nothing but looking over his shoulder and trying to stay hidden.

While he sat staring at the bustling southern shoreline of Key West, he forced down his last protein bar, then sucked his final bottled water dry. He needed to leave, yet at the same time, he needed to stay. This morning, he was far from fit. Yes, he'd eaten and rested last night, but he hadn't armed himself against Persia Coltrane, had he? While in her home, he hadn't felt the need to carry, even after he'd seen the pistol coyly trapped against her thigh.

Leave it to a clever woman to know how to seduce a man. But that lush, tanned thigh…

Most likely he'd decided to linger just because of it. The woman was well-endowed, soft in all the right places. But every FBI agent on earth had been trained at Quantico, and that training could get him killed. Which made staying with her another day or two impossible.

When she realized who she'd invited into her home, then slept with, there'd be hell to pay. This time around, he was the betrayer. The deceiver. He knew damned well she never would've slept with him if she'd known who and what he was.

Disgusted with himself for running out on her, Walker lifted to his feet, grabbed his bag up from the sand, and walked into the surf. The channel between Persia's island and the Keys wasn't wide, maybe a good hour's swim was all. Might as well get it done.

Steady, measured strokes took Walker to Geiger Key. Naval Air Station Key West lay to his left, Saddlebunch and Sugarloaf Keys to his right. Highway One connected them to the mainland. He could walk that distance, but Walker had something else in mind.

Before he did anything else, he tugged another light gray, ratty Ron Jon t-shirt out of yet another plasticized compartment in his bag. This was his last decent shirt. He'd have to do some real shopping before long. To finish the look, his Ray-Bans with black reflective lenses came next. Today, he was jut another bland, nondescript tourist.

He found what he was looking for on the eastern most tip of Geiger Key, where a streamlined row of high-priced yachts bobbed in the shallows behind a long stretch of security fencing, itself topped with concertina wire to keep guys like him out. Dusting the sand off his bag, he walked the boardwalk between here and there, with the nosey confidence of a lost tourist, sizing up the multi-million-dollar babies bobbing in their bumper-lined docks. Nothing dry-docked here, not with these expensive toys. No way. Only the best for the rich set, and that meant they were all in the water, probably gassed up, and ready to go. *Perfect...*

A couple tough guys in muscle shirts watched. Not that Walker gave them a second look. Mall cops didn't scare SEALs. Sure, they were packing heavy-duty holsters and over-sized pistols, and they did look big and burly. Walker just didn't care. He wasn't here to tangle with, or kill anyone. This was about getting away from it all, in his case, that meant America. Wasn't that what these yachts were for, to get their wealthy owners away from all those petty problems of being obscenely rich?

He brushed a hand over his chin when he'd nearly smiled. Then, because he couldn't be seen breaking into these secure slips, he headed back the way he'd come. Even waved at the two guys still glaring at him. Smiled like a tourist out for a stroll.

When he could manage it without being seen, Walker ducked out of sight. The beach was calling his name. Stripping off his glasses and shirt, he sealed them back in his bag, then walked into the surf, the bag over his shoulder. This next adventure wouldn't take long.

Out beyond the breakers, he turned east, maintaining strong, slow, powerful strokes. To anyone watching, he was just another swimmer plowing through the gentle swells beneath the bright Florida sky. He was no one. Just some guy.

Until he'd breached the supposedly secure dock. There were no fences or concertina wire out here in the water.

Like one of the pesky dolphins the Keys were known for, Walker arrowed through the shallows to the first yacht. Nope. It was a charter boat. Not what he was looking for. Moving on, he swam toward the next. But the Arabic script on the bow meant trouble Walker didn't need. The one-hundred-eighty-foot Benetti yacht at its side was too long. The next, an Oceanfast Superyacht sat too high, too visible in the water, and looked like a destroyer. Walker didn't want anything that hinted Navy. The damned thing was even painted gunmetal gray. Oh, hell no.

The next vessels were three Cantieri di Pisa yachts, all in a row. All sleek, white, and way out of his class. Each one-hundred-fifty-three feet long. Tonnage... He guesstimated four hundred fifty, maybe more. They probably all required a twelve-man crew to operate. Not only out of his class, but too much trouble. Someone would miss any one of these babies the second it pulled away from the dock and into clear water.

Walker kept going, not sure what he was looking for, but sure he'd know when he found it. Treading water now, he kept afloat even as his bag weighed him down. There were two rows of secure berths on this narrow peninsula, one on the south side, the other north. He didn't want to search all hundred or so slips, but he would if he had to.

Eleven yachts later, he stopped cold and swiped the water out of his eyes, not believing his good luck. A forty-five-foot Meridian Motoryacht. What was a vessel worth a measly two hundred K doing here among all these million-dollar yachts the caliber of Donald Trump's wet dreams?

A large, roomy cockpit sat high and proud above what was undoubtedly a lavish master stateroom on this white and black, all-polished, albeit much smaller, watercraft. Tinted windows lined the deck level. Security cameras blinked along each topside window frame. But Walker was willing to bet those were merely part of an onboard security system, that there was no one sitting in an office somewhere, actively watching this yacht twenty-four-seven, ready to spring into action and call the police if a seagull happened to sit on the yacht's rail. Or if a seal, pun intended, climbed onto the swim deck to, *ahem,* sun himself.

Bobbing there in the water with only his head showing, Walker took everything in. Black canvas roof on the cockpit. Black fenders kept the hull from scraping against the dock. Polished wooden rails from bow to stern. But the kicker? The godawful name stenciled in black vinyl lettering at the stern, just above the aft ladder. *Coronado's Sea Nymph.* Son of a bitch, this was Commander Goff's rig. Goff, as in the naval officer Walker had been convicted of murdering with his bare hands.

He glanced over his shoulder, feeling as if someone had just stepped on his grave—with six-foot-long, spiked cleats. H-h-holy shit. How could Goff's yacht be here?

Walker sucked in a slow deliberate breath. The upside? This craft was perfect for what he needed. Cummins engine. A fuel tank that held at least one hundred fifty gallons of diesel. He guessed it could top-out at seven hundred fifty horsepower, give or take a couple ponies. Didn't require a crew, not even a co-pilot. One man could handle it, easy. Bow and stern thrusters. Two decks, one upper—probably the master stateroom since it also sported an enclosed patio aft. One lower level, undoubtedly the forward galley and maybe a guestroom. Upper aft deck for lounging and watching the have-not's world go by. Then the swim deck and ladder, where swimmers could come and go, or where a guy could stand and fish from.

The up-top cockpit offered a full three-hundred-sixty-degree view. And this yacht was new. At least, fairly new. The damned thing glistened like a waxed, iridescent black-and-white pearl in the sun, which meant it hadn't seen much saltwater. Or use. It'd been stored, as in protected in dry-dock, when it wasn't being used.

The downside? Walker dipped his chin below water, blowing bubbles, trying to come up with any reason not to slip up and onto this craft, then set it and himself adrift. Except for getting caught and put in Leavenworth. That was a good reason not to abscond with a deceased man's yacht. But Goff was dead. How could fifty years hard time in Leavenworth get any worse? Walker was already in his late-thirties. He'd be eighty if he lived long enough to serve his sentence. There was no hope of being exonerated or pardoned. What did he have to lose?

Not. A. Damned. Thing.

Decision made. He closed the distance and climbed aboard. Next stop? Top off his tank at Key Largo. Spend a few days moseying south to Puerto Rico, then onto Barbados. Maybe refuel at Georgetown, Guyana. Contrary to popular belief, the straightest way across the Atlantic was not as the crow flew. Smart sailors took the longer route, down to the eastern most tip of South America to the westernmost tip of

Africa. Fewer miles. Less chance of running out of fuel or encountering US Coastguard. He might run into a few pirates, but Walker had no fear of pond scum. Not with the firepower in his bag.

He meant to leave the States in his rear view as fast as he could. To eventually end up in Europe where nobody knew his name, face, or what he'd been accused of. Might stop somewhere along the coast of Africa and linger. Maybe at Sierra Leone. Senegal. Or Western Sahara. From there, Morocco was a mere day's sail away, then Gibraltar, Portugal, and Spain. He knew a few people in most countries he'd deployed to. All except Ireland, England, and Scotland. He'd never been to the United Kingdom. Hell, now he had time. He might even make it all the way north to Denmark and Norway. The Baltic Sea and the Gulf of Bothnia. That'd be interesting. Cold, but interesting.

His heart rate quickened at the adventures still ahead. His life wasn't over, not by a long shot. NCIS might've thought they'd ruined him, but he wouldn't go down without a fight. If he had time, he might investigate them for a change. Wouldn't they be surprised if he uncovered a way to beat those dirtbags at their own lying game? If he found out who was behind this well-orchestrated plot to assassinate his character? That'd be even better.

His fingers curled into fists thinking of the day of comeuppance in his future. Truth did prevail, damn it, and he meant to make sure it did. Hopefully.

# Chapter Eight

It was the day after her hasty exit from the Keys, and Persia couldn't keep her mind on the briefing. Or her boss. Or on the upcoming, important powwow at the United Nations, New York City, her reason for hurrying back to Alexandria, Virginia.

Every president, prime minister, king, queen, and despot was coming together in NYC to discuss the ever-polarizing concept of climate change and the world's imminent demise. Environmentalists had become the doomsday prophets of the twenty-first century, all clamoring for governments the world over to shut down any and all manufacturing that relied on carbon fuels. To prohibit air travel, the use of natural gas, coal mining, *blah, blah, blah.* In other words, to stop living, producing, manufacturing, and go back to the stone ages.

Persia was surprised breathing oxygen and spewing carbon dioxide weren't on their hitlist of disgusting emissions. Cows were.

She'd worn a light dress this morning, a powder blue sheath with a simple, white knitted shrug covering her shoulders, offering a touch of professionalism to her casual attire. The TEAM's dress code was quite lenient. Unless they were on assigned operations, casual business was the rule of thumb, which meant most other agents wore black and their black TEAM polo shirts. But Persia was sick of looking like an FBI reject, and she hated black. After the fiasco in Brazil, she needed color in her life. Bright, airy colors. Any color combination other than red or black.

After a few meetings with The TEAM's physician on staff, Dr. McKenna Fitzgerald-Villanueva, Persia now realized she'd brought a couple triggers home with her from Brazil. It stood to reason, after working and living with a psychotic killer like Domingo Zapata. She wasn't the innocent woman she'd been before. Far from it.

Somedays, she suspected she bordered on the edge of a nervous breakdown. She dreamed of stepping right over that edge, by either screaming her heart out or drinking herself to death. Even now, a slim, easy-to-hide flask rested full and comfortably available in the over-the-shoulder crossbody bag beneath her desk. Because she, former FBI Special Agent Persia Coltrane, one of the Bureau's finest undercover operators, was hanging on by the thinnest thread. And an occasional shot of whiskey helped, damn it.

She should be high after the biggest, toughest success of her career. She had awards from the Bureau and the Agency. Fat lot of good paper certificates and bonus checks did. Instead, she was unraveling, blindsided by ghosts and monsters in the dark. By stupid *Crayola* colors!

Her nightmares had become unbearable, and she detested tiny, cramped spaces. Like elevators, even her sporty Toyota sports car seemed suffocatingly close once she shut the door and turned the engine. Not that she'd ever been caged or trapped like so many of Domingo's victims. But her empathy for those women and girls continued to replace them in her nightly dreams with—her. A night hadn't yet gone by that she hadn't woken up screaming, sure she was the one being assaulted or doing the assaulting. She was exhausted, reliving what she'd never lived through. Yet believing she'd indeed been tortured—or worse. That she'd killed…

Doc Fitz called it post-traumatic stress, but Persia knew better. Her nightmares were her just reward for not having helped those women and girls escape when she could. For following CIA protocol, instead of blowing Domingo Zapata's hairy ass to hell. *Just for being there…*

Except for that one night with Hotrod, she hadn't fallen asleep without a good stiff drink or two before bed, since she'd come home. Sometimes, she took the whole bottle with her. Which was worrisome, needing to numb her heart like she did. But as long as it worked, hey. She would self-medicate until the nightmares stopped. Or until Doc Fitz came up with a way for Persia to get out of her head long enough to rest her soul. Really, truly rest. To fall asleep and dream, instead of having nightmares. That'd be nice.

To be able to forgive herself. That'd be even better.

Persia left her lights on at night now. All night. All of them. Even her oven light, and how ridiculous was that? It almost made her sound crazy. Well, crazier. But she'd learned the hard way that what you couldn't see, would hurt you. Even something as small as that dark square place in her oven or microwave wasn't safe, daytime or nighttime. More than once, Zapata had introduced snakes and tarantulas into narrow dark openings.

*So, yeah. Let there be light, damn it. Lots and lots of light.*

But reds and blacks? All shades of Domingo Zapata. He'd always worn black. Even decorated his skin with the most horrific black ink tattoos. And fresh, red blood.

Her nostrils flared, remembering the septic stink of the wicked place she'd worked in for nearly a year. For a split second, Persia was back in Brazil again, fighting to keep her sanity, while she fooled Zapata into believing she wanted to work for him. Her heart pounded and she trembled. It was hard to swallow, much less think straight. Or listen to whatever Alex was rambling on and on... and on about.

Needing the sunlight more than this drawn-out, waste-of-time meeting, she stared out the window. What'd they call it? Mindfulness? Staying in the present? Letting the past she couldn't control, yet couldn't forget, go? Easier said than done. Persia required bright sunshine, a ton more space, and a little more R&R to get her head back in the covert ops game. And she would, by hell. She certainly would. Because panic attacks were surmountable. One only had to believe—

"You bet, Boss," Senior Agent David Tao replied, breaking up her therapeutic reverie. "I can have that back to you by noon. Soon enough?"

"Thanks, David, yes. I'd appreciate it. As far as your current assignment in Cambodia..." Alex's voice faded away.

Today's weather was bright and sunny on the East Coast, not a cloud in those blue skies. Which instantly reminded Persia of Hotrod, only his eyes weren't as vibrant. His were deep and dark, a seriously intoxicating midnight blue when he was focused. When he'd kissed her. When he'd made love to her.

She swallowed hard, remembering the weight of his all-male body on hers, the brush of his chest hairs over her sensitized nipples, and the slick, warm feel of his open mouth on her lips. His tongue sliding over her teeth to dance with her tongue. His breath. His fingers...

She still couldn't get the taste of him out of her mouth or her mind. Didn't really want to. The abrasions from his scruffy beard hadn't left her chin. Or in the hollow of her neck. Or on her lips. He'd left his marks all over her body and it had been everything she'd ever wanted. For once, she'd truly enjoyed time together with a man. In bed. In the shower. At her breakfast bar after she made pancakes for him. Even that crazy sensual story about the difference between cantaloupes and peaches. Hell, she'd enjoyed every second of whatever it was. Until the bastard left.

"Can you handle that, Junior Agent Coltrane?" Alex's snark was palpable.

*Ooops.* Persia looked away from the window and back into another set of deadly blues, only these were more like frozen Arctic icicles stabbing straight through her daydreaming heart. The sarcasm Alex had just hurled at her stung. She dropped her hand from her lips, embarrassed she'd been caught, by the leader of the pack, no less.

"Yes, sir," snapped out of her mouth, even as she cringed at her mistake. *Sir.* The salutation Alex detested more than he detested the person foolish enough to lead with it.

Closing his eyes, he ran a quick hand over his clean-shaven chin, no doubt struggling to not bitch her out for sir-ing him. Again. He could be such an ass about the simplest things. A badass, but an ass nonetheless.

"Yes, what?" he clipped out.

The entire room stilled and all eyes around the conference table turned her way.

"Boss?" she offered hopefully, though she suspected she'd made more than just the one mistake. Which she totally understood. Enlisted personnel did not mix well with officers.

Never had. Never would. Enlisted military worked hard for a living, while too many times, the officers who bossed them, simply sat back and took credit for everything the grunts beneath them accomplished. Cardinal rule number one: Never call an enlisted man, sir. It pissed him off. Alex more than most.

But she should've been paying attention, hanging on his every word. This was his TEAM, and he owned her during duty hours. She owed him that much.

At last he aimed those laser blues back at her, even as his lips thinned. "I said you're assigned to the Queen of England," he enunciated very clearly. Dressed in a business suit, he always looked dapper. Today was no different. Except that suit jacket was crisply pressed black linen over a burgundy dress shirt with a matching burgundy silk tie. Not bright red, but close enough to blood-red that it turned her stomach. Matching black slacks. Gold cufflinks. A USA flag pinning his tie over his heart.

Those. Colors. Looking at all that red and black had simply made Persia sick to her stomach, which was why she'd focused on anything but him. Still, her head bobbed in quick agreement. "Okay, thanks. Great. At the UN or—?"

"Mark…" Alex growled, his attention now to his right on Senior Agent Mark Houston. "I don't have time for this. Please fill Junior Agent Coltrane in on everything she's obviously missed. I've got a meeting with the Senate Majority Leader. We're done here."

Chairs scraped, as Alex collected his leather-covered planner, then stalked from the Situation Room. No one else moved, a signal everyone seemed to understand but Persia. Tired of her never-ending charade, she closed her eyes and ran her middle fingertip over her right eyebrow, covertly telling them and her boss to fuck off. Wishing she were anywhere else, but sure she was in for a butt-chewing in front of The TEAM.

Man, it was stifling hot in this conference room.

"You're distracted," Mark said quietly. He'd turned to her, his index finger tapping the worn corner of his planner. He had the darkest brown eyes that, thankfully, were never as cold or as icy as Alex's could be.

"She's been that way since she got back from Florida." Izza Maher snorted from the other end of the conference table where she usually sat with her hubby, Connor.

Only Junior Agent Connor wasn't here today. He and Harley Mortimer, one of the other senior agents on staff, had flown out earlier to the Islamic Republic of Afghanistan. Yesterday's 8.2 earthquake had wreaked catastrophic destruction that extended from Jalalabad into Pakistan, all the way to Peshawar. Connor and Harley had gone over to assist emergency efforts and to find their friends, to make sure they were okay. At least that was their cover story.

"Yes, Mark, I do have a lot on my mind," Persia agreed. Why lie? Her head hadn't been right since she'd left Brazil. Or maybe, since yesterday's flight from Florida. She no longer knew which pain hurt more than the other. Having lived through Domingo Zapata or waking up without Hotrod.

"I, umm…" Where to start? *I need an intervention? I'm afraid of the dark? I miss some idiot guy I only slept with once, and I'm pretty sure I'm turning into an alcoholic? Yeah. That ought to sit well with this group of polished professionals.*

Shoving his chair back, Mark lifted to his feet. "Step into my office. We need to talk. Dismissed, guys. You too, Izza."

Another snort. Persia loved Izza. Heck, she loved every last TEAM member. She was the problem, not them. Not even Alex. Dutifully, she trailed Mark to his private corner of TEAM-land.

"Mark! Mark!" Ember called from the customer service desk, where she worked IT issues with Agent Beau Villanueva, another over-the-top sniper.

One of those perpetually dark and gloomy guys, his brown eyes lit up when he caught Persia's sideways glance. "Good morning," he called out. Man, he was sexy as hell when he smiled, but he was also married to Doc Fitz. "Your new laptop just came in. Let me know when you're ready for a tutorial."

"Will do," Persia replied, wishing she could get her mind off—that man. That other man. The one with no sense in his hard, empty head. Sheesh. Hotrod Whoever-He-Really-Was hadn't even been able to perform! He was a loser! A nobody! Why couldn't she get him out of her mind?

Mark gestured her to go on ahead, while he diverted to Ember. All Persia caught was Ember excitedly telling him, "You'll never guess who just called!" Everyone loved Ember. She was pure sunshine. If she was that excited, the someone who'd just called must be quite the rock star.

With a long-suffering sigh that didn't begin to ease her deflated spirit, Persia sank into the wooden chair alongside Mark's desk. She tucked in her tummy, stiffened her spine, squared her shoulders, and prepared to be all she could be. No one needed to know her personal problems. Not even Mark. Especially not Alex.

By the time Mark entered and closed the door behind him, she was composed, back in the game, and ready to work.

"So talk," he said quietly, as he took his seat behind his cluttered desk. Persia didn't know all of Mark Houston's backstory, other than he and his wife now had five kids, all girls, and wasn't that amazing in this crazy, materialistic world? Plus, Libby Houston was not only a mom and a beautiful, svelte blonde, she was also a practicing physician. To look at her, you'd never guess she'd ever been preggo.

Mark himself was one of those tall, dark, handsome types, and built like a linebacker. He'd taken over for Alex Stewart a couple years back, during that dirty-bomb scare in DC. Which was why Alex could afford to spend time away from the office now. Like today. He had competent, well-trained staff. And he knew how to delegate.

Persia got right to the point. She meant to say just enough to get out of there. "I owe Alex an apology," she admitted brusquely, "but I need to be honest, Mark. I'm working through a couple issues since I left the Bureau. I'm not saying I can't work, just wanted to get that out in the open, so you know where I stand. Now, what did you need?" That ought to do it.

He nodded encouragingly. "Anything I can help you with?"

No, just no. She gulped. This wasn't going like she'd planned. Well, okay then. She'd give him the tiniest bit of intel. Nothing more. Nothing less.

"Could you please tell, I mean, ask Alex not to wear the color combination he had on today? I'm still seeing Doc Fitz." Mark already knew that; he just didn't know why. "And she's helped me realize that those colors, red and black…" A wicked shiver galloped over Persia's shoulder and right down her spine. It caught her unaware and she wiggled, damn it. "Those colors are triggers for me."

"Domingo Zapata," he said. Not asked. "His ink and the way he embellished his face, right?"

Embellished was too kind a word.

"Yes," she admitted, as a wave of anxiety swamped her. The four walls took a step forward, closing her in. It was suddenly awfully hard to breathe.

Mark was perceptive, maybe even intuitive. He was one of those indirect leaders who knew his people, and because he did, they loved him. Everyone loved Alex, too, just at a distance some days. Like today.

"What else should I know?" Mark asked kindly.

Taking a slow, deliberate breath, Persia rolled her eyes, not budging from her decision to stand fast. "Nothing. I'm fine. Honest. Hey, maybe I need to go shopping and buy something I don't need, huh?" She threw that feminine stereotype into the mix, still going for broke. Needing to divert Mark from getting any deeper inside her mind and her heart. Not going to happen. Her head had become a scary place lately.

He cocked his head, and man, this guy had the darkest brown eyes. "Take a deep breath, Persia..." His chest expanded, as if she needed to be shown how.

The way he drew her name out didn't help. She faltered. She liked Mark. He cared about people. That was his greatest strength and quite possibly, her greatest weakness. But her secrets were safer left unspoken. Not shared. She stared back into those brown eyes. Needing to run more than to breathe.

She honestly thought she could pull this act of invisibility off until he murmured, "We're all crazy, Persia, every last one of us. Some of us are still broken. We've seen and done too much. Don't feel like you're the only one who's been in combat hell, because you're not. And please don't isolate yourself, when you're obviously having a bad day."

A gust of breath burst between her lips. *Is that what I'm doing? Isolating myself? Am I that obvious?*

Mark nodded, as if he'd heard her self-doubt. *Is he psychic?* "You accomplished something in Brazil no one else could have done. The intel you provided your handler led US agents directly to Domingo Zapata. He's dead, and you're not. What's more, the work you did inside that hellhole, saved every last woman and little girl, as well as others he had his eyes on. Focus on the good you did. Let the rest go."

Like an idiot coming undone, her head bobbed and she sniffed. Just once. But he'd said too much this time, and most of it was right on the money. Sucking in another breath, she swallowed hard. "I know. I know. Let the rest go. I should do that only…" Her voice cracked. This was Mark, damn it. Not Alex. Maybe if she told someone besides Doc Fitz. "I… I still see them when I close my eyes," she whispered, her eyes on the floor like a damned little girl afraid of the dark. Which she was. "Every night, Mark. Those little kids. Those poor women." That sweet innocent baby lamb…

"Would you like to know why Alex is meeting with the Senate Majority Leader today?"

Well, ahh… that was odd. Mark didn't usually ignore anything Persia said. Maybe this was his way of distancing himself from a messy, tear-jerking, emotional confrontation with a seriously impaired female junior agent. Maybe he didn't care like she'd thought he did. She held her sharp tongue, feeling utterly stupid for thinking any man might actually be sensitive enough to care. Okay then. This wasn't his problem. Just. Hers.

She ran a hand over her eyes to brush that foolish notion away. *There. Gone. Moving on now.*

Mark stretched a hand across his desk and fluttered his strong, manly fingers for her to take hold. Like a drowning woman, Persia reached for him and took hold. By then, she was trembling. Talking was over-rated. Running seemed a much smarter option.

"He's seeking legislation to make it mandatory for every female or male agent sent into hell-holes, like Zapata's, to go in with at least one partner. With back-up," Mark told her, his eyes hard and serious, but his voice as warm as melted butter. "No man or woman should ever go undercover without close emotional, physical, and tactical support, the way you did. We don't send our TEAM agents out one by one. I don't know why the Bureau and Agency do. It's not smart, and it's not safe. USMC snipers always have a spotter. Alex believes every federal undercover operator should have someone on their six, too."

"Ohhhh," breathed out of Persia. She didn't know what to say. Alex was doing that? Now? It almost sounded like he was doing it just for her.

Mark's brown eyes softened even more. "It's called post-traumatic stress, Junior Agent. I know you understand the concept, but living with it is something else. Shit happens, and it's a good thing you're smart enough to be seeing Doc Fitz. Which is also why you and Izza are handling the Queen of England's security while this conference is in New York. It's only for a week, and it'll be fun. You'll see."

"Fun?" Persia hadn't realized how tense she was until that precise moment. Automatically, her lungs relaxed. It was easier to breathe. To think. "Oh, good. I mean…" She swallowed hard. "Th-thanks."

"You're welcome," Mark replied evenly, still holding her fingers. "And to be clear, Alex isn't angry with you, not at all. He's proud as hell, Persia. Of you and all you did for your country. You sacrificed plenty, and he knows it. But he's pissed with the Bureau for pawning you off on the Agency for this particularly brutal op. The Zapata brothers were despicable assholes, excuse my language. The Agency should've sent a damned army, not one woman. Not that you weren't capable, because you proved you were. But the cost was too high, wasn't it?"

She nodded. "I sleep with all my lights on," she confessed. "I… I…" Her mouth snapped shut, on the verge of telling him about that flask.

He squeezed her fingers. "I did that when I first came home, too. I think most of us did, maybe still do. Trust me, kiddo, you're not alone, and Alex is a hundred percent on your side. He, of all people, understands what you've been through. What you're still going through."

"He does?" She grimaced at how he'd stormed out of the Sit Room, though. Alex hadn't seemed to understand then. Just because she hadn't been paying attention. She blinked. Damn it. Tears. She had to blink fast or they'd get away from her. *What is wrong with me?!*

Again, Mark seemed able to read her mind. Opening the side drawer at his right, he tossed one of those small packets of tissues at her, and he was smart enough not to say a word.

Persia slipped a fingernail through the perforated *open-here* and tugged one, then two tissues out, wiped her cheeks, and blew her nose. Feeling like a loser. Nothing said unprofessional like whining and crying on the job. When she could finally speak without falling apart, she told Mark, "But I called him sir again."

Mark tipped his face to the ceiling and laughed. The guy had the nerve! "You have no idea how much Alex looks forward to jerking your chain. Hell, I had to be Santa after I called him sir. Consider it a rite of initiation. You passed. Now you're officially TEAM property."

That actually helped. *TEAM property, huh?* Precisely what she'd wanted to be when she'd signed on. Persia took another steadying breath. The knot in her chest that had seemed like a rock a moment ago, vanished. She might've shed a tear or two, but she hadn't made a complete fool of herself. That was Mark's unique talent. He made people feel important and safe. Like they could tell him anything.

Just not anything about that flask or Hotrod. Ever.

# Chapter Nine

Instead of moseying around the Caribbean, Walker made it to San Juan, Puerto Rico, the next day, without being caught. By then, he'd disabled the yacht's GPS and hard-broke the onboard computer to suit his needs. It took a minute or two, but SEALs were trained to cover all bases. That was when he discovered the hard drive had been wiped clean. No records. No apps. Which didn't stop Walker. Rebooting the computer, he focused on what little programming language he knew from college to access the internet. From there, he bought and downloaded everything he needed. Which was smart in the long run. Now, he was untraceable and, for the most part, untouchable.

Just outside of San Juan's busy harbor, he idled down and searched California's online motor vehicles database, hoping to locate *Coronado's Sea Nymph's* former registration, and change its status to salvage. Once he also altered the ID stuck on the yacht's prow, it shouldn't ring any bells if the Coast Guard came calling. Goff's Motoryacht would be just one of many forty-five-footers traveling south. It wasn't unique, and it hadn't been modified to stand out like larger watercraft were. If anything, it looked like any other intermediate size yacht. It looked ordinary, especially berthed alongside million-dollar toys.

At last, he located its current registration. *Shit.* His heart stuttered to a full stop. Owner was still: *Wallace E. Goff.* Address: *Saratoga Avenue, Ocean Beach, CA.*

Walker suddenly lost the ability to swallow. Even his tongue had gone bone-dry. It was as if the bastard he'd been accused of murdering were alive and breathing over his shoulder, when Walker knew damned well Goff wasn't. He wouldn't have been tried for murder unless there'd been a dead body, would he?

Sure, he truly wished he'd been the one who'd ended Goff. The man had deserved to die, a thousand times over, for all the ways he'd demeaned and abused his men. Problem was, Walker wasn't the guy who'd killed him. Neither did he know who'd had the balls to go after Goff and break his neck. Or who'd been smart enough to leave no fingerprints or other forensic evidence behind. Not that he'd seen the actual body, but he'd seen the morgue photos the San Diego Medical Examiner had presented at Walker's trial. Walker knew it to be true. Goff was dead. He couldn't hurt anyone anymore.

*Or could he?*

The oddest sensation slithered up Walker's spine and curled around his neck like an invisible, slimy noose. His lungs stopped working because his heart had suddenly gone gangbusters loud. Was Goff deceased or not, damn it? Walker *had* seen the medical examiner's photographic evidence. He had! That *was* Commander Goff's ugly gray face in the morgue shot. Walker was certain. Wasn't he?

Yet doubt niggled, like a drug under a twitchy addict's skin. Why hadn't the *Nymph's* new owner updated the registration? Was California DMV simply behind updating their records, or was more going on here than met the eye?

For sure, NCIS, the Naval Criminal Investigation Service, had failed to defend Walker, had, in fact, crucified him in the press during his court-martial. Hell, instead of defending him, they'd produced a neighbor and two sailors who'd willingly put their lying hands on the Bible and sworn they'd seen him at the scene of the crime.

But those two sailors and Goff's supposed neighbor had outright lied. Walker hadn't been anywhere near Goff's house the night of the murder, that much was absolute fact. He'd actually just returned to San Diego from seven days personal leave, which the Navy prosecutor should have known from the get-go. Yet, that lawyer had twisted the argument, denying any record of leave existed. Then, going one slanderous step further, he'd stated—for the record—that even if Walker had been on leave or out of the country, he could've easily returned and killed Goff. He'd had plenty of time. As a SEAL, he certainly had the skills. Why look for anyone else when the SEAL they had in prison was the obvious perpetrator?

Yet some Navy asshat had definitely tampered with his official Navy records. It was as if that leave request had never been granted, as if his written request hadn't been submitted. Since his Commanding Officer, CDR Wallace Goff, was dead, and since Walker had refused to explain where he'd been or why, he'd ended with nothing to substantiate his claim. Not even a receipt while he'd been undercover, albeit on personal business, in Guatemala. That would've betrayed a good friend's confidence and trust, something he'd never do.

Walker had simply set out on that unplanned trip to do a dirty job for his friend. He'd never revealed to anyone where he was going, what he'd done while in South America, or who he'd done it for. That man's little girl didn't need to become fodder for this country's vile, rapacious media. They would've turned her into a spectacle the minute they knew. A three-year-old kid, for hell's sake. So, they'd never, ever find out. Even if Walker had to spend the rest of his days in Leavenworth, he'd gladly bear the burden, rather than turn sweet little Emily Dooley over to media sharks for their predictable circus. Just for the fame and glory of hyping a story, true or not. Assholes, every last one of them.

Walker never understood what the nation's press corps had become. Not one of them were honest brokers anymore, neither were they held accountable when proof of their lies, slander, and contrived 'facts' surfaced. No, the bastards just spun their lies faster, turned on the next unwitting victim in sight, and started another feeding frenzy.

He would know. They'd pretty much trashed his twenty-year USN career and pristine reputation during his trial. They'd lied and invented salacious versions of a crime that had never happened, at least not the way they'd said. America's press was no longer about freedom of speech. They somehow twisted inalienable rights into weapons they readily wielded, to verbally assassinate anyone who spoke out against them, or got in their way. Hardworking people like him. Innocents like Emily. Hell, anyone they wanted to smear for the sake of sensationalism, they did it. Daily. Hourly! Hell, minute by minute!

So, yes. He'd take the hit for that sweet little blonde girl and her family. The Dooleys deserved his utmost respect, and they had it in spades. The press? They deserved to be held accountable. But that was another fight, and Walker had enough on his plate for now. Like what was really going on?

Who was behind this nightmare? And why was Goff's yacht in Florida, when it should've been docked in San Diego?

Walker's brain pinged from simple questions to crazier, more ridiculous ideas until Common Sense screamed, "Time out!"

Which made… sense.

For the moment, hw was a free man, and he had possession of Goff's yacht. A full tank. All the beer, wine, and food he needed were in the galley below. He knew how to fish, and he could survive on his own. Time was on his side.

Okay then. He settled down and changed the yacht's current DMV registration record from active to salvage like he'd planned. Then he changed the current owner from Wallace Goff to Ruby Hatfield. Don't ask where that name came from. Walker honestly had no idea. The only thing he knew was that it was past time to right the wrongs done against him. He meant to do that without outing Emily, her family, or what she'd lived through.

Feeling lucky, he took a chance and docked the *Coronado's Sea Nymph* at one of San Juan's busiest wharves. Donning his Ray-Bans with reflective lenses, Walker retrieved several large bills from his bag, ran to the nearest office supply store, and bought a couple sets of large, black, stick-on stencils. Only when he was back on board and had steered the *Nymph* south toward Venezuela, did he lose the sensation of being watched.

The criminal everyone thought Walker Judge was, for the moment, remained unseen and untouchable. Goff's yacht was off official records. Standing in the cockpit with his hand on the wheel, Walker took a long deep breath of freedom, even as he left the land he loved far behind. This was one of the downfalls to leaving. The other was an incredible, sultry woman named Persia.

Both now belonged to the past. Walker locked his heart yet one more time. Now was the time for clear, salt air in his nose, and getting his head on straight. He had to find out who was behind his multiple accusations.

To be safe, he kept the ship-to-shore radio on all that day. At sunset, before he lost what was left of the already fading daylight, he slowed the engine to idle and removed a coiled bundle of sturdy nylon rope from the cockpit supply locker. He had something to do that couldn't wait one more day.

At the prow of the *Nymph*, he tied a loop in one end of the rope, secured the other end to the polished starboard wooden railing, then adjusted the distance between loop and railing to the correct height. With the same agility that had earned him his SEAL handle in the Teams, he climbed over the railing to satisfy the gods of good fortune, sea, and wind.

Slipping one foot into the knotted loop for support, he dangled from the *Nymph's* prow, and scraped off the yacht's registration. But changing a ship's ID and name was serious business to superstitious sailors, and Walker was damned superstitious these days. Before the night was over, there'd be no more *Coronado's Sea Nymph* on the high seas.

"Hey, Poseidon. Hey, Neptune," he murmured to the ancient gods while he worked. "I humbly beg your favors and blessings upon this sea-worthy vessel as I rename her. I vow I will do no harm with this yacht, nor cause another sailor grief. Praise and thanks be to both of you for keeping her safe for me. From this day forward, let her be known as" —the new name came easily to him— *"Persia Smiles."*

And just like that, the superstitious chant changed to heartfelt prayer. "Let her be stronger than she thinks she is, Father. Let her always seek safe waters. Let her fly on eagle's wings. May the wind be always at her back. When sudden storms threaten her course, send your light to guide her home. Keep Persia safe, Father, please—for me."

He stuck the last of the scraped off, sticky vinyl into his rear pocket, then tugged the brand-new stencils from inside his t-shirt, where he'd put them to keep them dry. Carefully he removed the paper backing, then aligned the new letters and numbers.

The same job port side went easier. Quicker. By the time Walker was back up on the narrow forward deck, it was dark. The yacht's nighttime running lights had automatically come on. Hurriedly, he untied the rope and stowed it back in the cockpit storage locker. There was more work to be done.

Removing one of several LED lanterns from that same locker, he headed below deck to Commander Goff's well-stocked liquor cabinet. There, Walker requisitioned two bottles, one red wine and one champagne with an impressive gold label. Hmmm, *Louis Roederer 'Cristal' Brut*. Sounded decadently expensive. It would do.

On the swim deck at the rear of the yacht, he uncorked the pricey red first, and raised the bottle to the mighty gods of wind. Every sailor worth his salt knew them by name. "I call upon you, Boreas of the North, Zephyrus of the West, Eurus of the East, and Notus of the South. Hear me now. From this night forward, *Coronado's Sea Nymph* shall exist no more."

As if those gods were alive and listening, a breeze lifted Walker's hair, ruffling through it like fingers of approval from the great beyond. Like a fatherly pat on the head.

Pouring the wine off the side into the sea, he prayed, "This offering of red wine symbolizes the sacrifice and blood of virgins. I offer it to you mighty warriors, that you may blow away the stench of the old name and clean the wounds this vessel might have caused in her travels, through no fault of her own. I beg you to forgive her past, bless her future and her new name. Bless *Persia Smiles* with favoring winds and following seas, wherever she sails."

As before, the superstitious supplication led to earnest prayer. "Father, from this day forward, this sound and seaworthy vessel shall forever be known as *Persia Smiles*. Watch over her for me. Send Thy angels to guard her as she begins her new job with… with..." Damn, what was that guy's name? Oh, yeah. "Alex Stewart, in Somewhere, Virginia. Forever. Amen."

With his heart on fire for the woman he'd left behind, Walker knelt, facing the fancy script at the rear of the yacht's hull, just above the ladder that led to the upper deck.

One by one, the letters that had spelled out *Coronado's Sea Nymph* fell to the deck. As before, he rolled the sticky mess into a ball and stuffed it in his pocket. Then, tenderly, he blessed the stolen yacht with the name of the woman he'd left behind.

"Please forgive me," he whispered to her, there in the dark. "I hurt you by running out on you. I know I did. But if we're meant to be, I know we'll meet again. If and when we do, please let me make it up to you. Don't hate me. Until then…" He smoothed his fingers over the vinyl lettering of the name that had come to mean something to him. "Help her to forgive herself, Father. Heal her. Keep her safe. Thanks again. Amen."

Walker lifted to his feet, tired yet exhilarated. Back at the front of the yacht, he leaned under the railing, and struck the yacht with that pricey bottle of champagne, declaring loudly and proudly, "I christen thee *Persia Smiles!*"

The bottle shattered, and the golden, foaming champagne splashed into the sea, a just and holy offering. It was customary to toast newly christened ships, even if they'd just been renamed. It was a time for celebration, but Walker hadn't brought a third bottle with him, and he hated drinking alone. Instead, he walked to the cockpit and checked his bearings. Throttling the engine down to zero knots, he secured the stolen craft for the night.

He'd stopped worrying about the Coast Guard hours ago. Figured they had bigger fish to fry. Drug smugglers. Human-traffickers. Despicable miscreants like that. Besides, he was in international waters now, and the currents were calm.

Walker headed back to the upper aft deck, grabbed a woven blanket off one of the plush recliners there, made himself comfortable, and settled in for the night. He planned to fully investigate all drawers and cubbyholes of Goff's yacht come morning. But for tonight, he'd done all he could. For the first time since he'd left Persia behind, he was content. Well, semi-content. He'd accomplished a few things since he'd absconded with Goff's yacht. A hard day's work always felt good.

Staring up at the same stars that daring ancient voyagers had studied while they'd searched what they'd then thought was a flat Earth, Walker crossed his arms behind his head and took a deep breath. Being at sea had always soothed his soul. A man like him couldn't ask for more than the gentle give and take of waves slapping against the hull of a good ship. He knew better, but out here on the ocean, it was easy to believe he could live like this—forever free.

It had been a long day. He was emotionally, as well as physically, spent. Yet he cast one last thought to the myriad of benign stars twinkling in the dark night sky. "Forgive me for hurting her, Father. Thanks for keeping her safe."

It'd been a long time since he'd prayed as much as he had today. He just hoped he'd prayed enough.

# Chapter Ten

The Queen of England. The reigning monarch of all Commonwealth realms. An awesome, frighteningly powerful title that, frankly, stole Persia's breath, as well as robbed her companion agent's nerves. Izza Maher was close to hyperventilating. Not her usual reaction in times of stress. The battle-hardened Hispanic had a reputation for being tougher than most of the guys on The TEAM, probably meaner, too. But this morning, she'd morphed into a silly fangirl about to meet her all-time teen idol.

"Should I kiss the back of her hand or her knuckles? Her ring?" Izza whispered out of the side of her nervous mouth. "What do you think? Should I bow? Curtsy? Man, I hate looking stupid. I don't want to look stupid. Help me out here."

Persia couldn't keep from smiling. Just a little, though. Izza didn't usually reveal nervousness. To tease her now would surely land Persia's ass on the floor. Not how she wanted to be introduced to Her Majesty. Both had dressed in formal TEAMwear: black pencil skirts, crisp white blouses beneath pressed black blazers, The TEAM's golden logo high on their left lapels. They waited. And, apparently, Izza worried.

For the moment, they were still in the hallway outside the Queen's posh suite at one of New York City's finest hotels. The two bodyguards at the entrance to that suite had yet to acknowledge Persia's or Izza's presence, even after they'd introduced themselves. The men stood there like stern, unflinching statues in business suits, staring straight ahead, and hardly blinking.

"Repeat after me," Persia murmured to Izza. "Your Majesty. That's all you need to say when you're introduced. She'll have her own escorts and bodyguards. All we have to do today is stick with these guys, stay out of their way, and coordinate with Alex, Mark, and David. They're running this show, not us. Do not touch the Queen unless she offers her hand first, and don't hug her. Smile, but keep your grip light and brief. Bow your head in acknowledgment and step back."

"But when should I do all that? Who's going to introduce us? And when?"

"That, I don't know. But someone just as important as Her Majesty will surely make introductions. Maybe one of her grandsons. That'd be cool, huh? Being introduced by a prince."

Izza groaned. "I hate not knowing what's gonna happen next. Why didn't Alex tell us this crap yesterday?"

"Relax, girlfriend. You've been in tougher spots. You can do this."

"Yeah, but—"

Both golden gilded doors opened outward.

"Oh, shit," Izza gasped.

Damned if Alex didn't step into the hall first. He nodded once to Persia and Izza, then extended his hand back into the room and...

She. Walked. Out.

Persia's heart stopped beating. It really was her. Her Majesty. The one and only Queen of England.

"Your Majesty," Alex said respectfully, his right hand now cupping Her Majesty's left elbow, as if he did that every day. He bowed his head slightly. "May I present one of my finest agents, Junior Agent Izza Maher?"

Izza stumbled forward, but caught her balance before she face-planted, and just in time, she managed a breathy, "Your… Your M-Majesty."

The Queen grabbed hold of Izza's hand with both of hers. "I am so glad to meet a woman sniper! What a hard job you have. Thank you for keeping me safe," she murmured conspiratorially, her British accent perfectly clipped and so, so… royal.

She almost sounded like a regular person. Not like that calmed the flock of starlings flapping furiously to be free inside Persia's ribs.

"You're w-w-welcome," Izza stuttered.

Yet, the Queen still held onto her hand. "I'm having a private dinner in my suite tonight. Would you two join me?"

Alex had taken a step back while she spoke with Izza. Persia looked to him for direction, not sure if dining with royalty was something a bodyguard on duty should do.

He. Just. Winked!

Not what Persia expected. Then his head bobbed one curt nod of approval, and she started to breathe again. That he'd assigned Izza and her to guard this prestigious visitor still made no sense. But here she was, hyperventilating and fangirling as bad as Izza.

"S-sure," Izza answered, her dark brown eyes all but stabbing Persia to help. "I, umm, I mean we... We can do that, can't we? I mean, we've got time."

Which allowed Persia to reply graciously, "Yes, ma'am, it would be our pleasure."

With that, the Queen's sweet face broke into a gentle smile, and she released Izza's hand, which had to be sweating bullets by now. Persia's certainly were.

Alex stepped back to the Queen's side and gestured for her to step forward. "Ma'am, another of my best, Junior Agent Persia Coltrane."

He was so sure of himself. So confident. What the heck was he doing here, and how did he know Britain's royalty? It was no wonder he'd been uptight yesterday in the Sit Room. He had to do this!

And thank heavens, he'd dressed in simple gray and silver tones today. Not red. Not black. Yet Persia's heart still pounded when she stepped where Izza had just stood and accepted the Queen's hand. It was warm and soft and… She. Persia Coltrane. A nobody. Was touching the Queen of England!

Her eyes were royal blue, made more stunning by her silvery-white hair and the lovely teal business suit she wore. As she'd done with Izza, the Queen grasped Persia's hand with both of hers. "It is so nice to meet you. What a lovely name, Persia."

There were no words. Literally. Persia couldn't remember a thing to say.

"Your family must be from the Middle East, yet your surname is Coltrane. That's not very Middle Eastern, is it?"

"My m-m-mom," Persia stuttered as her brain came back online. "Dad's from the South, but Mom was born in Iran. You might have heard of her. Doctor Ahmadi."

The Queen's pretty blue eyes widened. "Ester Ahmadi? She's your mother? What a lovely coincidence."

Persia blinked. "You know Mom?"

"I most certainly do. Who do you think sent the armed guard that facilitated her safe escape during that atrocious war? Mustard gas, for pity's sake. That was supposed to have ended with the war that ended all wars. Not like that worked either, but really. Gassing one's enemies is unfair and inhumane."

"I… I didn't know you rescued her. Wow. She never said. Yes. Mom and Dad live in Mississippi now. My dad's Dupree Coltrane, but wow, I wish she were here now. I'm sure she'd love to talk with you." *I'm going to have such a long talk with that mother of mine. Tonight. After dinner. If it's not too late.*

"I'd love to meet her again. She is such a strong woman. Well, then. Yes. You'll do nicely. Plan to be here by six this evening, and Alex…" She released Persia's hand and turned to him. "Do bring Kelsey and that adorable daughter of yours. I brought Lexie something, Kelsey, too."

"Yes, ma'am. Kelsey has been looking forward to chatting with you again."

*Again?* This morning kept getting stranger and stranger. *Alex and Kelsey Stewart hobnobbed with British royalty? My Mom knows the Queen of England? Who knew?!*

"Well, let's get this foolishness at the UN over with, shall we?" With a smile, the Queen proceeded down the hall with Alex at her side, while her ten bodyguards, not counting Izza and Persia, followed.

Alex looked as if he'd done this before, as if the Queen were just another good friend. He was nothing like the curt taskmaster he'd been in the office the last few days. He almost looked good. The Queen and he chatted at the elevator. Then, while two guards stepped inside once the doors opened, he tipped his head back and laughed at whatever she'd said. Who was he?

"Sure didn't see this coming," Izza murmured out of the side of her mouth. "The Boss and the Queen? Sounds like one of those risqué romance novels Ember reads."

Persia shook her head, not able to reply. What Alex and the Queen had going on between them had nothing to do with romance. He was more like one of her faithful knights, sworn to fealty and prepared to die for her. Like Hotrod would do for someone he cared about.

Damned if that notion didn't drop like a rock in Persia's heart. The Queen had a knight like Alex, but who did Persia have? Nobody.

# Chapter Eleven

Walker would've slept better if he hadn't stared at the stars all night. Would've also helped if he could've gotten Persia out of his mind, once and for all. But he couldn't, and he hadn't. Instead, he was on his hands and knees in the master stateroom, going through bottom drawers in the long combination dresser/desk, with an LED flashlight stuck between his teeth. Exploring. Investigating. Searching for the elusive explanation as to how Commander Goff's yacht had been berthed in Florida, instead of sunny California.

He'd shut the engine down east of Grenada, where he intended to refuel come morning. A bill of sale, that was all Walker was looking for. But he had yet to find any official records pertaining to the yacht. Not registration papers or receipts for payment of that registration. Anything with the new owner's name on it would do. A restaurant receipt. A hotel reservation. Even a captain's log or address book. A fuel receipt, for pity's sake!

Tired, Walker rolled off his knees to his butt, needing a clearer head than the exhausted one currently sitting on his shoulders. "Where would I keep records and receipts if I were on vacation?" he mused aloud.

Obviously, not in the master stateroom. Not in the guest stateroom either, though both had enough high gloss cabinetry and closets for ten guests' clothing, shoes, whatever else guests usually boarded with, as well as enough room for a folder or file or… something. Most yacht owners kept captain's logs to document maintenance, repairs, or bills of sale. That there was no paper trail anywhere was disconcerting. Normal people left paper evidence wherever they went. Credit card receipts. Maps. But not this guy, whoever he was.

This stately accommodation included a bed right out of the best bed and breakfast, a lavish ensuite bathroom with, not one, but two private vanities. Plenty of storage, although Walker now knew most of the closets and drawers were empty.

It was obvious this yacht had been built for two, everything doubled, from the recliners on the upper aft deck to the umbrellas stationed beside those recliners, to this queen bed. A long mirror lined one entire wall in the head. The shower was another masterpiece all together, with two split showerheads, one on either side of the tiled-bench facing the sliding, double-glass doors.

Yet, there was no sign a woman had ever been aboard. There were no blouses, swimsuits, slacks, or dresses hanging in the closets or folded in the drawers. No flipflops, boat shoes, or heels. No sexy nightgowns, panties, or bras in any drawers. No make-up, perfumes, or other feminine items in the head.

Walker hadn't found a single file that might identify the yacht's owner. Which might simply mean that the owner had left California, and was on his way to somewhere else. Maybe he'd decided to sail around the world. New owners did stupid stuff like that. They thought they knew it all, when, many times, they didn't know a damned thing about the yacht they'd just bought. And this was the age where newer generations didn't rely on paper receipts. But there should still be some sort of written evidence of preparations for that voyage. Of purchases for extra foodstuffs. Additional tanks of fuel. Something!

With that lame what-if scenario in his head, Walker pushed up and left the master stateroom behind. The sun had been up for hours, and it was too damned bright. Pulling his Ray-Bans up from his shirt pocket, he protected his tired eyes.

The uniform of the day was exactly what he'd worn yesterday, and the day before that. Wrinkled khaki cargo shorts, the kind that came with extra pockets. A dull, gray, short-sleeve shirt. Nothing flashy. Nothing bright. No hat. He'd lost his ball cap somewhere in South America, and he wasn't about to wear anything he'd found on the yacht. He wasn't desperate, and guys just didn't do stuff like that.

His swim trunks were draped over one of the recliners on the aft deck where he'd tried to sleep last night, along with a towel. Right now, he needed coffee, maybe a breakfast of eggs and bacon from the galley. His brain ought to work better then.

Even if it didn't, he had time. He planned on docking somewhere along the coast of Guyana, then French Guinea in West Africa. Today's weather was perfect, and he'd been blessed with following seas. If these conditions held, before he headed to Africa, he planned to fill his tanks at a little fishing village out of Recife, Brazil, in a week or so. He had friends there. Not that he'd look them up, not on this trip. It was too soon to reconnect with people from his past. Better to cross the Atlantic, and stay ahead of the game. From Recife? Full steam across the Atlantic to the coast of Western Africa.

Someday, he'd like to visit Ascension Island, that tiny speck stuck in the middle of the Atlantic between South America and Africa, just south of the equator. Discovered by the Portuguese in the fifteen-hundreds, it was a barren, inhospitable wayside. Yet it was also rich with history. In the early nineteenth century, the Brits had garrisoned the island. Then, during World War II, they'd allowed the United States to build and man Wideawake Airbase there. It had been a strategic location during the Falklands War of 1982 as well. Walker could refuel there. Might even find a local shop to buy a few decent clothes. A cap.

He had enough cash to finance his current lifestyle, or lack thereof, hidden deep in the waterproof lining of his gear bag. If he needed more, he'd have no problem getting it. Out of sheer dumb luck, the inheritance he'd received when his grandfather passed years ago was safely out of NCIS's reach. He'd been smart enough to open an offshore account before he'd gone to Guatemala. Ironically, the same morning he'd returned from South America, NCIS had stormed his house and taken him into custody. They'd marched him into the street in shackles and cuffs. Like an already condemned criminal, instead of an innocent man under investigation.

You'd think under the umbrella of the United States Constitution, that everyone was innocent before trial and judgment. Not so. The minute he stepped foot in the brig, Walker never stood a chance. Someone in Navy ranks had condemned him before he'd gone to trial, maybe even before he'd returned from Guatemala. And like the bastard that person was, they'd fed the sensation-seeking press nothing but lies, then backed every lie with false witnesses.

Walker shook the shitty memories off. Somehow, he'd find a way to prove his innocence to the whole damned world.

*Deep breath. Let it go.*

Ascension Island was not in the plan. Walker wanted to cross the Atlantic sooner than later. Although, now that he had time to think, there was an airport on Ascension Island. He could catch a plane to Johannesburg. But that meant going ashore and through customs, where a man with no passport would be detained and…

"Stick to the plan," he hissed. "Be smart. Keep your eyes open. You can do this."

As always, it felt good to have faith in himself. Lonely. But good.

# Chapter Twelve

Dinner with the Queen was refreshingly enjoyable. She'd brought elegant gifts of Irish crystal heart ornaments for her female guests. Lexie Rose Stewart sat on her lap at the moment, chattering like little girls did when they had someone's undivided attention. Man, that little one was Kelsey Stewart all over again. Delicate frame, expressive eyes, and a dainty pert nose dotted with the tiniest chocolate sprinkle freckles. Shiny dark curls spiraled down her back, but those mischievous melted chocolate-kiss eyes sparkled more than the crystal settings adorning the elegant table.

The men and boys were dressed in business suits, and the women in dinner dresses. Little Lexie wore a lovely red velvet dress over black tights, shiny shoes, and a big smile.

Taciturn Hunter Christian and his pretty wife Meredith, sat at the Queen's left, with their two sons. Courtney sat beside his father. Little Robert sat next to his mother.

Kelsey and Alex sat at the Queen's immediate right, with Lexie's empty chair next to Kelsey. Persia and Izza were next to Hunter's family, while Eric and Shea Reynolds sat across from them, next to the Stewarts. Unfortunately, Eric's two-year-old triplet girls, Summer, Sage, and Lyrik, were home with a stomach virus, with Eric's mother watching over them.

The Queen had gifted each child a plush *Winnie-the-Pooh*, courtesy of A. A. Milne's vivid imagination. After Lexie had curtsied and told Her Majesty, "Thank you, ma'am," like a very good girl, she'd marched straight to the wooden rocking horse set out of the way, near the bay windows. To Persia's amusement, Lexie had argued strongly with Alex when it came time to dismount. "But, Daddy, I wanna ride the pony. Why else is it here if not for us kids to ride it?"

To which he'd firmly said, "After dinner, sweetheart. Let's sit down. It's time to eat. Now."

Lexie had pouted when he'd physically lifted her out of the tiny leather saddle and placed her on the booster seat next to Kelsey. Persia could've laughed out loud.

Only when the Queen asked if Lexie could, "Please, come and sit with me," did that little girl's smile return. Like a rock star.

Kelsey's lashes fell then, and Persia was sure she chuckled under her breath, at the power struggle between one hard-assed father and his stubborn daughter. Seemed like that apple hadn't fallen far from the Stewart tree.

Alex was a doting father, that much was clear. And Kelsey adored Lexie and him. The second he returned to his place, he rested his arm along the back of her chair and pressed a sigh and a kiss to her temple.

"Stop laughing at me," he growled, ever so softly, his attention again focused on the Queen.

"That little girl's as pigheaded as you," Kelsey whispered back.

"Yeah, well…"

Eric chuckled at their interaction. "Relax, Boss. You could've had triplets. Three times the fun."

"And we would've loved them!" Kelsey replied, her eyes bright as she elbowed her husband's ribs. "Admit it, Alex.

You'd love three more little girls just like Lexie running around the house. Or three sons would be cool, too. You need three Mini-Alexes following you everywhere you go. You could teach them carpentry."

He rolled his eyes. "One of these days…"

Which caught Shea's attention. Leaning over her place setting, she asked Kelsey, "Are you two pregnant?"

"No," Alex answered, a bit too quickly.

"Alex?" the Queen asked from her place at the end of the table, her arms still around his precocious firstborn's waist. "Are congratulations in order?"

My, how quickly that man stiffened to attention when she spoke, and Persia knew before he said one word. The biggest clue was that Kelsey had yet to say anything and her head was still down. No one could see into her eyes. *Yup. The Stewarts are pregnant!*

Persia elbowed Izza at her right to listen up.

"Err…" Alex took a deep breath. He licked his lower lip.

That man was stalling!

Then, he seemed to deflate, as if he knew he'd been caught and had no way out of answering. He took another deep breath before he finally said, "Yes, ma'am, we are. But just one," he told Eric and Shea quickly. "I don't know how on earth you handled three."

Eric beamed. "Simple. I learned early. When Mama ain't happy, ain't nobody happy. So I do what I'm told. I keep my opinions to myself, and I hop to it when my queen speaks."

"As you should," the Queen added regally.

Kelsey beamed.

"Plus, we hired two nannies," Shea added with a cute shrug. "I work at home, and one baby's a handful, but three"—her brows lifted—"is a circus. A good circus, but—"

"But all mothers need extra help, even if there's just one newborn in the house," Eric insisted, his big arm around his wife's slender shoulders again. "That's what husbands are for. We really are good for something."

Persia didn't know the Reynolds' story, but they couldn't seem to sit close enough to each other. They had triplets, yet they still acted like honeymooners. Loving glances. Soft bumps and touches. They were adorable.

Lexie tipped forward from where she sat on the Queen's lap. "Mama, what's pr… preg… preg…?"

"Pregnant, sweetheart," Kelsey explained, her brown eyes soft with emotion. "That big word just means Mommy and Daddy are going to have a tiny baby, and you get to be a big sister. Would you like that?"

Lexie's brows nearly reached her hairline. "Me? I get to be a sister?"

Alex winked. "Which means you also get to teach your baby sister or brother how to share toys. Can you do that?"

"Ah huh." Lexie's cute little head was bobbing now. "And I can teach her to walk the dogs with me and how to eat cheerios and not to eat mac-n-cheese like a little pig and—"

"And how to take naps and not give all our family secrets away?" Alex asked pointedly.

Persia nearly giggled when Kelsey elbowed him again. "Did you hear that? She didn't hear you say baby brother. All she heard was sister. We're having another girl."

When Alex put his index finger to his lips, Persia wasn't sure which of his girls he was shushing, Kelsey or Lexie.

Lexie ducked her adorably cute face into her shoulders, quivering with excitement. "Kin we get my new baby sister tonight? Pwease, Daddy?"

Kelsey grinned up at her man, her eyes bright and glimmering. But he seemed to be purposefully avoiding her.

Hunter laughed out loud. "Yeah, Boss. Explain that one, why don'tcha? When can Lexie get her baby sister? This I've got to hear."

Meredith leaned her chin into her palm, as she turned to watch how Alex was going to handle Lexie. How could he resist that precious little girl?

But it was the gleam in Kelsey's dark browns that Persia was watching. All of her heart was in those pretty eyes, now glowing up at Alex. Persia suspected Kelsey's left hand was right then splayed across his thigh, below the linen tablecloth. Her fingertips might even be tapping *I-love-yous* that she didn't dare speak out loud. But she didn't have to say a word. Her love shone like a bright, trusting beacon. Up. At him.

When at last, he sighed and looked down at her, Alex's handsome face blossomed with the loveliest, most rugged, manly smile Persia had ever witnessed. Yes, blossomed, and, yes, loveliest. Men might not want to be described that way, especially not badasses like her boss. But true love did that to even the hardest warriors, and that was what Persia saw now. Alex was all warrior, but one who obviously adored his wife above everyone else in the world, except for Lexie and her new baby sister.

Man, everywhere Persia looked, she saw gorgeous couples in love. Hunter Christian was one tattooed monster of a gentle man. The tattooed snake running out from under the white cuff of his dress shirt ended at the end of his middle finger, most likely with a not very nice expletive. Yet he still gripped Meredith's much smaller hand between their place settings, as if he couldn't bear to let her go.

And Meredith was just plain beautiful. Blonde, she was the perfect complement to Hunter's dark hair, deeply tanned skin, and coffee-brown eyes. While their oldest son Courtney was blond and blue-eyed like his mom, little Robert had the same dark eyes and hair, broad shoulders, and the cutest dimple in his cheek, just like his dad.

Then there were Eric and Shea, both dark-haired and obviously in lust and love with each other. Outright sexual tension radiated between them like a couple of horny teenagers who couldn't wait to leave. If he wasn't leaning a shoulder into her, she was smiling at him like they shared some deep, dark, naughty secret. Only it couldn't be dark, not the way their eyes sparkled at each other. No, it had to be love, and nothing about love was dark. Persia knew that for sure, because she'd grown up in a house full of it.

Even Izza had a man she adored in her life. Connor would be back from Afghanistan before long, and where would that leave Persia? Alone, damn it. Always alone. Suddenly she wanted to be back in her cozy Florida bungalow, snuggled in her bed with the handsome man whose name she knew… Was. Not. Hotrod!

Those darned tears glimmering at the corners of her eyes had to stop, before she lost her mind and gave herself away. She refused to waste one more tear or another minute, thinking about that loser. He was the one who'd ditched her, remember?

At last, Alex turned to Lexie and winked. "That, kiddo, is tonight's bedtime story, so eat all your dinner."

"Okay!" she answered, clapping with childish delight. "I get a new baby sister and a new story!"

"Hey," Izza muttered. "You gonna take this or not?"

Persia jerked her attention away from the sight of that grinning little girl across the table. Ah. The elegant crystal platter of boiled beef, boiled cabbage, and... were those boiled turnips? Just what she needed, flatulence on top of heartache. Cabbage, really? Who ate that stuff anymore? Only it did look good drizzled with browned butter and sprinkled with green herbs and onions. And the beef smelled divine.

"Yes, sorry. I was daydreaming. Got it," Persia whispered back. She took a tiny helping of each, then passed the platter. What would it hurt? Pushing the food around on her plate gave her fork something to do, while she pretended to be a happy, carefree professional.

Why not take another one for her country? Seemed like that was all she ever did.

# Chapter Thirteen

Walker worked his way up the African coast toward Portugal, where he spent a week lounging in the peace and quiet off the Azores. That week turned into two, then three. He was still a good thousand miles from anywhere. Communication with anyone in the States to the west, was sporadic at best.

For the first time since that night with Persia, Walker let his guard down. He left the security of *his yacht* behind, to roam the bustling docks of busy São Miguel, the largest island in the Azores archipelago. The last time he'd been here, he'd been with SEAL Team 18. The best in the fleet. Not that its reputation mattered now. Still...

Once upon a time, he'd been USN Lieutenant Walker Judge, and commanded the rowdiest, best, most honorable SEAL Team in the fleet. Not one of his guys had backstabbed him during his trial. How he ached to reach out to them. Just to talk, to see if they knew something he didn't. Just to hear their voices.

Lieutenant Junior Grade Ryder Dahl, Walker's executive officer and a damned good friend. Loyal, and built like a big, black refrigerator. Hence his handle, *Black Sabbath*, shortened to just plain Sabbath. But there was nothing plain about Ryder. Yes, he could make the ladies swoon when he wanted to, but the man had an uncanny talent for strategizing his team's way out of impossible situations. Which was what Walker needed now.

Then, the three ensigns on SEAL Team 18. Both Steel Arrington, aka *Frosty*, due to his shock of bright white hair, and Nguyen Li, aka *Trigger*, second-generation Vietnamese-American, were top-notch snipers and as deadly as they came. Ensign Dallas Perkins hailed from Austin, TX., hence his handle: *Tex*. As the Team's language expert, Tex had an uncanny talent with various Pashto dialects, a plus with as much time as Team 18 had spent in the Middle East. Walker never trusted the supposedly vetted local translators. Too often, those friendlies turned into assassins.

Petty Officer First Class Urban Sweeny, aka *Red*, because of his bright red hair and all those freckles, handled communications equipment. Petty Officer Third Class Amerigo Torres, aka *Scarecrow*, rounded out Walker's team. A proud Latino and a naturalized Mexican-American citizen, Amerigo was one of those ordinary looking types who could ghost in and ghost out without being seen or caught. Or remembered. Uncanny, was what he was. He was the one who'd taught Walker how to avoid making an impression, how to avoid being seen.

Walker missed his guys. They'd been through some stuff together, everything from taking out pirates on the high seas in Indonesian waters, to the grunt work still going on in the Middle East. How he wished the US of A would get out of Afghanistan, Iraq, Syria, and all those other tortured places where freedom, and doing the right thing, didn't stand a snowball's chance in hell of surviving, much less thriving. Walker's one take-away from the wasted years he'd spent in that part of the world, was that he couldn't change people.

Even when he'd just wanted to help. Or save them from themselves. Uh-uh. People had to want to change, and right now, that wasn't happening. The powers in charge of those Middle East kingdoms seemed intent on turning time in their countries back to the Stone Ages.

Every other civilized country had already deserted those desert climes. But not the noble United States. Which was too bad. Too many young men and women had died for what felt like nothing more than political bullshit, oil, and strategic military positioning. It all came down to greed and power, and Walker was sick of the continual one-upmanship American politicians played at the expense of military lives.

They'd play that game differently if their sons and daughters were the ones dying in the Middle East. Only they weren't. Elitists' sons and daughters were forever too good, too rich, and too privileged to ever have to fight for their lives or their freedom. No. That responsibility would always fall to someone else's children.

The plight of every good soldier was, it seemed, to die for the unthankful, unthinking masses. The power brokers who peddled their influence while others died in their stead. But for what? So they could get richer? More powerful? So they could flaunt their wealth behind ten-foot-high walls that protected them from having to see what their greed had done to America?

There seemed no end to it, no hope in sight. Yet reaching out to his guys was unthinkable. Walker wouldn't make them accessories after the fact. Yet he wondered how they were doing now, and if they were okay. If NCIS had targeted them or claimed guilt by association.

The last thing he'd heard on American radio was that military members everywhere were looking for him. He was on the FBI's top ten most-wanted list, which meant Interpol was looking for him, too.

But Walker was willing to bet his life that his guys weren't hunting him. That they still believed in him. They were SEALs. His friends.

He ran a quick hand over his head, needing a cut, but not willing to risk being recognized by some nosy guy in a barbershop. His beard had grown into a thick cover that bore as much darker browns as it did gray these days. Didn't that figure? He'd barely turned thirty-five, but he felt as weary as a ninety-year-old. Guess life was not what you made it. Not unless you'd intended it to run over you like a rogue wave, swamp your boat, drown your dreams, and wash your Trident overboard, as if it were merely another foolish trinket that stupid men lived and died for.

Christ, he was tired of life on the run.

Automatically, his fingers went to the scar on his chest, where his hard-earned Budweiser had been pounded into him by another SEAL, Adam Torrey. Now, there was a certifiable adrenaline junkie. Tall. Blond. A freak who'd once lived to dive out of perfectly good airplanes. Not Walker's forte, but Adam had certainly excelled at high altitude, low opening jumps.

Walker wondered where that diehard warrior had gone and what he was doing now. Was he happy? Had he settled down? Somehow, Walker doubted Adam ever married. Not in the cards for either of them. Torrey had always been one of those bigger than life, hero types. He was like Charlie Brown, aka Gregor Jorgensen, the Army Ranger who'd befriended

Walker during his trial, who had, in fact, been on the jury. A jury of Walker's peers who had actually advocated for more evidence. More transparency. More legitimacy. Instead...

Their wishes were ignored as much as Walker's sworn testimony.

He swallowed hard at the exile he'd been forced into after the farce of his much-publicized trial. In the end, the judge hadn't cared about evidence. It had all come down to who had the bigger dick and more clout, the as-yet unnamed person behind the scenes.

Strolling along the dock, Walker came to a gray-haired man sitting on a fold-up chair with a shaggy white dog lying at his feet. The old guy wore glasses, a tweed cap, tattered gray pants, and an equally tattered gray button-up shirt that bloused over his paunch. Bright smears of paint blotched the shirt, no doubt from the paintbrush between his teeth and the palette on his knee.

When Walker came closer, the dog barked and jumped to its feet, slapping its front paws on the boardwalk like it wanted to play. "Shhhhh," the old guy shushed even as he tipped forward into the wooden tripod where a small canvas rested. An easel, that was what it was. Not a tripod.

The dog barked and spun around, its voice ratcheting higher.

"Rover, no. I said be still. I'm working here," the old man groused. He looked up over his black, square-rimmed spectacles. "Are you bothering my dog, mister?" he asked around the paintbrush still in his mouth, his right hand suspended above the canvas, not a hint of friendliness in his dark eyes. A thick, gray, street-sweeper mustache covered his top lip. Longish gray hair curled over his ears. Walker put him in his high sixties, maybe low seventies.

"Just out for a stroll," he replied easily, as he extended a hand. "Name's Hotrod. You're American?"

The man's shoulders deflated, as if he'd lost the mood, or whatever it was artists needed to paint. With a sigh, he set the brush in his hand over the smear of bright blue paint on his palette, then removed the other brush from between his teeth.

"Yup, and you're another," he grumbled as he leaned forward and shook Walker's hand with one, short, there-now-leave-me-alone shake.

"Yes, sir. Sorry if I disturbed you."

By then the dog, a Labrador-sized welcoming committee, stretched to the end of the long leash tied to one foot of the man's chair. "Mind if I pet him?" Walker asked, not taking anything—like simple, every day courtesy—for granted.

With an annoyed sigh, the painter folded both arms over his barrel chest. "His name's Rover and he's a stray, but he likes me and…" He lifted both shoulders. "That's more than I can say for most people. Hotrod, huh? Your parents give you that stupid name?"

Walker had to smile. "Just a nickname from my job," he qualified, as he knelt to stroke his new friend's furry snout. Damned if the crazy dog didn't close his big black eyes and groan. "But it stuck. Guess I'm a stray like Rover."

Wasn't that the truth?

"Name's Brimley Scott," the old man growled as he extended his hand again. This time his grasp was strong and sure. "Pleased to make your acquaintance, Hotrod Who-Ever-The-Hell-You-Really-Are. Marine?"

"Navy," Walker admitted. It was always smarter to go with partial truths. Lies were too hard to keep track of. "Been out for a year now. Thought I'd sail the world while I still could." He jerked his head back toward the dock where he'd berthed *his* yacht. "You know how it goes. Might as well do something exciting before I settle down."

"Hmmpf. You even got a woman?" Brimley asked with a twinge of sarcasm. "As ugly as you are?"

Nothing said you're home free like a dig from a fellow smart-assed warrior.

With a sigh that came from the depths of his all-American soul, Walker nodded, his heart instantly flung across the ocean to the only woman he'd ever spent a peaceful night with. "Yes," he replied, then coughed and replied louder, "Yes, sir, I do." *At least, I wish I did.*

The older guy's lips twisted. "Good for you. See that you treat her right. Mine up and left. Guess she got tired of waiting." His shoulders lifted again. "But I had important stuff to do, and some things can't wait. So here I am. Me and somebody else's dog. But Rover doesn't give me any flack like she did. We're good for each other. You hungry?"

That segue was abrupt. Walker lifted to his feet. "Nah. I've got places to go." Too bad his stomach let out a growl that sounded like it came from Big Foot just then.

Brimley cocked his head, a spark of mischief in his dark eyes and a wrapped sandwich extended in his hand. "Want to try that again?" he asked as he glanced to the empty bench across from him. "I'm not going anywhere. Doesn't look like you are, neither. Take a load off."

Walker had to smile at the old guy. "Well, hell," he admitted ruefully. "Don't mind if I do."

Before long, he and Brimley were eating together and chatting like two old friends. Daylight stretched into dusk. Turned out Brimley was former Army, a draftee from the Vietnam era.

"Yeah. My PTSD wore my wife out. I don't blame her for leaving. Never could tell her what all that crap back in 'Nam did to me. Not like she would've understood anyway."

"So you kept it inside?" Walker asked, his sandwich gone, the bottled water Brimley had offered him gone as well, and the bottle crunched for recycling.

"Didn't seem much sense in telling anyone, 'specially her." Brimley's gaze stretched over Walker's shoulder to the sea beyond. "She wasn't there, was she? She never could've understood, and she sure as hell didn't need to know all the details of what I did or what I had to do there. Was bad enough I had to live with it."

Which was so damned sad. How could a simple, sweet woman ever hope to erase the horrors of war when the VA couldn't/wouldn't help the men and women who came home battle-scarred, unwanted, or afraid of the dark and loud noises? And to think most of those draftees had been mere eighteen-year-olds when they'd gone to war. Godawful shame was what the whole damned mess was. *What it still is...*

Yet Walker also knew there were good women who'd stood by their wounded warrior husbands when they'd come home, no matter what. Who'd fought their men's VA battles for them, bathed them when they couldn't bathe themselves, cleaned up their messes, even argued with them when those old farts wanted to give up and die. Women who'd loved those damaged guys with all of their hearts. Who'd never once thought of leaving them, just because those loved ones had done what their country had asked, and in the process, might've lost a limb or two—or part of their minds. Maybe equal parts of their souls...

He sucked in a deep, cleansing breath of crisp sea air. During his life, he'd learned to rely on the ocean's remedy for relief. *If you can't fix it, set it down and let the tide take it far, far away. Let it go and tell it goodbye. Give the unforgivable and unforgettable back to God. Grief, forgiveness, and vengeance were in His bailiwick. Let Him worry about those damned loose ends.*

"Your rig secure for the night?" Brimley asked. "You need some place to stay instead of that bobber you've got tied up at the dock?"

"You've seen *Persia Smiles*?"

"Persia who?" Brim waved Walker off. "Nah, I don't know which fishing boat's yours. She's got a pretty name, though. You name her after the woman you love?"

Excellent question, one Walker didn't yet know the answer to. And because he couldn't define his feelings for Persia, he changed the subject. "Why? You looking for company, old man?"

Brimley's gaze dropped down to his feet. "Guess maybe I am. Seems like you been in a few battles, too, and you're American. Sumbitch, a man gets tired of not knowing what folks around him are saying all the time. But if you'd rather not hang around with Rover and me, hell, ain't no skin off my nose. I've got somewhere else to be. Rover, come on, boy, let's git."

The Azores attracted tourists from all over the world, especially from Europe, Portugal, and Africa, even as far north as the Netherlands and Scandinavia. Walker had noticed more Japanese and Chinese tourists this time around. Which was comforting in a way. They might watch American news, but he doubted they paid attention to something as insignificant as US Navy trials. No one in America seemed to care about the military. Why would foreign tourists? But those differing nationalities also created language barriers. Not many people cared to play charades just to order off a menu or buy a trinket.

"You and Rover are welcome aboard my rig," he parried. "I've got lots of room. Spend a night on the water. Do a little fishing. Might do you and Rover some good."

Brimley stared straight at Walker. Two warriors, eye to eye. Two men too proud to take each other up on their offers of charity. At last, Brimley's gaze dropped to his faithful companion. "What you think, Rover? Should we trust this smart-aleck or hightail it back to our place?"

Rover's energetic bark sealed the deal. For at least one night, Walker had company.

# Chapter Fourteen

Persia smoothed one palm over her trim waistline, proud of the clean figure reflected back at her from her full-length bedroom mirror. Dressed in powder-blue today, she'd slipped into matching heels, then stepped up to make sure she looked presentable, professional, and able. She had an early meeting with her boss today, and this time, she would make a solid impression on Alex Stewart, if it was the last thing she did.

Since day one, she'd been on his bad side, and not just because she'd sir'ed him once too often. Even Mark's assurance that Alex had her six, seemed at odds with the way he snapped when she was slow to reply, even the morning she'd had a flat tire on her way to work. That hadn't helped.

"But shit happens," she told herself, then, "Get over it," she told Alex, though he wasn't there. Taking a deep cleansing breath, she left her boss's ornery imaginary image behind, locked her apartment, and marched to her car with her head held high. She'd brought bastards the world over, down. She could certainly handle one former Marine.

Her mission in NYC a month ago had gone without a hitch, mostly because Alex had utterly paved the way for her and Izza. How could anything have gone wrong? He knew the Queen of England, for pity's sake, and she hadn't really needed two TEAM bodyguards.

She'd had her own, ones Persia knew would've never allowed her or Izza, much less anyone else, to get close to their Queen. Yet Alex had given his only female operators that specific easy-as-hell assignment. Okay, so none of the other assignments he'd doled out to his male agents had been any more difficult, but Persia got the impression Alex didn't quite trust her. He'd set her up, that was all he'd done. Made her feel useful when he hadn't really needed her at all. The dirtbag.

Well, today was the day she changed that. "God help me if I sir him," she told her rearview mirror. "That'd be just my luck, so don't do it."

Too bad that determination to be all Alex expected her to be, didn't last once she hit the office. Ember and Beau were there. No one else. Persia greeted them with a casual, "Hey guys. Where is everyone? I was supposed to meet Alex this morning."

Ember didn't take her eyes off her monitor when she answered, "Mark's in Florida. Something came up, and Alex will be with Sec Def all day. David's out of the office TFN."

TFN was TEAM talk for until further notice, which meant Senior Agent David Tao was probably on his way back to Cambodia, and The TEAM safe house for sex-trafficked children that he operated there.

"And Zack had to run home."

"LiLi forgot her permission slip for her field trip to Gettysburg," Beau added, his gaze also on his monitor. "He'll be right back if you want to hang around."

Persia leaned over their customer service counter, wishing she could see what was on their screens that was so important they couldn't break away even to make eye contact. But all

TEAM monitors wore security screens to prevent the wrong person from accessing confidential information. Which, at that moment, was her.

"Okay, so…" She let those worthless words hang as she scanned the empty work bay that could hold forty agents, if and when they were all there at the same time. Not today. It looked like everyone else was out of the office on real work. Didn't that figure?

"Do you two need help?" she asked brightly, still determined to give this damned job and her equally damned boss her all.

Slowly, as if it were too hard to talk at the same time that he watched his screen, Beau shook his head. "Sure… don't. We'll call… if we need you."

Luckily, Adam Torrey burst through the fire doors then. But like a heat-seeking missile, he walked past Persia and zeroed in on Ember's counter. "You found it yet?"

She shook her head. "It's not where you thought, but I've got a lead. Singapore, I think."

"There's more than one and we're both tracking them," Beau added, his dark brows narrowed into a perfect V that made him look primitively angry all the time. "Can you give us anything more? A specific amount would be nice."

Adam rested his forearms on the counter. Persia had never seen him look so threatening. Blond and tan, he always cut a strikingly masculine profile, like most of the guys in this office. But today, he looked leaner and meaner, as if he were wound tight and was about to snap. His short-sleeved black polo revealed muscled arms lined with veins that pulsated with some internal angst. He radiated enough hostility to power Alexandria, maybe all of Virginia.

Persia tried again. "Anything I can do to help?"

He looked at her then, his eyes sharp and his face hard. "Sure. Pull up a chair. We're tracking a couple offshore accounts. Least we're trying to."

"Without knowing dollar amounts, bank account numbers, IP addresses, or fucking passwords," Beau intoned gloomily.

"Or the precise name on those bank accounts…" Ember murmured, her usual excitement dulled by her attention on her screen. "That last one took me all the way to Beijing, then Cuba, before it bounced me back to Key West. Lost it there."

"Which makes us think we're looking for an offshore bank somewhere in the Caymans. Maybe," Beau muttered darkly. Rolling his shoulder, he ran a quick hand through his thick, gorgeous, chocolate brown hair. "We just don't know anything for certain, damn it."

Beau and Adam were two of the hottest males on this TEAM. But the way Beau's hair settled back into a shiny mass that nearly tumbled into his eyes the second he leaned forward, made Persia's mind wander to Hotrod and his tempestuous, ocean-blue eyes. The scrape of his scruff on her tender chin and lips. The guy was as ordinary as guys came. Yet even there, in an office where Persia wasn't needed, maybe wasn't even wanted, she knew Walker had wanted her.

Then he'd left. But…

*No. Just no!* She swallowed hard, forcing herself to… *Let it go!* He'd made his choice, damn him, and she was making hers now, too. Enough was enough!

She drummed her fingertips to the countertop in case anyone noticed her momentary lapse. "Tell Alex I'll be home, if or when, he needs me," she informed Ember and Beau—or whoever was listening—with as much sarcasm as she could muster. She needed to work for a living, damn it. Not just show up and collect a paycheck.

As if he'd been waiting for his cue, Junior Agent Zack Lennox shoved the fire doors open with a boisterous, over the top, "Good morning, people!"

Gah. Just what Persia didn't need, another drool-worthy, muscle-bound male in her life. Didn't matter who they were, they all reminded her of Hotrod. The ass.

Zack was one of those chipper, early-riser types, always raring to go and forever on top of the world. Today, he wore the standard TEAM black on black, with the addition of a short-waisted leather bomber jacket. Open over his broad chest and trimmed with silver zippers up the cuffs, it gave Persia an idea. Line these guys up, and they'd make a perfect Chippendale-style, *Bad Boys of The TEAM* calendar. Or they could call it *Dark and Dangerous*, something equally panty-melting. It'd sell like hotcakes, especially if she talked these guys into showing a little skin. Would Zack be willing? Would Mark or Beau? Would their wives let them?

Her heart skipped a beat at the concept. These guys were all drop-dead handsome, and what woman didn't want a little eye-candy hanging in her office—or kitchen. All proceeds could go to a local charity. If she worked it right, this could turn into a yearly tradition. Might even go national. Maybe international. *Note to self: run this spectacular idea past Izza.*

"Hey," Zack purred, as he rested those incredible guns on the customer service counter. Despite being happily married and the father of three adorable daughters, his baritone was always a sexy rumble to Persia's ears. Better yet, he'd made eye contact with her, something Ember and Beau had yet to do. "You ready to go to work?"

Now that was a stupid question. Crossing her arms over her chest, she shook her head. "No, Zack, I get out of bed and dress up for nothing every day."

At that snarky retort, his dark browns sparked, then skated down and back up her body again. Like every other testosterone-packed male in this place, a smile simmered on his lips. She didn't know what ethnicity he was, but Zack's coloring matched hers. Yet he gave off more of an island vibe, as if his next stop was beach volleyball against a team of hot babes.

"I take it you don't care for TEAMwear."

"If you mean the black-on-black ensemble you guys all do so well…" She rolled her eyes. "Frankly, it's blasé. You people need to lighten up. You're not always on missions."

Which was not the brightest thing she could've led with. The work bay *was* empty. Everyone else *was* on a mission.

Which made Zack grin. "Get your gear, Junior Agent. You're with me today. We're escorting Frank Gibson to USP, Lee." As in the high-security federal prison for male inmates in southwestern Virginia.

"Doesn't that fall under US Marshal's purview?"

"Yes, ma'am, it does, but they've asked for our support, and we're giving it. Seems Gibson's buddies are making enough noise to be taken seriously."

Persia's instincts flashed on alert. "They're dumb enough to think they can highjack Federal Marshals?"

"That's the word on the streets. You in?"

Finally. Real work. "Yes, sir, I am."

"Good, then wipe that make-up off your face and change into real work clothes. That dress is a no-go where we're headed. We'll leave in ten."

Ten minutes? Persia almost opened her mouth to argue she could never be ready in that short amount of time, but by hell. This time, she would.

# Chapter Fifteen

Walker, Brimley, and Rover were on a lazy tour of the Azores, tying up wherever and whenever the need struck. After dashing down a nearby alley back on São Miguel, Brimley'd returned with a small roller suitcase, an armful of canvasses, a tote bag of dog food, bowls, and other important dog stuff. He'd been excited, if all his grumping and groaning could be construed as such. Yet Walker knew a hard man when he saw one, and hard men tended to disguise their feelings.

This morning, Brimley and Rover exited the guest stateroom below deck, with Brim dressed in a colorful red-flowered Hawaiian shirt that draped over his threadbare denims and dusty loafers, the sides broken in and broken down. Rover still wore his faded black collar. No tags. But plenty of happy barks.

Since the yacht came equipped with brand new, top of the line, commercial deep-sea fishing poles, including Shimano reels with one hundred thirty-pound lines, it seemed the perfect way to start the day. Fishing from the upper aft deck, aka the lounge, it wasn't long before they'd each snagged a few small tuna, mostly Blue Fish.

Everything was going smooth and easy until... *Zippppppppp!* Brimley's line raced off his reel and the tip of that sturdy pole curled into the water. Jumping to his feet, he pulled it out of the rod cradle before it got away. "I got me a fighter. Hang on, Rover. Don't let this beast get away from us!"

"Way to go, Brim. You land it, I'll clean it," Walker said as he stowed his pole alongside the rail and grabbed one of the two brand new gaffs. He'd already tightened his line and secured the hook inside the reel. They'd already caught enough fish to last a couple days. Whatever Brimley was hauling up now would be lunch.

Rover barked encouragingly, most likely because he'd eaten his fill of roasted tilapia the night before, and he wanted more. The goofy dog's paws were on the first rung up from the deck, and he was looking at the water where nothing had yet surfaced. Still wagging his tail and wiggling his backside, his tongue was a long, wet, red carpet. He was excited, because his buddy was excited.

"Hot damn. Think I mighta caught me a marlin," Brim muttered as, at last, a flash of silver broke the surface. "Wouldn't that be something?" he asked as he glanced at his dog. "I could get it stuffed. Maybe hang it on our wall." For some reason that soured his mood. "If we had a wall."

But Walker had seen the dorsal fin on that flash of silver. This fish wasn't going up on anyone's wall. "You ever do any trophy fishing?" he asked as he clapped a hand to Brim's shoulder and watched the pole dip again below the sea.

"Nah," the older man growled, tipping back on his heels, urging the monster fighting on the other end of his rod forward, reeling in a few more inches of line to make it so. "Don't even have windows."

"You've got no windows?" Walker couldn't imagine anything worse.

"So what?" Brimley jerked his pole to the side, the muscles in his tanned forearms tight and bulging. "'S all I can afford, damn it. I'm on Social Security, kid, not disability."

Which meant Brimley was living from paycheck to paycheck, hence the threadbare clothes, etc. Social Security didn't amount to a hill of beans, except maybe here in the Azores where US dollars stretched further, but where nobody cared about an ex-pat. Disability would've put a few more dollars in his pocket, but some vets were too proud to take what they considered was a handout. But that no windows comment...

Walker had to know. "Do you live in a tent?"

"Nope," Brim shot over his shoulder. "Basement apartment. One room. One door. Four walls. Don't need anything more, do we, Dog?"

Of course, Rover enthusiastically agreed with everything his best buddy said.

Walker kept his hand where it had landed on Brim's hefty, warm shoulder. For as old as he was, the man was no lightweight, yet he wasn't fat, either. Every muscle strained against the fish on the end of his line. Walker wished, for Brimley's sake, it had been a trophy marlin. That would've been cool.

But in the end, Brimley pulled a thirty-pound dogfish, complete with row-upon-row of razor-sharp teeth and plenty of fight, alongside the yacht. Walker stuck the yacht's gaff into the beast's gills and jerked it aboard. Sharks may not be trophies, but they put up one helluva fight, and Walker meant to celebrate the battle Brim had just won.

"Shit. That's all I got for working my ass off? A stupid shark?" Brim dropped the pole and sank onto the nearest recliner. "Rover. No. Get back from that bugger before the damned thing snaps your nose off."

Rover was dancing all over the deck by then, jumping up on the recliners only to jump back down and bark at the scary intruder. By then, Walker had a foot on the shark's angular head, holding the terror of the sea fast to the cedar planking while its vicious tail thrashed from side to side.

"What do you think?" he asked. "Keep it or toss it back? Your call." After all, it wasn't a marlin.

Brim's face was red and sweaty. He yawned even as he swiped a quick hand over his mustache, then over his damp hair, now matted over his skull like a wet towel. "Hell, keep it, I guess. Shark meat's as good as cod. You're still going to clean it, aren't you?"

Walker couldn't miss the hope in his buddy's tone. "You bet."

With that settled, he unsheathed the blade from his hip holster and deftly separated the shark's head from its wiggling body with one slice. While the body rolled over the enclosed deck, Walker dropped the toothy head into the sea, where smaller predators would soon pick it clean. Mother Nature had some amazing garbage handlers at her disposal.

Rover was still plenty excited, but out of danger of being bitten then. Walker made quick work of gutting the shark, then skinned its sandpaper-tough hide from the meat. In minutes, two hearty shark fillets glistened in the sun, ready for the spotless grill. He dumped the waste over the side, where seagulls screamed for more, more, more.

Satisfied at how this impromptu arrangement was working, Walker took a seat opposite Brimley and let Rover nose the carcass. Inviting Brim aboard had been a rash decision at first, but Walker was glad the old guy was there.

The best thing had happened after Walker'd told him to stow his gear in the guest room. The grumpy old fart hadn't been able to hide his delight. Nearly brought a tear to Walker's eye. Because the stateroom had portholes, where a guy could watch the rising sun spread over the whole damned ocean if he wanted. The room also accessed *Persia Smiles'* small forward deck. Brim and his dog could sit out there anytime they wanted. That was all Brim needed, by hell. Fresh air and the freedom to live like a man, instead of someone's poor relative.

Plus, the guest room came with a full shower, plenty of counter space for Brim's easel and paints, and a queen-sized bed. The cabinetry was polished cherry, and Walker doubted his basement apartment could compare on its best day.

"Thought you said you were Navy?"

That softly phrased question ricocheted Walker back to where he sat on the upper aft deck. And there it was. The dead giveaway. Dripping wet in his palm. Walker's brother's fixed-blade, six-inch knife, complete with USMC Corporal Kenny Judge's name stamped with pride on the leather-wrapped handle.

Once more, his lungs filled with bitter regret, remembering the day he'd received word that Kenny had been KIA in Yemen. Walker'd been on the other side of the world then, tracking a known terrorist in Somewhere, South America. Yet the pain of that soul-sucking personal loss stole his breath, as if it had just happened. He was a kid again, and his best bud was gone. There was no sun in the sky, no stars in the heavens. Just that black hole in his heart.

Kenny had loved the Corps, almost as much as he'd loved the dripping wet blade now resting in Walker's hand. Which was why Walker had it. Why he prized it above any other KA-BAR, Sheffield, or standard SEAL issue, Ontario MK III. Just because it had once belonged to Kenny, and he'd loved it. And because Kenny was gone.

"I am Navy. This blade… belonged to a friend." *My best friend,* Walker told the knife silently.

"Sure sorry," Brimley said, as if he'd heard the real truth buried in those few words.

Walker gave him that. Swallowed hard. Locked his heart up one more time and refused to share the worst heartache of his life. Yes, losing Mom and Dad to cancer within months of each other had been bad, but losing his brother shortly after was a hundred times worse. Kenny'd been so young, so green. So much a part of his big brother's dreams and hopes. But so hellbent on saving America. Shit, the pain never went away.

"You gonna put that shark meat inside before Rover drools on it, or what?"

With Brimley's dig, everything shifted back to normal.

"You bet," Walker replied as he dried the blade on the towel at his side, then stowed Kenny's treasured knife into the sheath on his belt. He'd stopped wearing his holster once Brim came aboard, but the knife was never far away. Walker hoisted both fillets off the deck and out of Rover's reach, then headed below deck to the galley.

Hurriedly, he rinsed the shark meat in the stainless-steel sink, then drained the rinse water. Refilling the sink, he left one fillet covered with cold water. He meant to grill it for lunch with the last of the tomatoes he'd picked up during their shopping trip to the latest village. Deftly, he wrapped the other fillet in the white, waxed butcher paper he'd found behind the galley door, then placed it in the freezer side of the full-sized refrigerator/freezer combo.

There was something about all the white packages in the freezer that made a man proud. Maybe it was the caveman embedded in every red-blooded male's DNA to provide for the future. Walker didn't know.

When he strolled topside, Rover was once again hanging over the rail, while Brimley pointed to the frisky pod of dolphins breaking through the rippling waves portside. "I'm going swimming. You with me, Rover, old boy?"

Rover barked because, well, that was what Rover did best. Whatever Brim said, he was quick to agree, always boisterously.

"Wait up," Walker called as he dug one of the yacht's two inflatable dinghies out of the upper aft deck's storage chest. "Let's give Rover a place to land in case he gets tired of puppy-paddling."

But by then, Brimley's toes were wrapped over the edge of the swimmer's deck, he'd leaned forward, and he was ready to dive in, clothes and all.

"You might want to change into swim trunks," Walker warned. "Those jeans'll turn mighty heavy when wet."

"Nah. I got nothing but lint in my pockets. Come on, Doggo," Brimley urged Rover. "Let's cool off before lunch. One. Two. Three!"

*SPLASH!* Both dog and man leaped overboard, the best way to end a successful fishing contest.

Walker hit the self-inflate tab on the eight-by-five dinghy, then dropped it overboard while it filled itself to the manufacturers' approved level. Tying the dinghy's drop-line to the railing, he tied another loose rope to the opposite rail, just in case someone needed a hand-up. One could never take enough safety precautions when swimming in the wild Atlantic. Shit happened, and Walker wasn't sure of Brimley's health or his swimming skills. Why take chances?

With one hand, Walker stripped his shirt over his head and tossed it to one of the recliners. He traded his khakis for swim trunks. Climbing onto the rail, he planted both feet and balanced there with his eyes closed, his face in the sun, and the ocean wind in his nose.

At the moment, *Persia Smiles* bobbed lazily between the northwestern end of the Azorean islands of Ilha do Pico and the southeastern edge of Ilha do Faial. Talk about fair seas and blue skies. Felt like paradise. Just what Walker needed, a different kind of peace and quiet. A better kind of calm.

It was good to be alive. So. So. Good. He relaxed. He could breathe. Most likely because he was the skipper of a fine craft, and he knew more about sailing, the yacht, the sea, and fishing than his companion. But also, because he wasn't alone anymore, and Brimley had been right. Having someone to talk with, someone who understood where you came from, was a relief. Didn't hurt that he and Brimley were both combat vets, even though they'd fought separate wars at different times. Warrior-speak was the same language the world over, and one war was as bad as every other. Which was just plain sad.

Tucking his arms over his head, Walker jack-knifed into the bluest waters on the planet. Just like that, he was back where he belonged, cutting through seawater like that shark had and scattering schools of sunny orange and vividly bright blue fish as he went. The sea would forever be his first home of choice.

Opening his eyes beneath the waves, he studied the seascape. To his right, a few large tunas mingled with remoras and smaller silvery fish. The dark shape of a turtle lumbered in the murky distance. To his left, the massive white keel of the yacht bobbed calmly in the waves. She might sell for under two-hundred K, but honestly, what more did a man need than a star to steer by and a seaworthy ship to see the world in?

*Only the one thing I may never have again. Freedom.*

There was that. But rather than dwell on the negative shadows stalking his life, Walker propelled himself topside, grabbed another lung full of air, then dived back down to inspect the Meridian's hull. Smooth and sleek, she was an excellent craft. Both props were clean of barnacles. All blades were in good shape. No nicks. No chips. No paint missing anywhere.

Overall, *Persia Smiles* looked fairly new and untouched. It'd be nice to locate her registration and confirm his suspicion that the yacht was only a couple years old. If that. There simply wasn't enough wear and tear to indicate she'd seen much use. Hell, her cedar decking wasn't sun-faded or water-stained. Even the recliners' cushions were still crisp and seemingly unused.

But enough worrying and wondering. Like a streamlined barracuda, Walker flattened his arms to his sides and arrowed back into the land of sunlight, where Brim was helping Rover into the dinghy. The dog had the widest smile on his wet, furry face. So did Brimley. He'd tossed his jeans into a soggy ball beside Rover.

Rolling over, Walker settled into a steady set of backstrokes that took him far into the ocean. This was all he needed. Blue sky overhead, deep blue sea beneath, and the taste of saltwater in his mouth.

About a mile from the yacht, he jack-knifed underwater and came up with his arms spread wide, ready to fly. The butterfly stroke turned him into a natural seal, with the crown of his head leading the way, dipping just below the waves to break the surface tension. His entire body streamlined close to the surface. His hips perfectly synchronized with the rest of his body. He was one with the sea.

Never mind that his arms weren't fins or that they stretched forward, then down and out, then backward, movements a seal didn't have to make. Never mind that his hands cupped the waves away, while the powerful downbeats of his feet propelled him forward. The butterfly was the most exhausting stroke for most swimmers. Yet with every forward thrust, he relished the natural undulation of his body in water. For these few private, intimate minutes, he was one with Mother Nature. And she was bitchin'.

Back again at the swim deck, he drew both hands over his head, rotated on his side, then planted his feet on *Persia Smiles'* ass. Automatically, both legs straightened, thrusting him away from the yacht as he moved into an easygoing breaststroke. By then, his chest muscles were feeling the burn. Going the same distance, he finished his drill with a lazy swim back to the yacht. Damn, he was sore, but he felt good.

Breathing deep and easy, he closed his eyes and imagined what it would be like with Persia swimming at his side. Her hair wet and pulled back from her face. Her skin like silk, smooth and warm. Her eyes, big and dark, full of promise. Her lips red and swollen, because by then, she would've been well-kissed. She might even be sore in all the right places.

His chest heaved with a satisfied sigh at his impossible dream.

It was time to get back on board, back to reality. Persia wasn't here, and he was a fool to have left her like he had. Good reasons or not, he'd hurt her, and Walker would spend the rest of his days wishing he'd done right by her. But life on the run was no life, and he wouldn't have done that to her.

Back among the living, Walker closed his eyes and bobbed along with Brim. Rover was still shaking seawater out of his ears and all over the dinghy, barking at seagulls that dived too close. He'd had his swim, yet his loyal black eyes tracked Brimley. Thank heavens, Brim had left his boxers on.

Walker leaned his head back into the water until it covered his ears. Stretching his feet, he stared at the blue, blue sky until he was absolutely prone, parallel with the universe above and listening to the sounds of the sea below. This would be heaven with the right woman bobbing beside him. Holding his hand. Playing with him.

Regret sucked.

His stomach let out a noisy growl. Walker had only eaten a bagel and fresh fruit for breakfast, peaches Brimley had bought at a produce stand in the last village they'd docked at for fuel. Peaches that would forever remind Walker of the lady he'd left behind.

Shit. Everything reminded him of Persia.

He'd never been the sort of guy to keep a girl in every port. Hadn't seemed fair or smart to treat women like that, which was why he suffered for his sin of that one-night-stand now. Persia hadn't been just *any woman*, and what they'd shared hadn't been *just sex*. Walker couldn't explain it, and he wasn't about to discuss his feelings with Brimley. But that tender Florida interlude had reached into the darkest parts of Walker's soul. She'd shone a light there that had warmed and touched him. Still did. The pain of knowing he'd hurt her gutted him all over again. Men were pigs, and he was the worst.

He'd read enough crap about love at first sight and other nonsense, yet this once in a lifetime encounter had surely felt like that. Simple sex had never mattered so much before. Never made Walker think twice about leaving, or once about staying. It'd been no different than eating, something a guy had to do. The animalistic, biological need to ease the build-up of semen and the angst that came with it. To fuck.

While it'd been a damned long time since he'd engaged in that activity with any of the barflies that hung around San Diego's notorious SEAL hangouts, his time with Persia had left him wanting. Usually, he'd be physically satisfied for days after a hot, steamy encounter, maybe weeks or months if he'd deployed right afterward.

But this time… It wasn't just good sex he and Persia had enjoyed. She'd fixed breakfast in the middle of the night. After their shower, man, her fingers running over his bare skin, rubbing lotion over his tired, salt-water battered body, had separated her from every other female in his past life. The empathy she'd shown him during their brief encounter had left him lacking and hungry. But not for food. Not just for sex, either.

He needed her sweet light again, the one she'd shone on him. That light in the darkness that had lurked within him these past months.

Persia might act tough. She was, after all, a former FBI agent and CIA officer, now some kind of covert operator working for *What's His Name*. Alex Stewart, was it? Walker hadn't cared enough to commit the guy's name to memory. Mostly because he couldn't keep his mind off Persia for more than a couple minutes at a time. Wasn't he the dumbest ass ever? Kiss a woman. Bed that woman. Then up and leave her, without having the balls to tell her a proper goodbye.

And then? Still want that woman more than he seemed to want his next breath. Since when had life become the mess it was now? Since when had he ever stuck his neck out as often as he had this past miserable year? And for what? For who?

*For love…*

*Yeah, right. Quinn Dooley, maybe. He's been a friend as long as I can remember. But Persia? That couldn't be love. Too soon. Too fast.*

Yet even as he swallowed that seemingly reasonable excuse, Walker ran a quick hand over his head, still thinking about Persia and the last time she'd smiled. He'd been on top of her then. She'd just come all over him, yet he'd failed at his own release. She'd known he was having performance issues, but her release had left her glowing. And knowing he'd put that pretty smile on her face had to be enough. Because Walker's life was full of more goodbyes than he cared to remember, now one that hurt the most. A brown-eyed beauty named Persia Coltrane.

But she would survive; she *was* tough. Yet she wasn't as tough as she'd wanted him to believe. Walker was sure he'd detected a shaky vulnerability to the hard edges she'd always led with. When she'd mentioned the Zapata brothers, he'd been more alarmed that she already knew about him and who he was.

But now that he'd had time to think, Walker worried what she'd suffered working alongside a depraved pig like Domingo Zapata. What had she said, that she'd infiltrated his lair, that desecrated patch of deep, dark woods north of Ouro Preto, Minas Gerais, from which no tender, living soul had ever returned?

That info-byte alone set Persia apart from most male operators Walker had worked with. But her infiltration into Brazil had to have happened more than two years ago. Hotrod knew that for sure. Domingo's crime spree in America had been intercepted during the infamous Portland, Oregon, debacle. In Montana, if Walker remembered correctly. Hell, he even knew the former SEAL brothers who'd brought the rat bastard down and sent him to the federal Arctic prison. Chase, Kruze, and Pagan Sinclair. The Sin Boys. Also Sullivan's men.

Not like their alliance with Sullivan was common knowledge. It wasn't. Walker just happened to know the Sinclairs from his Navy time. The man they'd ended up working for, Senator McQueen Sullivan, had also worked a miracle by hooking Walker up with the Army's Night Stalkers out of Fort Campbell, Kentucky. The Senator from Texas was a straight-up, gun-slinging, shit-kicking cowboy. He wasn't afraid to get his hands dirty, and he knew people in all the right, low places.

But infiltrating Zapata's lair had to have been a dirty, risky business, depending on what Persia had witnessed or done to maintain her cover. For sure, she'd said there'd been kids involved. *Too many kids.* She'd hated when they were hurt, which meant Domingo did the hurting. Yet Persia had held fast long enough to provide solid intel back to her CIA handler, which eventually, brought Domingo down.

Walker wondered how long that was. How many hours, days, months? What had she seen? What had she heard? Shit! What had her CIA handler been thinking—or sniffing—when he'd sent Persia into Brazil to do that job? Male and female gender roles aside, infiltrating Domingo was no work for a woman. Walker understood where that ache in his chest came from now. From Persia! From the suffering still bound up inside her. His soul had heard what his ears hadn't been smart enough to detect. She was still hurting and… He should've known!

*What an ass!*

Pissed for having been more worried about himself than for what she'd endured, Walker rolled over in the water and stared at the shimmering blue below. Damn it, he'd missed what she'd been trying to tell him. She'd said she'd wished she could've killed Zapata—which he now knew meant she'd been angry or frightened enough to have considered jeopardizing her mission. But why? What specifically had made her desperate?

Of course, she'd also claimed she loved Julio Juarez, and Walker couldn't blame her. Julio was one of those rare guys who never thought twice about dying for honor or country. But Orlando and Domingo were godless vampires who'd sucked the life out of their victims and their country.

Persia's remorse-filled words rolled over Walker with every lap of what had been, until now, soothing ocean waves. *'Still messes with my head. Makes it hard to remember why I was really there. You know. Part of me turns into a raging beast thinking about it. I wanted to kill anyone who touched them and save every last child. Only I couldn't. I didn't.'*

"Shit," Walker hissed, needing to call Persia, if only to hear her voice and tell her he was listening now. That he'd finally heard what she'd been trying to tell him,. That he knew the kind of pain she was in. That he was the biggest, dumbest ass on the planet for leaving her like he had, and that he was so damned sorry for not appreciating all she'd lived through. All she'd sacrificed for her country.

"You had enough?" Brimley's question jerked Walker out of his regret.

"Yeah," he replied gruffly.

He was done being a thoughtless, selfish bastard. Damn it, he'd missed the brokenness of the beautiful woman who'd been right in front of his nose. He should've been focused on her and truly listening. But no. He'd been more concerned with CYA, when he should've tugged Persia into his arms and held onto her until she knew for sure he had her back. That he'd never let her go alone into another Zapata-like shithole again.

*You love her.*

He shook that crazy deduction off. *Nah. This isn't love. It's… it's comradery. We're two of a kind. Warriors. That's all.*

*No, it's not, and yes, you do.*

Jesus! Now he was talking to himself.

Ten swift strokes took him to the swim deck, where Brimley was climbing aboard. The man was a hairy beast, from his skinny legs to his paunch, to his chest and back. His age showed like any Vietnam vet, in the flaccid bat wings under his arms, to the way he limped when he walked. To the stoop in his spine and the gnarled joints in his hands.

Rover had already scrambled happily aboard, but when Brimley's big flat foot hit the middle cedar plank, the opposite end lifted as if it were loose.

Walker wiped the seawater out of his eyes and off his face. "Do that again," he said, needing to be sure what he'd seen.

"What? This?" Brimley stomped the offending plank three more times. Again and again, the opposite end tilted just enough to make Walker wonder why only the one plank was loose. "Feels like your boat's got a loose screw, kiddo. Just like you."

Brimley thought that was funny, but Walker knew different. Scrambling aboard, he dropped to his knees to examine the loose plank. It was the only board held in place with flat-topped nails instead of weather-resistant, stainless-steel lag bolts.

Rover shook, then stuck his furry nose in Walker's face and licked his nose. Brimley chuckled as he hoisted soggy Rover up onto the upper aft deck, aka the lounge outside the cockpit. "Enough kisses. Now sit, Doggo. Make room for me."

Meanwhile, Walker lifted the loose end of that plank up as the rusted nails gave way with a raucous *SCREEEECH!*

"Whoa," Brimley gasped from the recliner where he and Rover sat peering down at Walker. "What the hell's that?"

Good question. "I'm not sure." He'd found a narrow piece of a metal something beneath the eight-by-one-inch cedar plank. On his hands and knees, he leaned closer. Looked like aluminum. No screws fastened it in place, neither was there a handle to lift it. It wasn't a sheet, nor a patch. More like the bottom of a box that had no reason to be on the swim deck, much less under it.

"You never told me this was a used boat."

*I haven't told you much of anything.* But for sure, this puzzle box hadn't been hidden here to keep miscellaneous receipts safe. "I'm still looking for the user manual." *And the registration. The real owner's name would be nice.*

"Well, you still got that fancy blade on you, don'tcha? Why not pop this gizmo and see what you got?"

Palming his brother's knife, Walker prepared to do the deed. But before he did, he shifted his body between Brimley and Rover. Next, he offered a quick prayer, this time to the God of all gods. *Please don't let this be a booby trap.*

# Chapter Sixteen

Fundamentally, Persia knew boring operations were the best. This drive to western Virginia should've been a relief after all she'd done for the Agency. It would give her more time to decompress, but would handling a routine op put her back in Alex's good graces?

"You're sure antsy," Zack murmured. "What's up?"

Still dressed all in black, from his work boots to his leather jacket, he was an easy traveling partner. They'd split the driving, with him behind the wheel following the US Marshal's armored transport west. On the return trip, she'd drive. They'd stop for lunch then.

"I can't get comfortable," Persia admitted. Truth was she was more afraid she'd fall asleep. The steady hum of tires on the road and the gentle sway of the vehicle was working its magic. Especially since she hadn't slept much last night. Guess she needed more rum in her coke, or less coke in her rum. Which actually made sense.

"You want the wheel?"

That was tempting, but, "Nah. I'm good."

This unincorporated part of Lee County, Virginia, was mostly rural and fairly barren. Wide-open fields with lush green, woodsy backdrops stretched along both sides of the two-lane highway. It reminded her of home, where her parents still lived. Quiet. A lot less traffic. And it smelled better than the city.

The penitentiary had been built in the middle of Nowhere, Virginia, to enhance the state's most western county's dirt-poor economy. In other words, if they weren't farming, most able-bodied folks worked at the prison.

"So, tell me about yourself," Zack said as he tapped the earpiece snugged deep inside his left ear. "Where'd you go to school?"

Persia wore a matching earpiece, but so far, there'd been nothing from Ember or Beau, and thank heavens, not a terse word from Alex.

"DeSoto Central, Southaven, Mississippi. Home of the Jaguars. Then the University of Memphis, Tennessee. Go Tigers. It's less than an hour from home. That way, I went back any time I wanted."

"Sounds like you were… what? A cheerleader?"

Pressing the silver butterfly switch on her door panel, Persia activated the window to let some air in. Instantly, the vehicle filled with the rich loamy scent of freshly plowed fields, someone's cut grass, and wildflowers. "Good guess, but I have more brains than that. But I did play basketball in high school and during my first year at Memphis. That was fun."

"Ah, a full-ride scholarship then," he surmised correctly.

"Of course." She turned in her seat to really look at Zack. He was as easy to talk with as Mark. But those guns… His biceps stretched that leather jacket to the max. This guy worked out.

"You're close to your folks?" he asked.

"Sure, aren't you?"

"Hell, yeah. They'll be in town over Labor Day. I'll bring them by and introduce them if you're around."

That was a good three months away. She grunted. "Where else would I be?"

"We never know with this job, do we?" he murmured as the van ahead slowed. Orange barricades lined the shoulders of the road, then construction cones. A flagman at the right side cautioned them to slow down. "Doesn't it figure, roadwork ahead."

"So… Where are you from?"

He shot her a quick grin. "America."

"Me, too. But you know what I meant. What ethnicity? Your skin color is quite lovely."

That made Zack laugh. "Me? Lovely? Don't go spreading that around. Mom's full-blooded Irish, but Dad's from Jamaica."

"Hmmm. That explains it."

"Explains what? That except for my big nose, we could pass for brother and sister?"

"You don't have a big nose. But yeah, we have similar traits, only you seem to really enjoy life. You're always easygoing and…" She lifted both shoulders. "You smile all the time. You seem happy every day. Are you?"

He shot her a toothy grin. "Life's too short to be miserable, you ought to know that by now. Why not be happy while you're here?"

Her lashes dropped, and she wished she hadn't started down a road that would most likely lead back to Alex. He and Zack seemed more like old friends than boss and employee.

Zack's big hand dropped over hers on the console. "You're not Joan of Arc, Persia."

"What does she have to do with anything?"

"And you're not Jesus Christ."

Okay, that made her laugh. "You've got that right." *Because if I were, I would've snuffed the Zapata brothers the minute they opened their killer-baby eyes the day they were born. Or hatched. Or spawned or whatever.*

Zack's fingers squeezed over the tops of hers. "I've seen just as much shit as you have, but the secret's in how you choose to handle it. Let it go, or it'll fester inside until it drives you nuts. Trust me. Back when I first encountered the Black Dragon Syndicate—"

"You did what?"

His head bobbed as he kept his eyes on the road. "That's where my little girl Song came from. She was one of those Chinese orphans." His fingers squeezed harder. "That's also when I met Mei."

"Your wife?" Why didn't Persia know his backstory?

His head bobbed, but his Adam's apple seemed stuck in his throat "Yeah. Back then" —he swallowed hard— "Mei hated everyone, including me. We didn't know it then, but LiLi's father had her kidnapped, smuggled her into France. Mei got it into her head that LiLi's disappearance had to do with the influx of illegal Chinese orphans. All she wanted was her daughter back, and everyone else was in her way. She had a lot of nerve back then, even butted heads with Alex. It took us a while to learn how to work together."

"What did you do?"

His lips pinched together. "We went undercover, acted like a married couple out to adopt a kid, and desperate enough to take one illegally. Had to." His belly expanded with a long, slow breath. "All those little girls… Took one helluva chance. Thought Alex was going to fire my ass for sure."

"He wouldn't."

"Oh, yeah, he would have. I screwed the pooch big time. Made a lot of trouble for him. But the boss is also a sucker for little kids. In the end, I thought he and Kels might adopt one of those girls. I think they were looking into it, but the one they'd fallen in love with had parents who were looking for her and wanted her back, and…" He shrugged. "Things don't always go the way we want, do they?"

*Wasn't that the truth.* "How many kids?" Persia needed to know.

"How many Chinese baby girls, you mean? Hundreds," he whispered, then coughed and said, "We save big kids and little kids one at a time, Persia. We don't work miracles. That's not our job. We just do the best we can every day. Haven't you always done that?"

She nodded, staring out the front window, finally understanding that Joan of Arc reference. Joan had actually saved the world back when she'd lived. She'd been a French heroine, which had made her England's enemy. When the English captured her, they'd tried her on trumped-up charges, then burned her at the stake at the tender age of nineteen. She'd been a teenager.

Somehow, all that Persia had accomplished in her years seemed so much less. She was no one's hero, and she'd done things no one knew about, things she wasn't proud of. Things she'd never tell. Which was why she slept with a nightlight—when she slept.

Her lungs filled with the fresh air blowing through the window. "I've always done my best," she said resolutely. "I'm no slacker."

"Never said you were. So, how much do you drink every night? Do you always carry a flask?"

The vertebrae in her neck damned near snapped like a whip when her eyes flashed back to him. Zack kept his focus on the road, as if he hadn't asked the mother of all questions. But he knew. *Damn him, he knew.*

"As much as I need to," she confessed with a titch of attitude. Yet she knew better. Sometimes, that bottle she took to bed wasn't enough. And lately, she worried she was sinking into no man's land, where unemployed, unemployable alcoholics roamed the streets, looking for a bed or a bottle— or both.

Zack's big chin dimpled when his lips pinched. "Been there. Done that.

"You're…?" This conversation had gotten way too intimate. "You're an alcoholic?"

"Nah, but I've drunk myself stupid enough. Before Mei and the kids came along, I lived to party. Not proud of it, but after what I'd survived, I figured I deserved a break, so I took one. A long, damned hard one. Do me a favor?"

The breath she'd been holding eased out of her. "Sure. What?"

"Invite me over next time you decide to drown the pain. I'll bring Jake Weylin. He's been right where you are. We'll get you through it."

Tears sprang to Persia's eyes so quickly she had to look away. "Thanks. I just might do that." Might not, too. Inviting friends to a pity-party didn't seem smart, and she'd already said too much. Zack was no dummy, and he wasn't asking questions just to be nice.

Two motorcycles zoomed past, one on each side of the SUV, the loud clamor of their bikes startling Persia back to reality. Both took to the shoulders, kicking up gravel as they passed the federal van in a cloud of dust.

"What the hell?" Zack stepped on the brakes.

Persia peered out her open window to see if she could get a good look around the van. Both bikes had come to a screeching halt, nearly running over the team of road workers and orange cones lining the road ahead. Only these road workers were all young, white, and covered with enough black ink to rival Zapata's disgusting artwork. Just as she turned to tell Zack that she thought something was wrong...

*BOOM!* The federal van lurched off its tires.

Zack jammed the brakes, bringing the TEAM SUV to an abrupt stop. Rapid gunfire popped ahead, as the Marshals' van's taillights signaled flashing reverse, get-the-hell-out-of-my-way! Its rear-end fishtailed, its bumper now aimed at TEAM SUV's grill.

Still cursing, Zack slammed the vehicle into reverse. Throwing one arm over the seatback, he revved backward off the pavement onto the graveled shoulder.

Persia tapped her earpiece to alert TEAM HQ, "Taking fire. Request immediate assist. I repeat, we are taking fire. US Marshals are under attack!"

"Sending back up now," Beau snapped. "How many, Persia?"

She told him what she knew. "Only saw seven, but there may be more. All young men, look like gangbangers. Any TEAM agents within distance?"

"Alex is in the air," Ember stated loud and clear, her voice steady where Beau's had been tense. "Sheriff and Medics are in transit."

Which meant Alex had already been headed this way. Why? Didn't he trust her?

Straight ahead, the red sedan that had been ahead of the Marshals' vehicle now lay on its side, smoke billowing from its sky-facing windows. The motorcyclists and construction workers now brandished rifles, pistols, and other weapons. All seven bastards advanced on the TEAM SUV, which had landed sideways after that backward drift, and also, put Zack directly in their line of fire.

Persia scrambled out of the vehicle and into position on the passenger side. She fired a warning shot over the SUV's hood and over Frank Gibson's homies' heads. TEAM protocol demanded it. According to Alex's rules, these idiots deserved one last chance before she ended them. "Stop, or I'll shoot!"

Like a pack of in-sync killers, they'd doffed their orange vests and now advanced in matching black wife-beaters and leathers. The macho chicken-shit swagger and all those tattooed faces reminded Persia of another asshole and his gang in a different country.

By then, Zack was out of the vehicle and on his feet, facing the killers down. "US Marshals!" he announced, his pistol on target. Which was true. She and he had been deputized for just this scenario. "Drop your weapons! Do it now!"

When the tough guy on Persia's far left sneered and jerked his short-stock rifle into his shoulder, Persia crouched and steadied her clenched weapon on the SUV hood. The idiot answered Zack's demand with a wicked spray of hellfire that spattered the SUV's grill and spiderwebbed the windshield.

Persia came up shooting. Zack engaged as fervently. Both their weapons of choice were SIG Sauer P226s, and both made quick work exacting law and order.

Too bad Gibson's homies weren't trained former military or equipped for the fight they'd started. All the ARs in the world couldn't stand up to the highly-honed reflexes of battle-hardened warriors, or to Persia and Zack's combined years of muscle memory training.

For a few seconds, it was all noise, mayhem, quick thinking, shoot-'em-up, and gunsmoke.

While Frank Gibson's boys kept walking, Persia's pistol kept talking. Only when the fourth wannabe-hero bit the dust in a dramatic spin, followed by an, 'I'm dead' face-plant, did numbers Five, Six, and Seven drop their weapons and raise their hands.

Seven cried, "Don't shoot! Please. Don't shoot us!"

Which sounded just plain pathetic. What'd they expect? To simply stroll up to a federal transport, pop the two well-armed officers inside, then head into the sunset with big brother?

With her weapon still exhaling a steady scent of lovely vaporized gunpowder, Persia stepped away from the TEAM SUV and, with her SIG snapped onto the whiner's face, bellowed, "Hands up where I can see them!" She would've used expletives, but she was still trying to make a good impression on Zack. Maybe score a couple brownie points even while she walked steadily into the body count.

Zack was already there, his pistols pointed on both Five and Seven, both face-down and squirming in the gravel.

"I've got the one on your right," she told her Agent-in-Charge.

"Copy that," he replied as he roughly cuffed Five and Seven, then stepped back to wait on the Marshals to read their rights.

The Marshals' van was now safely off-road yards behind the TEAM SUV. One uniformed officer had stayed with their prisoner, while the other approached, his weapon drawn.

"Marshal Goodwin, everyone okay?" Persia asked, as she crouched beside the bleeder long enough to cuff him, roll him over onto his belly, and leave him face-down in the road like his bros.

"Yes, ma'am, but that kid's Doogie Gibson, Frank's younger brother," he told Persia. "Wanna bet four of the others are Andy, Reese, Chip, and Mikey Gibson?"

Doogie twisted around to stare at Persia. His blue eyes were full of tears and his blond hair dripped sweat. Damn, he was just a kid, maybe sixteen, eighteen, tops. "You bitch. You killed my brothers."

"What'd you expect? You play with fire, you're gonna get burned. Didn't your mama teach you that?"

"But Frank's innocent! He didn't kill that lying whore and her kids!"

"Then why is she dead, and why did three witnesses finger your brother?" Marshal Goodwin asked, as he took over the scene.

While he commenced reading the kid his Miranda rights, Persia straightened and scanned the mayhem these guys had caused, in case there were other active shooters. From where she stood, she could see straight through the Marshals' van, since most of the windshield was gone. The armed officer inside was still in control of his prisoner. No trouble coming from there, well, except for Frank cursing his head off from inside his barred cage.

Except for the smoking sedan on its side, no other traffic cluttered this narrow stretch of road. A thick copse of scrawny, half-dead trees lined the far side of the plowed field to the north. No one there. On the south, another newly plowed field stretched for miles in all directions. No cover there, either. The confrontation was over.

Meanwhile, Zack moved silently from one downed shooter to the next, divesting them of weapons and knives, and checking for life even as he kept watch over his shoulder as well.

"I've already called this in," Goodwin said. "Help's coming from the prison. Sheriff and paramedics will be here soon."

"Thanks," Persia replied as she turned to Zack and said, "Alex is on his way."

Zack nodded. "I heard. Good thinking. Stay here while I check whoever's in that sedan."

"Copy that," Persia replied, but she couldn't reconcile what had just happened. It seemed inconceivable that these kids thought they could ambush federal Marshals. Yes, they'd packed some stout firepower, but this was not TV land, and there was nothing glamorous about having to shoot teenagers, even dumb-assed ones with guns. Because that was what Persia was looking at. Three still alive, uninjured kids. Four down, soon to be sporting toe-tags. And one arrogant son of a bitch, manacled and bellowing from his caged bench seat in the rear of the Marshals' van. "You bastards killed 'em! You killed my brothers!"

Well, yeah. Self-defense worked like that. *You shoot at me, you can be sure I'll shoot back.* Persia shook her head at the twisted mindset of murderers, rapists, and warlords the world over. Yes, she'd killed these armed and dangerous children. When it came down to them or her TEAM, she'd do it again.

Zack waved from the red sedan. "One driver. He's alive and conscious. Just scared."

Nothing boring about this day.

# Chapter Seventeen

True confession time. "I knew it. You're a damned Navy SEAL!"

"Was. USN Lieutenant Walker Judge. I commanded SEAL Team 18, and I'm damned proud of it." Former military members often raised salutes or used active duty rank designations as signs of respect, long after a warrior retired. Walker wasn't about to correct Brimley.

Still on the upper aft deck with the lockbox out of its hidey-hole, but as yet unopened, Walker nodded from the recliner, where he sat with his hands loose between his knees. He'd figured it would be a matter of time before Brimley connected the name on Kenny's knife to the man with the yacht. He just hoped Brim took the revelation in stride when he did.

Like a wise old man who'd seen war up close and personal, Brimley touched two fingers to his brow and answered smartly, "Proud to meet you, LT. US Army Sergeant Brimley D. Scott at your service, sir. Tell me what you need, and I'll make it happen. I may look old, but I've still got plenty of fight in me. Just ask. You'll see."

Goose-flesh rippled up Walker's arms and across his shoulders at that undeserved respect and unearned devotion. Instead of recrimination, he'd been idolized. Which made him wonder if Brimley had even heard of his trial in far-off

America. Not that it mattered. Walker certainly wasn't going to out himself. But it would've been nice if everything were out in the open. Brim seemed trustworthy. Walker just couldn't take the chance.

He decided to go with partial truths that would afford his friend a healthy dose of plausible deniability if the day came he needed an out. Friends didn't betray their friends, but should Brimley choose to turn Walker in, he intended to do all he could to protect his buddy. Regardless. Call him a fool. Call him a bastard. That was how Walker was made.

"First of all, I don't believe there are gems, diamonds, or gold in this lockbox," he stated quietly. There probably weren't any receipts, registration papers, or grocery lists, either. Not as well-hidden as this lockbox had been. "No treasure maps. No stock or bonds."

Brimley never batted an eye. "'Course not, it's too small and too flat for all that. But whatever's in it's got you spooked. Spit it out, son. You think it's worth opening now, or should we hand it over to the cops soon as we dock?"

*We.* Such a little word with such a wealth of consequence behind it.

*If one hangs, we all hang…*

"No cops. No authorities." Walker licked the corners of his mouth and squared his jaw. He didn't want to open the box with Brimley watching over his shoulder. Things would be easier if diamonds and jewels were in there. He'd gladly return that crap to the real owner, once he knew who that mystery person was. But he kept thinking of the name on the registration in California's Department of Motor Vehicles' database. The last registered owner. *Wallace Goff.*

Everything that man had ever touched had turned rancid and had gone just plain wrong. Goff had never been a worthy leader of warriors. As odd as it seemed, he'd also worn the Trident, which should've made him the best commander in the fleet. But not once had he served in any significant battle. Yet he'd never had a problem sending his teams into hell without proper intel, equipment, or sufficient manpower. The three friendly-fire incidents to his credit should've put him behind a desk long ago, but until the day he'd been murdered, he'd still controlled Team 18 with an iron fist.

It was as if he'd been Teflon-coated his entire Navy career. Walker wanted to know why that chicken shit had been promoted as far as he had. Commander, for hell's sake. Who had he known? Which Admiral had covered his ass and paved his way? Or was he just one lucky son of a bitch?

Now this odd little aluminum lockbox showed up on Goff's yacht. The width, length, and depth of the thing equaled the size of five, maybe six legal-size tablets. While the plank above it had been hollowed out to make room for it, the lockbox itself was just plain worrisome. Its locking mechanism looked simple, yet Walker worried it might be booby-trapped. That aerosolized ricin, or some other just as diabolical chemical weapon, might lurk behind one twist of his knife's blade into the lock's aperture.

It could very well happen. Anyone devious enough to hide something that well, had to have been desperate. And desperation made people nuts. But if that person was Commander Goff…?

Walker ran a quick hand over his beard at the ridiculous way his mind was working. *No. Just. No.* He'd seen the pictures. Goff *was* dead. Dead and buried. The body in those morgue shots was definitely his CO. There wouldn't have been accusations or imprisonment, otherwise.

*Yet pictures can be doctored. Witnesses can be bought. And anyone with a brain knows your trial was a sham.*

*Yeah, yeah, I know.*

Walker's imagination seemed to have developed a nagging voice that wouldn't let up. Not about Persia, and now, not about the man Walker knew for certain was dead and buried in the National Cemetery in Point Loma, CA.

*Or was he?*

*Yes. I saw the morgue shots with my own eyes, damn it. I was there.*

*But did you witness his burial? What do you really know?*

Damned if his imagination didn't make a good point. *But shit!* To further silence that nagging voice and all his suspicions, he leaned over the damnable box, took firm hold of the lid so it wouldn't slip, and stuck the shiny tip of Kenny's knife into the zig-zaggy aperture.

*POP!* The lid jack-knifed open—but only because its hinge was spring-loaded. There was no pressurized anthrax dust lurking inside. No whirling razor blades either.

"Well, that sure was anti-climactic," Brimley grouched.

Glancing upward, Walker grinned at the older man's dry wit. "What were you expecting? Jack-in-the-box? Freddy Krueger?"

"Hell, yeah. 'Least a midget ninja with a handful of Chinese stars, tense as you were." When Rover barked, Brim smoothed one hand over his bristly head. "'S okay, Dog. Sorry I got you upset. Nothing scary here. So, what's in it?"

"Nothing, just a bunch of maps, love letters, and—"

"Riiiiiight. And Romeo and Juliet kept a lockbox just like this one before they poisoned themselves in the name of looooove." Brimley rolled his eyes and fluttered his fingers over his chest, which made Walker smile, considering all those gray chest hairs showing. "Quit your stalling. What's in the damned thing?"

"All right, all right, keep your shirt on." Walker removed the only thing in the box, an accordion-pleated cardboard wallet. Unsnapping the elastic cord that bound the thing, he peered into the first pocket. Looked like receipts, some folded, some dog-eared. Second pocket, a handful of black-and-white photos. Third pocket, more of the same, only those photos were in color. Fourth and fifth pockets held one eight-by-eleven tablet with a BIC pen stuck in the spiral. Sixth pocket, two, make that three, USB flash drives.

With a deft sleight of hand, Walker palmed those last three items. What Brim didn't know couldn't hurt him.

"Well? Any gold or silver coins? Pieces of eight? Doubloons, for Christ's sake?"

"Afraid not, just a bunch of papers. Looks like receipts. Might make good reading over lunch." Walker held the cardboard wallet over his head to validate what he'd said. "Man, I'm hungry. Feel like grilling that trophy shark yet?"

Brimley's eyes lit. "Hell, yeah," he said as he slapped both palms to his knees and lifted to his feet. "Come on, Dog. You're in for a real treat now."

"I'll secure the plank. Be right there," Walker said as he closed the wallet, then secured the swim deck, fastening the loose plank with the same rusted nails. They'd have to do until he located a couple water-proof bolts.

Once inside the relative solitude of the cockpit, he rifled through the wallet's pocket of what looked like receipts. *Jesus H. Christ.* They weren't receipts for fuel or food. He was looking at handwritten orders—for blondes, redheads, brunettes. Detailed, numbered, inventoried purchase requests. For females! Short-haired. Long-haired. Caucasian. Asian. French. British. Egyptian. Shit! Twenty-one handwritten orders that included girls as young as six months, toddlers, and teenagers. *Children!*

Walker pursed his lips, his heart pounding. He'd run across a thieving pack of sex-traders once before, oddly, just before he'd been illegally incarcerated. That visit to Guatemala had been on his own dime, because he'd volunteered to follow up on a kidnapping. His best buddy's wife was from Guatemala, and she'd gone home with the kids to visit her folks. While there, Quinn's darling three-year-old Emily Dooley had gone missing during what had become a disastrous family picnic.

When every avenue failed Quinn and his wife; when he was up for the naval commission of a lifetime, Walker had innocently strolled into his office one day. Just to shoot the bull. To catch up on each other's lies. But he'd known something was wrong the moment he'd looked Quinn in the eye. The man had barely been holding himself together.

Haltingly, word by word, Quinn had told Walker what no one else had yet known, that his youngest child was missing. He hadn't wanted America's out-of-control press corps involved, so he and his wife had been working every back channel they knew to get Emily back. But they'd gotten nowhere, and Quinn was beyond desperate.

Finally, he'd broken down and revealed the sordid details of the alleged gunfight between two rival gangs on a Guatemalan beach. The staged battle had overtaken a simple family picnic on a bright, sunny day. During the gunfire and ensuing chaos, his wife, their three daughters, and her parents had run for their lives. His wife had taken the two oldest girls with her. She'd thought her parents had the baby, Emily.

But Emily wasn't with her grandparents, and as the nightmare wore on, it turned out the gang war was a front. A lie. Once the local police had shown, they'd explained how those particular gangs actually worked for some bastard running a sex-trade operation out of Cuba. He'd paid them to stage fights, brawls, and outright warfare, in order to herd prospective victims away from their families.

Terror worked that day. Poor little Emily had run for cover, only to be snatched by the thugs working for some pedophile in Cuba. No one had heard her screaming because whoever'd grabbed her had chloroformed her, then stuffed her limp little body into the back seat of his jacked-up, POS, American-made truck.

Luckily, the man had thought himself above the law; he hadn't moved his merchandise quickly enough. When Walker arrived a couple weeks later, he'd first tracked down the police officers who'd been at the scene the day Emily went missing. When the bored sergeant he'd spoken with merely shrugged as if a wealthy American losing his child were no big deal, Walker waited until shift change. Then he followed the man home. It took a few rounds of musical chairs, knuckles, and a righteous game of *talk-or-I-will-kill-you*, but at the end of that long, sweaty night, Officer Bruno had squealed like the pig and coward he was.

Walker left him bleeding and without a way to warn his good buddy Renzo, aka, the Guatemalan child predator with a basement full of women and children in his fancy house on the beach. Renzo, it turned out, worked for the guy from Cuba, which to Walker, meant the source of Quinn's trouble probably lay farther north in America. Needless to say, the conversation with Renzo was short and to the 'point.' But among all the sputtering, bleeding, sniveling, and lying, he eventually told Walker that his buyer was running late. Guess some business transaction had gone sideways.

Once he'd felt certain Renzo told the truth, Walker had bound and gagged the jerk. Then he'd gone into the basement and assured the women and children there that help was on the way. Once they'd settled down, he'd contacted a friend of a friend who'd instantly put him in touch with honorable men on the same kind of mission. *'The Good Guys'*, an organization of former SEALs, US Marines, and other USA law enforcement officers, who were out to change the world of sex-traffickers. Disgusted with what they'd witnessed happening to children all over the world, they'd joined forces with aid organizations from other countries to recover exploited and endangered children and women. In hours—hours!—the Guatemalan team of saving grace arrived with vans, first-aid, food, water, comfort, and their army of carefully trained volunteers. It took the former SEALs and Marines a couple hours longer, but they'd showed before sunrise. Renzo went to jail that day. Which was too bad. Walker had still wanted a piece of that asshat—preferably his cold, dead heart.

But all those children…

Seeing the condition the frightened women were in was bad enough, but the terror in all those little ones' eyes had gutted Walker in ways he hadn't expected. After a short, hysterical talk with Emily, then a heartfelt conversation over the phone between Quinn and his little girl, the Guatemalan authorities put her in Walker's custody and allowed him to escort her back home.

At first, in Renzo's crowded basement, she'd been hysterical, afraid to even look Walker in the eye. She'd screamed and cried, and he'd cried with her. It had broken his heart that she'd been so frightened of him. At last, out of desperation, he'd dropped to his knees and told her who'd sent him to find her and take her home. He'd told her how much he loved her daddy. Finally, the elfin three-year-old had sucked up her courage and ran into Walker, burying her skinny body inside the sweaty warmth of his arms.

He'd bowed his head, and there she'd stayed. While *'The Good Guys'* arranged a flight back to California, via the US Air Force, Walker took Quinn's baby girl to the beach, needing to move her as far from the house of horrors as he could. For the rest of the day, he'd done nothing but sit in the sand and hold her, because she'd needed that the most. He wasn't her daddy, but he'd sure as hell called Quinn and made sure Quinn knew his baby girl was finally safe and coming home. Walker'd made sure Emily knew she was safe, too. Just by being there with her. Just by rocking and softly singing every damned song he could remember.

Best, worst, hardest flight of Walker's military career. Emily'd cried the entire time, and once again, he'd cried with her. Despite what nourishment he'd offered, the gourmet cookies, pretzels, or sodas the guys onboard had brought with them, she wouldn't eat or sleep. Hadn't wanted anyone else to touch her or talk to her, either. Didn't look at anyone, not the worried pilot or the anxious co-pilot. Only Walker. And mile after mile, she'd made sure he knew she didn't really want him, just *"Crissy and Sissy and Mommy and Daddy!"* And Walker wanted them, too. For her sake.

"Don't worry, they'll be there, sweetheart. They're waiting for you right now," he'd assured her a thousand times. Overall, she hadn't been physically hurt, which was damned lucky for Renzo. But she'd been so thin, and twitchier than hell. Walker was positive she'd been drugged. Her sad blue eyes were faded and sported dark, black circles beneath then. Her pretty, long blonde hair had been cut short and dyed bright red to suit some pervert's idea of a dream girl. The bastard. A tattooed number had been inked into the delicate skin on the top of her poor left foot. Guess that meant something to Renzo, but not Walker. Pissed him off. Made him wish he'd ended the conniving jerk before the Guatemalan task force had ever arrived.

Justice would've been served then, and Walker had been angry enough to have taken matters into his own two hands. He could've ended Renzo. God knew he'd wanted to. But Emily had needed him more.

By the time the AF transport landed at Naval Air Station North Island, Coronado, CA, Emily had been emotionally drained, so had Walker. But when Quinn broke down the second he'd spotted Emily… When he'd finally had her in his arms… When she'd acted like she'd wanted to crawl inside her daddy's skin and never be seen again—Walker'd known he'd do it all over again. That was what friends did for friends. He was just damned thankful he'd gotten to Emily in time.

But the next time around? If ever Walker were to 'bump' into Renzo again? The rat bastard wouldn't stand a snowball's chance in Hell. As it had turned out, Renzo's posh beach home had only been a temporary staging point, a quiet, out of the way place where he'd collected his buyer's *assets*, and where those human *assets* had been drugged, dressed up, paraded, displayed, and auctioned off to buyers all over the world. Via freakin' satellite.

Some perv in far off China had *'ordered and purchased'* Emily. Walker planned to visit China someday, soon. He didn't know how; he didn't know when. But he *would locate* the entitled Mr. Su Chen Fong. Walker only needed to see the guy once. At a distance. Under a damned dim light. In his fuckin' crosshairs.

Oddly, the morning after Walker had delivered Emily into her father's and mother's safekeeping, he'd been rudely awakened by the local Navy MPs, who had already been inside his house. Wasn't that a kick-in-the-gut coincidence? Walker knew he'd been targeted the second he'd destroyed that perverse human supply line in Guatemala. He just hadn't known by whom. Certainly not Quinn. Sure wasn't his brothers from Team 18. Walker wanted to meet whoever was behind his sham of a trial. He wanted the name of the bastard who'd benefitted from the torment he'd encountered in that dark, crowded basement, where blankets and tears had covered a dank, concrete floor. Then he wanted Mr. Asshole Fong. In that order.

Yet here again, another human tragedy lay in his hands like a horrid gift. As if she hadn't done enough, Karma seemed to have tagged him for a repeat performance of what he'd found and done in Guatemala.

Caught between the Devil and the deep blue sea, Walker set the disgusting stack of human purchase orders aside, then spread out the black-and-white photos from pocket number two. He counted twenty-one. All little girls, each photo assigned a three-digit number in the upper back corner, which coincided with the number of digits inked onto Emily's perfect little-girl foot.

Jumping out of the chair, Walker strode back to the door and flipped the switch that opened the ceiling vent. The cockpit was suddenly too warm.

Back at the desk, he lined up the color photos alongside each corresponding B&W. The same women and girls were in both sets, but the B&Ws were obviously preliminary shots of possible targets. The color versions were after shots. After the females were abducted. After they'd been dressed in scanty outfits, then posed as dreamy-eyed models. After they'd been drugged, then obviously staged to go to, or were already on, the black market.

*What a messed-up world.* He nearly choked on the thick bile creeping up the back of his throat. He hadn't yet found a clue that led to the person behind the scenes. Damn it. He couldn't show Brimley what he'd found, didn't dare take the guy into his confidence. Not about this. Yet Walker couldn't delay returning to the galley, either. Brimley was already suspicious, but holy hell! Why couldn't one day pass without turning to shit? Made him think of Kenny's sardonic philosophy, that no good deed ever went unpunished. Wasn't that the truth?

In the end, Walker repacked the wallet, then hid it under the mattress in the master suite where he slept. It'd be safe and out of sight there. After he swapped his swim trunks for khakis and a clean shirt, he slipped into his boat shoes and headed for the galley. Before he could make any decisions, he needed to know precisely what he'd found and who he was really dealing with. There had to be a name in that tablet or on those flash drives. There just had to be.

# Chapter Eighteen

Did anything ever, ever make Alex Stewart happy? At least momentarily pleasant? Guess not. But just once, couldn't he be pleased that the operation to USP, Lee, hadn't ended with innocent lives lost? How hard could it be to pull that bullshit stick out of his ass?

Persia rolled her right shoulder to force the cramp out of her neck. It had gotten tighter with every passing minute. What more did Alex want? Her blood on a rock? She and Zack had already surrendered their firearms to the local sheriff. They'd given statements that should've matched the Marshals' statements.

Yet there Alex stood alongside Zack, in a terse conference with Warden Everest over at the burned-out red sedan, while she cooled her heels inside the TEAM helicopter. Waiting for what she didn't know. Yet when Alex had told her to climb aboard, she'd obeyed. Whatever they were discussing, it had better be good, and it had better not be about her. Alex, Zack, and Everest had been squared-off for a good fifteen minutes now. From where she sat, it looked as if the guys were going after each other. Which totally fit Alex's MO, but Zack and the warden? Persia had no idea what sparked this testosterone-filled confrontation.

*Oh, you did not just glare at me! Did you? Damn you, Alex!*

"Well, bless my heart," Persia muttered, stabbing a middle finger salute over her right brow, sending him precisely what she thought of him. *The ass!*

Yes, it was a passive-aggressive response, but she doubted he'd catch it. Or understand it if he did. She sucked in a deep, cleansing breath before she lost what was left of her cool, calm, and obedient demeanor. The last thing she needed was to scramble out of this chopper and tell him what he could do with his uppity, do-as-you're-told, I'm-the-male-here attitude. Luckily, he and Zack had just turned from the warden. They were marching her way.

Persia swallowed her snark. Alex's scowl couldn't have been clearer, nor his steps any quicker. Rapping a curt index finger in the air, he signaled his pilot to get ready for takeoff, then climbed aboard with Zack at his heels. Both men belted into the jump seats behind the pilot and across from Persia before they donned their ear protection.

Pissed at being treated like a novice when she was anything but, Persia glared right back at Alex. Sliding a pair of silencer earbuds into her ear canals to protect her hearing, and to make sure she connected with the helo's dynamic communication system—and her boss!—she crossed her arms over her chest, prepared for whatever nasty thing came out of his mouth next. How did Kelsey stand living with him? Yet they were having a baby. Their second child! Ugh. The thought of them procreating...

Persia banished the visual of her boss under the covers with any woman on earth from her mind. She couldn't imagine him ever being that kind of sweet or romantic. Annoyed that she might've jumped ship too soon, that she would've been better off staying with either the Bureau or the Agency, her foot set to tapping. *Still waiting.*

At last, Alex looked up from whatever had captured his interest on his phone and spared her one of those guy chin stabs. "Marshal Goodwin says you saved his life, that you hit all your marks. Good work."

So not what she'd expected to hear. "Excuse me?"

"Yeah, but now, Warden Everest wants you on his payroll in a bad way," Zack growled, as his brows clashed like two streaks of dark lightning across his forehead. He crossed his arms over his chest in the classic sign of 'the-subject-is-closed.' But it wasn't. "Said he's prepared to offer you whatever it takes, that you deserve a hiring bonus. Says you're the best he's ever seen, that you shouldn't be working for a contractor. Dumbass is probably calling his senator right now to make it happen."

"How would Everest even know who shot who?" Persia asked, not sure she truly understood what was happening. "He wasn't there. He was hiding back in their van."

"No, but he and Goodwin are tight, and Goodwin contacted Everest as soon as you guys had everything under control," Alex said as he flicked the speck of mud that had dared tarnish the sleeve of his tailored suit jacket into outer space.

For a former Marine, this guy sure didn't look the part. His agents dressed business casual most days, but Alex was always dressed for success. Color-coordinated, today in a dark charcoal linen suit, crisp white shirt, blue tie with a perfect Windsor knot at his throat. Always clean-shaven, his dark hair was perfectly trimmed and his nails were clean. But he was built like a brick shithouse, square and angular with wide shoulders that made him look more like a day laborer in a fancy suit, instead of the savvy businessman Persia knew he was. Blue as icicles in the dead of an Arctic winter, his eyes could turn into glacier-sharp knives in a heartbeat.

Zack's palm came up into her face. "Nothing to worry about. Boss told Everest not only no, but hell no."

"Well, gee, thanks, *Boss*." Persia let her sarcasm stab straight to the heart of her problem. For added emphasis, and just because he'd made her mad, she gave Alex her classic eyebrow finger salute. "I get a job offer—me, just me—but you turn it down before I even hear about it? What the hell?"

Those ice-blue lasers ratcheted up to killer high-beams. "You want off The TEAM? Fine with me, just say the word."

"I didn't say that," she replied tartly. Man, he was always so abrasive. "But the decision wasn't yours to make, was it?" She leaned into the space between the seats, forcing the issue.

Alex tipped forward, more than meeting her halfway. "Anything that diminishes my TEAM *is* my call," he breathed, his tone chilled with a hint of spearmint she wished she hadn't noticed. On a good day, Alex was GQ material. But today? He was just another egotistical handler who thought he knew better than she did.

Persia cocked her head. "What am I? Your property? Nothing more than government issue? GI Jane?"

Darned if Zack didn't grin at her word choice. "To all us former Marines, hell yeah. You oughta know that by now, girlfriend. Us guys don't ever let a good thing slip away. Go on, Boss. Tell her the rest."

Persia felt like she was in a tennis match with Alex, only the ball was a grenade, and it was now in his court. Which would it be? An open stance forehand slam in her face or a killer lob that blew her out of her shoes? With Alex, probably a TKO, if he played tennis the same heavy-handed way he ran his TEAM.

"Hmmpf," he snorted. "Everest is an idiot. He offered you a fifty-K bonus, and he'll be calling you later today, because he sure as hell wouldn't accept my answer. But he can't top the benefits I offer or the raise I'm giving you."

Okay… That was new. "What raise?"

TEAM benefits were already unbelievably generous. Full coverage health plan. A life insurance policy to die for, no pun intended. Plus an employer-matched investment plan, on top of one heck of a lucrative retirement plan.

There went Zack's face again, cracking into another wide-open smile. "You're staying with us, Persia. No one takes better care of his agents than your boss."

*My boss, huh?* Again she asked, "What raise?"

Alex leaned back into his seat, closed his eyes, and replied, "The one I give every agent who measures up."

"Measures up to what?"

"My TEAM, my standards. You pass. Welcome aboard."

Persia hadn't seen the end of this tennis match coming so quickly. No killer lob. No hard-driven volley. Just a gentle drop shot with enough backspin that it whizzed over the net and landed like a feather in her court. She'd missed his intent, hadn't kept up with him at all. Damn. Alex was an excellent strategist.

"Well, err, okay," was all she could come up with. "Thanks."

Zack just kept grinning.

# Chapter Nineteen

Walker didn't share what he'd found with Brimley during lunch or dinner. Didn't see any reason to say anything. As far as Brimley knew, he was just some former SEAL out to see the world. No harm; no foul. It wasn't until the sun set into the west, and after Walker secured the yacht for the night, that he settled down in the master suite to investigate what he now knew was criminal activity.

From there, he could hear Brim's gruff voice as he talked with Rover in the room below. Walker locked himself in, then spread everything across the desk. At his left, he set the paper tablets and flash drives. The receipts went into a stack at his right. Most were fuel related, and all were date-stamped over the past year. Yet none were signed. The same last four digits of an x'd out credit card number were the only things they had in common.

Yet they told a story of every fuel stop it docked at along the Mexican Coast. And when. Several months ago, it had refueled outside San Diego, California, then again at Cabo San Lucas. Since then: Manzanillo, Acapulco, Salina Cruz, and—Monterrico, Guatemala. The same city where Quinn Dooley's mother and father-in-law lived. Where that simple family picnic on the beach had gone horribly wrong.

Hurriedly, Walker pulled up a map of Guatemala on the computer to check distance and location. *Holy shit.* Whoever had bought Goff's yacht had refueled within thirty miles of Renzo's beach hideaway. Had to be the son of a bitch running these sex-traffickers. The fat cat from Cuba, whom Walker was still convinced was an American, probably the same person who'd bought Goff's yacht after he'd died.

A dizzying wave of *déjà vu* slapped Walker upside his head. Stiffening his legs, he shoved back into the chair, the dominoes falling. Goff's yacht in Monterrico, Guatemala, where Emily's grandparents still lived. Goff's pricey house in Ocean Beach, CA. *Some guy* who lived in Cuba. *Some guy* who'd been delayed because of a business transaction gone wrong. Say… for instance… a desperate father who'd sent a trained SEAL with expert sniping skills, among others, into Guatemala to find his daughter...

*Plunk.* The last domino—what Walker's inner sniper had been trying to tell him for months—fell. Everything pointed to a dead man. Goff.

But those morgue shots... Could it be true?

*Yes.*

An uneasy chill shivered up Walker's spine, tap, tap, tapping at each vertebra with its long, twisted icicle finger. Not only *could* it be true. It *was* true. It had to be true. Goff had to have been behind all this human suffering before his death. So who was the son of a bitch running the show now? Whose credit card was that? Why Monterrico again? Was Renzo back in business? Lastly, who'd owned *Coronado's Sea Nymph* before Walker had turned her into *Persia Smiles*?

He lined up the black-and-white photos alongside their color versions. Both versions were of the same girls and women, but taken at different times. The B&Ws were grainy, as if shot from a distance. In them, the victims were still carefree, some taken with friends, some taken inside grocery stores or malls. The color versions were close-ups, after they'd been kidnapped. There was nothing carefree about frightened, crying females.

Walker flipped the spiral-bound tablet open to the first tabbed entry. Shit. Dates of surveillance and time of day each picture was taken. Location: schools. Location: homes. Location: girlfriends' or boyfriends' addresses. This pervert had known who each of these women and girls were, and where they lived, before he'd lured them away from their families.

The second tab revealed estimated delivery dates for each 'asset.' Names of buyers behind each 'order'. Details of precisely what they wanted, from age to hair color to nationality to status of virginity and...

*No!* Trembling with rage, Walker could barely go on. Yet he had to. He rolled his shoulder to keep his temper at bay. But the urge to avenge every last one of the hapless females in this disgusting inventory, burned hot and low in his gut. These women and girls were someone's children, sisters, mothers!

It took seconds to line up each matching set of photos with its originating order. Simple. Each order matched the three-digit tattoos on the poor women's and kids' feet. Whoever this bastard was, he was behind Emily's kidnapping. He was one of Renzo's bosses. What a deplorable supply chain these bastards had going.

In the end, it all came back to three-year-old Emily, and the one man Walker knew he could trust. Well, maybe two, counting Senator Sullivan. Make that four. Charlie Brown and Julio Juarez were honest brokers, too. But they were both

Sullivan's assets, and Walker couldn't ask more from Senator Sullivan. He'd already risked his career and reputation plenty.

Instead, Walker elected to contact the captain of the USS amphibious assault ship, the *Iwo Jima*. Wasp-class. Aircraft carrier. Currently on maneuvers off the coast of Brazil. Its CO Captain Quinn Dooley. It didn't take long to locate the secure chatroom Dooley had set up during Walker's previous foray into Guatemala. Thankfully, the site was operational. Dooley's last entry was still there.

Walker sent a quick: *I'm aboard Coronado's Sea Nymph.* Nothing too informative about that.

Instantly, Dooley came back with: *Wondered where she went.*

Ah, so he already knew the *Nymph* was no longer docked in San Diego. Good.

Walker replied: *She's been through the Canal. All the way to Cuba.*

*She stop in Guatemala?* came back quickly.

*You bet. Gotta love those beaches outside Monterrico!* Walker deliberately kept this communication obtuse. No sense showing his hand.

It took a few seconds before Dooley answered. During that time, Walker envisioned his friend suppressing the same mountain of rage that he had. Just the thought that Goff might've been behind Emily's kidnapping, that he'd sold a child as pure and sweet as that little girl to the highest bidder—

Dooley came back with two skull-and cross-bones emojis. Walker took that to mean he wanted Goff to die all over again. Walker got to the point. *Need a favor. Big time. Not sure you can assist with facial recognition, but I've got 21 females in the same sitch. Hope you might know a guy who can tell me who these ladies and girls are.*

*Send what you've got. I'll see what I can do.*

*Just want these gals home.*

*Understood.*

*And the bastards behind this POS enterprise in jail or dead.*

*What's going on? How did you come across this information? Where the hell are you, brother?*

Walker swallowed hard at that unexpected endearment. *Brother.* How he wished. His reply would've been spontaneous if Kenny had been doing the asking. No doubt at all. The question was one any concerned friend would ask. Yet Walker hesitated, his fingertips ready to send the answer that could betray him. He trusted Quinn, he truly did, but to send a reply that would out him—

*Never mind. I trust you, Walk. No worries. Send what you've got, but watch your six. As soon as I have something, I'll be in touch.*

*Will send everything I can in a couple minutes.*

*Copy that.*

Walker signed off, his fingers trembling, making it hard to type the right keys. It was a sorry day when he couldn't trust a Navy brother.

He hadn't yet powered up the flash drives. Didn't know if he had the stomach for it. What type of files could be so large they required that much storage? They had to wait until morning. Right now, he needed to send those photos to—

"Hey! You still awake?" Brim bellowed at Walker's door. "We got a helluva lot of flashing Christmas lights headed our way."

It took Walker mere seconds to secure the evidence back in the wallet, then run a quick program to erase the computer's hard drive. But the incriminating information inside the wallet could put him in prison, if those Christmas lights belonged to the local authorities. Which meant trouble.

Stuffing the wallet inside his shirt, he jerked the door open, the lockbox in his other hand.

Brim's face was red and sweaty. "Listen, young fella. I don't know what you pulled out of that contraption, but something tells me it's gonna cause us a heap of trouble. What's say we put it back where it was before these hotshots get here?"

Peering through the porthole, Walker took in the two rapidly advancing police cruisers. In a twist of sheer luck, the prow of the boat now pointed toward the quickly advancing boats. A demand bellowed over their loudspeaker, probably for them to desist and allow the authorities to come aboard.

"Good thinking," Walker said as he all but ran aft. Jumping down from the lounge area, he dropped to his knees on the swim deck and lifted the loose plank. Like before, the rusted nails screeched. But time was running out. Swiftly, Walker put the box back where it had been.

Brim caught his arm, as the plank settled back into place. In his hand: three weather-proof lag bolts and a flex-head ratchet. "Figured them nails need replacing," he muttered. "Why don't I head these jokers off at the pass, while you make things pretty back here?"

"Thanks, Brim. Whatever you do, don't resist. Let them come aboard. This is probably just a routine safety check. No worries, okay? We haven't done anything wrong." *At least you haven't. Me? I'm just wanted for murder.*

Brim replied, his lips pursed beneath that street-sweeper mustache. "Whatever you say, Cap'n, You're the skipper, I'm just your crew. Sure hope you know that."

Back on his knees, Walker didn't have time to reply. The request from the Azorean shore patrol's bullhorn wasn't friendly. They'd soon be all over this yacht. His fingers fumbled the bolts. *Hurry!*

# Chapter Twenty

"Boss wants you in his office yesterday," Beau muttered darkly from his TEAM agent desk in the work bay, not from the customer service desk where he'd been working alongside Ember.

"What's going on?" Persia asked. "Did Ember get tired of you or are you headed out on another operation?"

"Just moving out and making room for Mother. Guess she's finally coming back. Took her long enough."

Persia had to ask, "I'm sorry, who? Your mother?"

"No, Mo-ther," he enunciated clearly. Like that told Persia anything. "You know, Mother. Sasha Kennedy. The real genius techie behind this TEAM."

"I heard that," Ember called out from her usual location.

A wave of red crept up Beau's darkly tanned neck and spread over his cheeks, turning them candy-apple red. "Damn it, woman," he called out in her direction. "You know you're the best there is. Don't go making me have to choose between you and Mother." To Persia he muttered, "Because I've never even met the woman, but everyone here says she's a genius and—"

"I'm waiting," Ember taunted loudly. A lot of tapping was also coming from behind her customer service counter.

Persia smiled at the banter between this easily riled-up guy and the bombshell blonde he'd been working with since Persia's first day on the job.

"Damn it. You!" he bellowed over his desk. "You're better than Mother any day of the week! Is that what you want to hear? I'm in love with you! Just you!"

"Easy, Beau. You do know you're professing love to my wife, right?" Rory Dennison, Ember's hubby, chimed in. His desk was to the immediate left of Beau's.

"Yeah, big guy," Zack teased from the cubicle behind Beau's. "You don't want to make Rory mad. Last guy who did that is still looking for his teeth."

"And his left eye." Izza couldn't resist adding from the other side of Ember's counter.

"Excuse me?" That question came from Doc Fitz who was now standing at the open elevator door. "You're in love with who, sweetheart?"

Beau's bushy brows slammed over his equally dark eyes, turning them black. The veins in his neck bulged, as did the single vein that ran across his forehead when he was about to lose his temper. Which he did regularly. It didn't take much to push this guy's buttons, and apparently, everyone in the office knew it. Even his wife.

He exploded to his feet. "Shit! I don't even know Mother, damn it! I've never met her. She was gone for months before I ever…" His gaze landed on McKenna's pretty face.

As usual, she smiled in that I-could-just-eat-you-alive way she had.

Ember giggled.

Rory grunted like a pig.

Zack just stood there. Crossed both arms over his chest, and grinned. Why hadn't he made senior agent yet? He had all the makings of a great leader, yet there he sat in the work bay with the junior agents, as if he were their equal instead of, well, Alex's.

Persia's gaze strayed back to Doc Fitz, still standing at the now closed elevator and watching her out-of-control husband. There was a perfect example of opposites attracting. Persia had never seen McKenna upset or her feelings hurt. But Beau? He could flip a switch from smiling to nasty at the drop of a hat.

As if to prove the point, he sucked in a breath and growled, "Why'd you have to hear that, huh? What do you want?"

"You," McKenna replied evenly, her hand outstretched and her fingers fluttering for him to hurry and join her. "I need a ride into the District, remember? I have an early meeting with FBI Special Agent Duff on the forensic evidence we're working. But if you're too busy—"

Beau all but jumped over his desk to get to her side. "No! 'Course I remember. Let's go."

The moment he was at her side, he gave her a quick peck on her cheek and the starch went out of his shoulders.

"Excuse me?" Ember had come around her counter by then, both hands on her hips. "Where do you think you're going, Junior Agent?"

The dreaded junior agent ploy. Ember could be such a brat. The one and only eclectic dresser in an office of casual black, today she'd shown up in what looked like a Catholic school girl's uniform. Complete with a short-sleeved white blouse with Peter Pan collar, pearl buttons that complemented her full bustline, a short, red and black pleated plaid skirt, and, of all things, saddle shoes with bright-yellow, rolled ankle socks.

"You're going to walk out on me? Just like that?"

Persia wasn't sure who Ember was taunting, Beau or her husband. Rory hadn't taken his eyes off his wife, and the glitter in his dark eyes spelled L. U. S. T. in bright flashing neon blue.

McKenna had already called the elevator.

"I, ah—well, err, yeah." Beau looked so damned confused, as if he really had to choose between Ember and McKenna. One look down at his wife, and he turned that frown into a grin aimed straight at Ember. "You don't need me. You're the best, remember? I'm outta here." Then to McKenna, he declared, "Let's go, babe."

And off he went with his wife tucked under his arm. The elevator doors had no more than closed when everyone burst out laughing.

"You guys are so mean to him," Persia exclaimed. "What'd he ever do to you?"

"Aw, it's good for him," Rory replied, his gaze still on his sassy wife. "Trust me, this is nothing. When he first showed up, Beau was a pain in everyone's ass, but now—"

"We're pains in his," Izza said saucily from Ember's side.

"Oh, look." Ember pointed at the elevator.

Persia looked, but didn't see anything. Until Zack shook his head, still grinning like a Cheshire Cat, and muttered, "Those two."

Then she looked harder. Oh. The elevator had gone up, not down. To the vault? Not to underground parking? But why…? Never mind. Stupid question.

Persia grinned then, too. But what would it be like to look at a man like McKenna had looked at Beau? To love a man so much that your countenance shone with devotion?

"Coltrane! My office! Now!"

"Yes, sir!" she bellowed back at Alex. Then winced so hard her teeth hurt. Damn it. She'd done it again. "I mean…" Oh, hell, who cared what she meant? She was in trouble now. Again. Whatever!

Out of breath, and with everyone in the office most likely laughing at how Alex pushed *her* buttons, Persia hustled into his office and closed the door. There was no need for everyone else to hear what he said next.

"You growled?" she asked, then slammed her big mouth shut. *Did I really just say that? I am so dead.*

"Sit," he ordered, stabbing his chin at the chair beside his desk. Not the one in front of it, which always made her feel inferior for some reason she didn't want to explore or understand. She wasn't intimidated by this guy. Much. Until she called him sir… That was a hard habit to break.

"I've got a job for you," he muttered, shuffling over the few papers on his immaculate desk.

Wow. Papers on this obsessive-compulsive guy's desk. That was odd all by itself.

Persia ran her palms over her thighs to calm her nerves. She'd dressed for spring weather this morning. Light gray linen pencil-skirt with a pink, cotton, short-sleeved blouse, white pearls at her throat, and low pink heels, to avoid more back pain than she already had. Namely, Alex.

"Are you familiar with The Hague Invasion Act?" he asked, still not meeting her eyes.

"Yessss," she hissed, inadvertently drawing out that reply instead of compounding her error by calling him sir.

"Tell me what you know."

She swallowed to compose herself, licked her dry lips, then replied evenly. "The Hague Invasion Act is also known as the Service-Members' Protection Act, and was signed into law in 2002, by then President George W. Bush. The law authorizes the United States to use military force to free any of our citizens or service members from foreign incarceration or hanging by the International Criminal Court, the ICC, in The Hague, Netherlands, for alleged war crimes."

She took a deep breath and continued. "While its main intent is to protect our military members from indiscriminate trials and persecution, it can and will end all military assistance to any allies who refuse to agree not to extradite American citizens to The Hague. In effect, it ensures our troops are guaranteed immunity from prosecution for alleged war crimes. This law also prohibits the ICC officials from conducting investigations on American soil. For your information, the ICC was established by the Rome Statute treaty in 1998, which gave that court authority to try any individual in the world who had been accused of genocide, war crimes, crimes of aggression, crimes against humanity, or basically any crime that had no statute of limitation. Currently, I believe there are one hundred thirty-eight signatories to the treaty. Anything else?"

"One hundred thirty-nine," he muttered, still shuffling through those few papers.

She rolled her eyes at the insignificant mistake he'd insisted on pointing out.

"And it allows our military to contract for that protection when necessary."

Which meant she was going to the Netherlands. "If I may ask, Alex…" She refused to call him Boss. "What are you looking for?"

Another growl. "My contact. Damned thing popped out when I blinked. How the hell am I supposed to find it when I can't see it?"

Jumping to her feet, Persia scanned his tidy desk and easily located the missing lens. "I didn't know you wore contacts," she said, pointing her index finger to the tiny rounded, blue disk that, fortunately, wasn't near any of those papers, but perched on the framed portrait of his family. Right below Kelsey's smiling face. Wasn't that a peculiar coincidence?

"Infection," he grumbled, opening his pencil drawer and pulling out a small tube of contact cleaner. Or something. It must double as cleaner and moisturizer, she thought, as quickly as he spritzed a few drops of liquid between his index finger and thumb, then tilted back, blinked at the ceiling, and placed that puppy right back on his left eyeball. "Lexie came home with pink eye and I caught it."

Ewww. Persia couldn't watch the harsh way he handled that puffy red eyeball. Ouch. Her eyes hurt in sympathy. She could never wear contacts. Couldn't stand to touch her eyeballs like that. Just no.

"Who has the ICC incarcerated this time, and what's he or she accused of?"

Several ICC member countries had recently targeted US troops in Afghanistan, by name, claiming they'd committed genocide, when they'd bombed certain terrorist cells. Which was just plain hogwash, as her father would say. American troops were only in the Islamic Republic of Afghanistan at that current president's request. He'd wanted assistance routing the latest swarm of infidels invading his country. The USA had complied. He'd asked for help, and that was what he'd received. If he'd wanted to play politics, he'd chosen poorly. Because the current United States president stood by his military. Every single time.

End of story, as far as Persia was concerned.

"Former SEAL, Lieutenant Walker Judge," Alex answered, still blinking, but still keeping on. "Just got word today that he's in the ICC's detention unit. What do you know about him?"

A tiny voice whispered in a darkest corner of Persia's mind. *Walker Judge... Hmmm.*

"Not much, other than what I've seen on the news, only you can't trust anything coming from our media these days, so I'm still not sure what I know. A former Navy SEAL, Judge was tried and convicted a year ago, I believe. I was in South America at that time, so I'm not up to speed on all the details surrounding his crime or his trial. If I remember right, there was questionable doubt as to the validity of the prosecution's evidence." She wanted to ask. 'Right?' but didn't dare.

Alex simply nodded.

Persia searched her mind for what else she knew on the subject, but honestly, that didn't amount to much. "The buzz over at The Agency focused on the man Judge was accused of murdering, USN Commander Wallace Goff. Another agent in my office, a former SEAL, worked under Goff's command." *Man, who had that special agent been? Think, Persia. Think!* "His name will come to me later, and I'll let you know who it was when it does. Anyway, I recall him saying Wallace Goff was a flaming jackass. He blamed Goff for his SEAL team's increased attrition rate. He hated Goff's guts, and said he was known for getting good men killed while he got his face in the Military Times."

"Goff also wore a Trident."

Okaaaaay, so he'd survived Hell Week and he was a SEAL, that was good to know. Big deal. How did that fit into this discussion about Walker? "Are you saying that Judge murdered his CO because of Goff's leadership style?" Commanders had been fragged for less.

Instead of answering, Alex said, "Goff never saw battle. Not once."

Persia cocked her head, trying to understand where he was going with this train of thought. But really, a SEAL who'd never seen battle? Not just any SEAL, but a commanding officer? How did that work? Was it even possible to achieve that high rank without filling the *'armed conflict'* square during his pre-CO career?

Better question, what leadership style could any CO have had if he'd never fought alongside his men? But again, Persia opted for silence instead of opening her mouth and proving how little she knew about military mindsets. She was, after all, one of the few civilians working for Alex. Doc Fitz didn't count because she ran the onsite TEAM clinic. Didn't need to be former military for that. And Beckam's wife, Camilla, was currently on extended family leave. No one was sure if she'd ever come back after the birth of their first child, so Persia didn't include her, either.

Alex ran a careful fingertip under his sore, puffy eye. "Goff was a typical officer. Educated. Book smart. Overpaid and over-appreciated. Sponsored and groomed and some Admiral's pretty boy. Yet untried where it counted. Inexperienced when it mattered. The man didn't have a clue what it meant to stand and fight. To lose the man fighting beside you. To bleed or cry or curse or die. Always a REMF. Never a warrior."

Alex had just made Persia's problem with him crystal clear. It wasn't that he disliked her or was dissatisfied with her job performance. He just didn't respect officers. The way he'd said REMF, proved it. REMF stood for Rear Echelon Motherf-er, a crude term for guys who'd stayed in the rear, as opposed to those who'd fought on front lines. In some cases, it also stood for coward, yellow-belly, and chicken-shit, especially among the men who'd done all the bleeding and dying. 'Sir-ing' had Alex put him in the same category as the officers he despised. There had to be a story behind his strong emotional response, but Persia had no intention of asking about it today.

"What are you telling me, *Boss*?" Okay, he'd earned that one.

"I want you in The Hague, at the ICC, before sunset tomorrow. Bring Judge home. No one is to know. If you run into reporters, shoot the sons of bitches."

She nearly laughed out loud. "Yeah, I don't think that's legal. How do you want me to travel, and who am I traveling with?" Zack would be nice. Or Beau. He needed a good stiff mission after playing computer geek, didn't he?

"Might not be legal, but The Hague Invasion Act allows you to use any means necessary to free our SEAL. You're on an express flight from Reagan National into JFK at 1500 hours today. There you'll connect with a flight into Amsterdam.

Grab a train from there to The Hague. That gives you five hours to get ready. Pack light. Izza Maher's going with you. I briefed her earlier. She knows what else you'll need, and who you'll talk to once you arrive. Whatever happens, do not take no for an answer and don't come back without Judge."

Persia nodded, just once to acknowledge her implied 'yes, sir!' Finally. A real mission. But first… "I'm sure you've already vetted this through President—"

No one but the President dealt with ICC matters concerning US service members. Before she went anywhere, Persia needed official permission, preferably date-stamped and signed in crisp, blue ink with President Adams' *John Hancock* on it.

Alex snapped his fingers. "Adams is very much involved. I asked. He approved us bringing Judge home. Check with Ember on your way out. She'll have the file on Judge and all the paperwork you'll need. Anything else?"

"No, Boss," Persia easily replied as she lifted to her feet. Addressing him was going to be easier now that she knew what made him tick.

"Be safe," he ordered, as if she had to be reminded.

"Always. See you the day after tomorrow." Or sooner, she thought, as she shut his door behind her. Escorting an alleged war criminal back to the States was an easy job. This wouldn't take long.

# Chapter Twenty-One

Walker stared at the bright orange, too small, and flimsy as hell tennis shoes on his feet. No socks. Just cheap footwear with no support. No cushion. Hopefully, they hadn't been used before. Or if they had, at least they'd been washed, sanitized, maybe disinfected. But he doubted it.

They did match his jumpsuit nicely, though. Nearly matched the color of his swollen left eye, too. Only it was more black, blue, and yellow than orange. Although the broken blood vessels in the sclera did lend a definite crazy red-eyed, Frankenstein-ish vibe. As did the neat row of butterfly bandages taped over that same tender eyeball. Trick or treat, anyone?

He didn't remember who'd doctored him or which dumbass had thrown the first punch back on *Persia Smiles*. But there'd be hell to pay when he caught up with the jerk. At the moment, Walker didn't know where Brimley was, if he was okay, injured, or dead. He didn't know anything about Rover. Hadn't yet been able to get a straight answer out of the burly guard with the assault rifle standing outside his cell.

At this point, he figured some know-it-all must've recognized him on the dock in São Miguel the day he'd run into Brimley. Of all the stupid luck. No doubt, the jerk had followed Walker back to the yacht, then tattled to the local authorities to *'hurry, come nab the dangerous American killer.'* He'd thought his beard, ballcap, and dark glasses would've kept him safe. They'd worked before. Not like he'd ever see that ballcap or those Ray-Bans again. Worse, the local chief of police had made him shave. What a mess.

What Walker hoped would've been a simple, routine visit by the authorities on the high seas, had turned into a brouhaha that hadn't needed to end as brutally as it had. But when one of those loud-mouthed Azorean police officers kicked Rover, well, Brimley had taken offense. As he should have. One thing had led to another. Someone threw a punch. Brimley went flying over the railing. The next thing Walker knew, it was lights out, and he was picking himself up from a concrete floor in a cell in Somewhere-Other-Than-America.

It'd been a long time since he'd been ambushed. But while he'd knocked two of those bully cops on their asses and sent one flying overboard, another had come up behind him and clubbed him. He remembered the sound of his skull cracking, but after that—nothing. Until he'd come to behind bars. By then someone had treated the raw cut on his forehead, but the knot on the back of his head was still touchy as hell, and he'd learned quickly not to make any fast moves. Dizziness had become a constant, annoying companion.

After an intense grilling session under bright, hot lights, during which Walker quickly admitted that, yes, he was the Navy SEAL who'd escaped USA custody, the Azorean officials had quickly washed their hands of him. Within twenty-four hours, they'd transferred custody to a five-man squad of armed, stone-faced guys, each the height, width, and breadth of Goliath. Made him feel like David when he'd stepped out of his cell and had to look up at them. What he would have given for a slingshot. A few smooth stones would've been nice, too.

They'd never cracked so much as a lip twitch. It was actually funny, the way they'd treated him as if he were lethally dangerous. Which he was—when he wasn't hampered by a screaming migraine, metal cuffs, and weighted shackles. Nice touch, them. Weighted restraints made his feet and legs feel heavier than they were. Or maybe they weren't weighted at all, and his feet really were that heavy. Because his head certainly felt like it was somewhere up in the clouds. Man, a handful of Motrin would sure come in handy.

The speed with which they'd moved him out of that cozy island jail had concerned Walker at first. He'd thought he was on his way to a firing squad, or worse, given to ISIL. Instead, they'd marched him to a long black limo parked at the curb, which took him to the local airport. Only when he'd seen the bright blue KLM logo on the bird's tail he was being steered toward, did he realize how bad things were. He was being shipped off to the Netherlands, home of the infamous International Criminal Court in The Hague. The intergovernmental organization that had, over and over again, attempted to apprehend, jail, and prosecute US military members, citing alleged war crimes allegedly committed in Afghanistan.

Which, in some cases, may have been accurate. Men cracked in battle, and untreated PTSD was a raging nightmare during any firefight. Not that those reasons absolved anyone, but they did provide understanding. And then, there were also those guys who'd enlisted just because they enjoyed the killing. Walker had always been on the lookout for those types. He didn't need psychopaths on his team, and he'd refused to work with the only one he'd ever come across.

At its core, the ICC was biased against Americans. In the few cases they'd apprehended US soldiers, those innocent men's names, faces, and alleged crimes had been splashed across European media outlets, and the suspects were considered guilty before their cases were even heard. Which, now that Walker thought about it, wasn't much different than what the US Navy had done to him. *Feed the media frenzy first; then conduct a rigged trial. Way to go, Navy.*

So here he was, behind bars again, this time in the bowels of a hostile foreign detention unit, where anything could happen. He would soon be facing the same court that had indicted the likes of Libyan President Muammar Gaddafi and Sudanese President Omar al-Bashir. Not like either of those 'gentlemen' had accepted the ICC's judgments or arrest warrants. But still.

Being lumped in with the likes of the ruthless dictator who'd sheltered those responsible for bombing Pan-Am flight 103 over Lockerbie, Scotland, in 1988, and killing two hundred seventy innocent passengers, was disconcerting. Especially since Walker hadn't yet been read his rights and didn't know precisely what charges he faced. Didn't know if the ICC provided public defenders, either, not like some weak-kneed lawyer in a three-piece suit would care about an American warrior. Most American's didn't. Why should the rest of the world?

But it'd be good to know if he were being charged for war crimes. Most SEALs were. Or if the ICC was simply detaining him, pending his extradition back to the States. That was the scenario Walker hoped for, though he wasn't sure why.

Leavenworth was no picnic. It'd be a hard sentence to serve, but at least he'd be in America. The land that he loved.

Because Walker did love the country he'd bled for—the land of the free. He still upheld the concept behind that often misused *'We the People...'* closer to his heart than did most Americans. Because he *had* killed for his country, and in the process, he could've died, too.

Everything he'd done came back to the decision he'd made the day he'd enlisted, when he'd promised: *I, Walker Judge, do solemnly swear I will support and defend the Constitution of the United States against all enemies, foreign and domestic; that I will bear true faith and allegiance to the same; and that I will obey the orders of the President of the United States and the orders of the officers appointed over me, according to regulations and the Uniform Code of Military Justice. So help me, God.*

The crisp slap of dress shoes on concrete interrupted the trip back in time. Interestingly, the cells across from him were both empty, and he couldn't tell if the cell next to his was occupied. Concrete walls made good neighbors. When those footsteps ended at his cell, he looked into the face of a tired-looking middle-aged man who might be his lawyer. The guy said something to the guard, who nodded, then unlocked the cell door. Walker stayed put, his cuffed hands between his knees and his shackled feet in those ridiculous clown shoes.

"Sir," the man said from the doorway. The round spectacles perched at the end of his nose needed a good cleaning, and he kept flicking his tongue over his lips like a nervous, pale, gray-haired frog.

"Yes?" Walker replied, keeping his voice steady, so he didn't scare the guy more than he obviously was.

"I am Hans Koning. I am what you Americans call a public defender. I will represent you at your trial."

"I'd say it's nice to meet you, but we both know that's not true." Regardless, Walker extended his arms, intending to shake hands. Real men didn't kick against the pricks. If Hans was his lawyer, he meant to be as compliant, forthright, and helpful as possible. Going caveman on pencil pushers never solved anything. Certainly hadn't worked on Lieutenant Cameron Kroft, Walker's JAG appointed attorney.

The man's heels clicked together as he bowed, then straightened, instead of accepting Walker's offer of civility. Okay then. He dropped both hands back to his knees.

"We have just received word from your government," Hans said in perfect, quiet English. Flick, flick went his tongue.

"Finally," Walker breathed. They might not like him, but someone from the States was coming for him. Small consolation, but he was relieved nonetheless. The Navy had no doubt sent a couple Masters-at-arms to escort him home, where they'd march his ass to Leavenworth. It wasn't the best scenario given the evidence he'd found on the yacht, but he had contacts in the States. One of his guys would eventually find where the Azoreans had docked *Persia Smiles*. Maybe they could also locate the evidence and the bastards behind those kidnapped women and girls. "When will they be here?"

"Who?" Hans cocked his head, the light from the florescent tube overhead reflecting off his glasses, giving him a deer in the headlights look. "Excuse me? No. You misunderstand. Yes, we have received word from the United States, but no one is coming for you." He pulled a piece of paper from an inside suit pocket and held it for Walker.

Still seated, he stretched forward and took the single sheet, then quickly read the Navy's response. DISAVOWED had been stamped across the paper in deep, dark, blood-red stencil font. Like an insult. He should've known. The USN had betrayed him yet again. They meant him to rot in this foreign jail, face a firing squad, or hanging. It all depended on what crime he was charged with.

Without letting his disappointment show, Walker handed the paper back. "Thank you, sir. I appreciate you taking the time to meet with me. Can you tell me why I'm being held? On what charges?"

"Yes, oh, yes. You are charged with the murders you committed in Jordan. War crimes, sir. Surely you did not think you could get away with that?"

Jordan? That was new. "Who exactly did I murder?"

Hans blinked as if he couldn't believe Walker was that stupid. "Why Prince Jamalud Khalid and his entire family. Do not act as if you do not know. I have seen the proof. There are many pictures of you walking into the wedding tent with the bomb that day. I have watched as you set it on the wedding table. The prosecutor has a very solid case. He has witnesses. Lying will only create more trouble for you."

"I killed a family in Jordan?" Interesting. Walker had never set foot in that country. Had always wanted to, but Jordan hadn't been part of his orders. "May I at least see the photos and proof? You do have evidence, don't you?"

Hans' head bobbed. By now, he was wringing his hands, twisting the gold band on his ring finger around and around. "Yes, you may see it. All of it. Tomorrow morning. But I must ask you, sir. I must know in order to prepare a proper defense. Why did you do such a heinous thing? You bombed a simple family wedding. You killed over a hundred people. There were children there. Babies. Grandfathers and grandmothers. How did their deaths serve your needs?"

Wow. Over a hundred innocent people. If this were an actual event, it must've happened while he'd been on an operation. Walker had honestly never heard about it. "When did this supposedly happen?"

"Last year. January."

That explained it. The same month Walker had been on those three weeks' leave to Guatemala. "The exact date?"

"January 30th."

The day before he'd come home from Guatemala. He'd spent that first night in America with Quinn Dooley and his grateful family in Norfolk, Virginia, then flown to San Diego the next day. Only to be arrested and incarcerated in the Navy brig in Miramar, San Diego, before the sun came up. Had the official record of that confinement been expunged like his Navcompt 3065 request for leave had? "Sounds like you're already convinced I'm guilty. Are you?"

The man ran a nervous hand over his thinning hair. "No, b-b-but…" Hans should never play poker. His expressions were dead giveaways. The current one clearly said, *'You're a liar and not worth my time.'*

Walker went for slow and easy. "But what, Hans? You want me to talk to you, well, I need you to talk with me, too. If we're going to work together, we need to be honest with each other."

Hans looked like he needed to sit down before he fell down. "B-b-but…"

Walker cocked his head, trying to get a read on this guy. Hans was too edgy. Something was off. That prickly sensation of being watched tickled the short hairs on the nape of his neck, until they'd turned into tiny, hyper-active radar dishes. Of course he was being watched. He was in prison. Yet this feeling was more like a premonition. A sniper's internal sense of something coming for him. But how could things get any worse?

At last, Hans looked Walker dead in the eye. "Because it is your Admiral Pickering who provided the video evidence. He is a very powerful man in your government, yes?"

Walker never flinched. Didn't bat an eye. But his instincts snapped to attention at the revelation. *Pickering, huh?* So that was how far up the chain this betrayal went, all the way to a four-star commissioned naval flag officer. Shit, an O-10, the highest appointment a man could reach in the US Navy, for Christ's sake.

At last, Poseidon's stars were beginning to line up in Walker's black-as-ink sky. Wanna bet Admiral Edgar Pickering was also the bastard behind Goff's white-gloved rise to power?

"Are… are you okay, Lieutenant Judge?" Hans asked, fidgeting with his glasses. But the eyes behind those smudged lenses were bright with concern for a change. Almost interested.

"Actually, I am," Walker replied evenly, intent more than ever on proving to his lawyer that whatever so-called evidence Pickering had provided was fake, photoshopped, or straight-up CGI. If Walker believed in anything, it was that truth always prevailed. Eventually.

Admiral Pickering might've thought he'd covered all his bases, but he hadn't met Navy SEAL LT Walker Judge yet. But he would.

He sure as hell would.

# Chapter Twenty-Two

After she boarded KLM's Airbus bound for the Netherlands, Persia planned to spend the seven-hour flight between JFK International and Schiphol Airport, Amsterdam, researching the escaped convict, former USN SEAL Lieutenant Walker Judge. She hadn't yet perused the intel Ember had provided, not with the tight schedule she and Izza had been on. Between their quick hop from Reagan National to JFK, then the agonizingly long line through security, followed by a breathless sprint across the terminal to catch their flight, she'd barely had time to grab the bottled water she'd tucked into her bag.

Sinking into her seat, she took a deep, cleansing breath, thrilled that Ember had secured first-class tickets for this seven-hour flight. *What a day.*

"Man, I hate fast turn arounds," Izza muttered, "especially when Connor's out of the country."

"You've got a good babysitter, don't you?" Persia asked as she eased her bag under the seat ahead of her. She'd changed into TEAM casual, and now looked very much like Izza's twin sister. Same black polo with the gold TEAM logo high on her left chest, same long, dark hair pulled back in a ponytail. They even had nearly the same dark brown eyes and olive skin tone.

Yet they were nothing alike. Izza had motherhood stamped all over her. Everything she said revolved around something her husband Connor, or her kids, Jamie and Jax were doing.

"Sure. They're staying with Zack and his girls until I get back. His wife Mei is always good to take any TEAM kids when quick trips come up. Just… You know… I don't get to hear what happened at school today, and Jamie wanted to get a haircut, and Jax gets blue whenever his daddy's not home to read him a story before bed, and…" Izza stretched and yawned. "I hate it when Connor's overseas. It's not like I can't handle things by myself, because I'm no wuss, but…" Her shoulders scrunched. "Guess I just miss him."

Izza was so much in love with the man she'd married. Automatically, Persia's mind went to Hotrod. Despite the fact that he was a jerk from the ground up, he would've been damned nice to wake up to in the morning. He'd been so tired that night, and she *had* loved rubbing Aloe Vera gel all over his body. Heck, she'd loved every second, every rub, and every purr spent on him. All over him. The prickle of his recently shaved neck under her palm. The sensual glide of her hands over all those muscles and ridges, dips and bulges. His chest. Man, he had a gorgeous set of well-defined pecs. And that seductive trail down his belly. The man was made of steel in all the best places.

"What on earth are you thinking, girlfriend?" Izza asked. "You didn't hear a word I said, did you?"

Persia blinked like an idiot caught daydreaming. "Yes, err, what?"

"I asked if there's someone in particular that you miss? My hell, you're blushing! Come on, spill. Who is he? What's his name, and why haven't you told me about him before?"

Persia shook Izza's astute deduction off, not confessing to anything or anyone. "Who, me? Ha! I wish." Wished for someone like Hotrod, but not Hotrod. Someone better. Kinder. Someone who would stay... "Trust me, Iz, you'll be the first to know if that day ever comes." *Which it won't, because who the hell knows where Hotrod is now? Not me. And who cares? Also not me.*

"Aw, it'll happen. It's just not your time yet. But you'll know when it does."

"I will, huh? How did you know Connor was the one for you?" Persia blinked her lashes and widened her eyes like an owl's, teasing her friend to spill her own secrets.

Now it was Izza's turn to blush.

By then the aircraft was in the air, and it was *'Amsterdam, here we come!'* The flight attendant stopped by and asked if they wanted drinks before dinner. Persia asked for champagne with the promise she'd keep them coming. Izza ordered a hot fudge sundae. *Extra fudge. Hold the nuts. Two cherries, please.* They settled back for girl talk then.

Persia slid into her talk-show-host persona. "Don't hold back, Agent Maher. Please. Tell your viewing audience all the juicy details. How'd you snag a hunk like Connor? Was it love at first sight? A blind date? And who set you up? But most of all, precisely when did you know he was the one for you?" Because Persia had the sneaky suspicion she'd already met her once in a lifetime. And the jerk had left her behind like a discarded banana peel.

Again with the coy lift of a shoulder and that bright, sassy smile. "It just happened," Izza murmured, "one day when we were out on patrol together."

"And where was that?" Persia snapped her fingers under Izza's nose. "Details, Izza. We want the deets. Your adoring fans have a right to know." It felt so much better badgering Izza about her love life than dodging questions.

"Will you stop?" Izza giggled. "And keep your voice down. People are watching."

"Of course they are," Persia stage-whispered. "You and Connor are better than Brad and Jennifer ever were. You stayed together."

"Okay, okay, but hush. If you must know, it happened while we were deployed to Camp Baharia, Iraq. We were both USMC sergeants, only he was short, nearly ready to go home. I had a couple more months left in-country."

"Whoa, Baharia? Really? Was he part of the USMC plus-up in Fallujah after those American contractors were killed?"

Izza nodded. "Yup. Him and my brother, Jamie."

"And...?"

And Izza's cheeks ballooned as she expelled a big breath. "We got a tip where several IEDs were placed, so we were part of an eight-man patrol. But the tip was a lie, and we were ambushed. Everyone else got away, but Connor and I got separated. Had to hunker down in a bombed-out, POS barn. Things just kind of happened after that. One minute bullets were flying, and I was so scared I was afraid I'd wet my pants. But I didn't, you know. And I didn't scream, either. I'm tougher than most grunts, but the next thing I knew, Connor had his arms around me, and I was... and he was..."

"He kissed you," Persia hissed. "Didn't he? Connor kissed you in the middle of a firefight, and that's when you knew!" How incredibly romantic was that?

Again, the loveliest blush climbed up Izza's neck. She made a funny face, stuck her fingers under her shirt collar and scratched her collarbone. "Actually…"

Persia couldn't help it. She nudged her shoulder confidentially into Izza. "You didn't... You did! You kids made love in a bombed-out building? While you were being shot at?" This story was so much better than any Harlequin romance on the market.

Izza nodded, the cutest smile tweaking her lips. "Yeah. We did. Right there in the hay, while those assholes were lobbing mortars at us and screaming bullshit about American infidels and fatwas and crap like that."

How romantic! Scary, but still… so, so romantic.

"Yeah," Izza whispered. "I knew it then. I was going to marry Connor if it was the last thing I did, only…" The smile dropped off her face. "Things got kind of complicated after that. My brother Jamie, uh, was killed the next day in a different firefight, and Connor was there and—"

Persia let her hand fall over Izza's on the armrest between them. "I'm so sorry, honey."

She shrugged. "Thanks, but I…" Both shoulders lifted into a resigned shrug. "It took me a long time to forgive him for not saving my baby brother." Izza swallowed hard. "I was so mad that he chose to save some strange Iraqi woman and her kid instead, that I quit the Corps. Actually, I was kind of forced out, because of my, umm, unresolved PTSD. But then we ended up working together for Alex, and Connor found out I was pregnant, and—"

"You were what?" Persia about dropped her teeth.

"Yup. I was prego." Izza nodded as if she needed to confirm her story. "That didn't help. By the time I told Connor, I looked like I was hiding half a watermelon under my shirt. And I was bitchier than hell because, well, because he'd lived, and Jamie didn't, and I was still so mad and so, so hurt."

Persia hated to ask. "Umm, so… who's the baby's fa—"

"Oh, she's Connor's all right. That's why we named our little girl Jamie, after Connor's best friend, my brother. Only Connor didn't know I was pregnant when he first saw me afterwards. We didn't get to say goodbye in Iraq and…" She rolled her eyes. Izza had the brightest, sparkly eyes. "Men are soooooo dense! I swear. I was as big as a blimp, but he never suspected. And I was damned if I was going to tell him, because then he'd feel responsible and think he had to do right by me and marry me, and, shit. I didn't want to be any guy's obligation. I'd never planned to fall in love or have kids, it just happened. But then I hated him, and, you know... Somehow things worked out."

Persia's brows lifted as she squeezed Izza's hand. "No, I don't know that. I'm twenty-nine, and sure, I've kissed a few guys, but there's only been one man I thought cared for me as much as I cared for him. But he was just another ass who walked out on me. So, no. I'm not looking for love or romance. It's not worth the pain or trouble. Life sucks, and then you die, that's my motto. But good for you. You've got Connor, and it's so obvious he adores you."

Izza flipped her hand over and interlocked her fingers with Persia's. "Life does not suck, girlfriend. It's damned hard sometimes, yes, but it's also damned great most of the rest of the time. I know that, and so do you. Don't lie. I saw the way your eyes sparkled before. You were thinking of that man you cared about, weren't you? Confess."

*Yes!* "Nope. Nada. Not me. I'm done with the dating game," Persia insisted, shaking her head vigorously to emphasize to Izza, and maybe to herself—and Hotrod, the ass!—that she meant what she said. "You've mistaken me for Ember or Kelsey or Mei Lennox, or heck. Even little Lexie. She has such a crush on her father."

"Alex does have that effect on women." Izza sighed. "You should see him in a tux. Oh, mama, do females heads turn when he walks by. Mmm. Mmm. Did you know he gave me away at my wedding?"

"Really? Alex? He did that for you?" How sweet. Which was not how Persia would've ever described her cantankerous boss, even on a good day. Abrupt, maybe. Driven, absolutely.

"He lost his first wife and daughter to a car crash years ago," Izza said quietly. "I didn't know him then, but I know Kelsey's the reason he's the man he is today. And now they're having another baby. That was the best news I've heard in a long time. Hope it's a boy."

"I didn't know that," Persia murmured. "He was married before? He had another family? Wow. No wonder he looks at his wife and little girl like he does. They're his second chance."

"Then I'll bet you didn't know Kelsey had two little boys before she met Alex, but her ex murdered them,"

"Oh, my, no!" Persia couldn't imagine. "How can they stand to be around each other? Isn't that too much personal tragedy for one couple to overcome?"

Izza shook her head. "Not when you love each other. I think they might even love each other more because of what they've survived. No one understands another person better than someone who's walked through the same kind of fire."

Persia had no words. Alex a grieving widower? Kelsey a mother of murdered sons? Yet they seemed so upbeat and happy when they were together. And Alex almost acted nice—then.

Izza patted Persia's hand. "The point is, we only see the tip of the iceberg, not what's going on beneath the surface. Alex is a really good guy. He's just been through a lot of shit like the rest of us. Give him time. He'll grow on you. I promise."

"Okay, sure," was the best Persia could offer on that subject.

Despite this enlightening conversation, Alex was not the problem her brain was currently stuck on. It was that other badassed guy with blue, blue eyes. What had Hotrod been through? Was there a legitimate reason he'd up and left her without saying goodbye? Or was he just another loser who used women, then tossed them aside?

As fast as that thought crossed her mind, Persia discarded it. Yes, Hotrod had left without saying a word, but he was no slouch. No man who could swim from Cuba to Florida, was. That long-distance swim had required discipline, a shitload of endurance, and the sheer determination to never quit.

When the flight attendant came back with Persia's flute of champagne and Izza's three scoop sundae with extra hot fudge and a mountain of whipped cream with a cherry at the peak, conversation ceased. And that was okay. Persia lifted the champagne to her lips and sipped while she stared at the clouds beyond the window. Night had fallen, but the moon was high enough that it cast a silvery light over the few wispy clouds, making it seem like the moon was racing the jetliner.

Soon, dinner would be served, then another round of drinks or sundaes. Before long, cabin lights would dim. Pillows and blankets would come out, and seats would be tipped back for a good night's sleep. The flight ahead was long, and she was exhausted after the day she'd had. But Persia had work to do. Might as well get at it before dinner.

How she wished she'd never met Hotrod. He'd been stuck in her head, messing with her concentration since that foolish one-night-stand. But man, could he kiss. Her tongue ran a full lap around her lips, remembering. Like it or not, every time she turned around, her mind took her back to the sublime cinna-minty taste of his mouth and the sweet musky scent of the all-male body he'd rubbed against her. The feel of those hard ridges beneath the sensitive pads of her fingertips. The warm, wet suction of his mouth when he swallowed her nipple.

That same old ache started low in her belly, then morphed into liquid heat further below. Persia crossed her legs, wishing her body would stop betraying her. Okay, so that one night with Hotrod had left an indelible mark on her psyche—or something. But it hadn't marked her heart, because it couldn't. She wouldn't let it. She refused to fall for another loser. She'd had that wake-up call during her senior year in college. Once was enough.

She was so over Hotrod. So what if he had a killer bod. Only…

He had left his mark on her, hadn't he? No woman was completely over a man if she couldn't get him off her mind.

But he was the one who'd run out on her, remember? After she'd given him everything. Her body. Her marmalade. Her pancakes. Bacon. She'd all but gushed all over the ass! Even anointed his handsome body with her healing Aloe Vera gel because—

"Oh, my gosh, you're doing it again," Izza murmured, her drop-down tray stowed, and a crisp blue blanket pulled up to her chin.

Persia cast her the most sarcastic glare she could come up with. "No," she told Izza very clearly. "For the last time, I'm not thinking of any man. But I am going to finish this drink and read about the idiot SEAL we have to escort back to the States. You look sleepy."

"Yup. Think I'll catch a few winks before dinner. Wake me when they start serving."

"Will do. Sleep tight and stop worrying about me. I'm fine." *Just peachy.*

Speaking of peaches… Hotrod preferred peaches over melons. Firm, fragrant, delicious peaches that fit snug inside his hands. *'Makes me want to rub them all over my face. Can't do that with a pair of melons.'* Which was precisely what he'd done with her breasts. He'd rubbed his face all over them. Between them. He'd slathered them with wonderfully wet kisses and—

*Oh, for hell's sake. Stop already!*

"Hmmpf," Izza mumbled. "That's what I used to say. See you in a few."

Persia nearly snapped a vertebra looking at Izza to make sure she wasn't replying to what Persia wasn't sure she hadn't spoken out loud. Sheesh! Hotrod was driving her nuts. She had to stop thinking about him.

"Go. To. Sleep," she growled at her traveling companion. *And stop reading my mind, you crazy woman, you.*

With one last swallow, Persia finished her champagne and set the glass aside. Time to work. Dinner would be served soon enough, and she had a lot of reading to catch up on. Walker Judge, huh? Why did that name feel more than just a little familiar? Persia was certain she'd never met the guy. The only SEAL she knew was retired Navy, currently working for the Bureau.

Her fingers trembled as she tugged her computer up from her gear bag, then dropped her tray and set the laptop front and center. She'd already set her display for night reading, so the monitor wouldn't disturb others in the cabin. Not that she meant to work all night. But she'd stashed Ember's file under the laptop's lid in her haste to get out of the office in time to catch that express flight. Intent on reading as much as she could before dinner, Persia laid the file on her computer, flipped it open, and started reading.

Navy SEAL, check.

Nearly twenty years serving his country, check.

Various commendations and medals, not only check, but wow. Eight Bronze Stars with Valor, two Joint Service Commendation Medals with Valor, four Presidential Unit Citations. One Purple Heart. All these and still the Navy prosecuted him?

No wife. Both parents deceased. One brother, also deceased. Check, check, and holy shit. Some serious deployments into hot spots all over the planet. This SEAL had one hell of an honorable record.

Bless her heart, Ember had also included the details of Kenny Judge's obituary, as well as a brief rundown on

Walker's family. Seemed he'd come from a long military history. He'd followed not only in his father's footsteps by joining the Navy, but his grandfather's and great-grandfather's, as well. It was very apparent that Judge had always known what he'd wanted to do with his life. Interesting factoid for a Navy SEAL convicted of murder.

Next, his lawyer's brief on the trial. That took a while to read through, but it was interesting.

Walker's JAG NCIS attorney had readily declared Walker's exemplary service record, yet Navy brass had consistently ignored the medals for heroism above and beyond the call of duty, that they themselves had awarded him. Over and over, the JAG prosecutor had blatantly disregarded Walker's constitutional right to innocence before being proven guilty, as well. Through well-timed, albeit illegal leaks to dishonest reporters, NCIS had succeeded in trying him in the press. Even the men and woman selected as peers for his jury had been hand-picked by Navy brass. Yet, they'd actually done an honest job. Something his defense attorney hadn't.

The more she read, the more unanswered questions Persia had, and the more she believed something was fundamentally wrong with the Navy's top echelon. His new lawyer, a civilian attorney out of San Antonio, Texas, seemed to think that as well, and had already petitioned for an appeal.

Without having met the man, Persia leaned toward Walker Judge being the real deal, the ideal warrior. He could've been that face on the Navy's recruiting posters. So what if he liked to rough-house and had gotten into a few brawls over his career? Wasn't that what SEALs did?

The real problem here seemed to lie within the Uniform Code of Military Justice, the military's criminal justice system. Vastly different from the civilian system, the UCMJ had its own body of laws, and military tribunals were *supposed* to interpret, enforce, and protect those laws. They were *supposed* to be impartial and fair. They were *supposed* to be founded on truth.

Yet Persia knew all about those sanctimonious military tribunals. If some pompous general or admiral wanted a lower-ranking lackey to end up in Leavenworth—*wham, bam, yes, sir, it's done.* Good men and women didn't stand a chance against the butt-kissing and rule-bending that went on behind closed Navy and Army doors these days. Not unless they were wealthy and could afford the best lawyers, which most sailors could not. Even then, those lawyers had better watch their backs. Heaven help anyone who didn't kiss the right ass in the current vicious, highly-charged, political clime.

Ember had included other clippings of military ops Judge had been on. But faces were blacked out and the details had been heavily redacted.

The cabin lights just flashed on. Dinner was on its way.

Hurriedly, Persia leafed through the rest of the file. A photo of Judge would've been nice. It'd be good to know what this guy looked like. She was about to call it quits when she came to another folder tucked into the first. Interesting. She thumbed it open and—

*No way...*

Her brain registered the prong fasteners at the folder's top. Her eyes noted the color of the folder. Blue, for common missions, not black, for classified, eyes-only missions.

But her heart...

*OhmyGod!* That face. That handsome, stalwart, sexy, scruffy, irresistible, handsome face. It was him. Walker Judge! Only Walker Judge looked exactly like Hotrod. His lips, so perfectly set with silent determination. So… damned… kissable.

Those incredible, crystal blue, as pure as the ocean before the morning rain, eyes. Even now, they seemed to be looking straight through her.

Those perfect, kissed-by-the sun, sandy-brown brows. His thick eyelashes made him just plain little-boy adorable. Even all dressed up in what appeared to be his official USN photo, he looked as if he, too, remembered their one night together.

Like a complete idiot, Persia lifted that wonderful file to her nose, sure she'd detect the same luscious hit of wind, sand, and sea, combined with the distinctly male musk that had rolled off his skin that day. His mouth. The cinnamon on his breath.

She couldn't breathe deeply enough. Didn't dare swallow. None of this was real, not the hammering in her heart, most assuredly not the eight-by-eleven glossy portrait of USN Lieutenant Walker Judge staring up at her from Ember's meticulous file.

Talk about being ambushed!

But it *was* him. Persia would know. No other man could steal her breath like this guy had, when he'd first stalked out of the ocean like a svelte, sexy, dripping wet predator. To be honest, she'd been enthralled the moment she'd seen him. He'd put on one helluva strip show peeling out of that wetsuit. He'd been exhausted. That had clearly shown in how his shoulders slumped when he'd dropped his ass to the sand.

How he'd sat there staring at the surf for so long, as if he'd just wanted to breathe.

But those tanned, chiseled shoulders... Wide. Thick. Impressively bulged and muscled. Capable of sweeping her off her feet. And yet, he'd rolled to his hands and knees, and he'd kissed the sand the moment he'd cleared the surf, like someone who'd been away from home too long. Someone who'd been emotionally impacted by that homecoming, obviously overjoyed to be back in America. Which told her how much he loved his country. Made her wonder now why he'd been in Cuba. She hadn't thought to ask. Now she wished she had.

Also made her think of that sandy, but heartfelt kiss to America's farthest southern shore. Did murderers love their country like Hotrod loved his? Did they swim a hundred miles just to get back to her, risking life and limb through shark-infested waters?

There was something—not right—about this man being anywhere on the FBI's most wanted list, much less in the top ten. Spec Ops guys were a different breed of American. She would know, since she'd also served her country in ways most people could never understand.

Infiltrating Domingo Zapata's perverse world of child slavery and all it entailed, had been a damned tough physical war for Persia, as well as an excruciating, daily mental struggle. Yet every second, and with every breath of her time there, she *had* fought valiantly to keep not only her sanity and perspective, but her soul.

Persia swallowed hard, remembering the smell of those blood-stained concrete walls. The memory of the despair etched within those walls was still so sharp and bitter, she could taste it. But all those poor, helpless women and children…

Domingo Zapata hadn't tortured anyone during the months she'd worked for him. But he had terrorized them. Living under the gruesome death threats he promised was enough to drive anyone insane.

Yet she'd had the balls to face that horrible monster, and she'd done it alone. Without any backup. How? She'd arrived at his bunkers dressed in rags, begged a handout, and acted as if she had no idea who he was. Then she'd convinced him that she was just as sick and perverse as he was. How? By killing a lamb, then licking its blood off her fingertips, painting her face and dancing, laughing like a maniac. To this day, she didn't eat anything mutton-related. Never mind that the lamb she'd killed was destined for stew after she'd killed it. Lambs cried for their mamas when they were hurt, did you know that? And their mamas bleated for them once those babies were dead. They mourned for days and sometimes they died because they just stopped living. Because of her! She had that baby's blood on her hands! The whole damnable mess still turned her stomach.

Automatically, Persia clapped her palms over her ears, denying yet again, the quivering fear in that tiny animal's bleating cry for help. Wishing she could go back in time and tell her FBI handler, 'No,' that she didn't want to work for the CIA. Not in South America. Never in Brazil. Never, ever with a psychopath like Zapata!

Despite her night terrors now, she *had* brought him down. The bastard *was* dead. With her own eyes, she'd watched Julio Juarez put two hot rounds straight into Zapata's brain. She'd seen the blood splatter, and she'd rejoiced in every single drop of it. Because Persia had also watched while Agent Juarez's wife had played games with Domingo when Julio'd thought she'd been kidnapped. Persia knew for a fact that Bianca Juarez had willfully, and with malice, deserted her husband and her only child—Julio's one-year-old boy, a toddler, for fuck sakes!

It took a few moments of mindfulness and steady, slow breathing to banish the ugly memory again. Yet reliving those awful months made Persia realize that Hotrod, err, Lieutenant Walker Judge, a decorated USN SEAL, must've done things just as difficult, maybe even harder. Yet not once had she gotten an unsettling vibe or an ugly feeling from Hotrod, err, Judge. Damn it. He was Walker Judge. *Walker, Walker, Walker!*

If anything, he'd impressed the hell out of her that one night. He'd been sweet and gentle and… okay, he'd also been too tired to perform, which might explain why he'd left before dawn. Maybe he hadn't been able to face her? No. Uh uh. Not Walker. Tough, confident guys like him weren't afraid to face their mistakes. And they didn't usually have performance issues—not unless they'd just swum a hundred freakin' miles to get back to the land they—he—loved.

Yes. Loved. Guys like Judge didn't kiss just any stretch of sand. And they didn't leave the kind of impression behind that he had left with her.

Lieutenant Judge sure cut a handsome profile in those crisply pressed dress whites in this official photo. Persia had always been a sucker for a man in uniform, but knowing what lay beneath this particular uniform, and knowing this guy… *Ahh.* Persia wanted to eat him up all over again. For breakfast, lunch, dinner, and a tasty, lip-smacking midnight snack.

On his left chest, above the placard of six rows of campaign and various USN ribbons, rested the proud, gold Trident that declared the Navy SEAL's creed: *'In times of war or uncertainty there is a special breed of warrior ready to answer our nation's call. A common man with an uncommon desire to succeed.'*

Only this common man had made the tenderest, sweetest love to her—before he'd walked away. How many weeks ago had that been? She couldn't think. Only wanted to sit here and breathe the essence of this damned troublemaker back into her life. If that were even possible. If only she could go back in time and—

"What's up? Is it dinnertime yet? You okay?"

"No! I mean, yes! I mean, no, it's not dinner yet, and of course I'm okay. Why wouldn't I be okay?" Wow, how insincere was that? Persia slammed the folder shut, rattled at what Izza might've seen. That she might've been watching the whole time.

"Oh, okay. No worries," Izza mumbled sleepily. "I've already read that jerk's file, so you don't have to if you don't want to. He's a Class A ass, and according to Alex, ICC's got him cuffed and shackled. If he tries anything, we'll just taser his ass and take him down like the dog he is. Right?"

"Umm, yeah. Sure." *Take him down.* All the ways Persia had taken Hotrod down, in her bed and in her shower, stormed her poor flustered heart. It fluttered like a giant butterfly with B-52 wings stuck in her chest. Who would've ever guessed Hotrod was Walker Judge?!

"Go back to sleep," Persia urged her friend as calmly as she could. "S-s-sorry I disturbed you."

"You didn't. Just had a funny feeling. You ever get one of those?"

Persia nodded, but Izza's eyes were already closed, so she lied and said, "No. Never."

And then she cracked that file and began reading every single page again. Persia didn't just have a funny feeling. She had a full-blown premonition. Walker Judge would yet prove his innocence. And by hell, she'd help him do it.

# Chapter Twenty-Three

Morning came too early when a guy had to pee, but couldn't. Walker stood over the hard-water-stained steel toilet bowl, poised for action, but getting nowhere fast. Massaging his aching lower back while cuffed had proven miserably impossible. Didn't help that his cuffs were in front of him with a chain running to his shackles, or that the current guard on duty watched every move he made.

But it'd sure be nice if someone turned the thermostat down. Better yet, off. It was early summer, for hell's sake, and Walker was sweating like a pig in this cramped, airless cell. But there was no relief. Not from the oppressive heat, nor from his kidneys.

When it became obvious he'd had a total failure to launch, Walker closed up the Velcro fly on his ridiculous clown suit, and did a quick two-step shuffle back to the board in the wall called his bed. The shackles on his ankles seemed heavier this morning, and he was frustrated with the unnecessary restraints while he was behind bars. Everything was too damned much.

Still dizzy, he leaned his aching head onto the flat pillow on his bed. It was strange how simple things like pillowcases mattered to a guy with no future. But the lack of a case on this sweat-stained pillow brought back the sweet memory of better times. Of being with Persia Coltrane in her bed. Of her hair spread out like an ebony fan on her pure, white, *Pottery Barn* pillows.

He could still smell the luscious fragrance of her sun-warmed skin. The flowery scent of her silky hair. The barest hint of whiskey on her breath. Interesting. Whiskey instead of wine. He would've pegged her a Napa Valley girl. Not a Valley Girl, but one who was a helluva lot smarter. Which Persia was. One who enjoyed the finer things.

Walker lifted his cuffed hands together, slid his wrists one over the other, then dropped both over his eyes to dim the light. There was no privacy in this closet of a cell, no way to turn the light bar overhead off or down. He'd become an insect, caged and spotlighted for dissection. But at least the chain between shackles and cuffs allowed this much relief.

He hadn't felt this bad since he'd been a kid at home with the flu. Kenny'd been sick the same week. They'd missed five full days of school, but had both felt too bad to celebrate their good fortune.

Kenny. Damn. Thinking about his kid brother was not what Walker needed right now. Besides, he wasn't sick with any flu bug. This holding cell was small and there wasn't enough ventilation down here in the basement. That was all. Guess the ICC didn't believe in A/C. Or prisoners' rights.

Disgusted with the shitter his life had devolved into, Walker rubbed the heels of his hands into his eye sockets. Man, he was tired of running, just as fed up with fighting the whole damned world. Hans said he'd come back this morning, that he'd bring all those incriminating files and photos that showed Walker bombing a wedding in Jordan. But what did that matter? If Goff was the bastard who'd altered Walker's

OMPF, his Official Military Personnel File, he was powerful enough to rig another jury and alter the ICC's evidence, too.

Everything seemed hopeless. Hopeless and too damned hot!

"Hey! You! Jerk-off!" the latest moron on duty bellowed, while he battered that expensive weapon on the metal bars like it was a baseball bat. "Is time to wake up, lucky American pig. You got company."

Walker rolled to his feet. Might as well rise and shine. A man who couldn't pee sure as hell couldn't sleep, not with this raucous idiot standing guard. "I'm up," he replied to get the guy to cease the racket.

"Stand back!" the guard ordered, as he unsnapped a ring of shiny silver keys from his belt. He managed to unlock the cell with one hand, while pointing his rifle at Walker with the other. Which was a stupid move since Walker was still sitting on his bunk. "I will take you to another room, but you must not try anything. I know how to kill."

*Well, so the hell do I.* Was that supposed to be a threat? Walker could barely climb back to his feet and walk in these shackles, much less try anything that would get him out of this detention unit. His head and lower back hurt too damned much.

Man, he hoped it was Brimley in that other room. No one else knew he was here. But now that Walker had time to think, how'd Brimley know he'd been shipped off to the Netherlands or that he'd been detained by the ICC? Even if he'd somehow found all that out, how'd he get to The Hague from the Azores? Was he secretly a rich millionaire with a fast jet at his beck and call?

Nah. No guy who lived in a cheap, rundown basement apartment, was a secret anything. Brimley's being here didn't make sense, but it'd sure be good to see the old fart again. Walker wanted to know what happened to Rover. He hoped Brimley had gotten to his doggo in time after they'd both gone overboard. They had a bond, those two. It'd kill Walker if Brimley lost his best friend because of him.

"Halt!" the idiot with the rifle bellowed the second Walker made it into the hall.

Man, these people liked concrete. Nothing but cold, gray walls and floors stretched all the way down the hall. And yet Walker was burning up. For the first time, he worried his problem might not be the lack of proper ventilation. Might actually be the flu. Damned disconcerting.

While his guard fumbled to snap that silly key ring back onto his belt—*Shit, it's not rocket science!*—Walker focused on staying upright. But gray on gray on gray didn't have a soothing effect on his gut. Despite the weighted shackles at his ankles, his head seemed heavier, yet lighter at the same time. Try making sense out of that. He couldn't. When the world tilted sideways, he slapped both palms to the wall beside his door to steady himself. It was that or fall down.

"Stop!" the guard bellowed as the business end of his rifle snapped to the center of Walker's back, pressing hard between his shoulder blades. "I will kill you if you make another move!"

There was no way Walker would ever admit to this idiot that he might be sick. Comprehending that might take more brain cells than the guy had. So he sucked it up, nodded his compliance, and replied in a clear, subservient voice, "Sorry, sir. It won't happen again."

Bullies loved to be obeyed and made to feel important. Which was why the 'sir.' It worked like a charm.

Appeased, the big, tough guy with the only weapon in the hallway gave Walker his chin. "Turn around. We will go see your visitor now, but just one move…"

*Yeah, yeah, yeah.* Walker stopped listening. At the moment, he needed all the strength he had just to about-face and walk a straight line. Seemed like he and his handler walked for miles, but it was only down the hall and around the corner. By the time he stood at yet another closed door that had to be unlocked by the man with ten thumbs, Walker'd had it. He swallowed hard, which was difficult to do with a dry throat. But he did resist the urge to grab the wall again.

Finally! The freakin' door opened to reveal an average interrogation room.

Metal table bolted to the concrete floor. Drain beneath the table. Rings in the concrete to lock shackles in place. More rings on the table for handcuffs. Two-way mirrors, one to the left of where Walker was obviously supposed to sit, since that was where the only metal chair in the room had been bolted to the floor. The other straight across from that same uncomfortable looking chair. Closed-circuit-TV cameras blinked from all four corners of the ceiling. Bright florescent light tubes glared down at him.

With all this concrete, you'd think this basement room would've been cold. But Walker felt as if he were walking into a square, gray sauna.

"No!" his personal moron bellowed the second Walker cleared the doorway.

What now? All he wanted to do was sit in that damned chair before he fell down.

"We wait out here. You will stand until I allow you to sit."

Walker closed his eyes at the idiocy of yet another stupid command, even as he stepped back beside the guard. What did it matter if he sat in the chair or fell on the floor?

"Stay standing," the guard threatened, "or I will exact swift discipline you will never forget."

Which meant he'd use that bully club dangling off his belt alongside his key ring—if he could get it unclipped fast enough—on a prisoner he assumed wouldn't fight back. Walker almost wished he'd try it, see how that went. Sick or not, he'd feed that club to this over-confident asshat in a heartbeat. Maybe two, given his current shaky condition.

"Yes, sir," Walker replied, breathing shallowly through his mouth now. SEALs didn't give in, or give up. He'd survived Hell Week. This was nothing. It was simply a matter of who would outlast the other. A step-by-step endurance test. *Just. Keep. Going...*

An hour later, which was probably really just five minutes, the steady drumbeat of soles on concrete headed his way. Thank God. Stiffening to attention, he prepared to look whoever this visitor was in the eye. It'd sure be good if it were Brimley. Then Walker could find out how Rover was.

Damn. It was Hans Koning rounding the corner. Business suit. White dress shirt. Black tie that matched his black shoes. The second he came into view, his head canted nearly to his shoulder. His entire forehead furrowed. "Why are you standing out here? Go inside. Now. Sit. Please sit," he said, gesturing to the empty room. Then to the guard, he spoke a few tense, very short sentences in Dutch.

The guard grumbled back in the same language, but snorted at Walker to go in.

Not willing to admit weakness or defeat, Walker marched into the blistering hot room with his back straight and sank onto the designated metal chair. It should've been cold to the touch, but like everything else in this miserable dungeon, it was sticky and too warm. He put both hands on his knees to still his trembling.

Hans disappeared, while the guard dropped one knee to the floor at Walker's feet. "You think you are going home, but you are not," he growled as he removed the cuffs, then the shackles, with all the gentleness of Attila the Hun. "Not while I work here, buddy. Not today."

*Buddy?* "Do I know you?" Walker had to ask as the man scraped the shackles sharply across his ankle, as if to make a point. "Have I offended you somehow?" *Because I'd sure like to. You're as big an ass as my CO was.*

"All you American Navy SEALs offend me," he hissed. "You think you are so much smarter than the rest of us."

Ah, so that's what this was about. A WWE wrestler wannabe challenging the reigning champion. Walker had no response for that. He'd let Karma take care of this guy.

Very shortly, Hans returned, pushing a comfortable leather chair on wheels through the doorway. "Sit. Here, please," he told Walker as he rolled the chair far from the interrogation table. "Please. I am sorry you had to wait so long for me. My supervisor detained me. Your guest will be here soon."

He shot a few more terse words at the guard, who had no problem tossing them right back. After a quick exchange, Attila bristled. Hans' entire demeanor darkened, but whatever he'd said seemed to end the power struggle. Like a petulant child, Attila stomped around the corner and out of sight.

Walker had yet to move. He was weak, but he was damned if he'd admit it.

"You are not well, sir," Hans said quietly, his head tipping toward the chair. "Please take a seat."

"I'm fine. Who's my guest? Wouldn't be an old guy with a dog, would it?"

"Hey there, LT Judge," a woman called out behind him. "Happy to see me?"

Walker looked over his shoulder. Suddenly he couldn't catch a breath. Felt like he'd been sucker-punched. Or shot point-blank. The walls spun. Stumbling forward, he sank into the chair Hans had offered before he fell on his face.

The person now entering the interrogation room with her sexy hips swaying and her luscious lips smiling was none other than—

*Oh, sh-sh-sh-sh-shit!*

The anticipation of finally seeing Brimley and Rover faded into outright terror. This was his guest? The woman who hated him? The goddess he'd dishonored by walking out on? Could this nightmare get any worse?!

"Per…Per… Persia?" he croaked, sure he was delirious and seeing things. Wishing he were seeing things. This couldn't be happening!

When she headed straight for him, he turned his head and closed his eyes, prepared to get slapped, punched, or spit on. He deserved whatever she dished out.

Instead, Persia dropped to her knees, her palms clamped over his thighs with a breathy, "Hotrod."

In his wildest dreams, he'd never expected to see her again, surely not here. But the way she'd said his handle when she knew his real name… He turned his head and looked at her. Then he felt worse. He didn't want her to see him like this, not so weak, certainly not in this damned clown suit and beat half to death.

But what a sight for sore, tired eyes. Persia looked so damned pretty it hurt his heart. Dressed in black jeans and shirt, she'd already shrugged a hefty bag off her shoulder, unzipped it once it hit the floor, then pulled a bottled water out. Twisting the cap off, she offered it to him.

His hands were shaking so much, he couldn't get a good enough grip on the damned thing. Walker set the bottle on his knee to keep from dropping it and to keep him from looking weaker.

Those deep, dark chocolate eyes might as well have been razors. She knew who he was, damn it, or she wouldn't be here. Yet she seemed genuinely happy to see him. Not pissed off. Not hateful or mean. Her fingertips on his thighs were so gentle, he wanted to cry.

"I'm sorry," he told her sincerely. "But I—"

"Shush," she replied, glancing over her shoulder. "Mr. Koning's giving us a few moments of privacy, but we have to hurry. Can you walk?" She leaned between Walker's knees, almost against his cock, her gaze slipping over his face, diagnosing and inventorying all she saw.

"Who are you? Persia? R-r-really?" Not just anyone could get into the International Criminal Court building. It was too well guarded.

"There'll be time for questions and answers later. We have to go now. Stop shaking, so I can unlock these stupid cuffs and shackles."

"You've got keys?"

"No, I've got a hairpin, shit. Of course I've got keys. Hans gave them to me."

"Hans is working with you?" Nothing made sense.

"That's what I said, isn't it?"

"Okaaaaay." He was all for leaving. "But where are we going?"

"Out," she growled, glancing at the door Hans had left open again. "The prosecutor overseeing your case is an insensitive ass, and the judge is an idiot. But Hans Koning believes you. He's on your side, and I'm breaking you out."

Walker closed his eyes, sure he was out of his mind. Persia, here? Couldn't be. Hans letting him go? None of this was real. Had to be hallucinations, which meant he was damned sick.

"Where's Brimley?" he asked the first random question that popped into his head. "And Doggo? Have you seen an old guy with a big dog around here?" Because they'd be real. Not—Persia. Her being here and being so nice made no sense.

"Please shut up, Hotrod. You're running a fever, and you're talking nonsense. We really have to go. Now!" When the cuffs and shackles clattered to the concrete floor, she ran her tongue over her bottom lip, and damn...he was distracted. That sweet, honeyed tongue. Those lush, red lips. Her mouth. He wanted another taste of that wine. Oh, wait. She was a whiskey girl. But if this were just a dream...

"Did you hear me?" she snapped, tugging him out of the chair by one hand, the other clamped tightly around his waist. "We don't have much time. Alex doesn't want anyone in the press to know you're here, so Izza's upstairs, creating a distraction. Come on, Hotrod. You're a big guy. You have to help me do this."

*Alex who? Izza? What kind of name's that?* "I am," he muttered as the concrete floor danced beneath his stupid orange shoes. "But I look like Bozo."

"Yeah, well, I happen to like clowns." She huffed, dragging him toward the table, where she opened her bag. "Here. Put this on."

Damned if she didn't pull a lovely pink poncho stamped on its back with *DIVA COMING THROUGH!* out of that bag. Instead of tossing it at him, she lifted his arm and started to dress him like a kid.

"I've got this," he murmured, then struggled like hell getting the hole in that plastic thing over his head and facing the right direction. In the end, Persia's dogged persistence was the only reason *DIVA COMING THROUGH!* ended up on his back, not his chest. Small consolation. It was still pink and clashed with his orange jumpsuit and shoes and... *Who cares?!*

"There," she said, her bag on her shoulder again, her arm around his waist and her wonderfully soft-in-all-the-best-places body pressed flush to his side. "Let's go."

Too late. Attila was back, his rifle pointed in Walker's face, and yelling, "Stop, or I'll shoot!" loud enough to wake the dead.

"Will you shut the fuck up?!" Persia hissed as she let Walker go, and... *BAM!*

Whoa. She'd just cocked her fist back like a prizefighter and punched Attila's square, ugly face. After he dropped his weapon and accordion-folded to his knees, she kicked and nailed his family jewels. He curled, whimpering into a fetal position.

"I think I love you," Walker mumbled like an idiot.

"Will you move it?" she snapped, pulling him past a drooling Attila, into the hall, and away from the interrogation room and his prison cell.

"Where we going? Really. You can tell me," he murmured as he stumbled along. Not like even then, he would know where he was.

"Home," she snapped, her hand on his chest, keeping him upright and walking. "But first…" She rounded the corner, and he found himself pushed up hard against the wall.

He cringed like a pussy. *Here comes the slap down.* Either that or he'd wake up back in his cell, and this would all be a dream and—

One of Persia's soft sweet hands cupped his jaw. Her fierce gaze scorched him, but her other hand on his chest was so gentle. So warm. The air between them seemed somehow full of flowers and stardust and hope. Then she was in his face, and her mouth was on his, and she swallowed every last one of his worries. He didn't deserve her kindness or her sweet breath or her tongue in his mouth—but he took it.

Grabbing hold of her biceps, he held her fast while he gave back what he could. A rumbling, throaty growl moaned out of her, as she returned the favor with vigor, damned near eating him alive. Walker wanted to fall on his knees in adoration of the amazing woman who was swallowing his worry. Unless this was all a dream. The one he'd had every night since he'd walked out on her. *I suck. I deserted this woman. I don't deserve her rescuing me now. Why the hell's she here?*

She didn't let up on him. Just kept rubbing her palms over his shoulders and down his arms. When she growled again, he was all in. Walker tilted his head to access more of her mouth.

Only when both his eager hands dropped to her black-encased backside did she break the connection.

Without saying anything, she jerked her bag off the floor, and then they were speed-walking down that long hall to nowhere again. Her pulling him along; him trying to keep up because, besides being sick, he was now dizzy from that steamy kiss.

Then they were around another corner and running up concrete steps. Her taking two at a time; him holding tight to the handrail, so he didn't fall backward and die before he got away. Another long damned hallway that, thank heavens, was empty of armed guards.

Suddenly, a siren blared overhead. The overhead lights started flashing yellow. A pair of twenty-foot-high doors with long push bars blocked the exit at the end of this hallway. And Walker knew he had to save Persia. She was the important one, not him.

"Run," he told her. "Get out of here!"

"Will you knock it off? I'm here to save you!"

"But you need to leave."

"Not without you. Keep moving," she ordered, her tone as hard as steel, "or neither of us will make it."

"Who's gonna kill us? We're American citizens, for Chrisssst sakesssss." He was slurring like a drunk. Staggering like one, too.

"Tell that to whoever signed the ICC's warrant for your arrest. The judge upstairs refused to acknowledge President Adams' signed extradition orders, and your prosecutor's a Nazi moron. Your buddy, Hans Koning, got me into the ICC, but he told me you were in rough shape, that I might not be able to get you out. Also told me to watch out for the jerk with the rifle. Which is why I decked the motherfucker. Now move it!"

How Walker adored a woman who cussed like a sailor.

"Hans helped you rescue me?" Man, that sounded pitiful. Him, a SEAL, needing to be rescued by a wimpy guy in a business suit and a tie. What the hell? Had the world turned upside down and inside out?

"Yes. He's on our side." Persia shoved Walker through one of those gigantic doors and all but pushed him down yet another set of stairs. Outside. Where the air was cool and free. His lungs automatically inhaled freedom.

"That way. That one," she hissed, steering him toward a—

"What is it with these people? Is orange the Goddamned national color here?"

"Shut up and get in!"

Walker obeyed, ducking into the orange clown car parked at the curb. They'd exited into an alley. But it was a damned tight fit getting his long legs, big orange feet, and much too large ass into the passenger seat of a car the size of an extra-mini Geo Metro. "Didn't know they still made these things."

Persia climbed in the driver's seat and slammed the door. "We're in one, aren't we?"

"My brother bought one a loooong time ago. Only it wasn't orange. It was greeeeen. Hey, it's a stick." Walker cupped the plastic knob lovingly. You didn't see many manual transmission vehicles in America anymore.

"Yes, it is, genius," Persia breathed. Impatiently, she brushed his hand aside, pressed the ignition button, and stepped on the gas.

Just as Walker expected, gears screamed when the car lurched forward and died. "Take it easy. On standards, you got to use the—"

"Don't tell me how to drive," Persia snapped, restarting the car, shifting swiftly from neutral to first gear, her left foot pumping the clutch pedal smoothly. Man, she worked this baby like a guy.

Walker slumped into the seat when she hit second and stepped on the gas, cranking the wheel while the car squealed away from the curb. His knees were in his chest, but his eyes were still on Persia. "I think I love you," he murmured, mostly to himself. He thought.

"Heard you before," she hissed, the tiny toy car hurtling at warp speed and straight into oncoming traffic.

"You're on a one-way street!"

"Yeah, well..." Tires squealed, and she was now fishtailing on what looked like a busy frontage road paralleling train tracks. "Hang on while I lose our tail."

"What—?" *Oh, that tail.* The puke green sedan on the other side of the tracks where a silver bullet train was suddenly blurring by.

Silver bullet... Hmmm. His dizzy head jumped to the memory of icy cold beer and—

"Hold tight!!" she ordered.

"Y-y-yes, ma'am!" he yelled back.

The clown car drifted into a perfect one-hundred-eighty-degree turn, just as the final train car rumbled by, sending them back in the same direction they'd come from. No sign of puke green then, only another dizzying turn and squealing tires, followed by a thousand blurred buildings and more course corrections than Walker could track. Too many bikes and canals and…

Automatically he slammed both palms to the dash when she brought the car to a sudden stop and yelled, "Get out!"

If only he could make his fingers work to open the tiny handle to his door. Shit. He was all thumbs, and that was kind of funny—him being in clown shoes like he was—

Until she jerked it open and hissed, "Do I have to do everything?"

*Umm, yeah. Maybe.* Instead of saying that, he manned up and said, "Almost had it."

By then, Miss Impatience had a stranglehold on his scraped raw wrist, and he was on his feet. Just a little too quickly. He didn't see the curb because he was looking at her. One clown shoe landed sideways in the gutter; the other only half made the curb. His ankle collapsed, and over he went, on Persia.

They fell onto the sidewalk together, but somehow, he managed an outstanding quarterback save that put him on his back and her core on his belly. And just that fast, he was home safe with his nose buried in the wonderfully warm valley between her pillowy breasts. He loved it there.

His lungs reacted instinctively, inhaling deeply and sucking in every last glorious feminine pheromone. Clean womanly sweat. Fresh laundry detergent. Some kind of flowery, female deodorant. Walker stretched his neck, his tongue ready to lick those tantalizing scents off of her body.

But just as his hand cupped her ass, she pushed to her knees. "Knock it off, Hotrod. We need to get inside and you out of sight."

"Yeah. Right." He knew that.

Once she'd climbed to her feet, he rolled to his knees. Shit. The thousand step staircase ahead of him might as well have been to the stars.

# Chapter Twenty-Four

Man, this guy was heavy. But at least Hotrod was on his feet and moving forward. Mostly. But he was damned sick, and everywhere she touched, his skin was burning hot. Had to be running an awfully high fever. But that poor eye. And his forehead. Who had he been fighting?

"One more step," Persia urged encouragingly.

Her left hand was now splayed over the center of his chest, her other hand clenching a balled-up knot of his pink poncho. She'd dressed him in that because the orange, government-owned jumpsuit beneath it had *ICC Detention Unit* stamped in bright red on his back. Guess the ICC wanted to make sure escapees would be easy to spot in a crowd. A big guy like Walker certainly would have been.

At last, they were at the front door to the safe house. "Lean against the wall here, and please stay on your feet. I might not be able to get you up again."

"Won't have to. I'm...I'm not going anywhere," he huffed, even as he leaned backward and his head hit the doorjamb. "I'm good."

*Good and stubborn,* she thought.

They'd known they'd get separated after running into the media mob camped outside the ICC, so Izza had ordered Persia to locate Hotrod and break him out, while she created a distraction. It seemed reporters from the entire world had shown up today. Evil, nasty, lying sharks, all of them. *Wonder who they're after? Couldn't be Hotrod, could it? How'd they know he was there? Who told?*

Ignoring her panic, Persia pushed the door open, then shrugged her bag off her shoulder and let it hit the floor. Thank goodness, she'd brought a ruggedized TEAM laptop. It was unbreakable. "Okay, let's do this, big guy. Slow and easy. I've got you."

Hotrod palmed the doorjamb over his head with one big, sweaty hand, then ducked into TEAM safety. "Christ, it's freezzzzzing in here."

"No, it's quite stuffy, but you're sick. You've got a fever, and you're chilled. Bed. Now."

Persia led him to the first room down the hall and pointed him toward the double bed against the opposite wall. "My room's next to yours, so if you need help, holler. Izza's is across from mine. We're here to get you out of the country and back home."

Like most TEAM safe houses, this one had no windows except for the bullet-proof, darkly tinted, four-paned one alongside the front door. But what it lacked in see-through glass, this home made up for in security cameras and a wealth of other failsafe measures. Like a steel-walled safe room, which seemed redundant to Persia. A safe room in a safe house? That was Alex for you.

Hotrod muttered something as he fell face down across the bed. Sounded like, "Good night."

Man, he was a long drink of water, as her father would've said.

"Oh, no, you don't. Out of those clothes first," Persia ordered as she undid the Velcro on his ridiculous shoes and let them drop to the hardwood floor. How embarrassing to outfit an adult man like a clown. "Let's get you undressed, so I can see what we're dealing with."

She'd meant if he had any other injuries, but that might not have been the best way to have said it. She already knew what she'd dealt with in Florida, and it was f-f-fine with a capital F.

Persia shook the delicious memory out of her head. Now was not the time for daydreams. She needed to take stock of whatever antibiotics Alex kept in this safe house. She'd brought her own first-aid kit, but he was a bugger for details. Surely, he'd provided plenty of first-rate supplies and, hopefully, stronger antibiotics than those she always carried.

The second Hotrod rolled to his back, she tackled getting him out of his pants, which were simple orange pajamas with an elastic waistband. Would've been easy, but he decided to help. With a growl, he lifted his backside and scraped those britches over his hips and off. *Wayyyy off.*

The orange pajama top flew next, and there he was, sitting on the edge of the bed in his all-over tanned, very manly birthday suit. All of him. With his hands on his knees and his legs spread like every other guy on the planet. Totally unashamed of his nudity. Bleary-eyed and sick and smiling up at her like the bad, bad boy he was.

"Hey, Persia Coltrane," he murmured. "Sure is good to see you again."

Man, he was adorable. He'd shaved since she'd last seen him. His scruff was gone, but his light brown hair was longer and mussed, sticking up at odd angles. He'd been in the sun; strands of his hair now streaked with light gold highlights. His chest seemed wider. But those poor eyes were not only black and blue, the whites were red with blood. Two of the four butterfly stitches over that same puffy eye were half off. He needed a doctor, but he was only going to get her and Izza, when she returned.

Drawing the sheet over his lap before she acted on the feminine impulse to straddle him, Persia knelt trembling like an idiot at his knee. "Who… who did this to you, Hotrod? Who beat you?"

His shoulders lifted. "Not sure. Might've happened when they boarded the yacht. Or maybe in jail on São Miguel. Hell, I don't know."

"São Miguel? You were in the Azores? What yacht?"

"My yacht. Yeah. The Azores. Now the Netherlands." He cocked one arm behind his sweaty head, then ran a hand over his hair, his face pressed against his bicep. This man was one ripped badass, and that bicep was a taut bulge of bronze tanned skin over deeply-veined muscles. His chest was the same kind of tempting. "Some asshat got the drop on us. I honestly don't know who smacked my skull. Don't know much of anything."

Which meant he'd been beaten while he'd been unconscious. Which fit what Mr. Koning had insinuated that ICC guard might do to Walker again. "How long have you been in ICC detention?"

Hotrod squinted, his one good eye staring her down. "Two days, I think. Not sure. No clocks in there, and lights stay on twenty-four-seven. Jesus, my brain's killing me. Can I just sleep?"

"Not until I'm sure you don't have a concussion." She reached for that amazing hard head, threading her fingers through his wet hair for— "My hell. You've got a knot back here the size of a grapefruit."

Persia tugged his forehead against her collarbone, needing to see the back of his head. She parted swatches of hair to better see his scalp. The damned knot she'd felt was large and bruised, but not bleeding. "You've got a concussion, Hotrod—"

By then, he'd buried his face between her breasts, and a flood of memories swamped Persia. How could she hate the man who'd made sweet love with her back in Florida?

Gently, she cupped that hard head, and eased his nose out from her cleavage. "It's no wonder your head hurts. I'll get an ice pack, then we need to get your temp down. There's a tub across the hall. I'll run a cold bath, and then somehow, we'll get you into it."

"We," he breathed, his breath in her face hot and foul, smelling of infection. "You said we."

Persia nodded, not afraid of whatever germs this man might be carrying. He was in her custody now, and he was safe. That was all that mattered. "Yes, Hotrod. You and me. We're going to get you cooled down and then back to bed, where you can sleep the rest of the day, okay? We fly home first thing tomorrow."

"You know who I am." He hadn't moved, but those battered eyes glittered with what could only be tears. And that broke her heart.

"Yes, sugar, I know who you are. I use your SEAL handle because that's who you were the last time we were together." She hoped that made sense. "Let me help you up."

"But they took my Budweiser, damn it. I'm not a SEAL anymore."

"You are to me."

She had to keep him moving, though. But when she lifted to her feet and grabbed him, arm to the elbow, to get a better grip, he easily pulled her down onto his lap. Persia found herself snuggled inside the steel bands she'd been dreaming about for weeks.

"This isn't helpful," she muttered against the sweaty, solid strength of his chest, loving the feel of him beneath her as much as hating the less than professional position he'd put her in. What would Izza say when she found out that Persia and Hotrod had slept together? That they'd had one hot, steamy, glorious night together in Florida? And Izza would. She had a sixth sense for girl/guy stuff like that. What would Alex say? He'd fire her for sure. The implications…

*No. Just no!* Persia couldn't think about anything except getting this man into the tub, cooled down, then back to his bed, where she could finally replace his bandages and doctor him and kiss him better and… Man, this was going to be her toughest mission ever.

"But you know who I am," he growled. "You know I lied to you. And I left. I wasn't even man enough to tell you goodbye. Hell, I wasn't man enough all that night."

Easing away from her very secure location, she put a fingertip to his lips. "Yes, I know you weren't exactly honest with me, but I'm not mad. Not anymore. I was at first, but I think I know why you did what you did."

"Why… why aren't you mad? Everyone else is."

The anguish in his question was heartbreaking. "Because I'm not everyone else. I saw the man you were the night we were together. That, and I've been going over your transcript on the flight over. I haven't read all of it, but something about your trial isn't right. Come on, sugar. You're very sick. Talk can wait."

Those poor battered eyelids closed, squeezing one pinkish tear out. It trickled down his nose. It was as if no one had ever called him sugar before. *Well, good.*

"You came for me," he ground out, his eyelids squeezed tight.

Persia put her hand around his stiff neck and tugged until he had no choice but to face her. "Yes, I came for you, and we're going to get you safely back to the States. But you can't get on any flights out of here while you're sick. The altitude will kill you if you're congested. Let's do this. Now. Let me up."

He did let her up, but he didn't let her go. With one hand resting heavily on her shoulders, Hotrod allowed Persia to lead him across the hall. Which was an erotic treat all by itself, to be followed by a handsome naked man who dwarfed her by a foot and outweighed her by—a lot.

Most European homes came with tiny water closet bathrooms, hell, with tiny everything. But this safe house had been built American-style. The tub was extra-large, the tiled walls surrounding it fitted with handicap rails. One of those sturdy plastic shower chairs for people prone to fall, sat to the side.

Persia ushered Walker onto that chair, where he sat with a thump. She had to look away. This guy might not know it, but his body was definitely on alert. Her fingers trembled as she knelt by the tub and cranked the water tap to lukewarm, remembering how she and he couldn't seem to get enough of each other back in Florida. How heavenly it had been being inside his arms, with him inside of her.

Once again, she had to force herself back to her primary mission. Which was not about them. Certainly not them together again. She fluttered her fingers under the faucet. Cold water would lower his temp quicker, but the shock of it might be too much for him in his current condition.

When at last the two faucets doled out an acceptable mix of hot and cold, she turned back to Hotrod. "Up you go," she said, her voice as raspy as if she were the sick one. She cleared her throat and tried again. "Come on. We can do this."

He obeyed, lifting off the chair. Gingerly, he raised one muscled leg over the tub edge, then the other until he was ready to sit.

"Oh, my, stop!" She couldn't take in all she was seeing. Dark, ugly bruises blackened his lower back. "You're hurt. Hurry. Sit back down. Please. Let me—"

What? Reverse time? Make those ugly marks disappear? Go back to the ICC and exact vengeance?

"'S okay, princess," he told her quietly. "Sorry you had to see that. Must be pretty bad, huh?"

She could've cried. "It's bad enough. Aren't you in pain?"

"Yeah, everything kinda aches all over."

"Sit down, Hotrod. Please."

He turned back around again, and for one brief moment, he stood there with both hands flattened on the tile behind him, looking down at her on her knees. She looked up the entire length of that glorious all-male physique. His thighs. All those muscles. Velvet over steel. All wrapped in a battered shell that needed someone to care for him, to believe in him. But all that masculinity was so, so beautiful, growing longer and harder to resist by the minute. He had to get into that tub and sit down before she made a drooling fool of herself.

Persia lifted to her feet, drawn like a magnet to a man she had no business wanting as badly as she did this guy. "Sit down," she whispered. "Please. If you fall, you'll hit your head on the edge of this tub. You could kill yourself." *And what would I do then?*

She thought he'd offer some crack about the tub not being the only thing that was hard. Instead, he murmured, "Stay."

"Yes," blurted out of her mouth. "Oh, yes, sugar, I'm not going anywhere. See this chair?" she gestured to the handicapped seat. "I'll stay right here until you sit down. While you relax in the tub, I'll just be in the kitchen making lunch." Meanwhile, she seemed to be sweating. And drooling.

"'Kay," he breathed, as at last, he bent his knees and lowered his magnificent ass into the rising water. "Brrr. It's cold," he complained when his butt hit the chill.

"And I'm going to make it colder. Here," she said as she handed him the tiny plastic clamshell pillow from the counter to lean his head and neck against. Once he was prone, she increased the cold water pouring into the tub and turned down the hot.

"J-join me," he murmured, his head resting to the side on that pillow, his poor eyes already closed, and goosebumps popping up on his arms.

"Nope. Sorry. I—"

*WHOOSH!* He pulled her into the tub.

"Hotrod!" That was the last word she got out. He had her trapped at his side, one big manly hand under her now wet head, the other cupping her jaw, while he kissed the hell out of her. Germs and all, sick and exhausted and all—

He kissed her as if his life depended on it. Passionately and thoroughly. Desperately. His tongue turned into a wave of need and hunger sweeping over her lips, painting inside her mouth and behind her teeth with fire.

Yup, she was thoroughly contaminated now. But what a way to go…

Persia melted against him, aroused and aflame with mixed feelings for this brave, battered man. "You're sick and you're injured," she murmured around his prehensile lips. "This has to stop."

"Funny," he growled into her mouth, "I'm feeling a lot better. Might even be cured."

Lightheaded, soaking wet, and out of her ever-loving mind, she succumbed to the sweet kisses of this gentle warrior. Her body fit perfectly where she'd landed, her belly alongside his hip, and her breasts pressed against his ribcage.

But when he inhaled a ragged breath, she grabbed the opportunity and placed a stern hand between them. Too bad it landed on his right pec. Temptation flared all over again.

But somehow… common sense ruled. "No," she squeaked. Okay, that tone wouldn't work. Persia pulled her hand off that hot bod and boldly cleared the rasp from her throat. "Hotrod, no. Let me up."

"Awww…"

There was that little boy within the badasssed male again. He was incorrigible, and she was an idiot. Alex would surely fire her for fraternizing with his client now.

"Hot chicken soup!" she nearly yelled as she extricated her arms from his and climbed very carefully out of the tub. "I'm not going far, just far enough to fix lunch and soup and… and…"

Her gaze settled on the manly muscle between his leg, and she lost her train of thought. Hotrod might be sick, but he wasn't dead. There was still a lot of life left in this guy. In *that* guy, too.

He held one muscled arm out to her, his fingertips fluttering for her to come back to him. "I'll get better quicker with you in here with me."

*And I'm in trouble.* "No, sugar. Playtime's over," she said airily, before she changed her mind. Or lost it. "Bath first, then soup, then sleep. I'll see what else there is to eat. Wait here. I'll be right b-back."

Persia left him sitting with the water still running and her heart pounding out a snappy salsa tango. He needed to eat and she needed to get her head back in the game. The real game. The TEAM game. Not Hotrod's game.

Distracted, she walked to her bedroom, jerked her last set of dry clothes out of her bag, and all but tore the wet clothes off. Thank goodness she'd dropped her smaller bag back at the front door, or everything she owned would've been soaked and ruined. Speaking of which…

That man! Her sat phone had been in her jeans pocket. Damn! Hurriedly, she retrieved it, and thank goodness for ruggedized, waterproof equipment. It was none the worse from the impromptu dunking. Izza hadn't called yet, but she would.

After Persia dressed and made sure her phone was operational, she peeked in on Hotrod to make sure he'd turned the tap off. What a sight, all that lean muscle against the back of the tub, his long arms stretched along the edge, his fingers curled over the lip. His breathing was more even, but till raspy enough she could hear it from where she stood and ogled.

Walker's poor blackened eyes were closed, and the dark circles under them made his face seem gaunt. He looked tired and alone. She nearly ran to him when she thought of all those bruises. He'd been kicked when he was down. That seemed to be the vicious circle of life he was stuck in. But he also needed decent food in his stomach. Knowing what she now knew about the ICC, she doubted he'd been fed properly. She wondered about the yacht he'd mentioned. Where was the gear bag he'd been so protective of in Florida?

# Chapter Twenty-Five

Life sure had a way of crapping all over a guy, but for once, something decent and good had happened to Walker. Out of nowhere, Persia had stepped back into his screwed-up life, and she didn't hate him like he'd expected. She'd even let him kiss her. As sick as he was, she'd kissed him back. And her fingers on his cheek and in his hair? They'd felt so damned sweet and gentle, he'd nearly teared up.

Ducking deeper into the chilled water, Walker let it wash the sweat and those damned tears off his face. He hadn't been this sick in years, didn't want to be now. High fevers made a man weak when he needed to be strong. Being sick could get a guy killed. But the weight of Persia's lush body on his when he'd tripped over the curb, and the brush of her sweet breasts against his tender ribs when he'd pulled her into the water, had given him an odd sense of strength that had nothing to do with physical fitness or core workouts.

Persia trusted him. She believed him, and she believed in him; he could read it in her eyes. Yet he hadn't done anything to deserve it. She knew he'd lied, yet she wasn't angry? That alone didn't compute. Most women, like What's-Her-Name, his ex, would've been hysterical drama queens if they'd awakened to find the guy beside them was gone.

But Persia had been sensible and firm. She'd read his trial transcript, too. Why? Who the hell was she? On the surface, it was one twisted, ugly story of cold-blooded murder. But most of it had been fiction invented by NCIS and the Navy JAG. So why was she here saving his sorry ass, especially after the way he'd treated her? When even the FBI was after him? And now the damned International Criminal Court...

Yet she'd called him sugar, like she actually liked him or something. Him. The man the Navy had condemned to prison, then disavowed instead of making sure he served time behind bars. Did she care that no one wanted him, not even the country he'd given his soul for? And if she knew all that, why didn't it matter to her? Or was this all too good to be true? It did feel like a dream, him being here instead of back there.

In the long run, he was too weak to do anything that would change his ever-growing legal nightmare. More than anything, well, except for Persia, he needed enough downtime to recoup his energy. Then he needed to find his damned bag with his ammo and his cash. His pistols and his yacht. Man, he'd lost everything.

"Hey," she murmured from where she was standing at the half-open door with a bottled sports drink in her hand. "Soup's ready, but I thought you'd like something to drink first. You'll need it to take these pills, a good strong antibiotic and four ibuprofens. You're not allergic to anything, are you?"

"Nope." He had to know. "Why are you doing this?"

That question drew her into the room. Closing the door, she sat at the edge of the white, plastic shower chair and handed him the drink. "Take these first, then we'll talk," she ordered sweetly, her other palm extended with several pills in the center of it.

His arm felt heavy when he reached for the pills and the bottle, but, oh well. Tilting his head back, Walker tossed the meds down his throat, then emptied the sports drink. It was ice cold and felt good going down. When he finished, he wiped the back of his hand over his mouth and asked, "Why do you still call me Hotrod?"

"Would you rather I call you Walker?"

"That's my name."

"Okay then. Walker Judge. Why were you incarcerated at the ICC? How'd you get here to the Netherlands all the way from Florida? You mentioned a yacht, where is it?"

He stretched, needing to see more of her. "I have no idea. But one thing at a time. For starters, I was in Minas Gerais the same time you were, and Agent Juarez is a damned good friend of mine. Our helo went down off the northern coast of Brazil, where he and I took out a dozen or so Matryoshka Dolls. You know, those blood thirsty Russian assassins. But when the Army Night Stalkers came to rescue us, I split."

He let that settle. As he expected, she blinked those beautiful browns, while absorbing the minute intricacies behind his revelation. That was one of her tells, blinking. "I wasn't aware the Dolls were active in Brazil."

"They weren't until Orlando Zapata decided to trade one of his gold mines for three Russian ICBMs. That's why the Dolls showed. They must've known about the transaction, then tried to sabotage the deal. But Agent Juarez got to Oz and the Russians first. By the time the Dolls arrived, everyone was dead, and the missiles were leaking radiation. The Dolls set explosive charges to detonate the nukes, but Agent Juarez took the Dolls out before they could blow Minas Gerais off the map."

"They would've killed thousands if they'd detonated those ICBMs," Persia breathed.

It was good knowing she was up to speed on the latest terrorist threat out of old Mother Russia. The Matryoshka Dolls, so named because so many double and triple agents comprised their ranks, were one of the cruelest mobs on the planet today.

Planting her elbows on her knees, she cupped her chin in her palm. "I know Agent Juarez. I was there when he ended Domingo Zapata. He's a good man. I watched him step between the woman and little boy he loves, so they didn't have to watch Zapata die."

"I know. You told me that back in Florida."

"I made pancakes…"

"Blueberry pancakes…"

"You wanted peaches…"

Something sizzling hot arced between them. He let his gaze drop to the black polo that did nothing to hide her lovely assets. "I'll always want peaches." *And the rest of you.*

"But not now," she told him firmly, her pretty cheeks blushing like the skin of a succulent, sun-kissed peach.

Sending a wave of water splashing over the side, Walker rolled to one hip. "What else do you need to know? Oh, yeah. How I ended up here. It's been a long journey. Before I found the yacht, sometimes I swam. Sometimes I walked."

"Why'd you swim from Cuba?"

"Believe it or not, I love my country. I… I just wanted to go home one last time."

A different kind of light flickered in her eyes. "I saw you kiss the beach."

"I didn't murder those people."

"People?" Her head canted as if she didn't know what he was talking about. "There are others besides your commanding officer?"

Damn it to hell. She hadn't known about the other charges. But she did now.

"Never mind," he growled, closing his eyes against the inevitable. Christ, he'd had it. How could he stand against additional, bogus murder charges, when he couldn't even defend himself against the original charge? It seemed pointless to try anymore, and running for his life hadn't worked. Goff's ghost certainly had a long reach.

"I said I believe you, Walker Judge. Do you hear me? I do, but we're going to have to prove your innocence, aren't we? And to do that, we need to uncover the lies and find the real killer."

There went that trusting *'we'* again.

He opened his eyes to the light touch of Persia's sweet kiss in the middle of his forehead.

"I honestly don't know how." He lifted a hand and ticked his crimes off his fingers. "The FBI wants me for murdering Wallace Goff. After I serve that sentence in Leavenworth, Britain will extradite me for a terrorist threat against their queen. Then, the US Army wants my ass for the deaths of the thirteen Green Berets I allegedly killed during that same event at Buckingham Palace. And now..."

Walker couldn't bring himself tell her about all those deaths at the wedding in Jordan. *Enough already!* "Get away from me! Just go. Leave. I'm bad luck."

He would've pushed her out of his arms, but Persia pushed him first. Flat to his back, his head darned near going under water. Not breaking eye contact, she climbed out of her black jeans, ripped the black polo over her head, and tossed it onto the chair. Bending forward, she gave him an eyeful when she shimmied out of her bra and panties, her hot gaze still on his.

His heart stopped beating. "What are you doing?"

"Sealing the deal," she replied with a shy glance over his long, naked body. "Move over, Hotrod. I'm coming back in."

Walker couldn't move quickly enough. Extending a hand to make sure she didn't slip, he held her tiny fingers while she stepped into the tub. As if that wasn't tantalizing enough, she spread those long legs over him, bent her knees, and sat on his thighs. Which gave him a bird's eye view that stopped his lungs.

"I… I…" Damn, he couldn't speak! "I don't understand you."

"That's the point, isn't it? You think you know everything, but you don't, do you? And because you don't, you feel out of control and unbalanced. You've always got to be the top dog in charge. But this time, you're not."

No kidding.

Lifting one arm over her head, she closed her eyes and ran a hand over her sleek black ponytail, loosened the tie and—

Walker damned near swallowed his tongue. He'd forgotten how long her hair was. How luxurious it had felt slipping through his fingers. How much it had soothed him when it brushed over his belly and chest. How much he loved the shine and shimmer. The flowery scent of her…

Tipping forward, Persia aligned her core over his rigid cock, which, like the brainless idiot it was, still pointed at him, when it really wanted her. He couldn't make his eyes not watch the way the lush mauve tips of her breasts bobbed into the water.

"This might not be the best time to… you know. Do this," he reminded her even as his palms cupped those warm, swaying, seductive globes. "I wasn't much good in bed last time. Remember?"

"Men. You all seem to think intimacy begins and ends with an orgasm."

*Well, duh.*

Persia reached between them, lifting her backside as the water she displaced lapped at his chin, while her fingers curled around him. And Walker thought he'd died and gone to heaven.

"But sometimes, it's more about you and me connecting emotionally instead of just physically, don't you think?" That one long, languorous stroke from root to tip got his full undivided attention. Every drop of blood in his brain went south.

"If you say so." He was all ears now. All cock, too.

"This is just about us, Hotrod. You and me," she purred, her hair a gorgeous, glossy curtain of ebony spilling off her shoulders, the wet ends of it brushing over his belly and pecs like downy angel feathers from heaven. Tickling. Inciting him. Making him forget… everything.

"We," she breathed through lips as red and sweet as the first strawberries in spring.

"Yeah. Us." *Oh, God, kill me now…* He'd turned into a brain-dead moron. *Strawberries in spring? Who thought of crap like that?*

Positioning him at the entrance to heaven, where he ardently wanted it to go, Persia lowered her backside slowly.

The bathwater stilled. Her eyes fixed on him, she gradually impaled herself to the hilt. Sparks. He could've sworn he saw sparks when, at last, her body encompassed his dick, and they melted together. The water wasn't cold anymore.

Moaning, that sexy sound coming from the back of her throat, she wiggled her beautiful ass and seated him deep. Again they were one. No borders. No boundaries. No in between. Just skin to skin. Lover to lover. Hot, hard heat to slick, warm heaven.

His hips lifted, sealing them more fully together, just like she'd said. With him inside as deep as he could go, he watched her head and all that hair tip backward. With a feminine growl, at the same time, she thrust her plump, beautiful breasts more fully into his icy-cold hands.

Like a heat-seeking missile, Walker took control of the diamond peak within reach. Breathing hard, he sucked her nipple into his mouth and gave her what she needed.

Squirming over his hips now, she straightened and crossed her arms behind his head, trapping his face to her breast. Friction had never felt so damned good. So hot. Nor smelled as sweet. Tingles ran up the back of his legs, urging one hard thrust after another. Bathwater splashed. Walker didn't care. He had what he wanted, and injured or not, he would deliver this time.

Leaning back under water until his shoulders were covered, he pulled her down to his level, laving her other rosy-hued nipple. He hollowed his cheeks and suckled, flicking his tongue over and around it until—Persia's legs stiffened. That was what he wanted. Her to scream and smile.

Those amazing pelvic muscles of hers contracted like a fist, and 'Go time!' roared up his spine. It was all he could do to hold off and not blow his second chance to pleasure her. He didn't have to wait long. Groaning now, her frantic body took over, squeezing and melting and—

Persia growled like a wildcat! Man, he loved the throaty, primal rumbles coming from deep in her chest. It vibrated through her body and into his. When the unspoken command resonating from the depths of her body told him she'd reached her zenith, his body obeyed like the slave it was. With one last thrust, he exploded up and into her. Everything. He gave more and more until…

The power of that release all but took the top of his head off. He hadn't come this quickly or this hard since he'd been a horny teenager.

It wasn't simply sex, where one woman and one man experienced separate orgasms, this time. This was one magnificent coming. Together. Simultaneously, a cataclysmic clash of two dynamic halves joining into one magnificent whole. The exquisite power of it rippled through Walker. Like a powerful tsunami, it began at his toes, then climbed upward through his body, sweeping every last worry, thought, and care away. The oddest surge of tranquility invaded his soul as it ebbed, replacing his fear. He was a man again.

Like a mermaid out of Neptune's deepest depths, Persia arched forward, sending the long strands of wet hair over her head in a magnificent arc. Bathwater rained down on both of them as dripping wet black ribbons splattered against his face, and into his eyes. Walker smiled from within the velvet cage she'd just trapped him in. He was so damned bewitched, whipped, and lost. She was his goddess. His North Star. Maybe his everything.

His hands sank to the delicate curve of her waist, his fingers splayed over the plush globes of the tops of her ass. Her palms balanced on his chest, over his pounding heart. And suddenly, all his aches and pains and worries vanished. There was only Persia and this beautiful thing between them in this shiny, wet, new world. Their world. There was only hope and trust and this gift of the one woman who, somehow, believed in him.

Tears sprang to Walker's eyes. Persia Coltrane had saved him. Again. She'd reached out when all others had betrayed him, and she'd jerked his dumb ass up and out of the well he'd dug himself into. A woman he barely knew had just given him precisely what he'd needed to continue the fight. She'd given him hope and faith in himself.

Damn, she must've seen the raw emotion on his face. He couldn't have hidden it if he'd tried. Hadn't thought he needed to, not with Persia. Like one of those lofty angels of old, she bowed down from what had to be heaven and pressed the sweetest, lightest kiss to the center of his forehead—like a blessing.

He closed his eyes, not sure he wasn't dreaming. It seemed unreal, the woman he'd run out on, kissing him like he'd never been kissed before. So tenderly. With such kindness. Such—love.

Almost made him believe in happily-ever-after. Too bad he knew better, but for now...

Walker held everything he'd ever wanted in the palm of his hand.

# Chapter Twenty-Six

Easing away from the kisses she'd just rained all over his face, Persia looked down on the man she was beginning to care about enough to die for. Walker looked sad. Tortured. His eyes were closed, and those gorgeous laugh lines drooped down instead of up. She hoped she hadn't been too rough on his poor battered body.

But he'd seemed to need her, and she'd gotten carried away. At least this time, he'd had no problems performing. In fact, they'd both come quickly and at the same time, which was a novelty in the less-than-grand scope of Persia's limited, unsatisfying sexual experiences. Her previous male friends had usually left her feeling used and unfulfilled before they'd rolled over and started snoring.

Not Walker. She hadn't ever climaxed so easily or this fantastically before. Not once in her life, and she really liked it. Her entire body still thrummed with rippling waves of the sweetest pleasure. Yet this delicious encounter hadn't seemed to help him. His entire countenance had gone dark. He seemed totally bereft, lost, and lonely, as if he hadn't yet found whatever he needed to be whole again.

Which didn't sit well with Persia, not after the spectacular high he'd given her. Balancing on her knees and palms, she lifted her backside, intending to distance herself from him and let him finish his bath. She could take a hint.

But she didn't get far. "No, stay," he whispered, his fingers tight at her waist, his voice filled with anguish. "Damnit, Persia, don't go. I'm sorry it's over so fast, but I—"

"You're what? Sorry?" she asked as she settled back onto his still ready-to-go cock. "For making me smile like a starstruck idiot?"

He opened his eyes and looked up at her then. "But I thought—"

She dipped down nose to nose with him again, her muscles still quivering from that spectacular orgasm. "You silly, silly man. Relax. You just made my day in a big way. And I do mean big."

His chest lifted with a huff as his lips curled into a hesitant smile. "You're just saying that."

Persia grinned back at him. "Yeah. You're right; I faked it. All of it. And this amazing body…" An aftershock shivered up her spine from her core. So fast and so hot, it took her breath. She closed her eyes to enjoy the sublime sensation of it. "Whew," she breathed when it ended. "Wow. Now, as I was saying, my body doesn't exactly know how to lie, so—"

A genuine grin lit Walker's face. "You did?" he asked with amazement in his tone.

"Yes, I surely did. You did, too. And no worries, I'm protected."

His face paled. "Shit, I forgot—"

"No, you *got* exactly what you deserved," she purred, her fingertips fluttering over his flat, do-nothing nipples, teasing him. Wishing this was the start of something out of this world. "I make sure I'm protected because I never know when I'll have to go international. It's a big world out there. Shit happens."

He sank deeper into the chilly water, taking her down with him, his fingers firmly on her backside. "I think my fever's gone. What do you think?"

Her breasts flattened onto his chest when she wiggled her hands and arms around his neck. "You just want me to say you're still hot."

"Well? Am I?" That sexy smile curving his mouth did the trick. Those handsome laugh lines were back in full force.

Persia ran her wet fingers through his hair, careful not to manhandle the bump on his head. When she did, he closed his eyes. But this time, he had the contented look of a ferocious jungle cat that had just been tamed, and that loved being petted. She could've petted him all day. Or at least until Izza returned. Which wouldn't be much longer.

Leaning against his cheek, she whispered in his ear, "You're still hot. So's your soup. Let's eat."

Persia had prepared a thick, creamy roasted chicken soup, topped off with toasted cinnamon croquets and sliced hard bread on the side. Once again, Walker sank his tired ass to the stool at the breakfast bar, dizzy and not certain he could keep anything down. But going to try.

Dressed in her black outfit again, she'd wrapped her damp hair into a thick braid, then wound it high on her head. Women seemed to work magic when it came to their hair. He couldn't see a single pin or stick or one of those toothy clasp thingies in those shiny tendrils. Yet her hair stayed right where she'd put it. Only a few strands trailed down her neck. How'd she do that?

She unsnapped the metal clip on the dripping wet, turquoise bottle of water in her hands. "Drink," she ordered after she'd filled his glass.

Tipping his head back, he emptied the glass. But when he brought his head back down, the world spun. Shit, not now. He refused to pass out.

Yet Persia was no dummy. "Why don't you just get into bed? I'll bring a tray with—"

"No." He waved the notion off as if he were healthy. "I'm good. Let's eat."

Persia never sighed or huffed dramatically like she knew better than him, just took the stool at his left and lifted her spoon. "Alex stocks his safe houses with the best. You like?"

Walker nodded, focused more on proving he wasn't a weakling. "It's quite good," he said after one taste. Then another. "Remind me who Alex is."

"My boss. After college, I worked for the FBI, then crossed over to the Agency for a while. Problem is, when you're federal, they think they own your soul. I couldn't live like that, not after that last job in South America."

"I know, but how the hell did a contractor get you into the ICC? Your boss is just a defense contractor, isn't he?"

A curious smile tweaked the corners of Persia's mouth. "Have you ever heard of Jed McCormack?"

"Sure. The billionaire behind most of the failsafe military gear and equipment currently out in the field. Met him in Iraq a while back. Sure wish he'd run for president. Seems like he's the only real advocate us guys have."

"Well, word in my office is that Alex saved his son Brady years ago. Jed never forgot."

Walker took another spoonful, then dunked a slice of bread into his bowl. Not bad. Not bad at all. "I get McCormack. He's wealthy and powerful, but your boss—"

"If you ask me, Alex Stewart is just as powerful as Jed. He worked a covert op for President Adams a couple years back, and he knows the Queen of England. Might even be able to help you with that false charge of terrorism hanging over your head."

That reminder spoiled breakfast or whatever this meal was. Walker put his spoon on the counter. "You said you've read my trial transcript."

"Uh huh," she mumbled as she leaned over her bowl and angled a sopping slice of bread toward her mouth.

And Walker was entranced. Those lips. Every move they made turned his cock into a steel spike, that even now, wanted into that mouth and every last bit of her attention. Thank goodness for the thick cloth napkin on his lap.

Persia didn't seem to notice his arousal. Daintily, her tongue slipped over her bottom lip, catching that single drop of getaway soup before she turned her attention on Walker.

"Yes, I've read your transcript, and I know your background. You have no secrets with me. I know your record, and that's where things don't line up. The timeline in your OMPF isn't accurate with what the prosecutor told the jury. Yet not once did your attorney challenge anything the Navy brass said. He just kept rolling over, asking them to kick his balls again and again."

Walker bowed his head. "I couldn't afford some hotshot lawyer back then. I'm a frog, not Jed Freakin' McCormack."

"But you've got a private attorney now." She made that a statement.

"I do. My grandfather left me some money. It's all I've got left, only now…" Shit. He'd need ten times that much to prove his innocence.

"So where were you during that leave you requested, but which the Navy declares they have no record?"

And this was where the rubber met the road. Walker debated telling Persia why he hadn't produced receipts that would've, without a doubt, verified his trip into Guatemala. But he'd made a promise to a little girl, and he wasn't going back on his word just to save his ass. Emily was the important one, not him.

"I can't say," he told Persia honestly.

"Or you *won't* say," she corrected. "I get it. You were on private business. Never mind. Forget I asked. That's where my boss comes in. I don't know everyone for sure, but Alex has several of us working your case." She lifted one dainty finger. "Me." Then another and another, as she said, "Former USMC hardass, Izza Maher, former Navy Intelligence Officer, Ember Dennison, and I'm not a hundred percent sure, but I think former SEAL Adam Torrey's also working on setting you free. Don't worry. We'll find out."

Walker about choked. "Adam works for Stewart?"

Persia's head bobbed. "Of course. Only the best guys and gals work for Alex, and trust me…" She seemed to be saying that a lot. *Trust me.* Walker was beginning to. "Alex wouldn't be digging into your case if he didn't think you were worth it."

A shiver raced over Walker's shoulders. He'd been fighting this battle all by himself for so damned long. No one had stepped forward to stand by him or for him until now. A stranger. A guy he didn't know, had never heard of before, had suddenly stepped forward to challenge the entire damned Navy? Stewart thought a lot of him, some guy he didn't even know?

Walker stared at his soup. Afraid to hope. Afraid not to. "I know Adam. We've served together. He still jumping out of perfectly good airplanes?"

Persia's smile warmed him. "Of course. We all have to be HALO qualified, but he's our flying squirrel, and you should see him with Squeaks. You'd never know—"

"You? You're HALO qualified, too?" Unbelievable.

Her one brow lifted. "I'm qualified for lots of things, honey."

"But he's… Adam's a father? What kind of name's Squeaks?"

"Squeaks is Adam's son, and that's just his handle. His real name's Jimmy Malone Torrey, but he earned that name by living, despite being born two months premature, on the desert island where Adam and Squeaks' mother crash-landed. You might've heard of her. Shannon Reagan, the billionaire, Paul Reagan's daughter. Remember him?"

Walker certainly remembered the asshat who'd delivered more POS equipment than life-saving gear to the Navy before he'd died.

Persia continued, "I can't wait to get you back to Alexandria, Virginia. That's where TEAM headquarters is. Alex is a hardass, but I think he'll be thrilled to meet you in person."

That'd be different, someone 'thrilled' to meet him, not just glad they'd arrested him. Walker dared to hope. "But he doesn't know me."

Persia's pretty clean hand landed over Walker's battle-scarred knuckles. "When I applied to work for Alex, I was pretty sure he'd fire me every time I turned around. Whatever you do, don't call him 'sir.' He hates that. Just Mr. Stewart, okay?"

Her fingers fluttered over Walker's. "He's former USMC, and he's lethal. But he's got something against officers. I'm fairly certain he's been working your case for a while now. I'm just glad he asked me to come get you." Her voice softened. "And I'm glad I was smart enough to leave the Bureau and look for a better job, or I wouldn't be here right now…"

With every word, her head had tilted closer to his. Man, Walker wanted to kiss her.

"I'm glad you're here," he murmured, sure he shouldn't kiss her, but just as sure he would. There seemed to be nothing between them that they couldn't conquer together.

Until the front door slammed open and one angry Hispanic woman with fire flashing in her black eyes bellowed. "Get the fuck away from her!"

# Chapter Twenty-Seven

Persia nearly swallowed her tongue. "Izza! No! This is Hotrod. It's okay!"

"I don't care who he is, I said back the fuck off!" Izza kicked the front door closed behind her. "On the floor! Face down! Now, fat ass!"

Obediently, Walker lifted both hands and slid off his stool.

But Persia was quicker. Turning on her companion agent, she grabbed his arm before he made it to his knees. "No, Izza. You back off. You've read his transcripts. He's not guilty."

"I don't know that, and neither do you." Izza's pistol still aimed at Walker.

"Yes, I do," Persia declared sternly, her temper up now. "He's sick. For God's sake, look at him, Izza. He can barely sit up straight long enough to eat, and he shouldn't be kneeling. I've given him a first dose of antibiotics, but he's not strong enough—"

Izza's neck jerked so quickly around, her ponytail flipped over her shoulder. "You what?! You're playing doctor now? With this joker?"

"It's all right," Walker said as he clasped both hands behind his head. "Let me go, Persia."

"No, it's not all right, and it's not fair!" Persia told him even as he tilted forward. When his eyes rolled back in his head, she barely had time to slide beneath his head and shoulders to buffer his fall. With a grunt, he collapsed on her thighs, his face to her belly, one hot arm circling her waist. Man, he was burning up again.

"Damn it, Izza! You're a mother! You're supposed to be able to tell if someone's really sick or not! Can't you see he's injured? Maybe even dying?"

"He could be faking!"

Persia had her hands all over Hotrod's head, neck, and shoulders by then. "Get me the digital thermometer from my first-aid kit. I should've taken his temp before. He's hotter than hell."

"Why didn't you if he's *so-o-o-o* sick?" Izza had her full swagger on. Sometimes, she could be as dense as a man.

"Because I had to cool him down first, smart ass. He's been beaten, and he was already hot to the touch when we got here."

"What the hell have you done?"

"What you would've done if you'd been here. What took you so long?"

"That creep went after Hans Koning. I couldn't just leave him there holding the bag after you and Judge escaped, could I?"

"What creep? Where's Koning?"

Izza jerked her head toward the closed front door. "Standing outside. Waiting for me to let him in. One of the guards said he helped you and Judge escape. Is that true?"

"Yes. Let the poor guy in. He's the only reason I was able to get Hotrod out of that place. We need to talk with him."

Again with the cocky head tilt. "Not until you tell me why you keep calling that bastard Hotrod?"

*Oh, shit.* Persia's world was about to implode. She might as well come clean. *Okay then. Here goes.* "Because that man is Lieutenant Walker Judge, and Hotrod's his SEAL handle."

"And you know that how?"

Persia's heart stuttered up her throat, suffocating her. This was where she lost her new-found career and her hard-won reputation, and where Alex would fire her. But that rep was based on her spot-on instincts, solid undercover work, and the sheer willpower to get the hard jobs done. She could've walked away from that mission into Domingo Zapata's lair any number of times, yet she hadn't. No matter how ugly or tough that heinous cluster of bunkers he'd called home had gotten, she'd stayed true to the mission. She'd followed her heart and completed one helluva nasty-assed operation. She'd done the damned job!

Swallowing hard, she faced her best friend and answered truthfully. "Because I watched him come ashore in Florida. He'd just swum a hundred miles from Cuba, Izza. Without tether or one bit of back-up support. I saw him get on his knees and kiss America, and then I—"

"You. Kissed. Him." Every word out of Izza's mouth was a vicious shot to Persia's heart.

Squaring her shoulders, she raised her chin. Her mother had always said it was tougher to stand up to friends than enemies. "Yes, Izza, I did, and I'm glad I did. He's not who everyone says he is. I know."

"Because you kissed…" Izza's big brown eyes widened. "You think you know him? Oh, crap, you let him… You and he… You didn't!" The censure in her hiss could have melted iron. "What have you done?!"

"No, Izza. What have *you* done? Judge him like everyone else? Condemn him before you know what you're talking about or what's he's been through? Were you there when he allegedly murdered his CO? Do you know for certain he did it?"

"Crap, Persia, are you sure he's innocent?"

Easing Walker to the floor, Persia stepped into Izza's line of fire. "Yes," she said, pressing her hand to her heart. "I. Know. The same way I knew Zapata would believe me when I faced him down in his hellhole. The same way I was able to nail his ugly ass to the wall. Trust me. I know damned well that Walker Judge is innocent."

At last, Izza wavered. Her glance zipped to where Walker lay unconscious, then back to Persia. It took a couple more seconds before she lowered her piece. But her chest still heaved with every hard breath. Her chin was still up, and the weapon remained in her hand, challenging Persia to give her more proof than just her heart.

"Read the transcripts over again if you don't believe me," Persia begged. "Let me show you what I found. What I saw. I've marked several sections. It's almost as if Ember laid out a defense case for Hotrod. It's all there."

"You mean Walker Judge, damn it. Stop calling him Hotrod," Izza hissed. "Crap, yeah, I read his file. It's all there, and it's clear as day, Coltrane. Judge did it. Christ, there were witnesses who saw him go into Goff's home. Morgue shots of the dead body that he admitted, in court, were Goff's."

"But he wasn't even in the country when Goff was murdered."

"Is that what he said? How gullible are you?"

"But witnesses can be bought. Morgue shots can be photoshopped."

"The Navy doesn't want him back!"

Persia cocked her head. "Wait a minute," she murmured, her heart breaking all over for this unwanted, yet *most-wanted* man. "They disavowed him?"

Izza's lips thinned. "That's what I said. Nobody wants him. Shit, I'll bet his folks don't even want him back."

A wave of empathy welled in Persia's heart, crushing her. "They're both dead, Izza," she said quietly. "They died within months of each other a couple years ago. Soon after, his only brother was killed in action. He has no family."

Izza's olive complexion paled. "I... I didn't know that."

"It's in Ember's file, honey. Could it be you missed other things, too?" Which made Persia's case feel even more solid. "Think, Izza. If he were Connor, would you go along with whatever the Navy said, or would you know, deep in your gut, that they lied? That something was wrong if they'd accused a man like your husband of cold-blooded murder? Wouldn't you do everything you could to help him? Wouldn't you fight for him?"

Izza rolled one shoulder. "Connor'd never kill a man in cold blood."

"Not even when the woman he loved was being tortured by—"

"Yeah, yeah, stop it, all right. Just stop!" Izza bellowed, even as she waved Persia off. "Walker Judge isn't your husband!"

Izza might turn belligerent even when faced with reasonable explanations, but she couldn't deny the fact that Connor had run to rescue her from the Mexican drug cartel that had gone ape-shit crazy in Utah. How he'd been injured when he'd gotten there, yet had walked straight into the airplane hangar where she'd been held, bleeding and all, with a dozen murderers firing at him. With shotguns and rifles pointed at his head. But he hadn't gotten shot. Hadn't hesitated. Not even once.

Persia knew for a fact that Connor had mowed those bastards down, then cried like a baby when he'd finally had Izza's battered body back in his arms. When he'd been convinced they'd beaten her so hard that she and his unborn baby were dead… That they'd killed everything he'd marched into Hell to save.

One didn't have to work for Alex very long before hearing all The TEAM's legends. How tall, handsome Mark Houston had rescued Libby from yet another cartel, this one from Russia, who'd buried her alive. How affable, gentle Harley had interrupted a deranged FBI agent inside his apartment. The guy had been prepared to slice Judy into bite-sized pieces, then wash the remnants of her body down the drain. But Harley had busted his door down, then busted that murderer. Shot him dead, then broke down because he'd almost lost the woman he adored.

Then there was the story of stalwart Gabe Cartwright, who'd been so certain that he'd gotten Alex killed, that he'd sworn his soul to protect Kelsey. In the course of that warrior's vow, he'd met Shelby, the woman who'd challenged his warrior ethics, his second amendment rights, and ultimately, the woman he'd taken a bullet for.

But the legend Persia loved best was how Alex had rescued a complete stranger, a battered woman, in the middle of the great Pacific Northwest. How he'd sheltered Kelsey and protected her from that day forward. How that hard-assed jarhead had become Kelsey's most faithful servant and her best friend. Persia still couldn't comprehend how those two had ever made a child, but Lexie was proof that they had, wasn't she? And because there had once been hope for Alex, there could be hope for Walker Judge.

"Call it my sixth sense," Persia pleaded. "Hell, call it women's intuition, I don't care. But I do know Hotrod, and I believe him. He didn't do what the Navy accused him of, and it's up to you and me to prove it."

# Chapter Twenty-Eight

Walker smiled as he lay there with his sweaty cheek planted against the hardwood floor. He'd never felt so bad, nor so good, at the same time before. Persia believed in him enough to fight for him. How rare was that? Only Team 18 had ever fought for him as hard as she was fighting her companion agent now. Which seemed surreal, a mere woman who only weighed a hundred ten—if that—ready to take on the world for a man she—liked? Had she said love? His head was buzzing and he couldn't recall. She'd said a lot of nice things to him and about him. But he was pretty sure she hadn't said that word. Not love.

*But you love her…*

*Yeah, well…*

He squeezed his eyes tight against his insistent conscience. Or whatever that nagging voice in his head was. Love her? Hell, he didn't even know her. Not yet. But he wanted to. An ordinary date would be nice. Maybe two or three… Then maybe love might enter the picture.

She was at his side again, pulling him into her arms. Tipping his head to her chest. Breathing her sweet spirit over his forehead and into his face. "You should see the bruises on his back. This man's been beaten. He's injured and sick," she told her friend Izza in no uncertain terms. "Tell Koning to come in, then help me get Hotrod into bed. First bedroom on the right."

Walker stared up at her. "Hey, hey, hey," he huffed like an idiot. He had so much more to say, but the words wouldn't come. Even if they did, he wasn't sure they'd come out right.

Izza grunted. "Next to yours? Are you kidding me?!"

"Will you knock it off and help?" Persia's exclamation thundered through every cell of Walker's weary body. Felt warm and pleasant. But at the same time, it felt like a shockwave of what he'd always thought the word of God would've felt like. If God had ever spoken to him.

"I'm... good," he tried to tell her, but it came out unintelligible, sounded more like a horse talking. A *hoarse horse. Ha!* Now he knew he was delirious, and none of this was real. Too bad. But a beautiful, graceful, smart woman like Persia would never believe someone like him. Would she?

Then they were lifting him, and he was surprised how strong these two women were. Walker lost track of time and space, simple things like that. The bed beneath him was too soft and too warm. Too small for his long legs. Someone turned the sun off, and he was lost in a night with no stars. Cool, gentle hands moved over his body. His face. Someone pressed the sweetest kiss to his cheek. Then quiet, blessed darkness.

"So someone beat the shit out of him," Izza groused. "So what? That doesn't make him innocent."

By then, Persia had doctored Hotrod as much as she could. She'd changed the butterfly strips over his battered eye and left him in his room with the lights out, a cold compress under his neck, and a bottled water on his nightstand. He'd been talking out of his head, not making sense, and she regretted making love to an injured man. That hadn't been smart, and yet she couldn't have stopped herself, hadn't tried. He'd needed the reconnection and the intimacy. So had she.

Hans Koning sat by himself at the front room table, thumbing through his cell phone like a high school teenager after spring break on the beach with a new batch of porn. Izza had set him up with a bowl of soup, several slices of bread, and a bottled water, but he had yet to touch anything. All he seemed to want was whatever was on his phone.

"No, but maybe this transcript will," Persia murmured, setting Ember's file on the breakfast bar between herself and Izza. "I marked the places where, when the prosecutor CO John Cudahy finished questioning witnesses, and Hotrod's attorney, failed to cross-examine. He didn't object very often throughout the entire trial, but when he did, the judge over-ruled him anyway. It was as if Kroft didn't care whether his client was convicted or not."

"Ah, yes," Hans muttered from the front room. "Look at this, ladies."

Persia made room at the counter for him to stand between them.

"I knew I'd seen Lieutenant Judge before yesterday. Of course, back then, I didn't know I'd get to serve as his counsel one day. This is a news clip taken during the early stages of his trial. Tell me what you see." He turned the volume up and his phone on its side, so both Izza and Persia could watch.

The panoramic view of the courtroom on Naval Base San Diego, California, had been taken from the side of the courtroom. Whoever the cameraman was, he'd caught Hotrod's brave profile when he was led in between two USN Masters-at-arms and escorted to the left of the two polished wooden tables facing the bench.

He'd worn his dark blue uniform that day and was shackled with both wrists cuffed to the reinforced nylon transport belt around his waist. Yet he carried himself with pride, his shoulders squared and his chin up. He smiled and said something to his guards when he was seated and his cuffs were chained to the table. One guard clapped a hand on Hotrod's right shoulder, which, to Persia, looked like a show of sympathetic support.

All snapped to attention when the presiding judge, clean-cut Captain Spenser Cole, strode briskly in from a side door and took his place behind the raised bench. Polished wood panels everywhere. Witness box to the left of the judge's seat. Court reporter at the right of the bench. Jury box to Hotrod's far right. Two Masters-at-arms, one at each side of the bench. Five witnesses, two Marines, three sailors. Four males, one female Marine. Interestingly, no SEALs were present in the jury box.

That alone raised Persia's hackles. "According to UCMJ rules, he should've been tried by a jury of his peers. I don't see a single SEAL in that box, do you?"

Hans nodded. "That is true. Keep watching."

A young man in dress blues hurried up the center aisle to sit with Hotrod. Had to be Lieutenant Cameron Kroft, the JAG's defense attorney. Kroft and Hotrod conferred for a minute or two, then Judge Cole nodded for the prosecutor, USN Commander John Cudahy, to begin.

"Was this Judge's first day in court?" Izza whispered.

"It was," he replied quietly.

Persia watched Cudahy call his first witness, an older civilian named Steven Horowitz, who claimed to be Hotrod's neighbor. After he was sworn in, Horowitz testified Hotrod owned property on Ocean Beach, not far from Goff's home. He swore he'd seen Hotrod break into Wallace Goff's residence the night of the murder. When asked to point out the murderer, Horowitz boldly stabbed a finger at Hotrod and yelled, "You should be ashamed!"

That caused a stir among the spectators, but NCIS Kroft didn't object. Didn't even squirm. Other than leaning into Hotrod for a word, Kroft seemed content to watch, rather than engage.

Clearly aggravated, Hotrod rolled his shoulder when the first witness left the stand without being challenged. He tipped his head into his attorney, but Kroft waved him off without looking at him. Hotrod leaned back in his chair.

When Izza peered closer to look at the small screen, Persia shook her head, annoyed at herself. "Wait. I'll get my laptop. That way, we can all see better."

"That'd sure help," Izza grunted.

Persia brushed Izza's sarcasm off, retrieved her bag, and quickly returned to the kitchen. "Gather around, folks," she said as she set her laptop on the table, then took a seat. "If we're going to work together, we might as well get comfortable."

"Good idea," Hans replied, loosening his tie before he took a position at Persia's left. Izza sat at her right.

In minutes, Persia located the website for the San Diego paper responsible for the news clip footage. She started fast-forwarding to get back to where they'd been, until Izza's hand settled over her wrist. "No, let's watch from the beginning. Seeing the trial's a lot different than just reading the transcript."

Again, Persia watched Hotrod being escorted into the courtroom. But this time, she wasn't focused on him as much as the long-legged woman wearing cream-colored designer silk slacks, a slinky mint-green sequined halter top, and Jacki O sunglasses, in the last row of the spectators' section.

"I didn't know court-martials were open to the public," she murmured out of the side of her mouth.

"Only to those with vested interests," Hans murmured back.

"Like a wife?" Izza asked.

"Or girlfriends and family members, yes," he answered.

"Which is she?" Persia asked, pointing to the woman in question.

A curious half-smile curled his lips. "She is worth watching. Please continue."

Well, that was no answer. But Persia watched the woman closer while the proceedings dragged on.

"Crap, where the hell's Judge's defense?" Izza asked, her index finger stabbing at NCIS Kroft, "because that jerk isn't doing a damned thing." Almost sounded like she was beginning to care.

Hans smiled. So did Persia. If anything, NCIS Kroft looked relaxed. Unruffled by his client's growing angst. Where Hotrod's demeanor had changed from professional calm to frustration, Kroft appeared dead from the neck up.

"Who's that guy?" Izza asked, her fingertip on another officer in dress blues, also sitting at the back of the courtroom.

"I do not know," Hans answered.

Persia didn't know either, but whoever that officer was, he was now on her radar.

CO Cudahy called Miss Sunday Night Breeze to the stand.

Persia nearly gagged when Miss Breeze—which sure sounded like a stripper's name—flounced to the witness box on platform heels with three-inch soles. She was the long-legged woman at the back of the courtroom in those Jacki O sunglasses. Once seated, she removed her shades, raised her right hand to the square, blinked her overly kohl-smudged eyes at Cudahy, then solemnly gushed to "tell the truth, so help me, God."

"You've got to be kidding," Izza growled. "That's his ex? Sounds like *Jessica Rabbit*."

Looked like *Jessica Rabbit*, too, with all that red hair, mascara, and silicone. Her halter top barely held what had to be 44Ds, matched with a too-tiny waist that only made those puppies look bigger. A sick kind of feeling rolled over in Persia's gut. Hotrod dated a stripper? That was his ex? Had they lived together? What kind of man was he, an idiot? Besides being male, which all by itself explained everything Miss Breeze represented. Sex. Sex. And more sex.

Izza made a funny sound.

"Shut up," Persia ordered, even as the rock in her gut dropped into a bottomless pit.

"Can't help it," Izza mumbled, her fingers on her lips as if she needed to suppress the snotty chuckle emanating from her big mouth. "Sorry, but Navy SEALs have a chick in every port. Everyone knows that."

Persia wanted to deny the accusation, but SEALs were known for being some of the toughest, rowdiest men on the planet. They fought hard, played harder, and fucked like there was no tomorrow. Which for some of them, there probably wasn't. They loved to fight, probably started most of the trouble they got into. Probably liked to get down and dirty in other ways, too. Miss Breeze being Walker's ex, made sense. In the most disgusting, carnal ways. Generally speaking.

"Ladies, please," Hans whispered. "Listen."

"Yes, you could say I know Lieutenant Judge," Jessica Rabbit articulated in her affected cartoon voice. "Least I knew him in the biblical sense of the word, ya know?" She giggled. Even the damned prosecutor grinned at her cutesy response.

Man, how stupid was Hotrod? Miss Breeze dressed suggestively, and had no problem drawing the prosecutor's attention to her overly abundant cleavage. She talked with her hands and her bright pink fingernails. And fake eyelashes that Persia wanted to rip off her perfectly smudged eyelids, one by one. With pliers.

"You want to kill her, huh?" Izza whispered. "I can tell. I know you do."

*Yes!* "No," Persia replied calmly. "Shush." *Let's hear what else this lap dancing moron has to say.*

"Were you with Lieutenant Judge during the night in question?" Cudahy asked as he approached the witness stand.

"No, sir, but I was with him all day long. It was my day off, and, well, I missed him because he'd just come back from a really long deployment, and well…" She. Giggled. Again!

"You know how it is when a woman goes without her man's attention for too long, don'tcha?"

Cudahy hesitated. Was he seriously considering answering? That hesitation wasn't included in the transcript. Neither was the stupid gleam in his eye.

Persia looked closer, her chin on her palm now. According to Ember's record, Walker hadn't been in the country the day or the entire week before the night in question. Neither had he been deployed. He had, in fact, returned to San Diego late the night Goff was murdered. Interesting…

So why wouldn't he reveal where he'd been, even to save himself? It made no sense.

After a long pause, Cudahy cleared his throat, placed his hand on the witness stand, and asked, "Precisely when did Judge leave your home the day in question?"

"Oh, we weren't at my place, no, sir. We ate at his place. Over in Ocean Beach. See, most folks don't know Walker Judge owns a second home two doors away from the descendant."

Cudahy straightened his tie. "I'm sure you mean decedent, as in the deceased, don't you?"

Jessica Rabbit scrunched those tanned, bare shoulders. Ducked her empty blonde head, wiggled her boobs, and squealed, "You know what I meant!"

Something in the prosecutor's eyes glittered. Looked a lot like—lust.

"You can't cure stupid," Izza muttered.

"No, Izza. She's not stupid. Look at him. Look at Cudahy. Watch how she can't take her eyes off him. And the second he placed his hand on that stand—" Persia reversed the video clip. Sure enough. "See? Right there. Watch his hand."

"Crap, she's playing with his fingers!"

"And he knows it," Persia hissed. "That's why he rested it there. He's reaching out to comfort or encourage her. Wanna bet Cudahy's sleeping with Miss Sunday Night Breeze? She might be an airhead, but that woman's in love with that officer. Want to bet Hotrod picked her up at one of the local bars? And she's lying. So did Steven Horowitz, Goff's alleged neighbor. Walker Judge only owned one house, and it wasn't anywhere near Goff's in Ocean Beach. He couldn't afford that neighborhood. Ember already checked his financials. She would've caught that."

"There's more," Hans said solemnly.

What more could there be? First, a defense attorney who provided no defense whatsoever. Then an ex-girlfriend—Persia refused to refer to Sunday Night Breeze as Hotrod's lover—who obviously had a crush on the officer intent on putting him in Leavenworth.

Persia crossed her arms over her chest, her eyes wide open now. When Judge Cole asked Hotrod's attorney for the second time if he was sure he didn't want to cross-examine Miss Breeze, Hotrod stewed. He'd distanced himself from LT Kroft by then, had pushed back in his chair, the cords in his neck taut. Yet he still faced the man holding the gavel with respect. Not once had he resorted to calling his ex a liar, or other theatrical dramatics. But he should have. Persia was mad enough to do it for him.

Hans pointed to the guy seated in the far rear corner of the courtroom. Dressed in dark jeans and a dark blue sweatshirt, he sat with one elbow on his knee, his left hand shielding his face from the camera. Standard weight and height, at first glance, he appeared ordinary. Until the ring on his finger caught Persia's eye.

"Wait. Stop. Can we freeze this frame and zoom in?"

That same wise smile cracked Hans' lips. "I thought you'd never ask."

Deftly, he worked the keyboard and brought that hand up close and personal.

"Crap. That *is* a big ring," Izza declared.

It was that and more. Downright ostentatious. The face of the ring extended from the man's knuckle to the first joint of the ring finger on his right hand. A bright gold Navy SEAL Trident, complete with eagle, flintlock style pistol, US Navy anchor, and Neptune's trident, accented the hammered silver ring.

"Hmmm," Izza murmured. "Looks like somebody's got a bad case of penis envy if you ask me."

"Or stolen valor," Persia replied. Oftentimes, guys who flaunted jewelry like this were wannabes who'd never served a day. "I wonder if we can trace who bought that ring."

Hans slapped the laptop cover down. "Ladies. Thank you for allowing me to represent your friend. I leave him in your capable hands. I must get back to my office."

"You'll be better off staying here where you'll be safe," Persia insisted.

He shook his head. "I will be okay."

"Are you sure?" Izza asked, her head tilted.

He reached out and took her hand in both of his. "Yes, Agent Maher. Thank you for worrying, but it is what it is. I know the law. They can't hurt me."

When it came to her turn, Persia didn't release Hans' handshake. Instead, she pulled him in shoulder to shoulder.

"You need anything, Mr. Koning, you reach out to me immediately, you understand? I will come for you."

"Goodbye, Agent Coltrane," he murmured as he eased his fingers from her grip, then shook his hand as if she'd squeezed too tight. Which she had. She'd meant him to know he could count on her and Izza.

Hans Koning turned on his heel and walked out the door without looking back.

It was time to track down the man who owned that ring.

# Chapter Twenty-Nine

Walker faded in and out of darkness, not sure of the day or where he was. Sometimes, the ever-present floating sensation beneath told him he was back on his yacht. Other times, he just felt like warmed-over crap. But then, out of the murky darkness he seemed stuck in, Persia's pretty face would smile down on him like a tender ray of sunshine. She'd coax him to drink more than he wanted. Sometimes cool, cool water. Other times, a nasty tasting tea, or whatever that stuff was. Probably one of those *Soylent Green* concoctions health nuts raved about, that was made in a blender with spinach, okra, and that tasted like pee.

Persia was also the one who'd manhandled him into boxers and a t-shirt. She'd helped him the few times he'd struggled to his feet and staggered to the head like a drunk, desperately needing something to hold onto while he did his business. Which caused Walker buckets of regret for not having been there when she'd needed him. Not once.

Yet she'd been here every time he'd needed her, her shoulder snuggled up under his arm, making sure he didn't fall. She'd stand him in front of the head and make sure he wasn't weaving back and forth before she'd let him go. Then she'd step away and give him privacy. He'd palm the wall over the head and try like hell not to fall into it, while he waited for his body to allow relief. Which it did. Eventually.

Then more easily, but still pink. Then… finally… clear and free-flowing and… Ahh… He was going to live.

It should've embarrassed him, her in the same room, waiting while he dropped his boxers and did what he had to do. Her possibly watching, maybe to make sure he didn't fall over. Or maybe just to sneak a peek. Some ladies would do that. But if Persia did, it didn't embarrass Walker. He had more to worry about than someone seeing his bare ass or his package. A sick man instinctively developed a uniquely primal focus on survival. Tunnel vision came with it. He was willing to do anything if it got him better.

Mostly, Walker wasn't worried because he knew Persia cared, and because she did, he'd put his trust in her. His body, too. Maybe even his soul. During this time, he'd transitioned from one raging body-ache that seemed lodged primarily in his head, to a general overall weakness that left him shivering one minute, sweating the next.

But tonight was different. He'd heard something. In the middle of a dead sleep, he'd jolted upright and palmed his chest and thighs for weapons that weren't there. In the space of a heartbeat, adrenaline had him up and on his feet. His head pounded while he waited for—something—to happen. Anything.

He cocked his head, sure he'd heard a noise. Inside or outside? He couldn't tell. Didn't know if he'd dreamed it or not.

Dizzy, he swayed, then sat back on the edge of his bed, not sure he hadn't woken himself. The safe house felt quiet. Safe. Yet he sat there breathing hard, needing to make sure before he dropped back onto his pillow. Safe houses had been breached before. He couldn't take the chance that whoever was behind his being railroaded and condemned at every turn, hadn't also sent assassins to hunt him down. Mostly, he needed to make sure Persia and her prickly friend Izza were protected.

Now he felt stupid. No noise. No anything. He'd had enough nightmarish dreams these past few days, or nights or hours, it could've been him. But all was quiet now. So quiet, he could hear his adrenaline-fueled heart pounding like a drum. Damned thing felt like it meant to climb up his throat. Must've been a dream. Good deal.

Swallowing hard, he ran his hands over his head and through his hair, then sat there, wondering where he could get his hands on a pistol. At least a knife. Did Stewart maintain weapon vaults in his safe houses? And who the hell was the guy that he owned a safe house in a foreign country, the Netherlands for hell's sake? Persia had said he was former USMC and operated a business out of Virginia. Was he so rich that he'd gone international? Nah. Jarheads weren't that kind of smart.

Damn. There it was again. Not a scream, but a whimper. A sob. Someone in this house was not happy. Walker was back on his feet, lightheaded and unarmed, but on his way to somewhere...

Once out of his room, he palmed the wall to keep steady. The dim glow emanating from the kitchen area lighted the way, but he wasn't sure which way to go. Left or right? He couldn't imagine Persia or her belligerent friend crying out, which was what he'd thought he'd heard. But someone had.

With each step, the walls seemed to breathe, moving forward, then backward, closing in on him, then doing it again. He shook the eerie sensation away and held still, waiting for another sound. Once again, he doubted himself. Nightmares and fevers were tricky. They could make you believe things that weren't real or events that never happened. Like the shit-filled caves in the mountains of Afghanistan where terrorists hid and lived and plotted... Like Goff's ghost...

Another anguished cry sounded from the room next to his. Persia. Oh, yeah. She'd said her bedroom was next to his. Palming her door open, Walker peered inside. The nightlight across from him was a nice touch. And there she lay, tangled in a mess of twisted blankets and sheets, with one long leg and bare foot hanging off the bed. Her hair was spread over her face, a pillow on the floor.

Quietly, he crossed the room. Would've made it all the way to her side, if she hadn't suddenly sat up like a crazy dead woman with her eyes bugging out of her pretty face. She raised her hands, turned her head to the side in front of her face, and whimpered, "No, no, no! Don't make me! I c-c-can't hurt him! He'sssss sssso ssssmaaall."

Walker stopped dead in his tracks. Hurt him, who?

"Persia, sugar," he whispered, his palms forward to placate her as he took another step closer. "It's me, Hotrod. I'm here now. You're going to be okay."

Her head turned in his direction, but her eyes were blank and unseeing. Sweat darkened the center line of her pink tank top. The poor thing's chest heaved, as if she'd just run a marathon. Tears streamed down her face. She shook her head. "Pleasssse, I... I... I can't. I can't do it. Not to a b-b-baby. Don't make me..."

Thankfully, he was at the foot of her bed by then. Shaking like a damned pansy from his short stroll, Walker sat his ass down with an ungracious thump. He was out of breath, sweating, and dizzy, but he was here for her. He knew that he stunk. He hadn't showered in who knew how many days. But a man didn't have to smell sweet or look good to rescue a person. He just had to show up.

Walker placed a trembling hand over the mussed covers on Persia's ankle. Thank goodness, she didn't jerk away. "It's just a nightmare," he told her quietly, then pursed his lips to keep from panting like a beast and frightening her. "Wherever you are now isn't real. But I am. Come back to me. No one can hurt you, sugar. Give me your hand. Just reach out. Let me help."

Her nostrils flared, but her eyes were still bright black and wide. Her breaths came in hard, short pants. So much terror etched her sweet face that he hurt for her. Wherever she was, it had to be an ungodly place for her to be so frightened. Persia was not a fainting violet. The woman had grit and grace, and somewhere close nearby, a loaded Smith and Wesson, .380 auto.

"He's h-h-here," she murmured huskily, then licked her lips, her gaze darting back and forth, over Walker's shoulder and around the room. But who else did she think was here?

There was no sense telling Persia that what she was reliving in her mind, wasn't real. To her, right now, the monster she faced was alive and breathing. So, Walker held onto that delicate ankle. He rubbed his hand up her blanketed leg, then back down, again and again. Warming her. Pulling her gradually back from whatever edge she was standing on, taking her back from the demon threatening her. Had to have been that rat bastard, Domingo Zapata. She'd surely seen hell on earth while working with him.

Silently, Walker cursed the Bureau and Agency for sending a lone woman into Zapata's filthy lair. For ever—ever!—thinking a single woman should be sent to do a man's job. Just because no man had been able to do the impossible, did not make sacrificing a female a smart or good decision. Who cared that she'd been outstandingly successful where others had not? Who cared that, in the end, she'd brought Zapata down? Walker sure as hell didn't. Success was beside the point. Damn them all to hell. The mission had cost her, not them. And it had cost her too much. She might never recover from all she'd seen or been forced to do. Couldn't they understand?

But now was not the time to go off on what had happened in the past. She didn't work for the Bureau or the Agency anymore. Only Alex Stewart, and she seemed to like him.

Walker set his angst aside and coaxed her quietly. "Sugar, I'm here, and I'm not leaving without you. Wherever you are right now, I'm there too. You're not alone, okay? Feel the hand on your ankle? That's me, Hotrod. I've got you, Persia, and I won't let you fall. No one's getting past me. You're safe. Come on, let's get out of here. Let's go home."

She blinked as if she'd finally heard him. Those lovely thick butterfly lashes fluttered. But her eyes were still wide and unseeing. Trembling from the crown of her head to her toes, she bowed her chin to her heaving chest. Even the ends of her long hair had curled under her breasts as if trying to comfort her.

Taking a chance and hoping bodily contact would help her reconnect with reality, Walker shifted to sit beside her. She inhaled what sounded like a deep cleansing breath, but might've been panic. Slowly, carefully, he lifted one arm and circled her shoulder, then tipped her into his side. He used just one arm. Not two. Not yet. Frightening her, holding on too tightly when she was still in a nightmare's clutches, might make everything worse. Walker didn't want to force or fight her. The next step was up to Persia.

He took a quick time-out to smooth his other hand under her blankets, searching for that handgun. Ah, there it was, alongside her other thigh. He moved it to her nightstand.

When he turned back around, Persia was staring straight into his eyes. The muscles in her neck worked hard as if she were struggling to swallow. "I… I…"

"Hey there, beautiful," he said quietly. She was so damned gorgeous this close-up. Exotic didn't begin to describe her. Rare did. Rare and incredibly beautiful and strong and one-in-a-million. "Remember me? The idiot who swam all the way from Cuba just to kiss the woman of his dreams?"

She didn't answer, and the pulse spot in her neck still pounded. But she seemed to be pulling out of her nightmare.

Walker tipped her head under his chin, then took hold of her hand and held it loosely. So many men and women coming back from the sandbox hated to be touched, and he respected that fear-driven need for physical distance. But he and Persia had already come together with enough heat and passion for him to know she was not suffering from that kind of PTSD. If only there were just one type of post-traumatic stress, life for every returned soldier, Marine, sailor, and airman—and their families— would be so much easier.

"Did I ever tell you about my baby brother?" he asked quietly, needing her to come all the way back to him. "No? Guess it's time then. The dumb butt's name was, err, is,

Kenny. Yes, ma'am, USMC Corporal Kenny Judge. He was eleven months younger than me, you know, one of those baby brothers you want to hug one moment, smack the shit out of the next. Every summer, my folks went north to visit my grandparents in Ontario, Canada. Gramps owned a few hundred acres. Farmed wheat. Acres and acres of gold, he used to tell us boys. Kept a hundred head of beef cattle. Called them his hamburger herd. Always took us boys shooting varmints and squirrels and such. Sometimes, if we went up north over Christmas break, we might come across a snowshoe rabbit or a winter goose while we were traipsing around with Gramps. I never minded eating squirrel or rabbit for dinner, but you can keep those geese. Too tough. Greasy as hell. Not worth the trouble of plucking them."

"I had a brother," Izza murmured from the doorway.

Walker glanced up at his unexpected visitor, standing half-in, half-out of the room, dressed in running pants and some guy's blue shirt with USMC emblazoned in black stencils over her chest. The shirt hung to her knees.

Izza had made it quite clear she didn't trust him, and Walker couldn't blame her. Not with the conviction on his record, and all those other accusations hanging over his head. But here she was, come to save Persia, too.

"Come on in," he whispered, then let go of Persia long enough to wave her friend to join the party. Persia had settled down by then, but she wasn't fully awake. So he kept her right where she was, at his side, his voice low and steady.

"Older brother or younger?" he asked as Izza took his place at the foot of the bed.

Izza Maher was a tiny thing, six or eight inches shorter than Persia. Instead of an uptight ponytail, her hair hung in lazy black spirals over her shoulders and down her back tonight, making her look more like a little girl than a grown woman. Or maybe it was that too-big shirt that made her look smaller than she'd seemed before. Of course, she'd had a weapon in her hands then. That definitely would've made her seem bigger than life.

"Younger," she answered, her voice soft and quiet, as her coal-black eyes scrolled appraisingly over him holding onto her friend. "I heard what you said. You know, when you asked Persia to come back. That was… nice."

He shrugged, needing Izza to trust Persia more than him. "Baby brothers are the worst," he murmured, forever wishing he could have his back.

"Jamie," Izza whispered. "Jamie Ramos. That was his name."

"Army?"

She shook her head. "No, USMC, like me. Dumb butt never took anything seriously, though. Not his career. Not getting ahead. Not until" —she blew out a breath between pursed lips— "it was too late."

Walker knew all about eternally too late. "If you don't mind me asking, when did you lose him?"

"A couple years ago." She was biting her bottom lip by then, her eyes focused on the blanket not him. "Firefight. Twenty miles outside Camp Baharia. Iraq. You?"

He took a deep breath. With his parents already gone, he hadn't shared anything about Kenny's death with anyone. There'd been no one to tell. Guys were like that. Hiding behind false bravado. Holding back. Carrying on as if working were the only thing that mattered. Had to be some kind of primal defense mechanism, an instinctual need to never show weakness. To always be the baddest Neanderthal in the fight.

Truth was, when Kenny'd been killed in action, Walker had buried his pain so deep, most days he didn't feel or acknowledge it. He'd relegated those personal pains to history. He'd had men to lead and missions to fulfill. But night times…? All that buried shit floated back to the surface, like Halloween ghosts gasping and groaning out of a sticky black tar pit of lost dreams and grief. Memories. Who needed them?

"Yemen," he admitted, his arm tightening around Persia's waist. She'd relaxed, and he'd tipped back to the headboard with her. "Province of Marib. He was there supporting a UN Special Envoy. Drone attack by Houthi rebels, Iran's buddies. Took out Kenny and three others."

"Navy SEAL like you?"

He shook his head. "Nope. Kenny was dumb like you and Jamie. Had to be a Marine."

"The USA's involved in too many other countries' civil wars," she said, still talking to the blanket.

"True, but in most cases, we're the only support some of those smaller, weaker countries have. If it wasn't for us, Iran would've taken over that part of the world by now. The latest Khomeini in power already kills anyone who gets in his way. His own people included. Women and children alike." Which was true. One Khomeini was as bad as the next in Walker's book.

"I know, but…" Izza let that hang.

"Tell me about him," Walker urged gently. He didn't want to fight this impetuous woman. Hell, he didn't want to fight anyone. He just wished women didn't think they had to prove they were as tough or tougher than men. But the world had changed, hadn't it? To get ahead in any career, a woman had to work harder, fight longer, and run faster. He knew that. In most cases, she had to be willing to stand against slander, backstabbing friends, and continual character assassination whenever she pulled ahead of the pack and proved she was, in fact, a helluva lot better. Walker had certainly seen how hard men and other women were on any gal who stepped up and succeeded where they'd failed. Or where they hadn't even tried to go.

So... Izza was a jarhead, huh? As soft and pretty as she looked in the dim glow of that nightlight? Nah. He couldn't imagine her geared up like a guy, toting a hundred pounds of ammo, her face painted, and marching off to battle. Just didn't sit right with him.

Walker tried not to be sexist. He just didn't want women to have to fight to the death, not if he was around. That was a man's job, to protect home and hearth. To do the dirty jobs, so women could live gently and in peace.

Her shoulders lifted, but Izza seemed intent on smoothing the wrinkles out of the covers instead of looking at him. "He was all I had," she whispered to that blanket.

"And you miss him."

She nodded. "Yeah. I do. As big a pain in the ass as Jamie could be, as much as he liked to tease, that shithead was my brother, and he always stood up for me."

"That's what brothers do." All at once, Walker knew where Jamie was. Yet he asked, "Where's he buried in Arlington?"

"Section 60. With all the others."

Arlington's Section 60 was where many of those killed in Afghanistan and Iraq now lay in honored glory. Or so the poets said. Walker had found it a sad, wretched place where too many ghosts still walked and talked... and cried.

"Kenny's there, too," he admitted softly. Speaking his brother's name still felt somehow irreverent. But with Izza, someone who'd lost as much as he had, it felt okay. Maybe even good. "Want to bet those two boys are still telling lies and taking dares?" Kenny never could resist a dare.

Finally, Izza's chin lifted and her dark eyes zeroed on him. "You're not so bad, you know."

What could he say? Nothing. So Walker shrugged, content to be on her good side for now.

"Please take care of my girlfriend, Walker Judge. Like you said before, I mean. Don't let anyone take her. Persia thinks she's tougher than she is, but she's not, you know? Not really. Keep her safe. I don't know why but she likes you, and she thinks you're worth saving. I'm not convinced, but she is, so make damned sure you are what she thinks you are. Promise me."

He bowed his head in humble submission, never more sure of any other order in his life. "Yes, ma'am, I promise to keep Persia safe, always. Goodnight, Izza. I'm real glad you're here with us."

"Me, too," she said as she lifted to her feet and padded from the room, leaving him alone with Persia still in his arms. Which told him that Izza trusted him more than she'd let on. She was a lot like him. Too tough to cry. Too broken to let her heart show. But he also sensed there was more to that story about Jamie than she'd ever admit. He'd always stood up for her. Against who?

"You have a good friend in Izza Maher," he told his sleeping beauty.

"Drink. I need a… a drink."

"Of what?" he wondered out loud.

"Wh-whisssss-key…" —she hissed like a tire going flat— "…helpssss…"

That got his attention. *Whiskey helps, huh?* Also explained the hint of alcohol he'd detected on her breath the first night on the beach. "It helps what, sugar?"

She huffed, hard little panting breaths through her nose. "Nightsssss. Dreamssssss. All that sh-sh-shit."

"Of Florida?" He doubted that, but he needed her to talk to him, at least verify what he suspected.

Persia slapped one hand to his chest and pulled away. "No. Him. Poor, poor, babiesss…"

Walker froze even as he kept hold of her waist. Babies? She'd tortured babies while she'd been undercover? No, not Persia. "What babies?"

Another huff. Another hiss. Another sad, "Poor, poor babies…"

"What did *he* make you do to *them*?" He cringed at what she might say next.

"K-k-kill. I had to… h-had to…"

Oh, shit. Zapata'd made her prove how bad she was, and to maintain her cover, she'd done as he'd demanded. Or had she? "No, Persia. Sugar, I know you, and you'd never hurt a baby."

She nodded adamantly. "Yeah. Had to. Baby lambsssss…"

Oh, thank God! Lambs. Not children.

"Did you eat lamb stew afterward?"

"No. Never. The blood…" Whimpering, she rubbed a hand over her sternum. "So… much… blood. Babies bleed. It was everywhere. Too much…"

This courageous woman might've been able to take down killers the world over, but hurting a tiny creature as pure as a lamb was the straw that had broken her.

Walker pulled her against him and bowed his cheek to the top of her sweaty head, aware of how much she'd kept bottled up inside. No wonder she'd turned to alcohol. Sure explained her nightmares now. Stewart's safe houses weren't stocked with booze, and she desperately needed a drink.

"It's okay. It's over. You're with me now. Breathe, Persia. Wake up. Let the past go and just breathe. I've got your six."

"B-b-but… they c-c-cry when I hurt 'em," she sobbed. "They cry!"

"I know, sugar, I know," he murmured, rocking her now and wishing he had a time machine to go back and end Zapata before she'd ever met the bastard. She'd be safe now, not haunted by the ghost of a lamb.

Persia didn't reply, just turned more fully into his arms. Her breasts flattened against his ribs, and her nose landed in the hollow of his neck. She moaned and her breathing evened out again. Every soft puff of her breath over his still feverish skin tickled and chilled. Once again, Walker was lost in the mystery of Persia Coltrane.

Needing to be closer to her, he sank his nose into her smooth, sleek hair. It smelled of some kind of flower he'd never be able to name. Flowers weren't his thing. Firearms, warheads, and gunpowder were. Fire any weapon, he could name the make and model of the pistol, rifle, tank, or missile that fired it, as well as the caliber. Months and years spent training ingrained those skills into every warrior's head. Hyper-awareness only sharpened those details more. But death honed them laser-sharp.

Watching other warriors die was the epitome of a refiner's fire. Watching them give their all for an intangible belief as simple as freedom. Inalienable rights. All the things that made Americans different from so many other people in the world. To lose the warrior at your side honed your own instinct to survive. Made you a better, more deadly, killing machine. Also made damned sure you walked alone the rest of your days.

Until this woman had burst into his life like a falling star, war had been Walker's one true calling. But now? He was beginning to like flowers.

Smoothing his free hand over her head, he brushed the tangled strands out of her eyes and away from her face. He curled both arms around her, leaned back, and stared at the ceiling. The road ahead that had once seemed so clear had grown unbearably difficult lately.

First, losing his folks within months of each other. Kenny had bawled like a baby at Mom's funeral. Dad had gone three months earlier, but he'd known all along that smoking those damned unfiltered cigarettes caused cancer. Smoking had always been his choice and his biggest weakness. But when Mom died of lung cancer caused by Dad's second-hand smoke? It had damned near killed Kenny. In one fell swoop, the Judge boys lost everything. Violet and Booker Judge had been, hands-down, the best parents any kid could've asked for.

Yet even at his mother's funeral, Walker had held everything in. He'd been the strong one who'd handled both funerals, then handled Kenny through the depression and survivor's guilt that followed. Funny how kids blamed themselves when they couldn't rescue the people they loved most.

Walker stroked his fingers through Persia's soft hair, then lifted a handful of silky strands to his nose. Remembering always hurt. After Kenny's funeral, Walker had returned to Team 18. It felt good to be a winner-takes-all SEAL again, instead of a grieving son and brother.

It wasn't until Quinn Dooley reached out for an assist to get his daughter back that Walker had finally gotten his head back together. When he closed his eyes at night, he could still see sweet Emily's teary, red face mashed into her daddy's neck, while she sobbed and whined and clung to him. He could still see Quinn falling to his knees on the tarmac, cradling that girl against his heart like he'd never, ever let her go again.

He didn't blame Quinn for needing that assist. Couldn't. Everyone needed help some time, even hardguys like aircraft carrier captains. *Even hard guys like me.*

Sighing, Walker pressed his lips into Persia's hair, at last understanding what he'd seen written all over Quinn's face the day Emily came home. It was time to be humble. Time to admit... Walker Judge needed the woman in his arms.

# Chapter Thirty

Stretching, Persia ground her nose into the warm pillow beneath her. Took a few seconds before awareness seeped into her weary brain and told her this pillow smelled like a certain man…

*Oh, no!* But yes, Hotrod was in her bed. Cracking an eye open, she peered up at the scruffy underside of his chin. He was on his back with one arm curled possessively around her and snoring quietly. This wasn't good. If he was here… had she screamed or done something equally embarrassing? Her entire body cringed. Had she had another nightmare?

*Please, no. Not now when I'm finally on a real mission.*

Oh, my God, had Izza heard? Did she know?

Persia closed her eyes as a wave of fiery heat infused her body. How utterly embarrassing! This paranoia had to stop. As stealthily as she could, she lifted up on her knees just enough to ease away from under his arm and—

"Stay," he murmured, his voice deep and thick with sleep, and that arm around her now clamped tighter. "My turn."

Her heart jackhammered up high in her throat as Hotrod pressed her closer. Man, he looked good early morning with his hair mussed and all that scruff. "Your turn?" *For what?*

"Mmphmmph," he breathed huskily, his eyes still sealed tight, but his fingers rubbing small, warm circles on her arm. "Yeah. My turn."

"But I… I have to fix breakfast." *Or something.* "Now. Let me up." *Before Izza bangs on my door and wants to know where you are and what we've been doing.*

Hotrod rolled over, caging her beneath his entire, wonderfully heavy body. Man, he felt good. He hadn't showered while he'd been sick, but who cared? The pleasant weight of him pressing her flat to the mattress made her eyes roll back in her head.

If only he was in better shape…

If only they had more privacy, more time, and…

One of his big hands smoothed over her shoulder and down her arm, then shoved her tank top up to her neck, baring her breasts, at the same time, lighting a spark at her core.

Automatically, she slipped her fingers into his hair, the other hand under his t-shirt and over the smooth warm planes of his back. Then down his spine and beneath his boxers to his firm, muscular backside. There wasn't one part of this guy not padded with muscle over large, sturdy bones and heavy sinews. Everything about him was bigger and stronger and harder. And pleasantly warm.

His heady scent incited every last feminine hormone. Persia's body filled with streams of dancing flames that licked up her legs and pooled at her core. She gripped that fine ass, ready if he was.

She was on fire. Just the sight and scent and feel of Hotrod did this to her. With one touch, one glance, he'd turned her body into liquid heat, like the icy blue flames from lighted cans of Sterno. Persia forgot breakfast. She already had the sustenance she craved.

"Hotrod," she whispered, licking the curl of his ear. Breathing a soft sigh over it. Into him.

"Yes, ma'am," he replied as if her command was his ardent wish, as if she'd ordered him for breakfast, and he meant to comply. When goose bumps popped over his shoulders, his hips jutted forward. He easily pulled her shorts down, baring her ass, which only made her need him more.

Pressing a hand between their bodies, Persia smoothed her fingertips up that rigid wall of muscle. Touching him. Breathing him. Loving the crisp hairs over his pecs. His flat manly nipples. Needing him inside her.

Like a pair of dancing fireflies, their bodies vibrated together. Moving in sync, as if they'd done this a lifetime before. Their breathing joined into one single breath. Their hearts, a single beat. They became sunlight and stardust.

Out of breath, she parted her legs and let him slide between. He cupped her sex. Nothing more. Nothing else. The power he held in that hand, and all those callused fingers stood for—his country, his honor, his team—stole Persia's breath. He'd kissed America, for heaven's sake. He'd fought and been prepared to die for her ungrateful masses. That made him a one-of-a-kind hero.

Hotrod wasn't a lightweight by any definition of the word. Neither was he white-collar office material or GQ airbrushed. He was blue-collar all the way, from his hair roughened legs to the magnificent steel licking at her core, to the rasp of his fingertips. This man was a worker and a doer, and he was doing things to her body she'd never known were possible. He hadn't even kissed her yet, yet she was close to detonating in his hands.

How did he do that?

Automatically, instinctively, her back arched at the mere thought of coming without more foreplay, and… "Damn, damn, damn," she cried.

It was happening. Just like in Florida. So fast. So good. She bucked against his hand and… "Yes!" Persia shattered into a thousand brilliant bits of suns and moons and stars.

Hotrod covered her mouth with his, swallowing her scream and her tears. She clung to him, her body wrung out with a release without end, a chain reaction rippling through her. The fiery pleasure ended with her gradually settling back to earth, even as aftershocks sparked tiny fireworks.

"I need you inside," she whined, ready for more. Wanting all of him. "Hurry, Hotrod. Now."

"Yes, ma'am," he purred like a sexy, obedient beast.

Only then did she realize he was still dressed and her bare heels were dug into the small of his back. She'd officially lost her mind. Who had trapped who?

As if he'd read her mind, he peeled out of his boxers, then knelt over her while she relieved him of his t-shirt. Persia couldn't get him naked fast enough. Finally skin to skin, and oh, so damned warm under her palms, he hovered over her. Breathing heavy. His gaze powerful and hazy and harsh and kind, all at the same time. His hair was just long enough that short lazy bangs tipped over his forehead. Not into his eyes, just enough she could thread her fingers through those locks and pull.

Leaning over her on one arm, he breathed on her, his eyes sinfully, wickedly dark. Like a warrior of old, total male domination glittered in those deep blues. His gaze fixed on her mouth. He meant to conquer her and she meant to let him. Theirs was a once-in-a-lifetime kind of romance. And if this was all she would ever have of this man, this one sweet, breathtaking moment, she meant to savor every last second and heartbeat of it.

The Agency had taught her that, and her time spent with Domingo Zapata had literally pounded the lesson into her. Grab what you could, when you could, because life wasn't promised to anyone. Just time, and even that was finite. What you did with those few minutes, hours, days, and years you were given, was on you.

"Persia," he whispered, his voice a silky baritone balm that melted into the tiny cracks and wide-open fissures of her never-to-be-healed-again heart.

"Hotrod," she breathed up at him, lost in the ocean of his eyes, yet begging for rescue. To be saved, once. Just once. Could he be the one? Did he see what she saw? The futility of living just to kill and die?

Time stood still, like it did at pivotal moments in a person's life. Like death. Like that first step into Hell. Like surrender and anguish and too many memories to ever forget. Persia noticed that the pivot points in her career had all been beginnings or endings associated with her hardest fought battle in Brazil. Even dead, Domingo Zapata still had a stranglehold on her, and she needed that to end.

"I need this," she told Hotrod truthfully. She should've said *you*, not *this*. Because *just* sex she could have and she'd had, with others. But this brand-new thing between her and Hotrod was something rare and bright and—promising. It was also something she didn't deserve, hadn't earned, and wasn't sure she knew what to do with, if or when she claimed it for her own.

That was why Hotrod had walked away from her before. Karma's one and only rule: A woman couldn't reap what she hadn't sown. All Persia had sown in her life so far had been death and destruction, with a hefty dose of vengeance splashed over all of it. Like water poured onto the desert sand, her need for revenge against Zapata had sucked the life out of her.

Hotrod pressed his warm, moist lips to her forehead. "And I need you, sugar," he whispered, her breasts mashed like pillows against his magnificent chest. "I think I've always needed this bright, intelligent woman and the light she's brought into my life."

Tears sprang to her eyes. Her throat tightened. He obviously didn't know her very well, because Persia was more of darkness than of light. Which was why she was still an aunt, not a mom. She'd seen too much evil to ever nurture innocent new lives. A woman who slaughtered lambs didn't deserve to bear children.

Just as her pity party swelled around her like a cold, wet blanket, Hotrod sank into her, and Persia forgot about death and blood and all the bright, dying reds splashed against evil blacks.

"Come for me, princess," he whispered in her ear. "Come *with* me."

Her body responded to his friction with heat and tears. Yet like a freaking baby, she buried her face under his chin, her arm still crooked around his neck. Holding on. Forever fighting the good fight, forever lost to the dark.

Hotrod began pumping in earnest, his body a machine with one goal, to hear her scream and to make her smile. But she couldn't recover the high she'd had. She wanted to. She tried to. Yet every beat of their bodies was now out of sync. The friction between them hurt. She couldn't pretend. "Stop," she whispered huskily. "Hotrod, stop. I... I can't."

Instantly, he ceased moving. Still hard and thick, and wonderfully hot inside her, he peered down through hazy, oceanic-blue eyes. "What's wrong? Did I hurt you?"

She shook her head, afraid he might see more than she wanted to share. "No, I... I just can't."

The tenderest light glimmered over his face. In one fell swoop, he rolled onto his back, taking her with him. Persia found herself sitting upright and straddling his hips. In plain sight. Where he could see everything. All of her. Where she had nowhere to hide and nothing to hide behind. Yet his palms gently cuffed her wrists, and his full attention was on her eyes instead of her breasts.

"Talk to me," he said, his voice so damned soft and low she wanted to cry.

Persia shrugged, not making this any more personal than it already was. "Nothing. It happens."

"Something," he insisted quietly, tugging her down and flattening her to his chest. Hotrod tucked her head under his chin and crisscrossed his arms over her back, keeping one manly hand on each cheek of her ass. "Better?"

She nodded, struggling to hold herself together as she slipped her hands around his neck.

"I'm an ass. Should've let you sleep," he murmured, his skillful fingers kneading her backside, his heavily muscled arms around her, making her feel safe and protected. Her, one of the FBI's best covert operators. The woman who'd brought Domingo Zapata, one of the world's most evil villains, down. Needing protection...

"No. It's all right. It's just… I just… I had a dream," she whispered, blinking fast so no teardrops fell. *The same dream. Forever and always, the same dream.*

Reaching around her, he pulled the bedsheet up and over them, instantly easing her nakedness. "Want to talk about it?"

"Not really." Persia ran her tongue over her dry lips, afraid to admit her weakness, but wanting someone to know why she needed that silly nightlight and how dark the nights really were without it. Hoping that someone could *please*, be Hotrod. But afraid speaking the dream out loud would make it real.

Yet she couldn't go on like this. Forever hiding and running and falling apart.

The nightmare poured out of her slowly. "It's a crazy, weird dream, that's all. Stupid, really. I shouldn't let it upset me, but…" She hesitated, about to ruin her bitch-of-the-beach persona once and for all.

"I'm listening," he breathed, the warmth and feel of his male body so damned comforting.

"Okay. So… I'm running. It's night and it's dark, pitch black. Branches I can't see slap my face and whip my eyes," she confessed quietly. "They sting, but they're not why I'm running. I'm covered in blood, Hotrod. Painted red like… like a devil." *Like him…*

Persia closed her eyes, reliving the nightmare that had once been her daily life. Seeing Domingo's evil, tattooed face and his flat black eyes again. "Someone's chasing me. I look back and all I see are red and black shadows, a long black arm, and a big tattooed hand with short-stubby fingers. It's like one of those cartoon arms, long like stretched putty with a huge, inflated gloved hand at the end of it. Only it's not a glove. It's him, Hotrod. It's h-h-him." Man, she wanted to die of embarrassment, but her mouth kept talking. "He's reaching out to grab me. To drag me back. To make me see and do things—"

"Zapata?" Hotrod's question was a soft, gentle, baritone vibration under her ear.

Swallowing hard, Persia nodded. Her heart was pounding by then, just like during and after every nightmare. Pounding so hard, she thought it might jump out of her throat in protest of all she'd put it through. All she'd seen. If only she had a drink. That would steady her nerves. It always worked. Just one sip, one swallow, one bottle. What would it hurt?

"I could really use a drink," she murmured, inadvertently confessing another sin. What would Hotrod think of her if he knew how much she drank? Part of her needed him to know that, too.

His big, warm palms smoothed over her shoulders, warming her. Chasing the gooseflesh away. If only he could banish her demon as easily.

"I'm still here and I'm still listening," he whispered, his nose in her hair.

He probably thought she'd wanted a bottled water, so Persia left it at that. One sin at a time…

"I… I can't run fast enough. I never can. Something trips me, and I go down on my knees, and I'm holding a… a baby l-l-lamb." Her stomach pitched bile up her throat. She was shaking now, coming apart. Just one drink. That's all she needed! "The b-b-baby's looking up at me with his big, beautiful eyes, and he's crying and bleating, only he's bleeding and bleeding…."

She sucked in a deep breath as the nightmare rolled over her once again with all its Technicolor reds and blacks, crimsons and ebonies, mashed and dripping together. Willing the ugliness and her trembling away, Persia buried her face against Hotrod's heart, needing every last ounce of his will and his strength. His power. That was all she needed, just enough of him to keep her going.

When his arms wrapped tighter, she murmured, "And then… I'm looking down, but I'm not holding a white, fuzzy lamb anymore. His face… he… he changed into a b-b-baby boy with big, brown eyes, and I'm holding the knife that's cutting his throat, and… he's just a tiny, sweet, baby boy and… and… he's the one bleeding all over me, and it's his blood on my face and in my hair and… No more!"

Sobbing, Persia ground herself against the man she'd just made love with, her heart too raw to confess one more sin, and her nose running like a faucet. She clung to Hotrod, her fingertips dug into his shoulder muscles. She was that drowning woman in a very black, very bottomless ocean, grabbing onto the only man foolish enough to come close enough to reach her.

There was no sense going on. If nothing else, her nightmare confirmed she should stay far away from children, babies, and lambs. She'd murdered a defenseless creature that had just wanted its mother. She could still hear its frightened cries. She could smell its blood. The same blood she'd smeared over her face to prove to the monster she'd been sent to destroy, that she was just as bad a deviant as he was. And she had proven it! So why couldn't she defeat Zapata's ghost? Why wouldn't he let her alone?!

"Shhhhh," Hotrod whispered, still holding her as if he cared. As if he knew precisely how she felt and what she'd done. "It's tough, I know, I know. Honest, I do. War is damned tough, and I know exactly what the Zapata brothers did with and to their victims. That had to be one hell of an ugly mess you dealt with. I'm sorry I wasn't there. I would've stood beside you every step of the way. I would've held you when the nights got too dark, and I would've helped you bring that bastard down."

*I would've stood beside you...*

Not *I would've killed him for you...*

Somehow, him acknowledging her ability and accomplishment, helped. Whether he knew it or not, Hotrod had just given her part of what she'd needed to get back on her feet. Affirmation. Recognition. He believed in her capacity to get the hard jobs done. She squeezed her eyes tight, wishing she could slow the tears. Wishing she'd kept her big mouth shut. "Never mind. Never should've—"

"Told me? Oh, yes, Persia Coltrane. You did exactly the right thing telling me. You've never told anyone else, have you?"

She shook her head, ashamed that she'd given herself away to a man she barely knew. What would he think of her now? Yet he kept those incredibly gentle, warm hands smoothing over her back and up her neck into her hair, holding her close. Just being there.

"Let me ask one question," he murmured against her teary cheek. "Did you kill a human baby or an animal baby?"

"A lamb. A tiny, helpless, baby lamb," she whined. "I killed it and I smeared its blood on my face, just so... so..."

"So you could convince Zapata you were good enough to join his gang. I get that. But the lamb ended up in a stew or something later that day, right? Its sacrifice didn't go to waste."

"No, but… Yes, but… he didn't deserve to die like that," whined out of her.

"But, to be clear, you never hurt the human baby boy in your nightmare. Right?"

She was shaking like a leaf then. "Right. He wanted me to, but I… I killed the lamb instead."

"Instead of a baby? He wanted you to kill a baby, and you told him no?"

Persia could barely think by then. All her sins. Laid bare. Every single one. Her cowardice. Her lies. "I told him that I'd gladly kill a baby later, and I'd dance on its ruined body with him." *Like two sick miscreants, I promised I'd dance with the Devil Incarnate on an innocent child's heart.*

"Ah, sugar…" Hotrod whispered against her temple. "You've been running from this nightmare a long time, haven't you?"

"Yesssss," she admitted. Running and falling and falling apart. And running again.

"What would you do differently if you could go back into Zapata's lair? Would you save that lamb or would you save all the little ones he had trapped there? Would you sacrifice Tomas Juarez to rescue a lamb that was destined for the table anyway?"

Hotrod made it sound easy. Save the boy? Save the lamb? "Tomas. I'd save Tomas again. Every time."

Hotrod's chest heaved with a great sigh. Carefully, he cupped her chin, tilting her head until she had no choice but to look into his eyes. His teary eyes.

Persia sucked in a sob. She'd made him cry. "I'm sorry," she breathed, as she traced the wet trail of tears on his cheek, then wiped it away.

"Don't cry for me," he said as he kissed her fingers. "Life doesn't give us many options sometimes. War's never easy. Which is why the lamb in your dream morphs into a human child. Either way, you knew you'd have to hurt an innocent in order to complete your mission and end Zapata. Yet you also knew you could never hurt anyone or anything unless you absolutely had to. You should already be some little girl's or boy's mom. That's who you are deep inside."

He sounded so sure.

"You're wrong. I've killed men in self-defense and they deserved to die. A lot of men, Hotrod."

"And that's why you're so good at what you do. You're capable of making snap decisions and carrying them through, even when they seem impossibly difficult."

"I would've killed Zapata if Julio hadn't." God knew she'd wanted to end Domingo since she'd first set eyes on him.

Hotrod smothered her into his arms, his hands interlocked across her back again. "And I would've killed him for you if I'd been there," he breathed. "Women's bodies and souls were designed to bring new lives into the world. To nurture and care for babies. Men were made to protect those women, their sons and daughters. Might not be politically correct, but Mother Nature doesn't seem to care about PC politics. At our most primitive level, the human brain's primary mission is to ensure the survival of the species. Call it racial, prejudicial, or narrow-minded, it is what it is. Women and men will never be interchangeable. Yes, women make damned good soldiers, and yes, they have every right to be all they can be. Hell, some women I know" —he squeezed her tightly— "put a lot of guys I've worked with to shame. They're braver. They work harder. They're smarter, and I'm damned proud to work with every last one of them. But that doesn't make them men. It just makes them stronger women. Like you."

She had nothing to say, so Persia kept quiet, content to listen to his heartbeat and the vibration of his voice.

"You ever play with fireworks when you were a kid?"

"No," she whispered, "but Dad does. Every Fourth of July. Mom loves our Independence Day celebrations."

"See? That's another one of those guy things. Boys take risks while girls usually just watch. But if you take a couple of those spinning butterfly flares, wrap them in duct tape, then light the fuse, what do you get?"

"A bomb."

"Exactly. And do you know how many little girls end up in the emergency room every year because they held onto that Independence Day bomb a second too long? None. Well, okay, maybe one or two, but the point is, boys play rougher than girls. They take more chances, more risks, and they do a ton of stupid shit before they grow brains. But girls—"

"Watch dumb boys," Persia murmured, finally smiling again.

"Exactly! Girls are born with brains. Boys aren't. It takes years for their gray matter to develop. Sometimes, it never does. Bottom line, males were made to complement females.

Take your parents, for instance. What on earth did an Iranian scientist ever see in a Mississippi cotton farmer?"

Thinking of Mom and Dad made her smile wider. "Mom always said it was love at first sight."

"Does she drive the tractor, or does he?"

"He does, but I can, too."

Hotrod breathed into her hair. "I have no doubt you can, sugar. But your dad must think working the fields is his job, not your mom's, that's all I'm saying. Go easy on yourself. You did what you had to do, what most men couldn't have done, and you did it because you're female. You fooled one of the worst murderers in Brazil. Don't spread yourself too thin. Talk to me. Let me—"

Izza rapped on the closed door. "Hey, guys. Wake up! Hans is back. We've got trouble."

# Chapter Thirty-One

Walker rolled off one side of Persia's bed while she rolled off the other. Still weak but not going to admit it, he staggered back to his room, tore open the closet, and selected the first pair of jeans hanging there. Measuring it against his body for size, he guesstimated it was close enough. After grabbing one of the clean t-shirts hanging next to the jeans, he crossed the room, yanked a dresser drawer open, and took out a pair of socks and boxers. He dressed hurriedly, still needing a weapon or two.

He'd just located a decent pair of boots—this safe house literally had everything in his size—when Izza slammed his door open and tossed him a rifle. "You'll need this."

Walker caught it easily. Checking the weight, he slid the breech open, made sure the weapon was loaded. Bolt-action, .308-caliber rifle with a full magazine. Sweet. "How many rounds does this mag hold?"

"Ten. More ammo and mags are on the dining room table. Pistols, if you don't like a rifle. Take your pick."

"What are we looking at?"

"Ask Hans," she barked, already out in the hall on her way to somewhere else. She'd dressed for battle. Cammie pants, black wife-beater, and her hair tied back ruthlessly in a ponytail.

Persia stopped at his door, tucking a black shirt into her black jeans. "Are you sure you're up for this?" She looked like Izza's twin. Same outfit. Same hairstyle. Same hard glint in her eye.

"Never felt better. Tell me about this house."

"Walk with me," she ordered, that ponytail swinging as she led the way. "I'm only going to say it once."

Walker fell in line. It was hard to know who was in charge, Izza or Persia. She'd changed back into a domineering fighting woman, but Izza had, too. Out in the front room, Hans stood over the table loaded with enough weaponry to make a SEAL smile. He'd changed into jeans and a plain white t-shirt since Walker last saw him. A loaded ammo belt draped his shoulder. He carried another custom rifle in his hand, as unlikely a warrior as ever could be.

But that table was a SEAL's wet dream come true. Not only were there more rifles lined on it, but also a half dozen SIG Sauer P226 pistols. Designed for extreme military use, it had long ago set the standard for combat pistols the world over. Single, double, and thigh holsters lay stretched alongside the pistols. Then an array of six and eight-inch blades, complete with sheaths and holsters. Large ammo cans and wooden crates were stacked beside the table. And Christ, a tank killer, as in an over the shoulder M72 LAW, one-shot, 66-millimeter, lay at the far end. Izza had been busy.

Walker helped himself to an over-shoulder double holster, two P226's, and as many mags as he could stuff in his pocket. Strapping on a thigh holster, he added a six-inch blade, instantly regretting that he'd lost Kenny's. Another pistol got tucked into his waistband behind his back.

"People," Persia snapped as she stepped to the edge of the table. "This building was built to withstand everything but a 120-millimeter round. Two points of egress" —she pointed to the front and the back doors of the structure— "with steel doors like the ones you'll find on gun safes. Piano hinges. Reinforced door jambs. Digital locks. Security doorknobs. Only windows in this home are upfront, top of the door and to its side. Glass is bulletproof, tested to withstand any magnitude earthquake or any caliber munition. Roof is buttressed twelve-gauge steel. Outside walls were designed to look like every other house in this neighborhood, but inside, everything you see is fireproof. Fire suppression will engage instantly in the unlikely case a fire does start. At that point, the online system will notify TEAM HQ, and a team will be dispatched to assist. No one is getting in this safe house without one helluva fight."

"This house has an online security system?" He couldn't believe that. "Who's watching us?"

"Most likely junior agents Ember Dennison or Beau Villanueva back at HQ. Other questions?"

"What's beneath us?"

"Six feet of reinforced concrete. Down the hall is our last line of defense."

"Which is?"

"The safe room."

That surprised him. Stewart was damned thorough.

Persia turned smartly to Izza. "You want to add anything?"

"Just that I'm still waiting for confirmation on the intel Hans provided. Until then, we'll assume he's right, that a squad of armed mercenaries is headed our way. ETA in fifteen.

Load up, folks. Persia, you and Walker hold our frontline. Hans, you and I'll cover the rear until reinforcements arrive. No one gets inside. Shoot to kill. Hans? Is that clear?"

"Yes, ma'am," he said as he stepped to her side, cleared his throat, and turned to Walker. "I have gone over all the evidence the International Criminal Court has against you, and I find the timeline lacking in sufficient details and corroboration. It's as if someone has deliberately misled the ICC. There are distinct similarities between your physical description and that of the bomber, but now that I've met you in person, I see that you are taller, heavier across here" —he dragged his fingers over his chest— "than the man who killed those people in Jordan. Plus, your eyes are blue; his were distinctly brown."

"I could've been wearing contacts," Walker explained what any prosecutor would no doubt declare.

Hans nodded. "Yes. You could've been wearing contacts that day, but there are other dissimilarities that prove you were not there. When this is over, I will show you what I mean. But now—" Hans glanced over his shoulder at the front door. "Because you fled ICC custody, President Von Schtolz has declared you to be a fugitive of international justice. Every country has been alerted, as well as every bounty hunter. You are to be taken dead or alive—"

"Over my f-ing dead body," Izza huffed, jamming the bolt on her rifle forward with the cockiness of a pissed-off bantam rooster. She'd wrapped the weapon's strap around her fist, her jaw set, and her brown eyes gone mostly black. "Von Schtolz sends anyone, they'll have to come through me."

"And me," Hans said quietly. "I stand with you now, Lieutenant Judge. We are all accomplices."

"Then we'll all hang together," Izza declared.

Walker was beginning to recognize her signature head swagger. This woman was as ferocious as Persia. They could've passed for blood sisters. But in no way was he putting their lives in more danger. "Listen. Guys. I'm honored you all trust me enough to fight for me, but—"

"Shut it," Persia snapped, her pretty browns flashing lovely amber fire.

She had the nerve to flip him off with a covert middle finger salute to her furrowed brow. God, he loved her!

"Now's not the time to look a gift horse in the mouth. One fights, we all fight. Got it?"

"But—"

"Butts and assholes," Izza quipped. "You ain't gonna win this one, Hotrod, so shut the fuck up and do what you're told."

Man, he loved these women. Made him feel like he was back with his guys. Humbled, Walker reached across Hans' chest and released the safety on the man's rifle, just in case he didn't know what that lever was for.

A shy smile came back to Walker. A head nod. Enough that he now knew Mr. Koning had never held a bolt-action rifle before. Possibly not any other weapon, either.

Shit. Stewart had better be right about this building. Because there was no way to adequately protect this house if an ICC squad breached it, not with a team of three and a half against what would, no doubt, be experienced soldiers. Yet that was what Walker meant to do.

He cast a sideways glance at Persia. His dream. His goddess. Now his commander. Pointing to the front and back doors, he declared, "I'll move ammo to drop spots, front and rear, for quicker access."

"Then do it."

Immediately, Walker carried half the ammo boxes to the exit, the other half to the front door. As soon as he finished, he asked, "Which way's the safe room?" He didn't plan on saving himself, but Hans and the rest of his team would live to see another day. Absolutely.

Persia stalked into the hall, backed up to the linen closet, and slammed her boot, heel first, against it. Instead of opening outward, the door slid up with the slightest hydraulic hiss, revealing another vault, similar to the front door, complete with a retinal scanner array.

"Well, bless my heart. Are you telling me we're going to need this, soldier?" she snapped, her middle finger doing its thing again. Her eyes flashed the sexiest brown flames Walker had ever been blessed with. His blood thickened, and his cock sprang to hot-damned attention. She might think she was a weakling because she'd had a few nightmares. But no way. This woman rocked her authority with poise and enough confidence to inspire even Hans. Who, Walker damned well noticed, was staring at Persia, as if she were a movie star and he was her greatest fan. That crap had to stop.

"Not if yours are the only retinas that'll open it," Walker countered, used to leading, not following.

"Relax," Izza soothed. "We've got you covered, big guy."

Not what he wanted to hear. "Prove it."

"Fine," Persia growled without any hint she'd just shared intimate secrets with him. "I'll open it, just for you."

*Whoa, the sarcasm.* He loved it.

"For your information, this door stays unlocked until someone shuts themselves inside and locks it. Is that understood? All you need to worry about is how to hit the big, square, palm-sized button inside this room. Can you handle that, Lieutenant Judge?"

*And now I'm back in the Navy.* Every word out of her mouth carried an implied dare. That last one, *Lieutenant Judge,* was a glove slapped across his face, challenging him to a duel. *Not Hotrod?* She was steadily provoking him to question her authority.

And hot damn, he was falling farther in love with every snarky order out of her hot, wet mouth. He'd worked with female soldiers and jarheads before, but never one as sexy or as sure of herself as Persia, and none who'd been in charge or pushed his buttons like she did. Even the way she stood in the hall with her shoulders squared, her feet spread, and her chin lifted, declared, *'Just try me.'*

The rowdy caveman in him roared to life to do just that. The impulse hit him to step over the imaginary line she'd drawn, to try her. To throw her belligerent ass over his shoulder, smack that ass, then carry her back to his den. Make a fire, then make her his. In every position possible.

"I asked if you understand me?" And now she was being an ass. A sexy, dominant, drill-sergeant-worthy ass. "Does that suit your particular Navy skillset, LT?"

"Yes, ma'am," Walker shot back at her. She had never before looked as hot as she did right then. How was he supposed to fight ICC assholes, when he wanted to rip her clothes off and fuck the hell out of her? Make her scream?

The vibration of heavy equipment rattled the house, ending that daydream. Sounded like a tank had pulled up to the front door. Stewart had better be right about this safe house's ability to withstand 120-millimeter rounds.

Walker turned to his assigned duty location, as Persia strode past him, her head held high and the buttstock of her rifle pressed into her shoulder. This woman was ready to fight, and he could barely tear his eyes off her.

Until a shot splattered the front window, and a hail of gunfire erupted at both the front and back of the house. Sounded like an entire hive of killer bees had been set loose. Yet nothing breached the structure or came through the window. Tiny impressions, like rock chips on a windshield, were the only damage to the glass.

*And here we go…*

He took position to the right of the windowpane, with Persia at the left, nearest the front door. Peering out, it looked like a small army had arrived. No tank, but three armored vehicles, all black and lacking high-power armament. But deadly just the same.

"Persia?" Izza called from the rear door. "Report." She looked as steady as Persia, but Hans was plenty rattled, breathing hard and twitchy as hell. He held his rifle like a novice who was afraid of the weapon. Not good.

"Looks like BSB is knocking on our door, Iz. I count twelve men in flak jackets, all carrying tactical rifles and loaded for bear," Persia replied evenly. Man, her fingers weren't even trembling. "And you?"

BSB, aka the Dutch Brigade Speciale Beveiligingsopdrachten; in English, the Security Assignments Brigade. Consisting of military police and various commandos, BSB was known for its ruthlessness when conducting special operations. This group must be their arrest team.

"Dozen, near as I can see through this damned peephole. Might be more. Hans, what do you think?"

"More," he breathed. "The BSB is similar to your American SWAT. Only better. This must be their advance team. But their uniforms are strange..."

Walker didn't have time to worry about their get-ups. "If this place is as secure as you say, Coltrane, what do we have to worry about?" he asked under his breath, needing all the deets, not just the whitewashed, good-enough-for-Hans, version.

"Because every good plan turns to crap the second shit hits the fan," she told him out of the corner of her mouth. "If things go south, get your ass in that safe room. Take Hans with you. Lock the door and wait these bastards out."

He lowered his voice. "And let you die? Get over yourself, sugar. Be serious. What are you really thinking? That they'll hit this place with a Hellfire missile?"

She swiped a hand over her lips. "I hope not, but this place is seven-years-old, and The Hague has blueprints on file for every building in the city. I'm thinking if they know how well this house is built, they've already planned how to get inside. We've got no diplomatic immunity if they do. They'll kill us, no questions asked. Hans for sure. And don't call me sugar."

"But you've already called for an assist. Someone is coming, right, sugar?"

Her nostrils flared. "Izza did, but they're not here yet, are they? Stop calling me sugar."

"But sugar, that fifteen minute ETA was—"

"Not for us," Persia breathed, as another attack of killer bees hit the front door and window, again without causing any real damage. "And stop calling me sugar, Goddamn it!"

Walker couldn't resist. He puckered up, blew her a tiny air kiss, and winked. Just to piss her off. What was she going to do? Court-martial him?

She slanted one helluva an evil-eye at him. Which only made him smile wider. Until the house shrieked, shook and vibrated. Then—

"Scheisse!" Hans hissed. "They're taking the entire building!"

"They're what?" Walker bellowed as things inside cupboards shifted and everything loose on countertops crashed to the floor.

"Plan B! Engage!" Persia ordered as she jerked the front door open, grabbed another box of ammo, and stepped outside.

Walker followed, hard on her six. Several rounds zipped past his head the moment he cleared the doorway. So fast, that he stepped back just to let the bullets fly by. Sure enough. The ICC had brought in a giant crane, its massive claws clutched over the roof of the house. Bet Stewart hadn't thought of that.

Persia dropped one knee on the top step, already firing steadily, an open box of ammo at her side. With an inordinate touch of manly pride, Walker noticed she knew how to run her gun. The ultimate sign of a professional. Never took her eyes off her targets, as, one by one, four men fell to her well-placed shots. She reloaded, again without looking away or fumbling for ammo. In seconds, she'd dropped two more BSB guys.

But he doubted these men were BSB. Hans was right. None wore official BSB badges or any other identifying insignia. Instead, every last head out there was shaved, adorned with swastikas and tats. The bastards all carried AKs. The ICC hadn't sent them.

"Cover me," he told Persia as he ran into the fray, then slid to his knees on the front walk. He'd caught the assassins by surprise. Also put him in the middle, where the far-right group couldn't shoot him without taking out their far-left guys. Walker took advantage of that few seconds delay and took out the crane operator with one well-placed shot. Who would've ever thought to rip a house off its foundation to get at a wanted criminal? Guess the Dutch, that's who.

Izza bellowing and cursing from inside told him the rear exit had been breached. Sweating now and out of breath, he pushed to his feet and ran back to the house. Clean shot, straight through the front door and through the house. He nailed the guard struggling with Izza, then the guy aiming at Hans.

Surprised when that thug fell dead, Hans sent Walker a thankful nod. Izza was back in fighting mode. She shoved Hans out of her way and blocked the doorway with her body, firing like a madwoman. Which made her a target.

No way.

Walker charged into the house, determined to hold fast until that promised TEAM assist showed. Where the hell were they?

With both front and rear egress points breached and no assurance Stewart's TEAM would arrive in time to save anyone, Walker did the smart thing. The right thing. The only thing.

Ripping his t-shirt over his head, he wound one sleeve over the end of his rifle and backtracked to the front door. He had a bargain to make.

# Chapter Thirty-Two

"No!" Izza screamed from the rear exit. "Damn you, Walker. Stop!"

Persia glanced over her shoulder in time to catch sight of him clearing the front door, a damned white flag stuck on the end of his rifle. "Back inside!" she bellowed. "I didn't come all this way to lose you now!"

"I won't let you die," he answered calmly. "Tell your boss—"

*BLAM!* A round caught his left shoulder, twisting the upper right half of his body forward. A red puff of blood and tissue sprayed the wall behind him. He clutched her wrist and fell to one knee. That damned white flag kept waving like the surrender it was.

"You sons of bitches!" Persia yelled, firing one round after the other into the assassins headed her way. Going to kill every last one if it was the last thing she did.

Hotrod should've known better! Damn him! These guys weren't from the ICC. They were common thugs. They wouldn't take him alive. Every last one of them was after the bounty on his head. Jesus, what a way to go. Hunted like a dog. Bleeding like a stuck pig.

*Not on my watch!*

"Get inside, Persia," he pleaded. "Please. For me. This is the only way you guys are going to live. Don't you see?"

"No!" she snapped, never more sure than now that this was where she was supposed to be. At his side when he needed her most, with her sharp eyes picking off one damned varmint after another and covering his ass.

Another spray of firepower exploded the siding over her head. Slivers and chunks of wood rained down. With one desperate shove, he forced her backward and pushed her inside. Where she'd be safe, but he would not. The ass!

"Don't do this!" she ordered, even as she fell on her rear.

Hotrod slammed the door in her face.

Persia scrambled to her feet, rifle still in hand. Looking through that small square of bulletproof glass in the door, she stared into the stormy blue eyes on the other side. He knew he'd be killed. But he looked pissed, yet brokenhearted at the same time. A river of red streamed down his neck, over his shoulder and chest. The stupid ass's hard head had just taken a hit. He'd been grazed. He meant to die for her. *Like hell!*

"Let me out!" She jerked at the door handle. Then harder. It didn't budge. Hotrod held the other side of that knob.

"Damn you! Let me out!" she cried, frantic she'd have to stand here and watch while they riddled his body with shot after shot. As if on cue, another round splattered across the front of the house, etching the window panes, still not breaking through. Somehow missing him.

Hotrod never broke eye contact. Never blinked. Just stared at her, as if he were soaking up this last moment. As if this was the end and he knew it. He was going to stand there and die to save her.

Persia froze. For a millionth of a damned second.

"No! Damn you, no! You can't do this!" she bellowed, pulling with all her weight and energy to open that door. "I can help! I'm no weakling! You can't do this! Let me out!"

Tears brimmed with every unsuccessful tug. She braced her feet. Cursed brave men in general. Tried to overpower his hold again. And again! "I'm not giving up on you, damn it. Don't you dare give up on me!"

Yet there Hotrod stood, on the other side of forever. As patient as fuck! Tenderness gleamed like tears in his eyes. He was doing it again, walking away and leaving her. Only this time, there'd be no coming back.

Tires screeched. Thunder rumbled and—

*UMMPH!* She watched as a different heavy vehicle cleared the curb and slammed to a halt. Then another. Her heart sank. Someone's cavalry had arrived. Either that was a fresh batch of assassins and this was the end or—

The battle sounds changed from AKs screaming to the steadier, heavier growl of—custom made rifles? Yesssss! Those were TEAM weapons and TEAM vehicles! Damn them! They were late, but The TEAM was here!

Hotrod glanced over his shoulder, taking in the latest threat, as if he'd heard the change in artillery cadence, too. His split-second distraction worked for Persia. Pissed as hell, she jerked that door inward, enough to knock his arrogant ass off-balance.

"Damn you," she cried as she pulled this stupid, stupid man inside. "You'd better not die!"

"For you, sugar, anything," he wheezed.

Then she wished she hadn't screamed. Hotrod stumbled forward. His eyes rolled back in his head. With a grunt, he collapsed into her, a dead, bleeding weight.

"Thank God!" Izza exclaimed from somewhere behind her. "They came, Hans. The TEAM is here. We're saved!"

Persia sank to the floor with Walker, her rifle still at her side. "He's been hit, Izza! He's dying!"

Cradling him, she ran a quick hand over his sweaty head. Her fingers came away drenched with red. One round had definitely grazed his skull, but the other was a through and through, high on his left shoulder. Red rivers poured from both wounds. "Don't leave me, Hotrod. Walker, please. Don't you dare leave me again…"

"Crap! Stupid damned SEALs," Izza hissed as she dropped to her knees alongside them. "He saves my life, then throws his away? Dumb shit! I'll kick his ass if he dies!"

It was times like this that Persia adored Izza. With her blowout kit already spread on Hotrod's belly, she worked quickly and expertly. Fiercely, as if she were at war with yet another enemy. Izza applied a hearty dose of QuikClot to stop the flow pouring out of his head wound, closed it with a bulky, sticky pad, then went to work on that through and through.

"Here," she snapped as she handed Persia a small plastic bag of cotton plugs. "You know what to do with these. I'll take the exit."

"I've got the entry," Persia replied, her heart pounding at how much this was going to hurt him. Yet it had to be done. The plugs were compressed cotton. Designed to expand when saturated, they'd slow the blood loss until medics arrived. One after another, she pushed several plugs into the bleeding hole just under his collarbone. It was battlefield first-aid at its best.

Hotrod groaned and tensed every time her fingertip penetrated his muscle. But he never opened his eyes. A bullet to the head, even a near miss, a graze, still impacted a man's skull with enough kinetic energy to crack bones and cause concussions. He hadn't yet recovered from his first concussion. He needed real medics and a Life Flight helicopter, damn it!

"Harder," Izza growled even as she leaned down to peer at the exit wound she'd treated. "Men are so stupid."

"He sacrificed himself for us," Persia murmured.

"I know. I saw that damned white flag. Still a dumbass move." The harder Izza worked, the more she cussed. "Fuckin' hero move. Not smart, Hotrod."

"You've done this before."

"Too many times." For as tiny as she was, this fierce Hispanic woman didn't know the meaning of quit.

"Connor?"

Izza shook her head. "No. He was gut shot. Whole different dumbass. Whole different problem."

"When?"

Izza growled, pushed hard on Hotrod's shoulder while she compressed the last plug into his back. "During that same Utah op. We got into a little trouble with our Mexican friends. Had to fight for our lives. No biggie."

"Was that when he killed those guys in that hangar? The time he rescued you? You call that no biggie?"

Izza shrugged. "Yeah. I saved him first, then he saved me last. So what? That's the way it works, Persia. If you love a man, you'll die for him, cuz if he's the one for you, he'll die for you without thinking twice. This guy just proved that in spades, huh?"

Persia swallowed hard. "You could say that."

She couldn't look away from Hotrod's rugged face. He'd grown pale. Even his scruff seemed lighter. As if he were fading away before she'd had time to tell him how she felt.

But she wasn't ready to whisper the L word yet. Didn't know if she'd ever be ready. Commitment was one of those final absolutes. A forever. Like death. She'd seen so much heartbreak in her life, that she'd discounted the concept of forever as a myth. Didn't want to live more heartache than she'd already witnessed.

Life was so damned tough for some people. There were no promises, even with marriage vows. Julio Juarez was proof of that. He'd gone through hell on earth with his first wife and son, only to lose them in the worst ways possible. Yes, eventually he'd found Meg, and they were living their happily-ever-after. But what were the chances Persia would find that kind of connection? Even with the man who'd just taken a bullet for her? He'd already left her once. Why ask for a repeat?

Izza's head came up. "Boss is here. Beau and Adam, too. They've taken care of whoever those asshats were. Boss is on his phone. Looks pissed."

*As usual.* "Those guys weren't BSB. But I'll bet someone at ICC is behind them being here."

"Agreed. I'm just surprised it didn't happen sooner. Come on. Let's get your boyfriend here cleaned up and ready to travel before Alex wants a full Sitrep."

"He's not my boyfriend, Izza."

"Yeah, right. Try telling that to the guy who sat up with you all last night during the nightmare you had."

Oh, shit. The dimmest shred of Hotrod calling her out of a very dark place came back to Persia. In her usual nightmares, she would've been running from Zapata. Hotrod knew that now. Did Izza? Had she seen?

Gingerly, Izza tilted him forward so Persia could get to her feet. By the time they were both standing, Adam had run in from the rear door. Quickly, his eyes scrolled over Persia, Izza, then fell to Hotrod. "Walker got hit? Damn, how bad?"

"Took two hits," Persia reported as evenly as she could. "One grazed his head, the other's a through and through."

Adam knelt, a couple bandages in his hand. "Let me have a look. Hold him steady."

Persia knelt, then tipped Hotrod into her shoulder while Adam double checked the exit wound, then slapped pressure bandages in place. She cupped the back of Hotrod's hard head and pressed her cheek to his sweaty hair. How had this happened? Not the wounds in his body, but the holes in her heart? She'd never felt as close to any other man as she did Walker Judge.

A moan eked out of him when Adam pressed too hard.

Persia closed her eyes, feeling every last bit of his pain in that moan. Wishing she could go back in time and do things differently. Yet every decision point in her past, every pivot point, even her seemingly innocent choice of colleges, had brought her to this day and this particular wounded warrior.

Shuddering, he arched his back.

"Take it easy," she whispered. Somehow, his bloody hand found hers. Persia lifted that hand to her heart. "Adam's here to help. Relax, Hotrod. We're safe now, and I've got you."

When she opened her eyes, Alex was standing over her, those icy-blue, razor-sharp blues of his, slicing and dicing through her tough-girl persona. Looking through her.

Analyzing. Judging. Always quartering her like he seemed to do with everyone and everything.

Well, let him look. If he could dish it out, he could take it. "Boss, this is Walker Judge, aka Hotrod," she told him clearly. "He's injured, and I'm going with him."

Alex's lips pursed with what had, until now, always seemed like disapproval. Yet he growled, "You're damned right you are. Step aside. Let me at him."

Persia released Hotrod's hand as Alex took a knee, then lifted him into a fireman's hold. Without another word, Alex jogged out the front door with him.

"Ladies…" Adam's big, square chin jutted toward the front way out. "The authorities are on their way. We can't be here when they arrive. We have to go now."

"I never did like this safe house," Izza muttered.

But Persia took one last look down the hall. She'd conquered one of her demons in this house. In that room. It might be the right time to conquer the other….

# Chapter Thirty-Three

He'd turned into Bill Murray, and this was freakin' *"Groundhog Day."* Once again, waking up alone in bed, feeling like a Bradley tank had run over him, not knowing where he was, but knowing this shit had to stop.

Something beeped up beyond his head. Walker peeled one eye open. Shit. He was in a hospital this time, and that beeping noise came from the machine tracking his vitals. At least he hadn't flatlined, and he wasn't back in that ICC cell.

He took quick stock of the room. Standard hospital issue. Nothing special and no one in sight. Until the door hissed quietly open and—

"Son of a bitch! Trevor Duncan!" He reached a hand to his Army buddy. The man who'd taught him to fly Blackhawks, and who'd personally covered his ass during Walker's brief stint as a Nightstalker pilot.

"You ass!" Trevor growled, even as he took hold of Walker's hand and squeezed the hell out of his fingers.

Brought sissy tears to Walker's eyes, but that hard, tough handshake hurt so good. "Why are you here? How'd you…? Where's…? Shit, don't just stand there. Say something!"

Trevor dropped the toughest-man-in-the-room routine and let Walker's hand go. "Been tracking your stupid ass for weeks now."

"You rescued us? That was you? Where are Persia and Izza?"

Both Trevor's palms came up as if to placate him. "Slow down. Take it easy. I'm not who rescued you. That was another guy. He'll be in later. Guess he's got trouble with some ornery senator in Washington, DC. He's been on his phone all day. But listen… Someone's waiting to see you."

"Bring her in," Walker said. *Please. Bring Persia in, right damned now.*

"Her?" Trevor teased as he leaned out into the hall and waved at someone to join them.

In walked Smoke Montoya, the dark-haired SEAL from Texas, and a fuckin' legend.

"Hey," growled the man who had single-handedly ended more ISIL and Taliban terrorists than any other spec ops operator. Then walked away from America for some reason Walker had never known.

"Smoke…?" Man, he was all choked up. "Why…? How…?"

Rolling one shoulder, Smoke stalked to the bed like he was ready to fight. "Because you're my brother, that's why," he said as he took hold of Walker's forearm, wrist to elbow. Some kind of wicked SEAL magic passed from him to Walker. Choked a man up to be remembered by the hero America had forgotten.

"And SEALs stick together," another rugged voice muttered from the doorway.

Julio Juarez! "What are you doing here?" Walker croaked. Seeing these men—these brothers—was killing him. Stupid damned tears welled in his eyes, making him blink like a sissy.

"I've been looking for you since you left me stranded off the coast of Brazil," Julio answered quietly. Once Smoke dropped Walker's arm, Julio took possession, interlocking his wrist with Walker's, like Smoke had just done. "I may not be a SEAL like you, *amigo*, but I will always be your brother. Meg says to tell you it's time to stop running and come home. That you have more friends than you realize. That you're going to be our son's godfather." He tugged something out of his rear pocket and slapped it onto Walker's chest.

Holy hell, a one-way airline ticket to Dallas-Fort Worth, Texas.

"Dominic? That was that little guy's name, right?" His brain was still plenty fuzzy, but Walker was sure that's what Persia had told him the night they'd met.

Julio nodded. The man was another legend. Born in Mexico, he'd traveled north as a teenager to work the strawberry fields of California, then studied hard, finished high school early and entered a local community college. A year later, he joined the Navy to pay America back for his new-found freedom. Not only joined, but Julio had told his recruiter he planned to be a SEAL. That got him a SEAL mentor, who properly trained him to pass the rigorous BUDS PST, the physical screening test. He'd just been accepted for Hell week when Hell had literally come calling in the guise of Satan's most evil spawn: Domingo Zapata. The sociopath kidnapped Julio's family, which forced Julio to ring out and begin the arduous challenge of getting his wife and tiny son back. It took him five torturous years. But that was another story.

"He's home with Meg. What shall I tell her?"

"Tell her I'll try—"

Julio cocked his head. "You will *try*? You? A SEAL? One of America's best, you will only *try*?"

Walker got the point. Try was not in any SEAL's vocabulary. He slapped Julio's hand, hard. "I'll be there, damn it. Tell that wife of yours, yes. I'll be there, and I'm proud to be Dominic's godfather. You did marry her, didn't you?"

Julio shrugged. "Of course. As soon as I could. She and Dominic are *mi familia*."

"You're one lucky son of a bitch," Walker said, thinking of Persia and how lucky he was to have her in his life. It'd sure be nice if she stayed…

"Damned fuckin' straight." Lieutenant Junior Grade Ryder Dahl declared. Once Walker's exec, he filled the doorway. Could've blocked the sun. Big. Black. And one damned loyal friend, Ryder was smiling like a son of a bitch. "Got some assholes out here who've been waiting all day for you to wake up, princess."

"Ryder!" Words failed.

"Yeah, Boss, of course it's me. Where else would I be but on your six? Just had to find your dumbass to follow it."

Walker would've laughed if Ensigns Steel Arrington, Nguyen Le, and Dallas Perkins hadn't jostled their wide shoulders and skinny asses through the door. Ensigns, what's a CO to do with them? Then… *Shit*. Red-headed, First Class Urban Sweeny, followed by Petty Officer Third Class Amerigo. Things were getting crowded in this tiny, standing-room-only place. His guys. They were all here.

"You sailors on shore leave or something?" Walker asked, struggling to get his damned emotions in check and his voice back under control.

"Nah." Amerigo Torres shrugged. "We quit, Boss. Figured it was high time we followed our leader into Hell again. Where are we going this time?"

"Yeah, Boss. Since you couldn't seem to stay clear of the law," Ensign Dallas Perkins, aka Tex, drawled. "We decided to come help."

"You quit the Navy?" Walker had to understand what he thought he'd just heard.

"No, Boss, we didn't quit the Navy," Ryder said in his deep, clear-as-Michael-Clarke-Duncan voice. "The fuckin' Navy quit us the day they convicted our Chief and sent him to Leavenworth. So yeah. We're here for you and—"

"Figured you needed one of these to get your lazy ass moving." Steel Arrington produced a dripping wet PBR, as in Pabst Blue Ribbon beer, from the plastic bag under his arm.

Shit. That did it. Walker was too exhausted to keep the tears from trickling out of the corners of his eyes. But then it got worse. In walked Brimley Scott with his street sweeper mustache and those same round spectacles. He hadn't changed a bit. "Rover's waiting outside. Hospital rules, so I can't stay long, LT. Just want you to know not to worry. I got everything handled."

"Brim," Walker ground out, his arm stretched to his friend. "You're here."

"Where else would I be?" the old guy growled as he came to Walker's side and pulled him into a bear hug.

Walker was a mess by then, hanging onto his friend as if Brim were a lifesaver. Afraid to let go. So damned shocked and thankful and—broken. He'd been running so long, but this crusty old veteran had trusted him from the get-go.

"There, there, son," Brim murmured as gently as a father might.

"How... how's Rover?"

"He's good. They ripped you off that boat of yours so fast, I never had time to tell you a proper goodbye. Want you to know that me and Rover been taking real good care of your girl. She's docked safe and sound in Portugal. Dry-docked her, so no one'll see her, and no one can get at her. She's safe, LT. Like you."

Walker shook his head, fighting like hell to get in control before he let Brim go. It'd been a long damned time since he'd been safe. Brim's words almost made the concept seem real.

This reunion could only have been better if—

"Walker Judge?" another familiar voice asked through the crowd. "Is this his room?"

"Come on in, sir," Trevor answered. "He's over here, still laying around and—"

Walker eased out of Brim's hairy arms. "Quinn?" he croaked, so damned wrung out by this overwhelming show of support from the caliber of men crowded in his hospital room. He could barely speak.

"Hell, yes, it's me," Captain Quinn Dooley muttered. Dressed smartly in his official whites, with his cover tucked under one arm, he cut a proud figure. One by one, Walker's friends stepped aside and let the Naval officer elbow his way forward. Finally at Walker's bedside, Quinn told the room, "At ease."

Not like most of them hadn't already been at ease. Only the three ensigns, Steel Arrington, Nguyen Li, and Dallas Perkins, had snapped to when they'd seen him.

"What are you doing here?" Walker asked the man he'd once risked his life for.

"I've come to repay a debt that is long overdue," Dooley replied somberly. Damned if his eyes weren't sparkling a little too much. That didn't help.

Walker coughed. "You, sir, don't owe me any—"

"Wrong, sailor. I owe you everything," Dooley corrected sternly. He tugged a handful of pink and blue strings and beads out of his pants pocket and handed them to Walker. "Emily asked me to give this to you. She made it, and you'd better damned well wear it. That little girl loves you, Judge. Don't know why, but—" Dooley choked, because he knew precisely why Emily loved Walker. And why Walker would forever adore his little girl.

He blinked hard as he accepted the sweet gift, a bracelet made with pink and blue elastic strings and bright red hearts. He slid it over his left hand, the one without an IV line, and onto his wrist. By then he could hardly speak. Didn't dare.

Quinn grasped Walker's right hand. Like a brother, pulse to pulse, his fingers tight around Walker's wrist. "You saved her, buddy. You saved my daughter, and you saved me and my wife, too. Now, I'm here to save you."

Walker honestly didn't see how that could ever happen, not with all the bogus charges stacked against him. It was like betting against the house in Reno. The cards were already counted, stacked, the crooked die cast, and he was going down.

"And the next time you're on my ship, you'd better damned well introduce yourself," Quinn growled.

Walker nearly smiled. He'd been on Quinn's aircraft carrier during that covert op into Brazil to assist Meg Duncan, then Julio. He would've grinned at the scolding, but one of his guys, he honestly hadn't seen which, reached past Dooley and slugged Walker's injured arm.

"Shit! That's where I was shot, you ass! It still hurts like a mother—"

Every single one of those blowhards laughed. They laughed! Even Quinn!

And Walker laughed with them. Because, well, that's what tough bastards did. They pulled each other back from all kinds of dangerous edges, even when that edge was just a crying jag.

Captain Quinn Dooley leaned over and told him, "Get used to it, LT. We're not going anywhere. We'll leave now to give you time to rest and heal and get your head back in the game. But mark my words, we'll be back. You're not in this fight alone anymore. Get that through your thick SEAL skull, will you?"

Walker could only nod and blink, then blink again.

Until his XO bellowed, "Commander on deck!"

Every last one of his men snapped to attention. Even Smoke and Dooley. And Brim!

*Now who?* Walker sank back into his pillow, exhausted but so damned thankful for brothers-in-arms.

Turned out the commander on deck was a tall, deadly serious, badassed civilian, not an officer at all. Dark haired. Craggy face. Wicked blue eyes. This guy was decked in tactical armor, and he wore it like he owned every last one of their souls. The men in his way flattened against the walls to make room for him. On his six, the only woman in Walker's dreams peered around the guy's thick biceps.

Persia winked. "Lieutenant Walker Judge, may I introduce my boss and the man who owns the one and only TEAM, Mr. Alex Stewart. Alex, this is the SEAL I've told you about."

Stewart rolled his eyes. Grunted. Why Walker wanted to salute him, he didn't know. It just seemed the proper thing to do to the man who'd commanded this many warriors just by showing up.

"Knock it off," Alex hissed at the men still at attention. "I'm not a son of a bitchin' officer. Relax. Then get the hell out. Judge and I need to talk."

Just like that, the room emptied. Even Captain Dooley, a Navy officer, who should've been shown more respect, walked out without a word. The room was quiet for all of two seconds, until Steel Arrington dodged back inside and set that frosty PBR on Walker's nightstand with a wink and a cheeky, "Later, Boss."

Tired to his soul, Walker faced Stewart. Persia stood at this fierce man's side like an obedient handmaiden, and that pissed Walker off. He fluttered his fingers for her to come to him. Damned if a smile didn't brighten her face. Persia came straight to his side, took his hand, and together they faced her boss.

"You made all this happen," Walker said to the guy. "I don't know who you are, but… thank you."

"I'm your boss, is who I am." Stewart stuck his chin at Walker, like one of those arrogant guys who thought they knew more than everyone else. Maybe he did.

"My boss?" Walker could feel Persia beaming down on him, like a warm morning sunrise.

"You heard me," Stewart growled. "Take it or leave it, I don't give a shit either way. But Agent Coltrane is one of my best, and when she tells me I'd be smart to hire you…" —he spared a quick glare under his eyebrows at Persia— "I'm smart enough do what I'm told. Are you?"

"Just like that? You want me to work for you?" *What the hell?*

"I asked you, didn't I?"

Talking with Stewart was like playing with a buzz saw. Every comeback carried a potential threat and a lethal glare. He was Walker's USN drill sergeant all over again.

"Yes, sir, but" —Walker caught himself. Shit, he was damned near ready to bawl again. What the hell was going on? These emotions were way out of hand— "I mean, Mr. Stewart. How did you…? Why did you…?"

"How did I know where to find your men? How did I know to locate Brimley Scott and his dog on a yacht stuck between the Azores and Portugal? How do I know you went into Guatemala, without proper clearance or permission, allegedly on personal business, fifteen months ago? How do I know why the captain of the *Iwo Jima* aircraft carrier is here with you today, instead of off the coast of Brazil, where he's supposed to be? Is that what you're asking me, junior agent?"

*Junior agent, huh?* Stewart seemed to think he already owned him. He certainly knew a lot. But Guatemala? Quinn Dooley?

"How do you know all that?" Walker couldn't help that his voice sounded tighter than usual. Or that his questions had come out raspy and hoarse.

"Because it's my business to know. Anything else?"

"Why are you doing this? You don't even know me."

Stewart's hard-as-ice eyes softened. "Because that's what I do, Walker Judge. I take the cases no one else will touch, and my TEAM does the impossible. I've been in your shoes once or twice. I know what betrayal feels like. But you're like me, too stupid to realize how many friends you've got. So I decided to show you before you got yourself killed."

That, right there, damned near broke Walker's heart. "But I'm a convicted felon. I'm wanted by the FBI, the Queen of England, and…" *And shit, just about every lawman between here and Dodge City, Kansas.*

Stewart waved that off like it was nothing. "So? You're still breathing, aren't you?"

*Well, err…* "Yes."

"Then stop whining."

Walker didn't know what to say to that. "Doesn't it matter, you hiring a convicted felon?"

"Hasn't before."

Thankfully, Persia came to Walker's rescue. "Boss, were you able to get through to Senator Sullivan yet?"

"Yesssss," Stewart hissed as he crossed his thick arms over his massive chest. "Dumb ass. He'll get over it."

"Okay, stop!" Walker bellowed, fed up with the overload of too many bits and pieces of intel. "You know McQueen Sullivan, too? Christ, who the hell are you?"

A crooked smirk tweaked the corners of Stewart's lips. "Already told you. I'm your boss. Not Sullivan. Get some rest. I'll be back in three hours. Be ready to move then."

And he was gone.

# Chapter Thirty-Four

The excitement had worn Walker out, Persia could tell. He was pale and breathing hard, staring into space more than asking coherent questions about what had just happened. She pulled a molded-plastic chair over to his bedside the second Alex left, ready to answer all Walker's questions. It was time to call him by his real name. Alex certainly had.

"Hey, Walker. You okay?"

"So talk," he told her quietly. "Who's Stewart, and why's he really here? What's he want from me?"

"I told you about him once before, remember?"

Walker shook his head. Even his blue eyes were pale.

"Former Marine. Owns a covert surveillance company called The TEAM, in Alexandria, Virginia. Hates to be called sir."

Walker's fingers fluttered. "That I remembered."

"I noticed you only made the mistake once."

"Yeah. He's like me, hates officers. I'd like to know the story behind that."

"Well, you work for him now. Maybe someday, he'll tell you."

"Stop stalling, Coltrane. Spill."

"Okay. Well, I had no idea until he showed up at the safe house, but Alex has been working your case since he heard you'd been convicted of murder."

"But that was over a year ago. Does he follow every Navy trial?"

"No, but yours called to him. At least, that's what he said. He's had Ember Dennison and Beau Villanueva, they're The TEAM's technical wizards, following your former CO's money trail. They're like your Petty Officer First Class Urban Sweeny, only they handle more than just comm equipment, and… Don't tell anyone, but I think they're sharp enough to hack into a lot of federal systems but without getting caught."

That seemed to perk Walker's tired ears up. "Goff's money trail? Why?"

"Yes, Commander Wallace Goff, and because too many things didn't line up during your trial. I'll tell you what I know, but it'd be better if Beau explains everything. He's been on your case non-stop for months. You'll meet him as soon as you're up for more visitors."

"I'm up for it now. Bring him in."

"No, Walker. You need to rest or you won't heal. And you need to heal to fight. You've had two concussions."

His chest heaved. "I guess. But why me?"

"Why not you?" Persia asked as she took possession of his hand again and pressed his knuckles to her lips. "You have this crazy notion that you're expendable, but you're not, Walker Judge. Let me call Beau. He'll—"

"No," Walker ground out. "You're right. I've had enough for one day. But what the hell's your boss thinking? Me ready to travel in three hours? Shit, I can barely hold my head up."

"He knows full well what you need right now. He's got a jet on stand-by at a private airfield. I'll get a wheelchair. You won't have to do anything but come with us when we leave."

"Where are we going?" he asked, his eyes growing heavier with every question.

"To Ireland," Persia replied softly. "A good friend of Alex's lives there. We'll be off everyone's radar, and you'll be able to recover."

"Who… who's us?" he asked as his lashes fell.

Persia pressed his fist against her breasts. "Us is you and me. Us is your friend Brimley and his dog, your entire SEAL team, Trevor Duncan, Captain Dooley, Smoke Montoya, and…"

By then, Walker was out cold, breathing evenly, his hand slack in hers. "And a couple other experts you haven't met yet," she murmured. "Us is my boss and my friends, too. Beau, Adam, and Zack. We're all in this together."

Reaching her fingers into his hair, she smoothed it off his forehead, then slid her fingers down his cheek, loving the feel of his skin and scruff against her palm. He needed a haircut. She needed to kiss him.

Lifting to her feet, she leaned into Walker and pressed a fervent kiss to his forehead. "Sleep easy," she whispered. "I'll be right here when you wake up."

"Damned right you will," he growled as his arm circled her waist and up she went, into bed beside him. "Get comfy, junior agent. I'm tired, and you're not going anywhere."

Persia tipped her forehead into his cheek, not going to argue.

"You saved me," she told him breathlessly. "Back in that bedroom. After my nightmare. Izza told me what you said, and how you said it. She likes you, Walker."

"Izza's okay," he answered dreamily. "But you're the woman I love, Persia. Only you."

Her heart stopped. Love? Was he serious? Did he even know what he'd just said?

Opening his eyes, Walker shifted to face her. His free hand settled on her jaw. His thumb landed on her chin. He pressed his warm lips into her forehead. "Persia Coltrane," he breathed, then pulled back enough to look into her eyes. "It's true what I just said. I meant it. I do love you. Shhhhh. You don't have to love me back. I'm not asking for forever. I just needed you to know that my life changed the second I laid eyes on you. There you were, stuck in that ridiculous Adirondack chair."

That made her smile. "I looked stupid trying to get out of it, didn't I? Did I look like a turtle on its back?"

He grinned, his blue eyes soft and hazy. "You never look stupid. No way. Not you. If anything, you're a little scary sometimes. You're confident and strong. You're tough. Some would say you're bitchin'. It's obvious you're highly trained, just as lethal as most male operators I know. Plus, you like what you do. You're good at it. It shows."

"Women are strong, too."

"They are," he agreed on a sigh. His fingers lifted to her hair, threading through a thick chunk of it, shoving it back over her shoulder. "But you're more than just an operator, Persia. You're beautiful and you're mine. Stay with me tonight. I'll keep your nightmares away and you'll help me rest."

His breath was heavy in her face by then. Heavy, sweet, and male.

"Okay," she replied, easily snaking a hand around the back of his neck. "I'll stay with you, but just for tonight."

Walker pressed her into his side, his nose in her hair. "We'll see about that," he murmured thickly. "We'll see…"

The next day found Walker passing through a quaint Irish village in County Tipperary, Ireland. The ancient stone fortress known as the Rock of Cashel dominated what little of the countryside Walker could see from the side window of the SUV he was quarantined in. By then he'd met an associate of Stewart's, Senior Agent Murphy Finnegan. He owned the farm where Walker was now headed. It was Murphy who sat with Walker now. Not Persia.

She'd slipped out of his bed sometime this morning before two male nurses had arrived to get him ready to travel. He knew he had a concussion. Jesus Christ, what next? He hadn't yet recovered from that beat down inside the ICC, and the bullet hole in his shoulder was nothing to sneeze at.

Yet he was glad for the company. Murphy reminded him of Brimley. Damn, it had been good to see the old fart yesterday and to finally know what had happened, that Rover and *Persia Smiles* were safe. The first chance he could, Walker meant to get back on that yacht. He needed a better look at the evidence he'd found. He was sure it led back to someone Goff had known before his demise.

"How are you feeling, son?" Murphy asked from the driver's seat.

Walker was stretched out in the back seat, one boot on the seat, the other on the floor, and his head tipped back against a cushion, facing Murph. "I'm good."

Murphy grunted, his grin reflected from the rearview mirror. "I used to lie, too. Then I married my current wife, and Moira's a pediatrician. She's got no problem calling me a liar to my face. So be honest. I've got meds if you need them."

"I could use a couple aspirin."

Murphy tossed a prescription bottle over the seat. Then handed a bottle of water back. "Figured as much. You're looking a might green. You need me to pull over?"

"Nah," Walker said as he popped the cap off the water and swallowed the prescribed dose of little white pills. Pain pills were a necessary evil. Like now. But he'd watched too many guys fall to opioid addiction. He handed the bottle back to Murphy. "Thanks."

"Your head pounding, or is pain just tap-dancing up your spine?"

Murphy was one of those grandfatherly types who seemed to know how to talk to people, even hard-nosed SEALs. Which Walker surely wasn't at the moment. "Tap-dancing," he admitted as he leaned back and closed his eyes, shutting the bright, cheery sunlight out of his throbbing head. He'd never been carsick. Sure as hell didn't want to initiate Murphy's SUV by tossing his cookies. Walker swallowed hard and told his gut to man up. "How much farther?"

"Two clicks. You need anything else? I've got chips, crackers, beef jerky."

*Yes, Persia.* "No. I'm good."

"She's waiting at my place," Murphy replied as if he'd read Walker's mind. "Agent Coltrane. Alex is there, too. They went on ahead to get everything ready."

"That's nice," Walker murmured, the pain meds taking over what little resistance he had left.

When the SUV came to a gentle stop, whoever opened the back doors did it quietly. He vaguely remembered being laid on a gurney, then a smooth ride into a stone cottage that was as big as a barn. Then someone fussing over him, settling him into bed, wiping a cool cloth over his face and brow. Caring about him. "Persia?"

"Shush," she whispered. "Sleep, Walker. No worries. The *Irish Guarda* is onsite, along with several TEAM agents. They won't let anyone onto this property, not like people know where we are anyway. Alex will explain everything when he gets back."

That'd sure be nice. "Thought he was already here?"

"He's a busy man," Persia murmured into Walker's ear.

Walker let the soothing darkness take him.

A while later, he woke to quiet conversation coming from beyond his darkened room. Walker rolled to the side of the bed and put both bare feet to the hardwood floor, testing his head for dizziness and his gut for nausea. The side effects of concussion. When he felt neither, he inhaled a full cleansing breath. The tantalizing aroma of grilled meat filled his nostrils. Then... tacos?

It was time to get moving. Cautiously, he lifted to his feet, then used the en suite head, a nice touch with American-style toiletries. Once he'd showered and finished with the necessities, he took a look at his reflection in the mirror over the sink. Not too bad. He needed a shave and a haircut, but his skull wasn't pounding and his eyes were clear. He passed a damp, cool towel over his face, and folded it over the rack. After brushing his teeth, he made for the ongoing conversation outside his door. It stilled the moment he showed his face.

"You're up?" Persia asked with a surprised smile.

*You're gorgeous,* he thought. But he asked, "What's cooking?"

"The guys out back are grilling steaks, and Izza's making enchiladas and homemade tortillas."

His stomach growled. "She can cook, too?"

"I heard that," Izza called from the kitchen.

"You're a rock star!" Walker yelled back at her.

"Too little, too late, buddy. No salsa for you."

Damn, he would've begged for salsa now, but not in front of Stewart.

Persia, Murphy, Stewart, Quinn, Trevor, Brimley, and Ryder were seated in chairs and on couches around a massive wooden coffee table in the center of the room. The rest of Walker's men sat cross-legged on the floor between the chairs, all with brown bottles of Guinness in hand. Hans sat beside Persia, a scuffed-up satchel at his foot. Smoke Montoya sat cross-legged with Rover sprawled across his lap. The dog jumped up and bounced over Nguyen Li's legs on his way to meet and greet Walker.

"Hey, boy, how ya doing?" he asked as he stroked the happy, tail-wagging boy. "You missed me?"

Rover whined and wiggled like a big furry kid.

"No, he misses the shark we've been eating," Brimley announced, saluting Walker with his bottle raised high. "Come on in, son. Have a seat. We've been talking about you."

"I'll bet," Walker said as he looked to Stewart, who nodded sideways at the vacant chair next to him. Stepping over Amerigo Torres and Urban Sweeney, Walker made his way. Might as well get it over with.

"About time," Stewart grumbled the second Walker's ass hit the cushion.

"Yeah, well…" He yawned just to tweak the uptight guy. "You know how us SEALs are."

Those laser blues could've sliced titanium, but Walker wasn't up to taking crap from anyone. Especially not some jarhead with attitude. "What'd I miss?" he asked brightly.

Persia beamed from her place across the circle.

"Him," Stewart growled, his arrogant chin now stuck at the two men who'd just come from the kitchen. One as big, shaggy, and dark as a bear, the other—

"Adam!" Walker called out, back on his feet again, damned if he was going to sit like a weak-kneed pansy in front of his SEAL brother.

Adam cut through the circle with long strides. "You're looking good," he said as he pulled Walker into a manly chest bump, then gently cuffed his good shoulder. "Shit, it's been—"

"Three years," Walker said as he eased out of Adam's rugged embrace. "I hear you're married. You got a kid?" Man, this blond behemoth looked good. Tan. Broad across the chest and shoulders. Still grinning as if he were on top of the world.

"We do, yes. Stop by and visit once you're back in the States. I've been telling Squeaks and Shannon about you. They're dying to meet the man behind the myth."

Walker blinked. There it was again, the same brotherhood as the last time he'd worked with Adam. Front and center. Always faithful. Always ready to take a guy in. Feed him. Make him part of his family. "What the hell kind of name is Squeaks?"

A dimple dented the center of Adam's big square chin. "That's what he said when he was born. He squeaked, so—"

"Bullshit," Izza interrupted. "Shannon didn't even know she was pregnant when that plane crashed. But when her water broke, me and Connor were on the other side of the island. Adam was the only one there, so he delivered her baby. All by himself. Bet Squeaks wasn't the only one squeaking then."

Both Adam's shoulders lifted. "Nothing to it. Like catching a home run."

"Ha!" Izza barked. "That sweet little guy was just what we needed back then. Squeaks shouldn't have lived. He came two months early, and we were worried we'd never—"

"Ahem," Stewart growled impatiently.

He sure had a way of dominating—and ruining—a perfectly great reunion. Walker wanted to laugh in his face. Instead, he cuffed Adam's bicep and promised, "Later, bro. Drinks for sure."

"At my place," Adam added, his joy at being a husband and father so obvious, it stabbed Walker's heart. Man, he wanted what Adam had. That undefinable something that made this flyboy seem—grounded. Maybe anchored. As if he'd found something that mattered more than those risky HALO jumps and the adrenaline rush that came with them.

Persia had the funniest glow on her face. Her eyes sparkled. Light. That's what she was, an unexpected light in the middle of a very bleak year.

Stewart growled again. Walker turned on him with a great big grin. Apparently, he was part of Stewart's TEAM now, and his new boss expected him to listen. Wasn't that son of a bitch in for a surprise?

# Chapter Thirty-Five

Persia couldn't take her eyes off Walker. She wouldn't have, either, except Alex had tasked her to lead this briefing. Most everyone who needed to be here had arrived, thanks to Alex's private jet. If needed, Ember was on standby back at TEAM HQ.

Persia began with Hans. "Mr. Koning. Would you please tell us what you discovered while examining the International Criminal Court's evidence against Walker Judge?"

He turned to Beau. "I believe Agent Villanueva can show what I found better than I can explain."

"You bet." Beau flipped open the laptop balanced on his knees, then nodded at Walker. "I'd sure like to know what you did to piss off so many people."

"You're not the only one," Walker replied evenly.

"But you've got folks in foreign countries looking for your ass." Beau flashed four fingers. "The States, England, Jordan, and now, the Netherlands."

Walker shrugged as if he didn't care. But Persia knew different. He was suddenly as tense as he'd been before the safe house was breached. "SEALs are lucky like that. So what do you have on me?"

"Watch and learn," Beau replied as he worked the keyboard, then activated the mini-projector he'd placed in the center of the coffee table.

Heads turned, and people shifted positions to watch the video that sprang to life on the wall opposite Alex and Walker. Persia took in the panoramic view of what would have been a lavish wedding somewhere in Jordan. The day had been sunny and bright. A slight wind was blowing from the east, fluttering the hundred or so flags atop three magnificent stretch tents. Stone planters of pink, magenta, and cream-colored hibiscus flowers, along with small green palm trees, were set at the corners of the tents. An over-abundance of already lit string lights circled each tent support and lined the ceilings inside, as well as the roofs.

Stretch tents were designed to be airy, yet waterproof, more like ceilings without walls than actual tents. These three were constructed of light, weather-resistant fabric stretched between uprights that varied in height from the few twenty-foot tall center supports, to shorter poles and stakes set at various intervals on the periphery. Every tent allowed visibility from every possible outside angle. Every guest, coming or going, tiny or stalwart, was on view.

"Watch the tent on the right," Beau said. "That's where the marriage ceremony was supposed to take place."

Unlike the others, which were both massive enough to house three long banquet tables with enough settings and seats for seventy-eight guests, the wedding tent held a single ornate table. That was where the bride and groom would've eaten their first meal as husband and wife. Long cedar garlands stretched between crystal goblets and gold lanterns, all set on a pristine linen tablecloth. Small potted palm trees stood at each end of the table. An elaborate, aquamarine Persian rug, as wide and long as the tent itself, carpeted the ground beneath it. After the meal, the bride and groom would've danced the first dance of the rest of their lives on that plush carpet.

Walker leaned forward, his elbow on his knee and his chin cupped in one hand. But there was no light in his normally twinkling eyes. The laugh lines that usually spread like tiny rays of sun from the corners of his eyes, were missing as well. He probably knew more of Jordan's wedding customs than Persia did. Which was why he looked more sad than curious. To face all the dreams that this family had lost, had to be difficult.

Persia flashed her attention back to the video, which now showed crowds of guests mingling, all waiting for the bride and groom to arrive and the ceremony to begin. It seemed as if brown-eyed, brown-haired little kids were everywhere. Running. Squealing. Chasing each other. Playing tag. Just being kids...

The sight of all that innocence about to be annihilated was heart-wrenching. Her gaze strayed back to Walker. His eyes were on those little ones, too. But the hand that had cupped his chin before was a fist now. His right shoulder rolled, then rolled again, as if he couldn't sit still. Which was an interesting tell. Why did the sight of children about to die illicit the reaction to run? Did he want to run to save them from the carnage he knew was coming because he'd planned it?

That didn't feel right. When Adam told Walker about Squeaks, he'd looked thoroughly pleased. Delighted, even. Had Walker known this Jordanian prince and his family? Was that why he seemed ready to explode out of his chair? Or did he think everyone gathered here today would turn on him, accuse him of murdering those children? Betray him like the rest of the world had?

Once again, Persia forced her attention back to the clip, where nothing, as yet, looked out of place. But it was akin to watching the *Titanic*. She knew how this movie would end.

At last, the marriage procession arrived at the far side of the wedding tent. A quiet, pleasant murmur rippled through the audience when both the bride's and groom's parents and grandparents stepped onto the lavish Persian rug. This was an important day in their lives too. Rather, it would have been.

Next, the smiling bride and handsome groom entered their wedding tent. Her highness, Princess Mari Hajjar, and Prince Jamalud Khalid. Instead of a traditional Muslim wedding, this one was thoroughly modern European. All the men in the wedding party wore tuxedos; the women wore long gowns. The bride's beaded gown looked to be straight out of Paris.

Three little girls in long flowing, pink gowns danced around the group, twirling like ballerinas, as they tossed flower petals over their heads. The camera panned quickly to the right, then just as quickly back to the wedding tent. People were smiling. The music was perfect—

Until an explosive shock wave shook the scene.

Interestingly, where most amateurs would've dropped their cameras and run for their lives, whoever was behind this lens zoomed in on the fire and carnage. Where once a regal wedding tent had stood, now thick black smoke filled the air. The cameraman, or woman, panned out and captured the entire scene of mayhem. Then zoomed back in, onto the charred, bloodied faces of those screaming and crying and dying.

"Who filmed this mess?" Walker asked.

"No one knows," Persia replied. She'd reviewed this clip briefly when he'd been sleeping, but it still turned her stomach. Those poor people. Those dear sweet little ballerinas—all gone. "Admiral Pickering claims he received the video from an anonymous source. There was no name or note with it when it arrived, no fingerprints." *Or so he said...*

"Did NCIS investigate this, too? They should have. Do you know? Did they go to Jordan? Did they perform autopsies?"

She nodded, wishing there was a way to calm his rising panic. "That's what Pickering said, yes."

"But you don't believe him." Walker's vehemence rippled through his words. His lips were pinched and his jaw tight, as if he were biting back the words he didn't dare speak. If eyes truly were the windows to a man's soul, he was in Hell right now. Struggling to make sense of terrorist acts.

She heard the question he'd really asked. So she gave him the answer he needed. "To be honest, LT, I don't believe or trust anything Admiral Pickering or NCIS said or did during your trial." She nodded at the images frozen on the wall. "This was a despicable act of terror. If NCIS suspected any American was involved... if they lied and said they investigated the deaths of these poor people when they didn't—"

"I'll have their asses," Alex spat. "Senator Sullivan is already backtracking everything they said they did."

Walker's head snapped to Alex. "Sullivan?"

"Sullivan's one of the good guys," Alex replied. "You oughta know that."

Interestingly, Alex stretched one long arm along the back of Walker's chair. Which Walker had instantly sensed. He was on the balls of his feet, once again ready to run or fight.

Until then, Persia hadn't fully realized how deeply he'd suffered from the betrayal and lies, how much he distrusted others. How utterly devastating to know you'd been falsely accused by the command you'd fought for and were prepared to die for, the leaders who should've had your back. Then convicted and disavowed? She already knew that the decision to flee the country he loved had devastated him.

At last, the tight cords in his neck relaxed. He swallowed and told Alex, "I do know that. He set me up inside Fort Campbell. Gave me clearance to fly and a sound way forward."

And suddenly, whatever war Walker thought he was fighting, was over. His Adam's apple bobbed with relief. He licked his bottom lip and sent her the tiniest nod.

The compulsion to run to him, to run her fingers through his hair, to hold him close, and kiss him and tell him that she'd always have his back, nearly swamped Persia's common sense. She would've done just that, but Hans was back on his feet. "Excuse me, Agent Villanueva, but could you please play it one more time?"

The room stilled as Beau restarted the video. Hans stepped within the flickering images and pointed at the tall, brown-haired gentleman in a crisp, black tux. "This is who brought the explosive. Do any of you recognize him?"

"No," Alex clipped. "Never seen him before."

But damn. If Persia didn't know better, she'd swear that dapper gentleman was Walker's twin. Same proud bearing. Same short hair and clean-shaven chin. Same dark glasses.

Just as handsome. Dressed like the other men at the wedding, this guy strolled into the wedding tent and set an elegantly wrapped gift between the bride's and groom's place settings. Then he turned and chatted with the Jordanian couple at his left. Smiling. Congenial. Just like any invited guest.

"Freeze that frame, please," Hans ordered.

Beau did as asked, then enlarged the view.

"Now look closely," Hans murmured. "Please. See what I see."

"I see a murderer," Alex growled. Man, once he made up his mind, there was no dealing with him.

"Yes, sir. You are right. But look at this—" Stretching his arm into the image, Hans ran his index finger along the stranger's nose— "now please compare with the accused."

Every head turned toward Walker, but he had the good sense to look directly at Alex. Smart move. Never blinked, just stared at the man who could hurt him the worst—or help him the most.

"As you can see, Mr. Stewart, Lieutenant Walker's nose is as straight and unbroken as yours. But this man" —Hans tapped the image on the wall— "his has been broken before. It is slightly crooked. See the small knot and scar? See how it ends at rather red, bulbous nostrils, instead of nostrils that are finely crafted. And here" —Hans directed everyone's attention to the man's chest— "compare again."

Persia couldn't help herself. "That's not Walker Judge."

"No, it isn't. That jackass is barrel-chested. This jackass" —Alex stuck his chin at Walker— "is trim and fit. He works out, and it shows. That jackass eats too damned much."

"And that shows," Adam added. "He's got a beer gut."

"And that belly band didn't hide it," Izza added.

The barest smile creased Walker's handsome mouth. Persia bit her tongue. It was either that or run to the only man in the room she was beginning to love—yes, love—and kiss the hell out of him. Make sure he knew he'd never be alone again.

"One more item. Please, may I have your undivided attention?" Hans asked above the murmurs and grunts.

Again, Beau forwarded the clip to the point where the stranger had removed his sunglasses and wiped his wrist over his eyes. By then, sirens blared in the background. Dozens more men and women were now on the scene, running to help, or carrying charred, bleeding victims from the disaster zone.

"This is all we need to prove Lieutenant Walker's innocence," Hans told everyone. "This... right... here...."

Beau enhanced the image until—

"Walker's eyes are blue," Persia declared adamantly. "That liar's are amber."

"But the prosecutor will insist I wore contacts," Walker added.

"Doesn't matter," Alex declared. "That bastard is not you."

"Watch this." Beau reversed the clip, then forwarded it back to the frontal shot of the bomber looking directly at the cameraman. He'd known he was being filmed, and he knew the guy filming. The corner of his mouth twisted into a sardonic smirk. He nodded, as if saying, *Job well done, now let's get outta here.*

"Enlarge that son-of-a-bitch," Alex snapped. He'd tilted forward, his elbows on his knees and fire in his eyes. "There. Stop it right there."

Sure enough. In the reflective lens of the murderer's Ray-Bans, Beau had caught the image of a tall, blond male in a waiter's uniform, holding a palm-sized video camera.

"And he has a tattoo," Hans proudly announced. "Show them, Agent Villanueva."

With several deft keystrokes, Beau magnified the black-inked number seven over the man's left eyebrow and three equally black teardrops beneath the same eye.

"Run him through Ember's facial rec program," Alex ordered.

"Already did, Boss," Beau replied. "Name's Butch Costa."

"Track him down."

Beau actually smiled. "Already did that, too. He works for a security outfit out of Canada that handles search and rescues, hot target grabs, like missing wives or children who've been taken out of the country. All former military. FBI Director Chase is holding him for you in DC. He'd appreciate a call before he and his guys, ahem, interrogate Costa to get the bomber's name."

"Tell Tuck to do it. I want to know that bastard's name the minute he calls back."

Director Tucker Chase managed the one and only FBI psychic team in the country. Any one of his agents could psychically probe Costa's mind, and he'd never know it. They might even release him, then tail him, give him just enough room and rope to hang himself. But only because they needed actual physical proof, since psychic probes into alleged perpetrators' minds weren't admissible in courts of law. Yet.

"Copy that," Beau replied evenly, his sat phone already out of his pocket and at his ear.

Hans still stood looking across the room at Walker. "There is still more, Lieutenant. Much more."

# Chapter Thirty-Six

Walker couldn't believe all that Hans—his one-time court-assigned ICC defense attorney and a veritable stranger—had done for him. There was more, all right. The papers Hans distributed to the group outlined other discrepancies in the wedding video.

Number one being the accusation by the Khalid family that Prince Jamalud had been killed in the attack. Turned out he hadn't. Hans had located the security footage taken at a prestigious local hotel, where Khalid's parents had stayed the night before the bombing, then had the audacity to return to afterward.

Seemed Beau Villanueva was another stranger to be damned thankful for. He was good at video forensics, had used something called satellite triangulation, to zero down on the rear view of a man walking away from the explosion. The same man had also been caught on Costa's video during that quick pan from the murderer back to the disaster—the *'murdered'* Prince. Not only that, but the men and women walking away with him, were his parents and grandparents. This explosion wasn't the end of a marriage. It was Khalid's way out of that marriage.

Hans had dug deeper then, and discovered a link between Prince Khalid and Captain Spenser Cole, the Navy judge who'd presided over Walker's trial. They'd met during a

Foreign Military Sales Program Management Review, an FMS PMR, long before Walker was charged with murder. Poseidon's stars were beginning to shine even brighter.

By then, Walker had to sit back and just let the revelations come. It was either that or hit something. There were so many. Hans had uncovered quite a spider's web. He also knew the allegedly-murdered Khalid family had fled to Saudi Arabia and were in hiding at one of the reigning king's many palaces. Living in luxury, while what was left of the bride's family truly grieved.

Then there was Adam. He'd located three off-shore accounts in Goff's mother's maiden name: Wallace Bernadette Samar. After weeks of tracking down the elusive woman, he'd located her grave in New Jersey. Then backtracked through city, school, and hospital records to prove that she was, in fact, Goff's mother. She'd been born in Jordan, came to the States with her parents when she was a young child, and had died of pancreatic cancer the year he'd graduated from high school. So how was a dead woman still depositing thousands of dollars a month into her off-shore accounts? And did she have anything to do with the Khalid family?

Back to Beau. Somehow, he'd gotten into the USN personnel system and had photographic proof of Walker's Navcompt 3065 leave request when he'd gone to Guatemala. It *was* in the USN personnel system. Yet, both Prosecutor John Cudahy and Walker's defense attorney LT Cameron Kroft, had denied any record of it. They'd claimed Walker lied, that he hadn't requested, nor been on leave during that time.

Beau had also dissected the backstories to every individual who'd ever attended Walker's trial. Not only was his former girlfriend Miss Breeze friendly with Prosecutor Cudahy, she was sleeping with him. Also noteworthy and profoundly disturbing, USN Admiral Pickering had attended the hearing more than once. He'd always sat in the back of the room, so Walker had never known he was there. But he'd always worn his uniform. Damn the arrogant ass.

"I wondered who that was," Persia commented.

"You've seen the footage before?" Walker asked.

"Yes, parts of it. Hans shared the court video with Izza and me the first day at the safe house. I didn't realize that was Pickering, though. I couldn't see his rank insignia clearly."

"That son of a bitch!" Stewart hissed, "Peckering had no business showing his face at your trial. No wonder these bastards never stood up for you. They were too busy kissing ass!"

"Pickering," Walker corrected. "He's Admiral—"

"I said Admiral Fuckin' Peck-Er-Ing..."

*Well, okay then. Peckering it is and would forever be.* Walker was beginning to like the hardass sitting at his right.

"Understand, people," Stewart continued earnestly. "His presence in any courtroom, at any trial, means he's watching, that he has a vested interest in the outcome. Every brown-nosing, weak-kneed moron will skew the truth just to look good in front of the boss."

"Or because he was following orders," Persia added.

"You think the Secretary of Defense is behind this?" Walker asked.

"Someone with a lot of clout certainly is," she answered.

Stewart turned on Walker. "Your son of a bitchin' attorney should've had the balls to declare a mistrial."

"The jerk barely spoke with me. Said he was too busy, that he had other clients, and he'd already spent too much time on my case."

"They had you right where they wanted you," Adam added, "headed to slaughter."

"Yes. I was…" Walker could barely go on. "Where were you guys when I needed you?"

"Looking for your dumb ass the minute you left Juarez and me standing on that fuckin' sandbar," Trevor growled. "What were you thinking? Swimming alone in the ocean at night? Are all SEALs as stupid as you?"

"I had no choice—"

"You swam over a hundred miles to get to shore," Julio murmured. "I would've helped. I told you that you had more friends than you realized. You said only Sullivan and Charlie Brown were your friends, but when I mentioned that Chief Warrant Officer Trevor Duncan was in transit—"

"Why the hell do you think I came all the way from Kentucky, in person! Just to save your sorry ass!" Trevor thumped his chest with his fist. "I had contingencies in place, damn it. I could've gotten you back to the States! Hell, back to Fort Carson, and no one would've known."

"I… I…" Walker couldn't speak. Acting tough was difficult in the face of so much overwhelming loyalty. But it'd been tough asking for help back then. It would've put Julio and Trevor at risk, and Senator Sullivan at more risk. They'd already done so much.

"Who do you think was behind the empty gas tank in that rental the day you escaped custody?" Adam asked quietly, the light in his eyes so damned tender, it hurt to look at him. "Who do you think slipped magnesium hydroxide into those two Masters-at-arms' sodas when they weren't looking?"

Magnesium hydroxide was the active ingredient in OTC stool softeners.

Walker swallowed hard. "You?"

"Hell, yeah. Me. I added a touch of flavorless *Ipecac* to their sodas, too, just to make sure those guys weren't going anywhere but to the head. Alex and I have been on your butt since the day that kangaroo court started. We even had a plan to break you out of the Navy brig, but I ended up following your dumbass all the way to Kansas. I was on the same flight as you and your guards. But then you disappeared into thin air—"

"I didn't know there was such a thing as flavorless *Ipecac*," Walker muttered, needing everyone to focus on something besides what an idiot he'd been. He'd sure been called dumbass a lot lately.

Adam lifted one shoulder like the big kid he was. "It worked, didn't it?"

Walker nodded, so damned humbled.

"Senator Sullivan had a plan, too," Stewart added quietly.

"He's in on this, too?" Walker had to ask, fully aware of that muscular arm behind him. What'd Stewart plan to do? Knock him senseless or… knock sense into him?

"He and I have been at cross purposes a time or two, yes. Now we coordinate our operations, at least we try. Apparently, McQueen didn't think to advise me he'd sent Kruze Sinclair to retrieve you from The Hague. By the time I found out, Persia and Izza were already in-country. They got to you first. Kruze spent two days hunting you down. By the time he located the safe house, I'd already been there and gone."

"Senator Sullivan installed me at Fort Campbell. In plain sight. It worked for a while."

"I know he did. But then he lost you, didn't he?" Jesus, who was this man that he knew so many powerful people? "Kruze just landed in Dublin. He'll be here before nightfall, and he's not going to be pleasant when he arrives."

Walker couldn't believe it. "Why's he coming here?"

"Because Senator Sullivan and I had no idea the Navy would ever let this bogus charge go to trial. But when they did…" Stewart blew out a long, deep sigh. "We had to do something. Hell, don't ask me why, but Kruze wants in on this mess with the rest of us idiots."

"Because he's a SEAL," Julio murmured, his dark brown eyes zeroed in on Walker. "And SEALs stand together."

Walker stared back at Julio. Behind that gentle Mexican/American's quiet demeanor was a will of iron. Julio might not have finished BUD/S, but he was every bit a SEAL, right down to his soul.

It seemed unimaginable. All these brothers and sisters…

All ready to stand and fight for him.

As always, Walker's gaze ended on Persia. Like the sassy warrior she was, she gave him her chin, that cocky show of attitude and courage.

"But that makes each of you" —Walker scanned the room, making eye contact with everyone— "accomplices."

Julio shrugged. "No, *amigo*, it makes us *familia*. If that makes us accomplices, it is only because we have chosen to be your brothers and sisters."

"And I have proof positive that Cudahy's office leaked deliberate misinformation about your case to the press," Adam interrupted. "Only the press didn't choose to investigate that. They just ran with it—"

"And ran your good name into the mud," Persia said quietly.

Walker stared across the room at the woman he adored. He needed a moment with her. Maybe a lifetime.

"And those two ensigns who testified against you, Chief?" Ryder asked, the whites of his eyes bright against his dark skin. "I had a little talk with them once you disappeared. They're ready to recant, but someone's threatening them. They won't say who, and they're scared. Once we clear your name, I've got a feeling you'll see them again."

"NCIS has some explaining to do," Stewart added.

"I never stood a chance—"

"No, son, you didn't," Brimley offered quietly. He hadn't said much throughout this meeting of minds. He'd just sat back in the recliner next to Murphy Finnegan's, his hands clasped over his belly, while he'd absorbed every last piece of evidence. Every lie and every twisted fact.

Rover was still making rounds, collecting ear scratches, belly rubs, and leftovers, but Brimley and Murphy looked calm and serene. Neither said a word until now.

Walker looked at the Vietnam Vet who'd befriended him. Brim had endured his own share of the mighty free press's backstabbing, name-calling, and slander. Hell, he'd been spit on when he'd come home, character assassinated by the media, and hung out to dry by the country that should've had his back.

"Let me guess," Walker said to Murphy. "You're a Vietnam vet, too."

Murphy murmured with a sly smile, "*Mi casa es su casa.*"

"It's sure good to get these facts out in the open," Brim said matter-of-factly. "But who said what and who did what doesn't get you where you need to be, does it?"

"It sure as fuck matters to us," Ryder Dahl roared. "We stand with our Chief."

"I get that, sir, I really do," Brim replied evenly, his palms forward to placate restless SEAL Team 18. "Loyalty's a damned noble thing, and you're right to stand by your chief. Walker's one helluva good one. But what he really needs to know is precisely who's behind all these lies. He needs to know why he's been targeted." Brim looked around the room as if letting that sink in. "Seems to me, all we're looking at here is plenty of means and opportunity. But we ain't yet uncovered intent or motive. Sure, some fat-assed admiral jerked a few chains and a couple of his boys yelled, *'Yes, Sir!'* Then bent over and asked for another butt-reaming. Some chains of command work like that. But we still don't know who's behind this particular blanket party."

"Peckering," Izza cut in. "Look at the jerk. He's breaking USN law like its nothing, and he's proud of it."

"Maybe," Stewart replied quietly. "But we need to keep our eyes on the real target, not the smoke and mirrors."

"And who would that be?" Izza growled. She seemed more than willing to square off with her boss. "Who's got enough power to influence a Navy trial, plant evidence to incriminate him for crimes committed in England, at Buckingham Palace, for crap sakes? Then all the way across the ocean with the ICC? If it's not Peckering, who the hell are we looking for, Boss? The President?"

"I've got a yacht," Walker announced a little too loudly.

Stewart looked at him as if he'd sprouted two heads. "So?"

Walker ran a hand over his face, wishing he felt better. He might've thought of that earlier. Might've sounded smarter now. "I found something." He stared into Brim's knowing eyes. "I think I can prove intent. Might even be able to prove who's pulling the strings behind this mess."

Brim nodded. Just once. A silent affirmation of agreement and solidarity.

"Is that the one dry-docked in Portugal?" Stewart asked.

Walker nodded, then looked across the room at Persia. "I stole it on my way out of Florida, then changed its registration and name to avoid the Coast Guard."

"To…?" Stewart asked pointedly.

"To *Persia Smiles*," Walker whispered. "It's Goff's yacht, *Coronado's Sea Nymph.* But I took it and I changed its name to… to *Persia Smiles*."

Stewart sat back with a growl, but Walker didn't care whether Persia's boss knew how much she meant to him or not. There, across the room, sat the only one whose opinion mattered. And she was smiling.

# Chapter Thirty-Seven

As soon as the meeting broke, Walker headed straight to Persia. She couldn't get to her feet fast enough before he latched onto her hand and said, "We need to talk."

He took her through Murphy's kitchen at a fast clip, past platters of grated cheeses, lettuce, and chopped peppers and tomatoes. Past crocks of steaming black beans, chili, and seasoned ground beef. Out the back door and into what looked more like an expansive meadow than a backyard. What a view. It was a charming quilt of crooked green little pastures tied off with rows upon rows of stone fences. The Rock of Cashel, high on the hill, lorded over the quaint village below it. It'd be nice to visit that castle someday. Just. Not. Now.

"Oh, hi, Zack," she said as she was hurried past one of The TEAM's baddest bad boys. "This is Walker. Walker, Zack Lennox."

He acknowledged Zack with a perfunctory, "Ah huh. Pleased to meet you." And kept going.

"Don't go far, Persia," Zack cautioned. Decked in tactical armor and armed with a short stock rifle tucked barrel down and against his chest, he'd only allow them a short moment alone before he broke up the party. Eric Reynolds was also out there somewhere. And, if Kruze Sinclair had caught an express out of Dublin, it wouldn't be long before he showed, too. There wasn't much privacy on Murphy's private estate, and Persia didn't want to be caught in a compromising position. Which she was pretty certain she would be. Compromised. Soon.

"We need to stay within sight of the house," she told Walker when he pulled her around the corner of Murphy's garage. The only cover there was an overgrown rose bush to her left and the thick branches of an old oak tree overhead.

"We're close enough," he muttered, then jerked to a quick stop.

Before she knew what he had planned, he'd backed her against the side of the garage. She barely had time to ask, "What's wrong?" before his mouth mashed onto hers.

"This," he ground out, his fingers in her hair, holding her head steady as he deepened the kiss, turning it wet and wild and desperate.

She was instantly in heaven inside this man's arms, encased in sheer muscle. Raw, feral energy rolled off him, engulfing her in their own private bubble of passion and lust. His shoulder muscles bunched with latent power, and that chest... Her nostrils flared, breathing in the scent of the same soap she'd showered with. Only on Walker, it smelled so much better.

He should still be flat on his back in bed. "Talk to me," she murmured around his lips.

"This," he growled more earnestly, as if that one word explained everything.

Persia knew then she'd made all the right choices during her life. Because here and now, she was filled with Walker Judge. Tenderness for this lonely warrior crashed over her like a soft ocean wave. Canting her head, she opened her mouth wider to give him better access.

His kisses turned ravishing, as if he couldn't make love to her mouth fast or good or deep enough. She melted against him, matching her softness to the rigid, hard angles pressing her to the wall. This was physical communication at an elemental level, and she gave back as good as she got. He needed to understand she'd always be there for him. No more words. No need for talk. Just him. Just her.

Growling, his hand slid under her shirt, then swiftly breached the lacy barrier of her bra, pushing it up and out of his way. Cupping her bare breast in his palm, he moaned into her mouth. His callused thumb worked her nipple with sure quick strokes, turning the sensitive bud into an express line straight to her core. Just that sweet, forbidden, carnal touch, with Zack and Eric within shouting distance, changed this reckless rendezvous into something intensely erotic. Excited shivers danced up the insides of her thighs. What if they were caught?

Lifting one knee, she wrapped it around his thigh. Which didn't get her precisely where she wanted to go. Walker solved the problem. Still squeezing her breast, he hooked his free hand under her knee, pulling her in close and tight, grinding the most incredible hard-on against her.

"Not here," she tried to tell him, but her words and willpower were lost in his passionate kisses. Each stroke of his warm, wet tongue over hers was an internal branding, as if he needed to control something. Or someone.

The instant she realized that, Persia calmed. She trusted this man more than she'd ever trusted anyone else in her entire career. Whatever internal battle he was fighting, it was her battle, too. That's what this was about. She was his anchor in the storm. So be it. Her inner goddess stepped up to the challenge of standing with and for this warrior. She was proud to carry his mark.

At last, the sweet mauling slowed. Then ceased. Heaving hard, breathy pants like a draft horse that had just run a race, Walker lowered his forehead to her shoulder. "You have no idea what you mean to me. You just don't know."

"Try me," she whispered as she came back to earth, then ran her fingers through his hair, holding him to her like she'd never let him go. "Maybe I'm smarter than you give me credit for."

"It's not that. I already know you're smarter and braver than most people. And I know the guys here are all trying to help, and I appreciate it, I do." A gust of heated breath landed inside her shirt. "But you have to understand, all this time, I've been running. I've been alone. I didn't dare trust anyone. I couldn't. Only Brim. Only you. Then suddenly I'm surrounded by an army that's ready to go to war with me. But it was like a gauntlet in there. I felt like I was taking a beating. I had no idea… Hell, I don't even know anyone on your team. But shit." He ran a hand over his sweaty head. "They're all crazier than I am."

"Why?"

His brows went up. "Do you think I'd let them go through with whatever they're planning? They can't come to Portugal with me. Neither can you. It's not safe. I'm not safe. It's just a matter of time before—"

She pressed her finger over his flapping lips. "Try and stop me."

Walker cocked his head, his eyes pleading. "No. You have to stay here where it's safe. I can't hurt anyone else, especially not you. Whoever's behind these accusations against me is one powerful man. He's willing to kill, and I won't let him get to you. Not any of your guys, either."

Rolling her shoulder like a bantam-weight prize fighter might before she delivered a knock-out punch, Persia shifted out of Walker's embrace. She needed space to fix her bra and straighten her clothes. "I'm not asking, Hotrod, and neither are my friends in there. I'm going with you and Alex, and you can be damned sure Izza doesn't care what you think, either. She's going, too. So are every last one of those guys. They're your guys now, too. So, get over yourself. We're on your side. Deal with it."

Damned if he didn't slip a hand around her neck, and double damned if his eyes didn't tear up. Instantly, Persia felt bad for picking on an injured man who obviously needed a good long nap instead of more confrontation. Walker wasn't thinking right.

"You really believe in me, don't you?"

She hadn't expected that question. "Why shouldn't I?" she asked as she smoothed the wrinkles out of her pleasantly man-handled clothes. "The Navy's way out of line, Hotrod. And we're going to prove it."

His shoulders shuddered with a drawn-out sigh. "You just don't know—"

"What? Tell me."

"What it's been like all these months. Even alone, I still had to watch my back. I couldn't let my guard down, and I couldn't trust anyone. The few times I did, I put them at risk. That's why I left Julio and Trevor on the sandbar that night. They'd already done more than enough, and how did I pay them back? By putting their reputations and their lives in danger. By making them targets. That's why I never reached out to Ryder or my team. How could I do that to them? To anyone?"

By then, his palms were warm on her hips, his thumbs stroking softly up and down her waist. "But then you came along," he muttered, his voice ragged, "like a bright shining star, and you changed everything. I'm sick of fighting the world, Persia. I just want to go home. I want to kiss America again and be able to breathe without watching my back. I want to be with you."

"When this is done," she told him firmly, her hands again around the back of his neck, "and it will be over soon, let's go back to my place in Florida. Let's both kiss the beach, then make love all day and all night under the stars."

A wan smile tweaked his lips. "That'd be so damned perfect, wouldn't it?"

"I think so."

"So, tell me." His voice turned hard. "Who is your boss? Really."

Persia looked at the blue sky shining down through the leafy branches overhead. Until then, she'd thought Alex was nothing but a hardass, with a soft spot for his wife and daughter. She knew better now. She'd just watched him work a miracle for a man he hadn't met until a day ago. She couldn't help the chuckle that bubbled up from her heart.

"Oh, you know the type. Former jarhead. Hard-assed, short-tempered troll. He's the same as you, Hotrod. He's willing to march into Hell for what and who matters."

"See, that's what I don't get. Why me?"

She couldn't suppress her tender feelings for this stubborn man. "Why not you—?"

"You do know the boss'll have your asses for this, don't you?"

"Eric!" Persia hissed, her heart pounding up her throat. She let her hands slip down Walker's chest to drop to her sides. "You just scared ten years off my life!"

Eric Reynolds was another tall, dark, and handsome warrior, only he worked out of the Seattle TEAM office for Murphy Finnegan. Outfitted the same as Zack, he stood calmly at the opposite corner of the garage, but she was certain he'd seen too much. "Kruze Sinclair just showed, and he brought someone with him."

"God, who now?" Walker snapped.

Persia smoothed a hand over his taut shoulder. Man, this guy needed a break. Even good news was stressing him.

"Senator McQueen Sullivan," Eric replied easily, his dark eyes warily quartering the scene, taking in the way Walker still had a good hold on Persia.

"Shit! Why's *he* here?"

She couldn't help but smile. Walker seemed to have a hard time accepting help from everyone. "What's wrong with Sullivan? I thought he was on your side."

"I… I ran out on him, too."

"You do that a lot, do you, Judge? Run out on folks who are trying to help you?" Eric asked good-naturedly, as he headed their way. "Bet I know what'll make you feel better." Reaching under his left arm, he pulled a pistol out of his holster and handed it over grip first. "There's gear, a go-bag, holsters, and plenty more ammo inside. It's time to get moving."

The moment Walker's fingers touched that weapon, he racked the slide and blew out a deep breath. "Thanks. And you are?"

Eric extended a gloved hand. "Former Navy medic, former USMC asshole, Eric Reynolds, on your six, Chief Judge. Damned proud to make your acquaintance and glad as hell we finally caught up with you. At least…" Eric winked at Persia. "Looks like she did."

She didn't hesitate, didn't let Eric think she was embarrassed, either. "Apparently that's all Walker needed, to be armed and dangerous again."

"As he should be. You ready to engage the enemy again, Chief?"

Persia answered for the man at her side. "Let's do this."

# Chapter Thirty-Eight

The meet and greet with Kruze and McQueen Sullivan ended up being more back-slapping than head-butting. For that, Walker was grateful. Then Stewart declared a moratorium on further action until everyone recovered from jet lag. The gang settled down for a day's worth of R&R at Murphy's. Because the house couldn't hold everyone, Walker's men camped in the fields and trees around the estate, along with Alex's male agents, Hans, Kruze, Brimley, and Rover. That left the guest rooms for Stewart, Senator McQueen Sullivan, Walker, and the two female agents, but it also provided a veritable ring of security around the place.

After the wear and tear of one hell of an intense day, Walker took a quick, hot shower and toweled off. He'd just gotten into bed when his door cracked open. He was facedown, too exhausted to care who needed to talk with him now. Until petal-soft angel fingers drifted over his shoulders, down his back and settled on his bare butt.

"That better be Persia touching my ass," he growled into his pillow.

"Of course it's me," she breathed as she climbed into bed with him, then covered them both with the blanket.

Still face-down, Walker breathed in her flowery scent. She'd settled against him, with one hand around his head, which put his face against the side of her breast. There he was within reach of the succulent skin he craved, but once again, his energy was flagging, and everything else along with it. She always seemed to come to him when he had nothing to offer. One of these days, he'd be Johnny-on-the-Spot, ready to perform at her beck and call. He'd jump her bones until he made her scream. But tonight, he was spent. This day had taken everything—even—that.

"I like the way you smell," he said as he wrapped an arm around her waist, hoping she'd understand. "What is it? Some kind of perfume from Paris?"

"Just the bar soap from the shower."

"I'm so damned tired," he breathed. Soap, huh? That meant she'd taken a shower and all that clean, sweet-tasting flesh was now pressed up against him and his for the licking. Damn. If he didn't have bad luck, he'd have no luck at all. "Raincheck," he mumbled to his pillow. "I want a damned raincheck."

"Sleep," she whispered, her fingers drifting through his hair. Over his head. Petting him. Softly. Tenderly.

He woke up the next morning to an empty bed. The day brought a couple more faces into the group. Another TEAM agent, Jordan Hannigan, who seemed thrilled to see Eric. Guess they'd worked together before, only Jordan had a definite Irish accent going for him. He'd come with a willowy blonde female medic who had no trouble telling Walker he was a "dumb arse and get back to bed, so I can treat you properly."

Turned out she was Murphy Finnegan's niece, Elsa Day, soon to be Elsa Day Hannigan. Blonde. Blue-eyed. Obviously smitten with the sturdy American male at her side.

She took her time redressing Walker's shoulder wound, using antiseptic packing that instantly stilled the throbbing pain of the through-and-through. As if one hole in a man's body wasn't enough, now he had two.

Then she patiently stitched the skid-mark the grazed bullet had left on the side of his head. Along with that came a warning: "You, boyo, have a lot of bruises on your back, and you most definitely have a concussion. I recommend you lay low and take it easy the next two days. You're not to lift anything heavy, nor tackle anything strenuous. You may only rest and sleep and eat. Do I make myself clear?"

"We'll see," was all he could promise. Taking it easy wasn't going to happen, not with the upcoming mission.

Ever since Persia had mentioned Florida and making love for days, Walker'd had his head on straight. He had a goal. No more pity parties. No more worrying about who was taking risks and who wasn't. With this particular team at his back, he could get to the bottom of the false charges against him. He would finally bring the bastard behind his misery down. Once again, Persia had given him a reason to hope and something to look forward to. Her.

"There you be, you poor, dumb lamb," Elsa said as she packed her medical bag and lifted from the side of his bed where she'd been working on him. "Miss Coltrane will be in soon with your breakfast. I know you won't, but it'd be wise if you stayed here with my uncle while your friends go off and do whatever it is needs doing. Two days, that's all I'm asking. Just rest for two days."

She kept coaxing, but Walker wouldn't promise anything. He'd eyed the pistol Eric had given him. Two loaded magazines now rested on his nightstand beside it. A box of ammo and a holster beside them. All he needed was Kenny's knife back, and he'd be himself again.

"Ah, I knew you'd ignore me. You're a man, after all, and since I'm just a woman," —Elsa stuck her chin at him— "you'll be stubborn and ignore my excellent advice. Okay then, if you have to go, go with God, and be quick about your business. It'd also be wise if you married that sweet thing who can't keep her eyes off you."

"Thank you, ma'am. I appreciate all you've done for me."

"Ah, the hard heads of hard men," she grumbled. "I'd knock on yours for good luck, but I'll wager it still hurts plenty, doesn't it?"

"I'm good," Walker replied. Headache or not, he was going to war.

He walked out of his room and into a flurry of activity. Stewart seemed to think he was in charge, so Walker let him run the show. By then, Stewart knew everything anyway.

"Persia and Izza, you're with me. Eric and Zack, accompany Mr. Koning back to—"

"I have a sister in New York," Hans interrupted. "Please, sir. I'd rather go to America, if it's okay with you."

"Good call. You'll be safer there. Eric and Zack, make it happen."

Eric gave Hans a thumbs-up while Stewart continued dispensing orders. "Captain Dooley, appreciate your support, but I know you're due back to the *Iwo Jima*. Safe travels and following seas, sir."

Quinn looked to Walker. "Trust me. I'd love to put a bullet through this bastard's head, whoever he is. Sure wish I could've identified the faces in those photos for you. But life on a carrier never slows down. Stay safe, Walk."

Walker shook hands with his long-time friend. "You, too, Q. Hug Emily for me. Tell her I'll never take her bracelet off. She'll always be with me."

"Good enough." Dooley nodded a respectful farewell to Persia, then stepped back.

"Murph, thanks for letting us crash here," Stewart said. "Jordan, you and your fiancé aren't invited. Go home. Beau, dig into Prince Khalid and Captain Spenser Cole. I want to know everything about their friendship. Adam, keep working with Ember to locate who's behind the deposits going into Goff's off-shore accounts. I don't care if you have to go to Switzerland, Germany, or the Caymans—"

"They're in Singapore, Boss. She's got several accounts," Adam said, "all in Singapore."

"Then get it done," Stewart replied crisply. "Julio and Kruze, there's a cab waiting outside to take you to Shannon Airport. I need you guys in Guatemala. Track down the gangs who staged the fights that enabled them to kidnap little girls. Locate Officer Bruno and Renzo, too. Make them talk. I want the name of the bastard behind this mess, damnit."

"I'd like in on that, sir," Smoke spoke up. "Got a lead from a sting operation in Texas. Found evidence that points to human trafficking coming north out of Guatemala. Hoping it leads back to the same person Judge is after. It'd be good to kill two birds with one stone."

"Or a fifty-caliber round," Stewart added grimly. "Julio? Kruze? You got a problem if Smoke teams up with you?"

"We can always use another gunslinger," Julio replied.

"They work for you?" Walker asked Alex.

"Hell, no," McQueen spoke up. "Smoke, Julio, and Kruze work for me. Always good to have the best on your side when you're fighting the Devil."

"Ryder Dahl stays with me," Walker said. Not asked. Just in case Stewart planned to send all his men running off on errands.

Stewart's answer came back sharp and crisp. "I don't need a damned army on my ass."

"Ryder stays," Walker repeated unequivocally. "He's my XO." *At least, he was. And him, I know and trust. You, I'm not so sure about.*

"Fine, but I need the rest of your men back in San Diego, guarding the ensigns who testified against you. They might as well watch over Miss Breeze, too."

"Are you thinking retribution, Boss?" Izza asked.

"I'm thinking we'd be stupid not to take care of the witnesses."

"What about Trevor Duncan?" Persia asked.

"No can do," Trevor answered gruffly. "Only got a two-day pass, Agent Coltrane. I'd love to join you guys and kick this bastard's ass, but I've got to be back at Fort Campbell come morning for a training program."

Walker had to ask. "Wait a minute. You guys came all this way just to—"

"Just to see you?" Trevor bit out. "Are you kidding? Hell, yeah."

"From The Hague, then here to Ireland? For me? Are you all morons?"

"I told you once that you had more friends than you knew." Julio said clearly. "Here we are."

"Brothers," Smoke added.

"To the fuckin' end," Adam growled.

"Hell, yeah!" Team 18 roared.

Walker couldn't speak. Physically could not make his tongue work in the face of so much blatant loyalty.

Leave it to Chief Warrant Officer Duncan to save the day. "Hell, yeah, is right. I came all this way just to tell you that you're the biggest, dumbest ass I've ever had the pleasure of working with." By then, he'd crossed the room and had a good grip on Walker's uninjured shoulder and hand. "My little sister Meg thinks a helluva lot of you, Hotrod. Don't ask me why, I sure don't understand it. But what Julio said is right. You're family. What'd he call us—*familia*? That's why we're here. For you, you idiot."

Walker didn't know what to say. Not even when Trevor crushed him in a monster bro hug, then slapped his back, stepped away, and growled, "Don't let Meg down, damn it. And you owe me one Blackhawk, you bastard."

Walker let that one slide. He had been at the stick the night Trevor's fancy experimental Blackhawk fell out of the sky and landed on that sandbar. Kind of. He'd actually been unconscious and drooling, after the Russian spy on board had stuck him with a hypo filled with Special K.

Trevor was the one who'd landed the high-tech bird—by remote control, no less—all the way from Fort Campbell, Kentucky. Walker'd been out cold, and Julio'd been about to have a heart attack.

By then, the room was nearly empty. "That does it," Stewart said.

"Brim and his dog are coming, too," Walker added.

"Can that yacht sleep eight?"

"It's a forty-five-foot Meridian, what do you think?"

Stewart's hard blue eyes skewered Walker once again, but Walker stood firm. It was his damned yacht. Well, not really. But he wasn't military anymore, and he was done taking orders and blindly following anyone.

After a few tense seconds, Stewart lifted his sat phone to his ear and turned away. He commenced making travel arrangements with someone he called Mother, and the stand-off was over. Walker shot Persia a look that meant *'join me in my room.'*

He had her in his arms as soon as she closed his door behind her. "Damn, your boss is an arrogant ass," Walker breathed as he captured her face between his palms and peppered her cheeks, nose, and mouth with tiny, moist kisses.

"I think he likes you," she murmured as her fingers roamed under his shirt, lighting him up like she always did.

"Soon…" he told her, needing her skin to skin. "We are going to be together again soon."

"Promise?"

He kissed her thoroughly. "Oh, yeah…"

The next day was a clear, sunny day for flying. Stewart had arranged transport to a private airstrip outside Cashel, and from there, they flew by private plane to Shannon Airport on Ireland's west coast. This multi-legged trip to Portugal had to have cost a pretty penny. Yet Stewart had provided for everyone, even had a crate for Rover. Once again, Walker wondered just who the man was that he could afford to move so many people and a dog by private plane. Transferring this small army was no small thing.

They landed at a private airstrip outside Lisbon. Then everyone climbed into the two vans waiting for them, while two male attendants loaded their luggage and gear, all without batting an eye. Since Persia had claimed the driver's seat of the nearest van, Walker took shotgun. Brimley, Rover, and Ryder joined him. Stewart commandeered the other van, with Senator Sullivan at his side, Izza in the back.

"You know where we're going, young lady?" Brimley asked once Persia pulled away from the airport and into traffic.

"Actually, no. I'm headed south on the highway that'll get us across the Ponte 25 de Abril bridge. I figured we'd find more boats and docks along the river." Ponte 25 de Abril was the suspension bridge across the mighty Tagus River, linking the cities of Lisbon and Almada.

"Smart thinking. I'll tell you when to turn."

Walker leaned back, content to bask in the sun pouring in his open window, since Persia and Brim had everything under control. He closed his eyes, taking in the smells of the nearby river and ocean. It'd be good to get back on the water again.

Persia was a capable driver. In short order, Brim told her where to exit. She turned off the highway and approached the docks.

"Turn at the metal gate up ahead, young lady," Brimley instructed, as he handed a ticket stub forward. "Here. This'll get you in. The storage number's 18B, right next to the hoist that'll put her back in the water."

"Good thinking." Walker peered over his shoulder. "How much do I owe you for storage?"

Brim waved it off. "Don't worry."

"We'll discuss this later."

"We'll see…"

*Like hell, we'll see.* Drydocking a forty-five-foot Meridian Motoryacht was no small thing. It required storage as big as a barn. She'd be on blocks or dollies, possibly suspended on industrial-strength belts designed to hold her tonnage. Yet Walker wasn't going to argue about money now. That would embarrass Brimley, who'd probably hocked his life's savings to store the yacht. But wasn't that interesting…? Brimley Scott had taken extra special care securing the yacht of a guy he'd barely known, had in fact, just met.

Walker ran a hand over his aching head. The flight from Ireland to Lisbon had done him in. Then the drive here. Now Brim's unexpected foresight and kindness. Possibly more secrets…

He was trapped in an upside-down world, where everyone he'd met lately was on his side. After a year on the run, that kind of loyalty made him antsy. He honestly still wasn't sure if he could trust everyone or what to expect from any of them. So Walker let Brim's comment slide.

Persia rolled her window down and presented the ticket to the sunburned, smiling guard at the marina's gatehouse. "The car behind is with us," she told him politely.

The friendly gentleman leaned out of his guard-shack window to peer into the van, then grinned when he spotted Brimley and Rover. The two exchanged pleasantries, and once again, Walker looked over his shoulder. Brim knew Portuguese? Rover barked, as if even he knew this guy.

The guard reached into his jeans pocket and pulled out a dog treat. Still grinning, he tossed the treat to Rover, then activated the metal gate and waved Persia through and for Stewart to follow.

She turned the corner at the end of a row of small storage units. Then Walker caught sight of the shipyard. Damn. *Persia Smiles* wasn't just docked. She'd been professionally stored, and that hoist Brimley mentioned was a massive floating crane that could probably lift three to four thousand tons.

"How big is that boat you stole?" Ryder asked.

"Forty-five-feet long."

"Is that crane going to be big enough?"

"Oh, yeah." And then some.

Brim and Rover hit the pavement before the vehicle stopped rolling. Brim strolled over to the hundred-foot high double doors, marked by a tiny metal sign with 18B printed on it, and punched a code into the keypad. The large metal door rolled upward, and there she was. *Persia Smiles*. In all her magnificent dry-docked glory.

Stewart's van had pulled alongside by then. "Everyone out," he ordered while Walker stared up at the tremendous size of his—boat. She was a monster on dry land, a sleek, beautiful lady monster. Man, her keel alone lifted her a good ten feet from the concrete floor.

Persia was standing aft, looking up at the lettering above the landing deck, now high over her head. "*Persia Smiles*," she murmured.

"You were always with me," Walker admitted easily. "Even when I left you behind."

Walking over to him, she linked her arm through his. "You only left because you were a hunted man."

His heart swelled at her easy forgiveness. Lifting her hand to his mouth, he closed his eyes and pressed a kiss into her palm. "You never cease to amaze me."

The light in her smile outdid the sun. "Then let's get this gal back in the water, sailor."

# Chapter Thirty-Nine

*Whew!* Getting *Persia Smiles* into the river was no small chore. Maneuvering her out of the storage building to the crane took the rest of the day. By the time the sun set, Persia was ready to leave Portugal behind. Walker's beautiful yacht bobbed placidly alongside the dock. He was antsy, ready to cast off.

Once aboard, he ran to the cockpit first, then returned to the aft deck with a screwdriver. Brim had called out to him then, "I moved it!"

Walker stopped in his tracks and cast a terse, "Where?"

"Sumbitch, can't an old man get aboard before you start bellowing?" Brim grumbled as he maneuvered across the gangplank, with Rover straining at the end of his leash.

Whatever evidence Walker had, it made him uncharacteristically tense. "Where'd you put it?" he asked the minute Brim's feet hit the deck. "Is it safe? Did you look at it?"

Brim cupped Walker's shoulder. "No, son, I didn't open or look at whatever you're hiding, but I wasn't sure it'd be safe where you'd left it. Those pirates boarded us so fast, we didn't get much time but putting it back where we found it, remember? Come on, son. I hid your bag, too. Let's go get your stuff."

While Walker went below deck with Brim, Persia helped Alex and Senator Sullivan transfer supplies to the galley. A few moments later, Walker was back up top, untying ropes from the dock and casting off.

He'd changed into khaki cargo shorts, an ordinary gray t-shirt, and boat shoes. Persia watched him turn from a hunted criminal to the captain of this yacht. The prestigious title fit. If she didn't know better, he'd gained two inches in height since he'd come aboard. Out here, he was king of these ocean waves, the master of his destiny. The wind off the river furrowed through his short, lush locks like wind through the stalks in a cornfield. She wanted to rake her fingers over that hair and smooth it down while she kissed that handsome man's lips.

It wasn't long before Walker cleared the congested confluence where the Tagus River emptied into the Atlantic. With him in the cockpit and the yacht aimed due west, everyone else took a few minutes to refresh and change clothes. It was good to see Alex in cargo shorts and an easy-going light blue t-shirt for a change. Man, he had some impressive calves. Which was par for all the men and women on The TEAM. Most still maintained strict physical condition, a prerequisite for job descriptions that included engaging with belligerents at a moment's notice, HALO jumping, or running into armed conflicts the world over.

The next thing Alex did was scan the entire yacht for bugs. Brim was at the wheel by then.

Walker couldn't have looked more shocked when Alex confronted him with a surly, "Are these yours?"

Confounded, he ran a hand over his head, which Persia wouldn't have noticed, except it gave her a good view of the underside of his impressive bicep. Smooth rounded muscle. Thick, overworked veins. Man, the guy was scrumptious, from head-to-toe and everywhere in between.

"That explains how the shore patrol found us. Where were they?"

"One in the cockpit, the other in the inflatable raft."

"Shit. He's known where I've been this whole damned time."

"Not anymore." Alex chucked both transmitters over the rail and into the ocean. "But whoever planted them knows you're on the move again."

"I… I don't know what to say."

Alex clapped Walker's back and walked away with, "Shit happens."

But Persia could tell Walker was stunned at the revelation. Just as stunned that Alex had touched him. When he finally stopped staring at Alex's back, his gaze zeroed on Persia.

She winked and mouthed, "He likes you."

He waved her off, and that was okay. There was a time Persia hadn't been sure of her boss, either. But he was beginning to grow on her, and she had to give Alex credit. He took good care of his people, and not once had he asked for any payment in return.

At the moment, he, Senator Sullivan, and Ryder Dahl were sequestered back in the cockpit with Walker. They'd left the hatch open, and Persia knew she should probably be up there strategizing with them. She had fought tooth and nail for Alex's approval. But the flight from Ireland and the hectic drive to the docks had left her bone-tired.

Izza had gone below deck to the galley. That woman seemed to enjoy cooking, so Persia let her. Brimley had taken possession of one of the recliners just off the cockpit. Rover was still roaming the ship like he was happy to be back aboard.

*Okay then. Why not?* She just needed forty winks.

Persia settled into the comfortable recliner opposite Brimley. He didn't seem inclined to talk, and she was glad for the companionable silence. The ocean air was cool and so, so easy to breathe. She hadn't been near the water since she'd left Florida, and she'd missed it. The busy Potomac River that ran between the District and Virginia, didn't count.

It wasn't long before her eyes grew heavy. The gentle sway of the yacht and the fresh salt air worked wonders. She fell asleep to the sounds of gulls and sea and freedom.

Walker couldn't have been happier. Finally. He was back where he belonged, at sea with his troubles behind him. The evidence of human trafficking he'd found was safe, and he had Kenny's knife sheath strapped at his side again. Brim had proven to be one helluva surprise.

For now, Walker wanted nothing more than to just stand over Persia and watch her sleep. Man, she was a beauty, with her long elegant fingers clasped together over her chest and her cheek tucked into her shoulder. She'd changed into cutoff jeans and a simple pink t-shirt. Her long, lush hair was tied in a ponytail, like Izza's.

To look at the two women, it was easy to think they were sisters. Both were olive-skinned, dark-haired, dark-eyed, and intense as hell when working. But Persia was sleek and tall, like a model straight out of a swimsuit calendar, whereas Izza was shorter. She was just as pretty, in her way, but she carried herself like she was always ready to pick a fight. Her husband had to be one pussy-whipped weakling if the rule about opposites attracting held true. Walker wondered who Mr. Maher was. An insurance salesman or some other pencil pusher? A wuss?

Not that it mattered. Walker needed to get this next meeting over with. The sooner, the better. Once he'd disclosed everything on those flash drives, he hoped to have the name of who was behind all those sad women's faces, and every last one of his false accusations. He'd know what to do next then. Even if there were no names on those flash drives, at least he now had a helluva lot of help. It didn't hurt that Senator Sullivan had stood up for him. Sullivan and Stewart seemed like two head-butting mountain goats, ready to run over anything in their paths, including each other.

Walker stroked Persia's shoulder. "Wake up, sugar. I need you in on this meeting."

"You got yourself a winner there, son," Brimley muttered softly. "Hope you know that."

"I do. You're invited to join us. We're headed below deck to my room, and you absolutely need to be in on what you and I found."

"Guess me and Rover'll be there then."

"Guess you'd better."

Persia shook herself awake. "Sorry, I drifted off," she said sleepily.

"Come on. Brim and I have something to show you." Walker tugged her out of her recliner and onto her feet.

Back in the master stateroom, he left the door open, so Rover could come and go. Senator Sullivan had taken the seat next to the desk. Dressed casually in jeans and a simple white t-shirt, his eyes sparkled out of his tanned, weathered face. This Texan carried himself with authority and pride. His trimmed, salt-and-pepper mustache wasn't the length and thickness of Brim's, yet it gave him the same distinguished vibe. He was older, yet still what women would call movie-star handsome.

Walker only knew him as the cowboy senator from Texas who'd tamed the wild Sinclair brothers of Montana—the Sin Boys. Former SEALs, Sullivan had enlisted the rowdy threesome into his team of covert operators. The SOBs were funded with dollars so black, they were redacted even on federal budgets. The man seemed to have complete power over his presidential assignment, a rare thing in DC these days.

It was Kruze Sinclair who'd come to San Diego the day before Walker's sentencing. By some miracle, Kruze had been allowed into the brig. Their conversation was quick, to the point. Kruze had simply shaken Walker's hand, then told him to keep the faith. He'd written a phone number in black ink on the inside of Walker's wrist and said, "You'll need this."

Then he'd walked away. Walker had quickly committed the number to memory, then scrubbed his hands and wrist clean. After he'd ditched the wretchedly sick guards taking him to Leavenworth, that phone number had taken him straight to Senator Sullivan's desk in Washington, DC. From Nowhere, Kansas, Sullivan had whisked him across country to Fort Campbell, Kentucky, where Walker'd met shit-eating, grinning Chief Warrant Officer Trevor Duncan. The rest was history.

Duncan taught Walker to fly the one-of-a-kind, experimental Blackhawk helo. Also taught him not to worry if the helo ever failed to perform. All he'd had to do, if or when that happened, was call Trevor and turn over the controls.

It was the wave of the future, where even big birds were unmanned drones. Where loss of life was, supposedly, taken out of the equation that had heretofore built massive federal defense budgets.

But Walker knew better. He'd lost his faith in elected officials long ago. Those pretty boys and girls didn't really care about the men they put in harm's way. If they did, they'd take better care of them once they'd returned home. There'd be no homeless vets on street corners, begging for scraps and loose change. There'd be no more suicide from untreated PTSD. No need for vets to fight for decent medical care. Besides, nothing provided accurate intel better than boots on the ground. End of that fairytale.

Stewart stood behind Sullivan, with Ryder seated on the easy chair to his left. Persia, Izza, and Brim sat on the bed to Walker's left. It was time. Swallowing hard, he retrieved the accordion-pleated file. Undoing the elastics, he moved the laptop aside and spread the incriminating photos across the desk. Made him sick to see them again.

Stewart was at his side by then, already had his sat phone at his ear. "Ember. I'm sending photos of…" He looked down at Walker.

"Twenty-one women and girls," Walker answered as he lined them up, so Stewart could take a better picture.

It took him seconds to send those pictures. "What else?"

Walker pulled the handwritten purchase orders out next.

"Jesus Christ," Stewart hissed, when he leaned in closer to take a better look.

"Shit," Sullivan growled.

Everyone was on their feet. Persia turned instantly hard. "I will kill this motherfucker, if it's the last thing I do."

Walker looked up at her. Man, he loved tough talk from this beautiful woman.

"I'm right there with you, sister," Ryder muttered, his deep baritone somehow calming in the middle of this view of hell.

"You have no idea how many times I've dealt with similar cases," Stewart breathed, as he snapped close-ups of several receipts. "Sex trafficking is the world's current Black Plague. It's everywhere. Interesting these are handwritten. That's different."

"Also interesting they're legible," Sullivan added darkly. "A handwriting specialist should be able to tell us who wrote them, provided we've got matching cursive. All the same penmanship. And they're numbered. At least whoever's behind this business kept records. Think your TEAM can narrow the playing field?"

"My TEAM works miracles."

"Good. Let's see how fast they can get answers, then."

"I think Wallace Goff is behind this," Walker offered. "Tell Ember to compare these receipts to his writing first."

"Might've been him," Sullivan drawled.

"No, sir, it *is* him. What I mean is, I'm sure he's still alive. I think he faked his death."

"Why would you think that?" Stewart asked, his sharp eyes scrolling over Walker like he'd been weighed and found wanting.

"Because there are just too many coincidences, Mr. Stewart—"

"Alex," the alpha hardass barked. "For hell's sake, if you're not going to call me boss, just Alex."

*Alex it is.* "First off, Renzo said something the night we… talked," Walker explained. "He said his buyer was late because another transaction had gone sideways. I think I'm what went sideways. His other POC, Officer Bruno, must've warned Goff that I was snooping around. Which was why I was able to rescue all those women and girls. If he'd been smart, he would've sent someone else to grab this human shipment, but he didn't, and he knew I'd recognize him. That's the only reason I was able to get Emily Dooley out of there."

"And…?" Alex prompted.

"And because…" Walker gritted his teeth, probably going to sound crazy, but still going full steam ahead. "Because this yacht's still registered in Goff's name. And the dates line up. The MPs were inside my house the morning after I returned from Guatemala. I was sound asleep. Hell, I still had jetlag, but there they were, arresting me for murdering my CO at 2100 hours the night before. Check my flight time if you don't believe me. I didn't arrive until 2030. Yet Goff's neighbor's testimony puts me at the scene before I'd even left the airport. There's no way I could've been in two places at once. Who else could've stacked the cards against me that fast? Had to be Goff."

"And…?" There went those sharp blue lasers again.

"I gave my leave request to Goff. He's got to be behind the sabotaged Blackhawk demonstration in Britain." Walker ran a quick hand over his too long for Navy hair. "And now that bombing in Jordan. Christ, I've been set up for every shit show that's gone down since I set foot in Guatemala. They can't all be coincidences. Who else could it be? Who else would've known?"

"You and he *ever* get along?" Sullivan asked sarcastically.

"Team 18 hated the son of a bitch, sir," Ryder piped up, his dark eyes hard and fast on Walker. "He played by the book and followed rules, but he never once backed us up. Never had a problem hanging us out to dry if it made him look good. Goff was a pencil pusher. Isn't that right, Boss?"

"Spot on," Walker agreed. "I can pin two deaths directly on false intel Goff fed us on an op in Algeria. We lost two good operators that time." Made him wonder what Goff might have had on them. Had they stumbled across his involvement in human trafficking? Was that why they'd died?

"And you…?" Sullivan pushed.

Walker didn't know what else to say. "Goff was plenty book smart; he just didn't connect with his teams like decent commanders did. He was too busy playing politics and kissing ass. None of us SEALs liked him."

"What do you know about the incident in Britain?" By then, Alex had crossed both arms over his chest, subtle body language for *'convince me, asshole.'*

"Only what I read—"

"It happened just weeks before the night Walker left Julio stranded on a sandbar off the coast of Brazil, Boss," Persia interrupted, her fingers still firm on Walker's shoulders. "The Nightstalkers were there demonstrating a hot infil from their

Blackhawk over Buckingham Palace, for the Queen. It was a big deal, and had been vetted through DoD. Media was everywhere. Security was extremely high. The Blackhawk had just cleared the palace roof when it exploded. Nine spectators were injured, one critically, and all thirteen Green Berets on board were killed. The Army pilot and co-pilot escaped with injuries, but the pilot is blind. He'll never fly again. Allegations surfaced instantly that escaped convict Walker Judge had jury-rigged a small explosive device onboard the helo. That he'd detonated it via remote control. Parts and pieces of a cell phone were found in the wreckage. A single fingerprint was on one of those pieces." She squeezed Walker's shoulders. "His."

"Where was he when this happened?" Alex asked.

"Working for me out of Fort Campbell," McQueen replied. "Already had him flying coach with Trevor Duncan. Learning to fly helos."

"He was in Minas Gerais, Brazil, Boss. I can prove it," Persia added.

"Who claimed the fingerprint was his?"

"Probably NCIS," Walker answered sarcastically, at the same time Persia replied, "NCIS, Boss."

When he looked up at her, it seemed her brown eyes were melting all over him. Man, he needed a break from all this cloak-and-dagger bullshit. Dragging her onto his lap and kissing the hell out of her would help.

"I'll check to see which NCIS agent handled that investigation, Boss," Persia told Alex. "I'll backtrack the chain of evidence, too."

"I'll check security footage at San Diego Airport, get a copy of our guy coming and going," Izza chimed in. "Want me to check with Buckingham Palace? See what Scotland Yard knows?"

"Do that," Walker said at the same time Alex barked, "Yes."

Alex shot him a dirty look. Walker just shrugged. "They didn't call me Chief and Boss for nothing," he offered semi-apologetically. Ideally, he shouldn't be investigating his own case. But he also shouldn't have had to.

"What I want to know is what motive NCIS claimed Walker had to execute those Green Berets. That's a damned stiff charge to make against someone they lost on their way to Leavenworth."

"Doesn't seem to me these yahoos needed honest proof or logical motive," Brimley added. "None of this makes sense, and it doesn't take a master's degree to see through all these bogus charges."

A gust of breath escaped Walker's lungs. There he was again, Brim coming to his rescue.

"Guys," he said, his voice hoarse. "For the record, I'm innocent of all these charges. I didn't kill Goff, those Green Berets, or the people at Prince Khalid's wedding. Do I know how to set remote charges? Yes, but I'll wager all of you can do that, too. Hell, I've never been to London or Jordan. Check my orders. Please, check everything I've ever done or said. I've got nothing to hide."

"Forget Khalid and that mess in Jordan," Sullivan muttered. "Alex and I already know who bombed the wedding. We can also prove Prince Khalid paid two million US dollars to erase his bride's family from the face of the earth. We have someone inside Saudi Arabia, sorting the details, right now. Just need to out whoever's hiding Khalid before we go to the AG and prove our case." AG as in Attorney General.

"My friend, the King of Jordan, will have something to say about Khalid murdering a prominent Jordanian family," Alex remarked drolly. "That'll be fun, watching the Saudi royal family facing off with him."

"What I want to know is how Captain Spenser Cole figures into this mess," Sullivan mused, twisting one end of his mustache. "Walker's right. Him being fingered for Goff's death the second his feet hit California, feels like a small part of a bigger plot. What are we not seeing?"

"Damned if I know," Alex replied, his sharp eyes all over Walker again, slicing him into bite-sized pieces. "Beau's working the Spenser Cole angle. My TEAM will get back to me with Sitreps before dinner. If they've got anything, I'll let you know."

Made Walker wonder if he had something stuck in his teeth the way Alex's gaze scoured his face, like he wanted to peel his skin away and dig a spoon into his brain. Just how powerful were these two men? "You know the King of Jordan? You guys have operators inside Saudi Arabia? Christ, how many agents are working my case?"

"All of them," Alex answered evenly.

Sullivan held up three fingers. "Just me and the Sin Boys."

Walker sagged back in his seat, humbled. Pride was a damned hard thing to swallow. "How... how many's that, Alex?"

He crossed his ankles and settled one hip to Walker's desk. "Let me tell you a story, Agent Judge. A few years back, my TEAM tangled with a syndicate out of China. The Black

Dragons. Worst damned case of child abuse I've ever seen. We rescued hundreds of little Chinese girls and babies during that op, but we lost thousands more, simply because we could only reach the ones in America. Which I find an intolerable end to any operation. But the hard truth is, there's no way to keep up with these human-trafficking bastards anymore. Much less get ahead of the game to save the women and kids before they get sucked into this shitstorm.

"The virgin trade and selling of minors is big business, even in the States. Guess you already know that, but know this, too. I've got a man in Phnom Penh, Cambodia, right now, who intercepts and rescues young girls and boys from sex-traffickers moving them into China. He runs my safe house. He gives them safe quarter, medical care, and a chance to just be kids. Usually, they were sold into prostitution by their families. But sometimes" —Alex nodded at the photos—"they've been kidnapped. Both ways are morally wrong, but I blame the assholes who buy these little ones, more. I blame the perverts and elitists who think they're above laws of common decency. They're the sons of bitches I'm after, and if it takes every agent I've got, and every dollar I ever make, I'm going to send as many of them to hell as I can!"

Whoa. Walker couldn't think of a thing to say after that impassioned declaration.

"To answer your question, Alex has at least eighty agents on his payroll right now," Persia spoke up, even as her fingers landed lightly on Walker's tense shoulders. "That's how many are working your case. Except for David Tao. He's the agent in Phnom Penh. I'm with you, Alex. I've seen the worst mankind can do, and it's time we end them."

"Me, too," Izza said staunchly.

"Me, three," Walker said, then quietly added, "Boss."

Alex skewered him again with a terse, "This is your yacht, Chief. What next?"

Walker ran a hand up the back of his stiff neck. Despite Alex calling him Chief, he felt more like a rotisseried Turkish kebob. "I appreciate everything you've done and are doing, Alex. Senator Sullivan—"

"McQueen. Please."

"Okay, well... McQueen, then." Walker sucked in a long deep breath that didn't come near to restoring his $O_2$ levels. "It seems like you guys have everything covered, even details I hadn't thought of. But I need to know who's in Wallace Goff's grave. We're going back to San Diego."

Damned if Alex and McQueen didn't nod in agreement at the same time. God, these guys were intense, and he hadn't even shown them the flash drives yet.

# Chapter Forty

Just as Alex and McQueen stood to leave, Walker said, "I still have a couple flash drives I believe are Commander Goff's."

Persia stayed where she was, on Walker's six, gently massaging the blood back into those taut neck muscles of his.

McQueen took his seat.

Alex ordered. "Open them up. Let's see who's running this shitstorm."

In seconds, the entire room had zeroed in on video clips of hundreds of girls and women who'd been surveilled and videoed in various stages of undress. At schools. At doctor's offices. Inside restrooms and dressing rooms. Some images were grainy and bumpy, as if the person taking the clips had used a cell phone or mini camera stuck under a dressing room or bathroom stall door. Other times, the pictures were crystal clear, which meant the perpetrators had been trusted doctors, nurses, teachers, or friends. Man, it was a sick world out there.

"Scan the rest of these son of a bitchin' files," Alex ordered as he scribbled on the tablet beside the laptop. "Send them to this number in Virginia. They'll go directly to Ember Dennison, who'll sort these through her facial recognition program."

Walker looked up at Alex then. "Thought only the FBI had software like that."

"Guess not," Alex replied curtly. Which Persia took as his stab at deniable plausibility.

Walker did as asked. When it became clear the first drive held mostly the same types of clips, he moved onto the second. Which was an entirely different video nightmare.

The scene was so dark that Persia had to lean over Walker's shoulder to see better. She blinked, not believing what she was looking at among the shadows. Women and children. Boys and girls. All behind bars in what looked like a dungeon. All frightened and crying. A dark-haired monster, his craggy features backlit by the blow torch in his hand. Another thinner man with an industrial-sized pair of bolt cutters...

*God, no.*

The evil spirit of the scene reached out and grabbed her by the throat.

"Is thisssss...?" She couldn't speak it. Didn't want to relive it! "Is th-th-that... him?" she asked, pointing at the monsters in the middle of the flickering nightmare. "That's him, isn't it? That'ssss...!"

Who else could it be? "Who took this picture? Is that Domingo? Is that his lair?" She was shrieking by the time she'd finished. But it looked like the inside of one of Zapata's demented cell blocks. So real, she could almost smell the fear again. The sickeningly sweet scent of burned flesh. The blood! Her heart climbed up her throat, as her stomach pitched its first attempt to vomit up that very same escape route.

Alex slapped the laptop shut, his other hand locked on her upper arm. "Not Zapata," he told her firmly. "That's old footage, Persia. Deep breaths. You can do this. Not Zapata, do you hear me?"

She nodded, embarrassed she'd freaked out so easily and so fast. But that place looked the same!

By then, Walker had spun his chair around. He pulled her easily onto his lap and wrapped his arms around her. "I've got you, sugar. Take a deep breath. You're here on *Persia Smiles*, remember? I named my yacht after you. Zapata's dead. Julio killed him. You were there; you saw him die. Breathe, sugar. Just breathe."

Swallowing hard to keep from projectile vomiting on her boss, she closed her eyes and breathed in the scents she loved best. Salt and sea and the slightest hint of aftershave. Shaking like a fool, she looked up into her boss's tender blue eyes. "I hate black and red," she told him as the first tears began to fall. "Don't ever wear those colors again!"

He had the nerve to smile, even as he cupped her jaw and wiped a finger over her sloppy wet cheek. "Yes, ma'am," he said with genuine kindness. "Mark already talked with me. No more power ties. Already threw them away. Didn't need them anyway. You're safe now. Both Zapata brothers are dead. So's the asshole in that horror flick. It's old news, kiddo. Is it still okay if I wear pink?"

She choked. Alex in pink? "Sure, but who…? Who…?" Man, this panic attack was so, so bad, she couldn't talk. She was making such a fool of herself. "Who was that?"

"Roland Montego, a sadist from Cuba. That was one of his holding cells," Izza said from somewhere behind Persia. "He can't hurt any more kids or women, because Seth McCray took him out a year ago. The fucker's dead."

"His sister Catalina's dead, too," Alex said quietly. "You can thank Renner Graves for ending that twisted sociopath."

"Both your agents?" Walker asked.

Alex must've nodded, because Persia didn't hear his reply. By then, she'd buried her face in her hands, so damned thankful Walker had a good grip on her. She was falling apart and doing it in front of her boss. In front of everyone! "I'm... I'm..." *Losing it.* "I'm sorry."

"Folks, we're all tired. We need to eat," Izza declared. "I've got chicken and cheese enchiladas in the oven. Quesadillas are up next. Anyone hungry?"

Persia nodded, embarrassed, but more aware than ever before how much she valued the men and the sister at her side.

The iron shackles of Walker's big arms clamped around her, holding her fast. "Roland Montego was another trafficker?" he asked Alex. "He worked out of Cuba? Are you sure?"

Alex glanced at Persia. "You okay if we don't go eat just yet?"

She nodded, her heart still pounding hard and heavy, but her paranoia back in its box where it belonged. Shoved down deep where it could wait for another day. Another stiff drink. Another entire bottle. "Yes, Boss. I'm good," she breathed, still clutching Walker's arms.

With a curt nod, Alex spilled the heinous story Persia already knew. How Roland Montego had trafficked human cargo to the most perverse buyers on America's Eastern Seaboard. How Alex had sent Agents Eric Reynolds and Cassidy Dancer Cannon into Cuba to end him. How Seth had been in Florida, at the same time, and had gotten involved in another privately-run effort to rescue those same women and children. One run by Cord Shepherd and his sister, Devereaux, the woman now married to Seth.

"I've got a good man still working in the Keys to bring down the bastards behind the sex-trade running between Cuba and the States," Alex said.

"Cord Shepherd?" McQueen asked, with something that sounded a lot like disbelief, in his tone.

"Yes, you know him?"

"Hell yeah, I know Cord." Grimacing like a bastard, McQueen scratched the end of his nose with a covert middle finger salute. Persia grinned. "You're either one lucky son of a bitch, Alex, or you really do work magic. Seems like you snap up all the good guys and gals before I even know they're alive."

"What can I say? I know people," Alex replied easily. "Plus, I've been in this business longer than you and your SOBs. Why don't you and your people come work for me?"

McQueen slapped his thigh and laughed. "By hell, you've got guts. But no, thank you. No, sir. I've got teams all over the world. Think we'll keep on doing what we've been doing."

"You do good work."

"Damned straight," McQueen shot back at Alex. "Your TEAM's not so bad, either."

"That night" —Walker interrupted the mutual admiration between these two alphas— "in Guatemala, Renzo said his buyer was from Cuba. And now we've got footage inside Montego's jail cells—"

"That looks exactly like the insides of Zapata's prison," Persia added weakly.

Another ugly coincidence…

Alex's head cocked. "You think Montego, Zapata, and Goff were working together?" His icy blues took on a faraway gaze. "The timeline sure as hell fits. You might be onto something."

"Unless Goff and Montego were part of something bigger," Walker replied. "When did you end Montego?"

"A year and a half ago," Persia answered for Alex. "Seth ended Roland Montego inside his own ugly lair down in Cuba. Then last December, in Virginia, Renner Graves took out Roland's sister Catalina."

"It was cold that night," Alex murmured. "And it snowed..."

Persia scrubbed her hands up her biceps, remembering how cold it had been, even in tropical Brazil. That night, no one at Zapata's lair had yet known the Sin Boys had apprehended Domingo Zapata in Montana. He'd gone there to kill Chance Sinclair and his pretty wife. But that was another story...

"What if these guys are all part of, I don't know, a bigger syndicate?" Walker asked. "A worldwide syndicate would sure explain these trumped-up charges against me. Hell, even the ICC's in on it."

"I'd sure like to know who bribed or blackmailed that judge," McQueen bit out.

Alex's eyes turned hard as steel. "Senator. We've been looking at this all wrong."

# Chapter Forty-One

They made it through the Panama Canal eight days later, then turned north and traveled up the coast of Central America, past Panama and Costa Rica. Nicaragua. El Salvador. It wasn't until Walker dropped anchor off the Guatemalan shore, that daily Sitreps yielded solid intel.

By then, he knew Hans Koning was safely at his sister's home in New York, and Quinn Dooley was back aboard the *Iwo Jima*. Trevor was somewhere in Africa, doing who knew what. Former Petty Officer First Class Urban Sweeney, of SEAL Team 18, had called to assure Walker they were watching Miss Breeze, as well as the sailors who'd testified against Walker.

Because Alex believed in transparency and made certain that every Sitrep was broadcast over the yacht's loudspeaker, Walker cringed when he heard his former mistake's name. Which Sunday Night had surely been. Brief. Exciting, for what that was worth. But the biggest dead-end of a relationship he'd ever encountered. Talk about bad timing, him being with a total airhead when this shitstorm started. Not one of his smarter alliances.

Worse, every time Persia heard that name, her eyes would search for him, and she'd wink, as if she knew what an idiot he'd been. The tease. He needed to explain that one, but with so many others on board, there hadn't been much time for privacy.

Izza Maher had contacted, of all people in the world, the Queen of England. She'd smiled coyly when she'd told Alex she had a confidential informant on the inside, working to clear Walker's name. That she'd get back to him the second she had actionable intel.

Of course, he'd asked, "That CI got a name?"

She'd given him a saucy shrug. "Sure. The Queen. Who else?"

Walker'd had to close his eyes and take a deep breath at that totally unexpected, downright impossible, reply. Seriously? Did this TEAM know everyone who was anyone? *Guess so.*

Everyone aboard looked more and more like a group of suntanned tourists, instead of special operators. Persia was dressed in cutoff jeans with a pink bikini top that revealed enough of her mocha chocolate skin, that Walker couldn't keep his eyes off her. He was hard for her from sunup til sundown these days. And there was no relief in sight. He was dying to go swimming with her, maybe duck out of sight around the bow. Fondle her. Slip the straps of that skimpy, sexy top off. Kiss the hell out of her. Grab a quickie.

But no such luck. It was Julio Juarez's quiet report coming over the loudspeaker now. "Senator Sullivan. Mr. Stewart. Kruze and I were too late. Officer Bruno has been reported missing, and Renzo was murdered by unknown assailants at his beach home."

"Obvious arson," Kruze cut in. "Nothing left but ash. They found him hanging from gallows behind the place. Birds picked the body clean by the time he was found."

Sullivan asked, "Is any effort being made to locate Bruno?"

"He went missing a year ago," Julio replied. "The police consider it a cold case."

"Someone's tying up loose ends," Ryder muttered.

"Any luck with the gangs who abducted Dooley's daughter?" Alex asked.

That caught Walker's attention. He lifted his wrist to his lips and kissed the red beads on the only bracelet he'd ever worn. Knowing Alex was as vehemently against sex-traffickers as Walker was—helped.

"There are currently no gangs in or around Monterrico," Julio replied. "A small army came through and assassinated all gang members over a year ago. Many people think it was the government's way of clearing the way for the new democracy."

"What do you think?" Sullivan asked.

"Not sure what to think," Kruze spoke up, "but the city's clean of all gang activity. People are pleasant, willing to talk and answer questions. It's safer now."

"That's one way to dispose of evidence," Alex muttered. "Clear out the rats in the name of public service. Find out who was behind that kill order."

"Yes, sir," Julio replied.

"Anything else?" Sullivan asked.

"We're still talking to people, sir," Julio answered. "Showing Commander Goff's picture around in case anyone recognizes him. We'll be in touch."

Sullivan signed off with a curt, "Copy that."

Adam Torrey was next on the horn with a casual, "Hey, Boss."

"What's up?" Alex replied evenly.

"Ember's still working her magic. I've got accurate account numbers, just need a way inside."

"You're breaking into a bank?" Walker asked. Unbelievable.

Adam's chuckle came through loud and clear. "Sure, why not? Goff's mother also retained a deposit box on site. I'd like to know what's inside that, wouldn't you?"

"Well, yeah, but…" What Walker really wanted was to be working *with* Adam. Like the old days. "Don't take chances."

"Are you alone?" Alex barked.

"Nope. Rory Dennison and Renner Graves are here in Singapore, too. Figured the more the merrier."

"Be safe."

"Copy that." Adam ended the call.

Beau Villanueva came online next, but he had nothing new to report in his quest to locate Prince Khalid and his family.

"Where are you?" Alex asked.

"Outside Louveciennes."

"You're in France?" Walker asked, as the very proper French pronunciation rolled smoothly off Beau's lips.

"Well, yeah. I've got good intel Khalid was spotted here. Where else would I be?"

It was common knowledge the Saudi royal family owned some of the poshest palaces in the world. But France? Really?

"Hmmm," Izza mumbled dreamily. "Connor's going to take me there some day."

"Stay in touch," Alex ordered.

And that was that.

"Were you planning on going ashore in Guatemala?" Persia asked.

Walker shook his head. "Not until we hit Mexico."

Which they did three days later. By then, everyone was antsy to get off the yacht. Since Puerta Vallarta was convenient and accessible, both by sea and by air, there were plenty of cruise ships docked and thousands of tourists. Walker opted to stay behind with Ryder.

"What's your real plan, Chief?" Ryder asked once Persia and Izza disembarked like two BFFs going shopping. Alex and McQueen had gone on ahead to replenish supplies. Brim had taken Rover for a walk to stretch their legs.

"Nothing," Walker replied as he watched the woman he loved turn around, smile, and wave. He waved back. She was grinning, and that had to be enough, considering it was the last time he'd see her.

"Come on," Ryder growled. "I know better. This is me you're lying to."

Walker turned on his XO. Sighed. Then admitted, "I can't put these folks in any more danger. Stay here and—"

"Bull to the shit," Ryder growled. "I'm going with you, Chief. Wherever you go, I go. You oughta know that by now."

"Thanks, but no, I—"

"Shut the fuck up. What's the damned plan?"

Walker knew there was no denying his best friend. "I'm going to dig up a body. I need to get there before anyone else does. You up for that?"

Ryder was taller than Walker by about six inches and brown as dark chocolate with shoulders as wide as a Notre Dame fullback. He was light on his feet and could personally pack more gear and ammo than any guy Walker had ever worked alongside. He not only had the vocal range of Michael Clarke Duncan, he was as kind and as humble. Had never let Walker down or questioned a single order. Just did what had to be done. Quickly. Expertly.

"How do you propose digging up a grave?" he asked now.

"With a shovel and Grave Finder," Walker replied. "I know right where the bastard's supposed to be. He'd better damned well be in the casket under that marker."

"Wasn't he interred at Fort Rosecrans?" The National Cemetery on Point Loma, the peninsula due west of San Diego, across from Coronado Island.

"Yes."

"How are you going to prove it's him? Won't you need a DNA test?"

"Embalmed bodies don't decay quickly. I'm pretty sure we'll both recognize the bastard once I pop the lid off his coffin, if he's even there. You can bet your ass he'll be in his best dress uniform and decked out with every last medal he never earned. You with me?"

"Yes, sir," Ryder replied quickly, "but that Stewart guy's going to be pissed when he comes back and finds us gone."

"Not worried about Stewart." Alex would be pissed, but he'd understand. And if he didn't? Didn't matter. Walker wouldn't risk getting anyone else hurt in the upcoming confrontation. Not Stewart or Sullivan. Yes, they were professionals, and they all had his back. Well, he had theirs, too. But leaving Persia would break her heart. That was the real problem, and why Walker hadn't already left.

He stared at the teeming throngs of visitors on the dock. Between the magnificent palm trees standing like sentinels along the hotels across the street and the revelry, there was a definite Rio Carnival feeling in the air. Street performers danced, mimed, or did magic tricks everywhere. Costumed vendors in kiosks hawked ice cream cones and aguas frescas, a non-alcoholic fruit drink. Others offered frosty beer and iced coffees. Further down, farmers' tents and EZ-Ups lined the way.

Two cruise lines currently docked took up the entire dock ahead of *Persia Smiles*. A fishing boat had just sidled in behind him. It had gotten a little closer to the yacht than Walker would've liked, but this was Mexico, where anything went. People were everywhere. Vendors. Tourists. Some coming. Some going. All distracted or causing distractions.

The longer he watched the sea of people, the more Walker wasn't sure he had it in him to walk away from Persia like he had before. Thinking about it was bad enough, but talking and planning another betrayal with Ryder made it real. And doing it—

The deck jerked forward, forcing Walker to grab the rail to keep from falling.

"Shit," Ryder hissed as he leaned hard to his left.

Walker looked at the fishing boat behind him. Its captain was swearing a blue streak, waving his hands and yelling at the yacht that had come in too quickly behind him.

"You see that asshat?" Ryder asked. "Probably some rich son of a bitch."

"It takes all kinds," Walker replied wearily. Which explained the sickening state of the world these days. It took a second for him to zero in on the elegant watercraft that had bumped the boat behind *Persia Smiles,* which in turn, caused the fishing boat to bump her aft deck. "Probably drunk. He'd better think twice before he hits my yacht again—"

Son of a bitch! That yacht's captain was Admiral Peckering. Dressed in pristine white slacks, a crisp navy-blue cotton polo, and boat shoes, he dashed off the gangplank, his head up, as if he were looking for someone. He threw a few bills at the kid he'd nearly run over on the dock. Must've ordered him to secure the yacht's lines, because the kid did just that.

"You seeing what I'm seeing?" Ryder asked.

"It's Peckering." The hairs on the back of Walker's neck were on end. The Admiral looked like he was in a hurry. But who was he looking for? Persia? His being here at this precise moment was no coincidence. Somehow, he knew losing her would destroy Walker. And if he was after her… shit. He was the bastard behind the human trafficking ring. It made perfect, scary sense.

"Stay with my yacht," Walker ordered.

"But—"

"Stay here!" Walker snapped, his eyes tracking Peckering as he dashed into the crowd. "I won't leave Persia again, damn it. Someone needs to be here when she comes back."

"You sure about this?" Ryder asked, a kick-ass tone in his voice even as Walker cleared the gangplank.

"Keep your ears on. I'll be right back." *And I'm bringing Persia with me.*

# Chapter Forty-Two

Izza went one way. Persia went the other. So many vendors clogged the winding streets and narrow alleys that she quickly lost sight of her friend. No matter. She tugged her sat phone out of her jeans pocket and dialed Izza. Hmmm. No answer. Just Izza's cocky voicemail: "You want me, you got me. Leave a number."

"Stop shopping like a mad woman and call me," Persia teased. "I'll wait for you at the fruit stand, the one with papayas and watermelon. You should see the size of these. I'm buying three. Don't be long!"

Izza had wanted to grab some small trinkets for her two kids. Persia wanted a bottle of rum and fresh fruit. She was weary of the steady meat, fish, rice, and potatoes diet. Men might be able to live on that, but she needed fresh vegetables and fruit. And it'd been weeks since she'd had a decent drink. Normally, she wouldn't mind going without while on an active operation. But after seeing that ugly video of Roland Montego's prison, she'd been craving one good burning swallow. That was all. Just one.

*Isn't that what all alcoholics say?*

"I'm not an alcoholic," she told herself. Because, well, she wasn't. One bottle did not an alcoholic make. But all the bottles lined up like prizes at the kiosk window ahead of her…

She pointed to the bottle of dark Jamaican rum, paid for it, then stashed it in the orange and pink cloth shopping bag she'd brought along for this precise reason. No one needed to know she was a closet drinker. She headed for the fruit stand beside the booze kiosk next.

"Three," Persia told the kindly dark-eyed little girl running the stand, even as she scanned the crowds swelling around her, keeping an eye out for Izza. Seemed like fruit was a popular item among more than a few lady tourists.

"Persia!"

She whirled around, expecting to see Izza winding her way through the crowd. Even though the voice calling her name had sounded like a guy.

"Persia!" someone else called at her left.

"Over here!" she answered, not recognizing the voices. But honestly, how many Persias could there be?

"Persia!"

Okay, that voice was definitely male. Not Walker, though. Not Alex, either. The sun went behind a cloud, casting an instant chill over her sunburned skin. A creepy sense of foreboding slithered across her shoulders. It was time to get back to the yacht. Like most women on the street, she'd only worn cutoffs and a bikini top. This was Puerta Vallarta, for heaven's sake. The vacation capitol of the world. But now she felt underdressed and exposed. She'd left her pistol behind to make room for the rum.

Concerned, she paid for the fruit, thanked the young girl, then turned in the direction she'd last seen Izza. Palming her sat phone, Persia hit redial. When she got Izza's voicemail again, she glanced over her shoulder. Call it instinct. Call it whatever you wanted. She called it intuition, the one gift that had kept her alive all those months in Zapata's lair. Someone was watching her.

Persia dialed Alex. He and Senator Sullivan had to be close. She'd no more than looked up from her sat phone, when a tall American male blocked her way. Gray hair. Impressive posture. Military bearing. Shifty eyes. He grabbed hold of her biceps as if he were simply making sure she didn't fall.

Persia knew different. Jerking away, she was pissed he'd touch her at all. "Do you mind?" He reminded her of… of… Oh, shit. Admiral Peckering.

Automatically, the middle finger on her free hand lifted to her eyebrow. "Well, bless my heart. Admiral Peckering. What do you want?" she asked, unable to answer the questions Alex was firing in her ear, her brain too flushed with a prey's instinctive need to run.

"You." Reaching both hands out, Peckering shoved her backward.

"Like hell…" she meant to say as she landed against another warm body. Her phone slipped from her fingers. Something stung her neck. Something very sharp. And she tumbled into darkness.

Walker ran into Izza first, standing in front of a busy fruit stand, a colorful cloth bag hanging off her shoulder as she stretched on her toes to see over the crowd. "Have you seen Persia?"

"No, and I've been looking for her. She left me a voicemail, said she was waiting here. You're taller than me.

Can you see another watermelon stand around here? Do you see her?"

While Izza dialed Persia again, Walker did a quick three-sixty. Nothing.

"This can't be happening," Izza whined as she stuffed her sat phone in her rear pocket. Leaning into the watermelon stand, she ripped off a string of Spanish at the young girl.

The girl nodded, then bent over and pulled an orange and pink bag from beneath her table. With a few words, she handed it over, then pointed to a monster palm tree and the alley hidden in the shade behind it.

"Gracias," Izza said, as she examined the bag. "Yup. This is Persia's. Three papayas. A bottle of rum. But no phone. Damn. She couldn't have gone far. Maria said she was just here. She dropped the bag when she ran into some guy. She sounded angry, but the guy grabbed her and wouldn't let her go. I asked what he looked like. Maria said he was tall and old. He had gray hair. He and another man took Persia this way. Follow me."

"It's Peckering," Walker growled as he followed Izza through the crowd, around more fruit and vegetable stands. "He docked behind us. He knew right where we were."

"How the hell'd he find us?" Izza muttered out of the side of her mouth. "Thought Alex scanned your boat for bugs."

"Only after we were at sea. Peckering must've had someone watching the marina."

"All this time? You think he's behind this? Really? A Navy admiral?"

"I know damned well he's behind it," Walker replied as they hurried into the alley. "Are you armed?"

"Always." Izza pulled a pocket pistol out of her bag. "You?"

"Yes." Reaching under his arm, he loosened one of the two SIGs he'd requisitioned at Murphy's from its holster. Lowering its barrel, he kept the weapon alongside his thigh and out of sight. No sense scaring the locals.

"I'll kill him," Izza promised, her piece hidden as well. "If that's who's got Persia, I'll fuckin' kill him."

"We have to find him first."

The narrow alley was crowded with more kiosks, more people, and plenty of shadows. Little sun filtered down between the twenty-plus-story hotels on either side of the alley. There were no cutesy outdoor cafes here. No welcoming lights or dapper entertainers hawking their next street performances. Just the raw, untamed side of a tourist destination.

Garbage was everywhere, some in overflowing waste receptacles, some scattered underfoot. The farther into the alley they went, the darker it became. Yet Izza walked as if she knew where she was going, so Walker let her lead.

Until he caught sight of the tall, gray-haired man up ahead. "I see Peckering," he told Izza as he dodged back and forth, straining to catch a glimpse of Persia past the crowd. "Can't see her yet. We need to split up. Take the next backdoor we come across. Go through the hotel and cut him off. Hurry!"

"Copy that," Izza replied. Turned out another, narrower alley branched off within seconds. She disappeared into the dark.

Walker dodged couples and families in his way, keeping his eye on the back of Peckering's well-trimmed haircut. Another man walked quickly at his side, but Walker couldn't tell if Persia was with them. There were too many people in the way. Apparently, the locals used this alley to avoid the congested plaza. He couldn't risk taking a shot.

In a dozen steps, Peckering would be lost, Persia with him. Walker took a chance and called, "Admiral! Is that you? Wait up!"

Like an idiot, he stopped just long enough to glance over his shoulder.

But that split-second distraction was enough. Instinctively, Walker's pistol came up. "Stop, or I'll shoot!"

The crowd parted like the Red Sea did for Moses. And there he was, in plain view. Admiral Fuckin' Peckering. The shorter, stockier, olive-skinned guy with him had one arm around an unconscious Persia. She appeared limp, draped against him. Drugged. A helpless beauty in nothing but her damned skimpy bikini top and shorts. *I'll kill him if he's hurt her.*

A crackling firework-like explosion rippled overhead. The crowd looked up. Peckering's toady stooped just long enough to sling her over his shoulder. She hung like a rag doll, her hands stretched limply over his butt.

Walker leveled his pistol at the Admiral. "Take one more step and I'll end you."

The light at the end of the alley beckoned, but Peckering had stopped just short of freedom. And now, he'd drawn on Walker.

Well, good. Walker had never let a challenge go unanswered before. Didn't plan to now. With calm, deliberate steps forward, he made himself a target. Buying time for Izza. Buying hope for Persia.

"Put her down, Admiral Peckering," he ordered loud enough for all to hear, his pistol warm and ready in his palm. His plan clear. One through Peckering's head. One through the asshole at his side. Catch Persia before she fell. Backstop was clear, and that made this plan perfect. No collateral damage. By the end of the day, she'd be back in his bed where she belonged.

But someone had called the local police. Sirens sounded nearby. If they arrived before this showdown was over, it'd be Peckering's word against Walker's. A United States Naval officer's lies against a convicted felon's truths. Walker would be disarmed, back in cuffs, and on his knees. Or dead. And Persia would be just another face in another accordion-pleated file.

*Not. Happening!*

Walker charged. Peckering's accomplice let Persia slide off his shoulder, his arm around her neck. Only then did Walker see the hypo he held to her throat.

"One more step, I kill her," the bastard hissed.

Peckering put himself between Persia and Walker. "You don't want Agent Coltrane to die, Lieutenant Judge," he said, his voice as slick as any politician's. "Put your gun down. Walk away."

"Take me instead," Walker said, his heart screaming like a Harley running full-out on warm blacktop. "I'm the one you've wanted all along. Look, I'll go willingly." He lowered his pistol, earnestly convinced he could persuade Peckering to let her go.

The sly monster's upper lip curled. One shoulder lifted like he was annoyed that he had to deal with an idiot. "Where's the fun in that? I can get good money for this whore.

There's no demand for men like you. No. What you're going to do, LT, is put your pistol on the ground, kick it away, then back off. You'll let me and Rodrigo leave. You'll walk away, wave goodbye, act like you never saw us. You won't look for this woman ever again."

*Like hell.* Yet Walker set his weapon to the ground, but he didn't kick it away, and he stayed crouched with one hand on the dirty cobblestone. "How'd a recognized Navy officer get mixed up with the sex-trade? It was Goff, wasn't it? This was all his idea. Is he blackmailing you?"

The damnedest smile tweaked Peckering's lips. "Yes, sure. Goff. It was all his idea. That's right."

The son of a bitch was flat out lying. But if Goff wasn't behind this—?

"You know damned well outside work pays a helluva lot better than Uncle Sam," Peckering continued. "You've been to Guatemala. You know what I'm talking about. Should've tried a little girl on for size when you had the chance. Then you'd know what it feels like to be a real man."

"You knew Roland Montego," Walker said, not asked, more and more disgusted with this cocky pervert. "You worked with him. Or did you work for him? Is that how this worked? You found the girls and he gave you a commission? Did you work with his sister, too? Or did he work for you?"

Peckering didn't confirm or deny, but Walker saw a glint of anger flash in his eye. Might as well get everything out in the open. The local cops might still get him, but Walker would know the truth. "I can pay for her," he wheedled. "Let her go, and you'll never see me again."

"You can't pay enough, LT. Hell, you're not even that anymore. You're ruined. Broke. Back the fuck off. Don't grovel. Weak men disgust me."

Walker was plenty disgusted, too. "I know you targeted Captain Dooley's three girls, Admiral Edgar Peckering," he declared loudly even as sirens screamed closer. People needed to know who this vile man was and what he did to children. "You sold little girls to the highest bidders. You killed United States Navy Commander Wallace Goff, and I can prove it."

"Can you now…?" The ghost of a smile shifted across the Admiral's face. He hadn't lowered his weapon an inch. Didn't need to. He had the one and only golden ticket out of there. He had Persia.

And suddenly, God bless her, there was Izza. Out of breath and red-faced, but fierce and sweaty and deadly at the other end of the alley. Her pistol was up and aimed at the back of Peckering's head.

"Move it, people!" she ordered as she stalked through the crowd. "Get the hell out of here! Vamanos!" Izza let out a string of Spanish invective, and the alley emptied.

He cast a casual glance over his shoulder.

"Let her go, asshole!" Izza demanded next, "or so help me, I'll splatter your brains all over that pretty brick wall behind you. I know who you are, *Peckering*. Soon the whole world will know."

"No," he said clearly. "Drop your gun and shut the fuck up."

Which only pissed Izza off more. "Give me a reason not to fill your head with lead."

"Because if you do," he drawled like a man who held the winning cards, "I won't give this bitch the antidote."

"You poisoned her?" Izza hissed.

"I poison all of them. It's the only way to keep them coming back for more."

Walker didn't think. Just acted. His pistol leaped up from the cold, hard ground, and—

*BLAM!* A single, deep-red rose blossomed dead center of Peckering's massive ego.

Rodrigo's eyes widened. By the time he dropped the hypo, Izza had her pistol pressed to his temple, her knee in his back, and Walker had Persia in his arms.

Izza punched Rodrigo's face. "Where's the fuckin' antidote?"

"I... I... I..." he stuttered, the whites of his eyes showing. What a troll.

Sirens were closer now. Walker grabbed the hypo, then gathered Persia and lifted to his feet. "We gotta go. Bring him with us."

Izza dragged Rodrigo to his feet. "You make one whimper, one sound, and I swear you're dead meat."

They'd no more than stepped out of the alley and into the light, when Alex and McQueen appeared out of nowhere like two pissed off guardian angels. Walker could've sworn they'd been sent by God. The sirens were up close and personal now, so close he could hear tires screeching and doors slamming. Time was up.

"Peckering's body's back there," he told Alex. "You might want to bring it with us."

"You end him?" Alex asked.

"Yes, I did. He poisoned Persia. Boss, we need to hurry."

"Back to the yacht," Alex ordered even as he lifted his sat phone to his mouth and ordered the person on the other end to secure Peckering's body. He'd no more than ended that terse call, when he took hold of Rodrigo's left arm. McQueen took the right. Together, they left Peckering behind and cleared a path for Walker and Persia.

"Hurry," Walker told Alex. "She's barely breathing, Boss. Hurry!"

# Chapter Forty-Three

They'd just cleared the gangplank. Alex and McQueen had released Rodrigo into Ryder's custody, when Izza pistol-whipped him. "Where's the antidote?" she bellowed, her weapon stuck in the back of Rodrigo's head. "What poison did you give her? Tell me!"

Ryder waved Walker to the nearest recliner. "You and your girlfriend, over there. Izza and I will take care of this idiot. You take care of her."

Gently, Walker settled Persia onto the cushion. Her beautiful olive complexion had turned pale, and she was clammy all over. Her fingers fluttered like she was losing control. "I need to know what kind of poison he gave her."

"We'll have that info in a minute," Ryder replied. "Stay with your lady, Boss."

Alex disappeared below deck, then reappeared with a first-aid kit the size of a monstrous ice chest. Slapping the cover up and open, he revealed an array of pharmaceutical supplies and medical equipment.

"Upper left arm," he ordered Walker, handing him a blood pressure cuff and stethoscope. "McQueen, I need you here."

"Copy that," McQueen replied obediently.

Alex tossed a clip-on oximeter, an IV set-up, and sterile wipes to him. "Prepare her right hand. She needs to be ready the second we know what poison we're dealing with. Start a saline drip until then."

Walker had the cuff in place by then, the stethoscope in his ears. "She's one-fifty over ninety-four," he reported. That high pressure put her in the hypertension range. On her way to hypertensive crisis. A stroke or heart attack.

Hurriedly, Alex tore open several packs of sterile cloth, doused his hands with alcohol, then used one of the cloths to pat them dry. Tossing the used cloth aside, he donned surgical gloves next and told Walker to do the same. "Step on it."

While Walker disinfected his hands and gloved up, McQueen swiped the back of Persia's hand and inserted the IV like a pro. He taped it in place and advised, "Her $O_2$ sat rate's dropping like a rock, Alex. Is there any epinephrine in that crate if she goes into cardiac arrest?"

"No worries," Alex replied calmly as he opened a pre-packaged sterile hypo.

"God, I hope you guys know what you're doing," Walker muttered, worried this was it, the end. That he'd never kiss Persia's sweet lips again or smell her warm breath in his face. Never feel the silky tease of her long hair over his bare belly or her fingernails raking through his hair. Never be able to tell her how much he adored her. How he meant to marry her...

Out of nowhere, a tear fell out of his eye, like a damned pussy. He brushed it away. "I can't lose her."

"Have faith," Alex whispered. "She's not going anywhere. Hold her arm steady. I need to draw enough blood to run a few tests."

Walker did as asked while Alex extracted a full vial of dark, red blood. Her life force. But it was too late. Persia stiffened. She was seizing.

"Hold her still!" Alex ordered.

"You're killing her!" Walker growled as tremors shook her like a dog with a rug. Thin strings of drool slid from the sides of her clenched tight mouth even as he held her steady.

Alex was already dripping blood samples into a small rack of previously prepared test tubes that Walker honestly hadn't seen until then. The man seemed prepared for everything. He'd better be!

With sweat glistening on her forehead and the loose hairs around her face frizzy, Izza intervened from her enthusiastic interrogation with an out of breath report. "Diethyl-meta-toluamide, Boss. He shot her up with diethyl-meta-toluamide. That's all."

"Christ, that's enough," McQueen ground out.

"You're telling me," Izza answered. "Now save her, Boss! Damn it, save her!"

Man, she was as pushy as Alex.

"Organophosphates…" he muttered as one vial turned bright yellow, then blue. "Confirmed."

"Insecticides?" Walker murmured. There were more lethal poisons, but those were bad enough, especially when administered directly into a person's bloodstream. "Does that bastard know which brand? What dosage? How much did Peckering give her?"

"Doesn't matter," Izza replied. "Rodrigo says Peckering shoots his girls up with this insecticide, then tells them it's delayed-reaction cyanide. That it'll kill them inside twenty-four hours if they don't do what he wants. He gives his new girls larger doses. Rodrigo didn't know the exact amount. Only knew Peckering wanted them good and sick and wanting to die before he—"

"Before he walks in and saves them," Walker interrupted, "and they end up believing him."

"Yeah, well, Peckering keeps his girls locked up tight. He only drugs them when he sends them out. They get the antidote after they return, after they've done what he wanted."

"Asshole," McQueen growled, his fingers on Persia's neck, checking her pulse even though the fancy oximeter on her finger was doing the same thing. "You have the right antidote, don't you, Boss?"

"Atropine," he answered, as calm as if this kind of thing happened every day. He'd set the test tubes aside, had already lifted another vial from the chest, tipped it upside down, and filled a new hypo. Man, even under pressure, this guy was a rock. His fingers weren't even shaking.

But Walker was coming undone. He'd treated numerous men and women from combat injuries, but this was different. This was Persia. He didn't want to think what would've happened if Alex hadn't come with him. Walker couldn't help it. His eyes brimmed at the gentle care these warriors were taking with her, the way they handled her with respect. The way they both knew just what to do. Both badassed men. Men who ruled the country in their own way. Without them—

"Thanks, you guys," he murmured, so damned grateful for men who lived to serve.

Alex never hesitated. Never answered, either. Just expertly eased the atropine into Persia's IV. In seconds, rigidity eased its stranglehold and her body softened. Her spine relaxed. She started breathing again. The caved-in, sucked-in hollow where her collarbones joined, vanished as her chest lifted with steady, calm inhalations.

"Breathe," Alex told her quietly even as one brow lifted and he asked Walker and McQueen, "Stats?"

Walker responded quickly. "Still elevated, but it's coming down." *Thank God.*

"Oxygen saturation's in the eighties now," McQueen said. "Looking better."

"She's off-duty TFN. Izza, she'll need some of your tortilla soup."

TFN was short for til further notice.

Tortilla soup was short for... Izza, as she wrapped both arms around her boss's broad shoulders and wept openly. "You saved her, Boss. You saved my best friend."

Alex patted Izza's back. "No, you and Walker saved the day," he corrected stoically. But who was he trying to kid? His eyes were as misty blue as Walker knew his were.

"How'd you know where we were?" Walker asked when he could finally speak. They'd been completely out of sight in that alley.

"She sent a panic call before I lost her," Alex explained, while Izza sniffed and dried her eyes. "I could hear her arguing, but the line disconnected before I could pin down her precise location. No doubt Peckering destroyed her sat phone once he disabled her. Never would've known there was an alley behind that hotel, until I heard your gunshot."

"Which one of you fired?" McQueen asked.

"Walker," Izza replied quickly, her eyes bright as she leaned away from Alex. "You shoulda seen him, Boss. Never blinked. Only fired once. Nailed the bastard. He's as badass as you."

Walker glanced over Izza's shoulder to where Ryder leaned against the aft rail. His XO smiled approvingly, as if he'd never doubted Walker's skills. Which he shouldn't. They'd worked enough missions. They both knew how lethal the other was. How loyal.

But Peckering's cohort looked like he'd seen better days. Rodrigo was face down to the deck, his hands cuffed behind his back, and his chin was bleeding from several lacerations. Walker wasn't sure what Alex would do with the degenerate once he came to. Shooting an unarmed asshole was a crime in any part of the world, but Alex seemed capable. If he wasn't, Walker was.

It was unfortunate Admiral Peckering hadn't spent more time working with and getting to know the men who served with him. He might've been a better commander. At least, he would've known not to mess with a SEAL on a mission. Because SEALs never backed down, never gave up, and that *'only easy day was yesterday'* bullshit was the fuckin' truth.

Walker avoided looking at Izza. He'd caught the love for Persia glowing from her dark eyes when she'd cried. That kind of love was pure, chocolate sunshine, if there were such a thing. If he looked too long, he'd melt like an M&M left in the sun.

A big, square, kick-your-ass fist caught his bicep. Instant agony radiated down from the still healing through and through, but Walker had no choice but to look his new boss in the eye then. He bit his bottom lip, not sure what Alex would see, but sure it wasn't a tough Navy SEAL.

"You took one helluva chance," Alex told him. "How'd you know Peckering was here?"

Walker manned up, sucked in his emotions, and filled in most of the rest of the story. How Peckering had forced his yacht into dock, then disembarked into the crowd. How

Walker'd known right then and there they'd been followed, that Peckering was going after Persia. How he and Izza couldn't locate Persia, wouldn't have known where she'd gone if Izza hadn't bullied the young girl selling watermelons for information.

"Thanks for that," Walker told Izza now. The only part he'd left out of the telling was how he and Ryder had planned to take off after Peckering by themselves. Wasn't Karma a capricious thing? By delivering Persia to Peckering, she'd also served him up to Walker. After, of course, she'd let Peckering's ego get the best of him.

Izza shrugged. "Just glad Maria saw what went down."

They were all sitting cross-legged on the deck around Persia by then. She was still unconscious but breathing steadily. Walker would've had her on his lap and in his arms, but he didn't think she'd appreciate the public display of affection.

"We need to get underway," Alex said as he covered her with a light blanket.

"One question, Walker," McQueen mused. "What's your plan once you're cleared of the charges against you?"

"I don't imagine that'll be easy or happen anytime soon, sir. As soon as the Navy knows I'm back in the States… If I even go back to the States—"

"You let me worry about that," McQueen drawled, his gaze never straying from Walker's worried eyes. "Let's say all this crap's behind you. Your name's clear. You're a free man. You were working for me at Fort Campbell, but that was just a short-term fix. What now?"

Walker leveled an index finger at Alex. "Sorry, sir, but I already work for him."

"Damn you, Stewart," McQueen cussed, raking a quick hand through his silvery hair. "What makes you think you deserve this guy? He's a SEAL, for hell's sake. My man worked with him in Brazil. Not yours."

"I asked first," Alex deadpanned, "and I pay more. You might be black world, but you're still civil service, Senator."

"You're a greedy son of a bitch, you know that?"

"I've been called worse."

But Walker knew better. He wasn't staying because of the money. Hell, he hadn't even thought of asking about salary or benefits. Hadn't cared. All he knew now was that Persia would be dead if he'd run out on Alex earlier. At the least, she would've been trapped in Peckering's ugly web. For the first time since he'd met her boss, Walker knew he was right where he belonged. He'd never heard of the guy or The TEAM before, but he wanted in on it now.

Automatically, he rested his fingers on Persia's shoulder, needing a connection with her. "Boss," he said as evenly as he could. "Peckering knew Roland Montego. I asked him. He didn't admit it, but I saw the look in his eye. They worked together. I don't know which one was the boss, but is it possible that Black Dragon Syndicate you were talk—"

*THUD.* Ryder hit the deck like a big bag of bricks. And there stood dripping wet Commander Wallace Goff with a hypo and a sawed-off shotgun in his shaky hands. "You're sure a Goddamned pain in my ass! Why can't you just die?!"

# Chapter Forty-Four

Jerking the pistol out from under his left arm, Walker jumped to his feet and put himself between Goff and Persia. "Stand back!"

"Drop it!" Goff ordered. "All of you! Drop your weapons, or I'll shoot!"

Walker had no choice. Neither did Alex or McQueen. Heavy hardware settled to the deck, but Walker only lowered his pistol to the blanket covering Persia. "You're supposed to be dead," he growled at his former CO. "I was convicted for killing your dead ass."

Goff raked a hand over his head, plastering his thinning hair to his skull in a foolish combover. "It was never enough for you, was it? First, China. Then Cuba. Then, that meat packing plant outside Joint Base Andrews. Can't you ever mind your own fuckin' business?!"

Walker didn't have a clue what Goff was raving about. "What meat packing plant?"

"Not you. You!" Goff bellowed. "Get the fuck out of my way, Judge!"

Alex took a half-step in front of Walker, blocking him in beside Persia. Shielding him. Wicked energy, like the dangerous voltage generated by Tesla coils, arced off the man. It whirled unseen, whipping out, making the tiny hairs on the back of Walker's neck stand up.

"You," Alex spat.

Goff rolled his eyes. "No, Stewart! Not just me! But I swear, every time I turn around, it's always just you. Dan Peters was right. We should've taken you out first."

"You sure as hell tried. Or don't you remember the pressure bomb you rigged in my elevator? All this time, Interpol Director Daniel Peters worked for you, didn't he?" Alex asked, his head cocked and his fists clenched. The man was a formidable force at rest, but his shoulders seemed broader now. Wider. As if Hercules breathed beneath his skin, aching to tear Goff apart, limb from limb. "You're part of the Goddamned, son of a bitchin' Black Dragon Syndicate."

"Not part," Goff sputtered. "Me! Just me! I… I am the syndicate!"

"You worked with Roland Montego and—"

"I don't work with anyone, Stewart! They worked for me. It was my idea. My dream. But you had to kill 'em. All of them!"

Everything became crystal clear when Montego's ugly name rolled off Goff's tongue. Without thinking, Walker elbowed Alex out of his way. "It was you that night in Guatemala," he accused Goff. "Renzo said his buyer was late. That buyer was you. You engineered the abduction and sale of Emily Dooley and all those women. Those little girls! Then you ran your own gangs down and murdered them to cover your ass. You accused me, so I'd never connect you with Renzo and Bruno. You've killed everyone you worked with!"

Alex put a firm hand to Walker's forearm, but the day for tolerance was long past.

He brushed the warning aside. He would've taken another step at Goff, but he didn't dare leave Persia. Goff seemed to be acting alone, but the man was unpredictable as hell.

"You murdered the Green Berets in London, too," he told Goff, his anger rising like mercury in the middle of a New York City heatwave. "It was you who sabotaged that Blackhawk, then sicced NCIS on me. You planted all that evidence. You sold Emily Dooley to some asshat in China. A three-year-old little girl to an adult male pervert!"

Goff's eyes narrowed. The man was flat-out crazy, and whatever swim he'd just taken had done him in. He didn't seem able to catch his breath. His hands shook, but the shotgun in his hand was still plenty lethal. Of course, a coward like him needed a double-barrel to hit his targets.

It all made sense now. In for a penny; in for a pound. Walker went for broke. "You stacked the court against me. You, along with your NCIS buddies, contrived evidence, then leaked that evidence to the press. You worked with Prince Khalid to murder all those people!"

Goff's cheeks puffed with an outrageous, annoyed exhale. "You still don't get it, do you?"

"What?" Alex asked, still as calm as ever and once more steadfast at Walker's side. "That you're behind one of the largest human trafficking enterprises in the world? That's how you did it, isn't it? You used Navy personnel and Navy assets to move your cargo. Most sailors onboard probably didn't even know what you were doing, but they took orders well, didn't they? You worked for Peckering, and together, you bastards created the Black Dragon Syndicate to—"

"He worked for me!" Goff bellowed. "Damn it! They all worked for me! That moron Khalid! Peters! Pickering! Who do you think bought the meatpacking plant for Montego's sister, just so she could tear assholes like you apart? That was her plan. Steal your wife and daughter. Sell them to your enemies. Capture you and chop you into fuckin' small pieces!"

Man, this guy was insane. Yet he couldn't seem to shut up.

"Who owns this…?" He waved his free hand at the yacht as if that explained everything. "All this is mine! I'm the one who makes everything work. I'm the genius behind this world-wide-operation. But you…" Once again, he narrowed down on Alex, the business end of that double-gauge wavering like the heavy end of a post. "You need to die. You're fuckin' bad for business."

Walker felt Persia stir beneath his fingertips. She was coming around. Good. But he needed her to stay down until this mess was—

*BLAM!* Goff had just fired a shot straight up in the air. "Get off my Goddamned boat!"

"We're not going anywhere," Walker replied, still shielding Persia from this madman's view.

"Leave the girl. She's mine now. All of you. Get in the water."

"We leave, she leaves with us," Alex growled.

The business end of Goff's weapon lowered on Walker's thigh. "Like I said, she's not going anywhere. But you four… Get the fuck off my boat or I'll turn you into shark bait."

Walker knew it then. One shot from that double gauge would kill him and Persia. If he reloaded quickly enough, the next would rip Alex, McQueen, or Izza to shreds. There was no choice. Walker had to leave Persia again. His heart climbed up his throat—until he remembered that rope.

He stabbed a finger at Goff. "This isn't over."

"Off!" Goff screamed, his face red, the veins in his neck thick and pulsing. "Not the dock! Over the side. Get in the damned water! Now!"

Walker shot a desperate look at Izza as, slowly, she climbed the rail and dropped feet first into the harbor. McQueen and Alex went next. Then Walker. The way Goff's shotgun tracked him as he climbed the rail, he wasn't sure he'd get off *Persia Smiles* alive.

Goff looked down at them from the aft deck. He had Persia now. The ass leered as if he'd won the lottery. "You're finished, Judge." His weapon tracked to where Alex bobbed alongside Izza. He aimed. The bastard was going to shoot!

"Dive!" Walker bellowed as the blast boomed like a cannon. He couldn't see through the diesel-laden murk that gathered alongside docks. The water was so dark and polluted, Walker couldn't tell blood from fish guts.

Still underwater, he arrowed straight toward shapes that looked like bodies, arms, and legs. But another blast peppered the surface tension directly overhead, sending a dozen or so pellets zipping into the dark.

By then, the yacht's props were churning, making visibility nil. Walker had no idea who'd been shot, if anyone. Quickly, he withdrew to the yacht's hull. Surfacing out of sight below the rail, he finally saw Alex, McQueen, and Izza alongside the fishing boat behind *Persia Smiles*. They weren't helpless and they looked uninjured. He should've known.

Something big splashed right in front of him. Ryder! Shit! Walker grabbed his buddy, rolled him over, then slung an arm around his neck and under one arm to keep him face up. The engines revved. And smooth as silk… *Persia Smiles* eased away from the dock.

Goff finally had everything he needed to hurt Walker. He had Persia.

*Like. Hell.*

By then, Alex had swum to his side. "I've already called shore patrol," he sputtered, treading water as the yacht's wake rolled over their heads and into their faces.

Walker shoved Ryder's limp body into Alex. "Take care of him."

"You'll never catch Goff," Alex growled as *Persia Smiles* puttered past the docked cruise ship on her way to open waters.

"Bet me." With one last look to get his bearings, Walker dived, then kicked upward and rolled his hips and shoulders into the same speed stroke that had brought him from Cuba to Florida not long ago. Once again, he was swimming home. Only this time, that home was Persia.

The world disappeared as his powerful arms pushed water and the futility of what he was doing, out of his way. He had room in his head for Persia. Only her. Walker filled his mind and heart with his one good reason to live.

Stroke after stroke took him closer, but he still had to slow every minute or so to clear the water out of his eyes and keep on target. The yacht had to move slowly through this crowded channel, but she was gradually slipping ahead, and, inch by inch, Goff was getting away.

*No. He. Isn't.*

Walker threw himself into his task. SEALs never quit. Goff should've known that. Throw a SEAL a bone and what did you get? A shiv carved from that bone and stuck in your gut. This was it. The day he'd been living for. The crime he'd been condemned for. The day he finally killed his CO.

As if on cue, a rusted garbage scow chugged between *Persia Smiles* and the end of the channel. The yacht slowed. Walker advanced. Powerful forward strokes brought him within reach. And there it was. The rope he'd draped over the rail the day he, Brim, and Rover had gone swimming. The just-in-case rope, dragging behind the yacht like a good luck charm.

*Shit. Where is Brim?* Walker cursed himself for not thinking about his friend until now. The last time he'd seen the old guy, Brim had been ashore and taking Rover for a walk. But finding Brim had to wait.

Silently, Walker took hold of that rope, looped it around his fist, and pulled himself forward. Timing was everything. He needed to breach the aft deck, make damned sure Persia was okay, then end Goff. He'd be in the cockpit, steering the yacht toward the open ocean. He'd never know what hit him.

The garbage scow must've cleared out of Goff's way. The yacht picked up speed. The gentle wake became a torrent. Hand over hand, Walker forged ahead. He kept his head down even as a deep burn began in his biceps and pecs. Burn was good. Every inch gained brought Persia closer. It did!

Fighting the weight and drag of the water rushing over him, at last, Walker was close enough. He slapped one hand onto the swim deck and dug in. Then the other hand. Like the SEAL he would forever be, he pulled himself aboard, inch by inch, then peered under the aft deck railing. Persia still lay on the recliner, out cold and covered. The weapons everyone had dropped were gone from sight, no doubt tossed overboard.

Goff wasn't in view, but that rat bastard Rodrigo was still belly down and out cold.

Running a quick hand over his face, Walker scrubbed the last of the seawater away. Over the rail he went, his eyes fastened on the cockpit door. Gently so as not to wake her, he placed a hand on Persia's bicep. She was warm and breathing evenly, and there was his SIG, right where he'd left it, hidden within the wrinkled blanket.

He palmed the pistol, checked the breech to make sure it was still loaded, then crept stealthily into the master stateroom. He'd left something hidden there, and he needed it now. The universe really did provide.

Back on deck again, he headed up the few steps to the cockpit, his pistol in one hand, the 'surprise' in the other. His way forward was clear. Goff needed his day in court.

He never knew Walker was behind him until Walker stuck his pistol in the base of his skull. One shot would sever his spine and blast one helluva hole through his throat. His twelve-gauge lay on the deck beside his foot.

"Stand up. Slow and easy. Don't even—"

"Like hell!" Goff slammed the throttle forward.

Lurching backward, Walker landed on his butt, but maintained possession of his weapons.

Goff crouched, scrambling for his double-gauge.

"Fuck!" Walker cursed, on his back now, the yacht's powerful engines screaming, and all that forward momentum holding him down.

Goff's fingers curled around the shotgun's barrel as he lifted it off the deck.

*No fuckin' way!* Fighting Mother Nature's law of physics, Walker pulled himself up onto one elbow, tipped forward, gripped his SIG, aimed and—

The yacht bucked, sending both men bouncing.

Goff lost control of the shotgun.

Walker rolled to his knees, clawing his way forward.

Too late. Goff already had the double-barrel staring down at Walker. There was no time to aim. Goff had the drop on him.

*No try. Just do!* Walker stabbed that hypo of Special K into Goff's meaty thigh. And—

*B-BOOM!* Holy Jesus, two weapons fired simultaneously.

Walker ducked and cringed, sure he was dead. Only nothing hit him. Not a single buckshot. No impact. Lifting his chin from his chest, he looked to Goff. A dark red hole blossomed in his left shoulder. He sagged to the deck, his knees folded under him, and his head lolled back on his shoulders. The man was going down.

Walker glanced up at the bulky shadow blocking the cockpit hatch. "Brim!" he bellowed as he clawed his way to his knees, then stretched forward around Goff's body and throttled back. Instantly the yacht settled, the backwash of her wake lifting her high on the billowing waves.

"Hey," Brim growled. "Looks like I got here just in time."

He was the one who'd shot Goff. But the pistol in his grip and that killer look on his face… So. Damned. Beautiful.

"Sure… good to… see you," Walker huffed, the adrenaline pounding through his head like a sledgehammer on a rampage.

Brim lowered his piece to his thigh, the barrel pointed safely down. "Always figured it was better to be seen than viewed. What'd you stab him with?"

"Special K. Same crap I got stabbed with a couple months back. Damn…" Walker breathed, shaken and stirred, by hell. Stirred to his soul that this old warrior had only ever had his back. Like Alex and McQueen. Like Adam and Smoke and… and… Trevor and Julio and… Zack and Eric and… And every single last one of them. He ran the back of his hand over his eyes, more emotional than he imagined he'd be when this nightmare ended.

"Son," Brimley said evenly. "You're okay, you know that?"

Walker didn't want to break down in front of his friend. But he'd been running on empty so long. Fighting lies and slander. Always alone. Looking over his shoulder, until… Persia! He had to get to Persia. She was his anchor. One touch from her and he'd settle down. He'd be okay.

"Go git your woman," Brim said softly. "She needs you, son, and by the looks of you, you need her."

Walker could only nod, his throat too tight for words. His heart was so damned full.

"'S okay. I'll take care of this jackass. You want me to toss him overboard?"

"Ah…" *Yes!* "No. Bandage him up. He's got to go back to the States. People need to see. People need to know."

Brim set his hand on Walker's shoulder. "Trust me. The only people that matter already know."

That did it. One minute Walker was on his way to Persia, the next, he was wrapped in one helluva bear hug, his eyes watering, and his man card in question.

"Thanks," he ground out, back slapping Brim.

"Aw, git," Brim growled, shoving Walker away from him as if he couldn't tolerate emotional displays when Walker knew damned well he could. "Go on, git. Give that sleeping beauty a kiss. Not me. I got a mess to clean up. Don't need you tracking anything up on deck."

"Where's Rover?" Walker had to know.

"Locked up below. Why? You need another snuggle?"

Walker had to smile at that teasing insult. "Man, I'm glad I stopped in São Miguel."

The left side of Brim's thick, gray, street-sweeper mustache twitched. A twinkle lit the dark of his eye. "Me too, son. Me too."

# Chapter Forty-Five

Persia couldn't remember ever feeling so bad and so good at the same time. Heck, she couldn't remember much of anything. Not where she was or how she'd gotten here. Her poor head pounded like she'd just come off a week-long drunk, while the rest of her aching self was deliciously cocooned between the warm arm wrapped around her shoulders and… Walker's chest? Well, that answered a few questions. As long as she was with him, nothing else mattered. Her cheek rested easily against the solid muscles she craved, her thigh and knee against his hair-roughened leg.

Peeling one eyelid open, she breathed into his neck. What a pleasant view, the scruffy underside of this man's chin. It embodied all that he was. Strong and brave and true. His show of defiance in the face of betrayal. He was her one true hero. The man she trusted with her secrets. Confided in. Wanted.

Her fingers were splayed over his belly, another fine way to wake up. For two cents, she would've let those fingers walk up his chest to cup that sexy chin before she covered it with kisses. Instead, she traced her fingertips through the trail of hairs leading past his navel to those hot, steamy parts below. Once her fingers slid over and around his manhood, he'd wake with a smile and a promise. Funny how that happy trail reminded her of *Men Working* signs. As if any woman needed a sign to lead her into temptation. Man working, indeed!

But why was he in her bed? Or was she in his? Okay, that was disconcerting. If they were still on his yacht, why wasn't she rooming with Izza?

Panic intruded like a thunderclap. Persia shoved away from Walker, needing room to breathe. To think! The last thing she recalled was—

Peckering! Where was he? *Is he here!* Her pulse spiked. Her fists clenched. She would not be taken again!

The same out-of-control fear she'd lived with in Brazil, roared through her now, lighting up every last panic receptor, sending her survival instincts into overdrive. Would she never be free from monsters? Adrenaline screamed, *'Run!'*

He'd caught her! She was sure. After all the good she'd done in Minas Gerais... After all the women and children she'd saved...

Hysteria lifted inside her chest, demanding to be heard. A scream crawled up her throat like a tsunami, blocking her good intentions and her last shred of logic. Drowning her. Suffocating her.

Just as quickly, a big warm wave slipped up her spine and tangled in her hair. "I've got you, Persia," Walker whispered, his warm, moist lips pressed against her forehead. "I'm here, and you're safe, sugar."

"I... I..." She couldn't speak!

"It's okay. You're okay. Alex and McQueen, me and Izza found you, and that asshat Peckering's dead now. Come on, try to relax. There's nothing you and I can't overcome together. Deep breaths."

His chest expanded as if he needed to show her how it was done. Which he did. She was barely able to match his breaths with her own.

"Slow down. One, in. One, out. There you go. You're on my yacht. You're in my room. Izza's on deck. Ryder's on guard with her. Breathe with me, baby."

Clinging to his broad shoulders like a crazy drowning woman, Persia mashed her face into his chest. "What…?" she squeaked like the timid little mouse she was not. "Guarding who?"

"Peckering's gopher, Rodrigo. He can't get you. Trust me."

"W-w-what happened?"

Walker held onto her so gently. So carefully. "Peckering poisoned you, sugar. Least he tried. But the rest of us saved you, and Peckering's dead, and his toady, Rodrigo, isn't going anywhere. Right now, he's shackled outside the cockpit and Izza and Ryder are keeping track of him. I'll gladly chain him to the anchor if you want. You can throw him overboard, or you can make him walk the plank. Either way, he's all yours. Alex wanted to call the authorities, but I'm captain of this ship, and you get first shot at him."

"H-h-he…" Shit, it was so hard to think. Persia licked her dry lips, sure she was making a fool of herself, clinging like she was to Walker. "He injected me with something, I think… In my neck." Her fingers drifted to the tender spot below her ear. "I… I lost my phone… and Alex… I called Alex because…"

Because she'd known Peckering was going to kill her for helping Walker. She'd seen it in his eyes. True evil, as wicked as the malevolence that had poisoned Domingo Zapata's soul, had stared back at her. Then he'd pushed her into… somewhere else. That was all Persia remembered. Admiral

Peckering shoving her backward. Her falling. The sting in her neck.

She'd only been in a skimpy bikini top and cutoff jeans. An overwhelming need to cover up and hide consumed her usual sass. Her bravado. The disguise that had worked until now.

"Yes, ma'am," Walker went on smoothly, his palms moving warm and sure over her body. Stroking calmness back into her. Smoothing over her jagged edges. Filling in all those damned cracks.

Anxiously, she fingered the hem of the oversized t-shirt someone had dressed her in, so glad she was covered and safe and… She mashed her face against Walker's chest, breathing him in. Of course she was safe. Walker was here.

He kept soothing. She kept trying not to fall apart. Why was she always doing that? She wasn't weak or cowardly or all that feminine. She could hold her weight against any man. She could, and she had, damn it.

"Rodrigo injected you with an insecticide, but you're okay now," he murmured, his voice caressing all her ruffled feathers. "Did you know that boss of yours carries a freakin' emergency room with him when he travels? Once Izza persuaded Rodrigo to confess, Alex administered the antidote, and here you are, safe and sound. Ready to fight another day." Walker's hands smoothed down her bare back again, both landing on her butt. He spread his fingers wide and cupped her cheeks, massaging a fraction more of her paranoia away. "How are you feeling?"

"Everything aches. My head the most." *But I'm scared, damn it. I hate being scared.*

Now she knew exactly what the women and children that Zapata imprisoned had felt like...

Their utter helplessness...

The defiling loss of personal power...

The shame and humiliation...

The degradation!

Like Domingo Zapata, Peckering had left his mark. Panic swelled again. He'd overpowered her. Would've killed her—or worse. He would've sold her into the worst kind of slavery imaginable—forced prostitution, enhanced with mind-numbing addiction. She'd been smug when she'd left her pistol behind on the yacht, so sure of herself, that she was smart enough to take all comers. That she was only going to be gone a couple minutes. What a fool!

"I've got just the thing for those body aches," Walker said as he rolled over and reached for something on his nightstand.

Persia couldn't help but take advantage of the view of his deliciously tanned, naked male body stretched like a feast before her. The way his ropey muscles rippled along his abdomen and chest, over his ribs. The way his coiled bicep flexed when he grabbed whatever he was after.

This perfect view of the man in her life always seemed to pull her back into the here and now. Tipping forward, she kissed a path up the taut column of his neck. Nuzzling into that neck, she closed her eyes and breathed deeply. This was all she needed. The scent of this man's skin in her nose. The salty taste of her very own SEAL on her tongue. His strength and every last bit of his kindness surrounding her.

With a playful growl, Walker caged her inside his legs and arms. He rattled a small green bottle in her face. "No sex for you. Not yet, sugar. You've been through hell, and you need a couple of these pain pills and nothing but rest and more rest today. All day. Maybe tomorrow, too." His lips brushed warm and soft over her mouth. "Trust me, Persia. I almost lost you. I'm not taking any chances."

"I don't want sex," she breathed into his chin. Yet even as she told him that, she cast her gaze between them and down the length of his magnificent chest past his belly. Walker was a gorgeous, handsome beast with his ass in the air like it was and his manhood just inches from her fingertips. "B-b-but… I'd sleep much better if we did. I mean, if you want to."

Her sexy beast smiled.

"Oh, come on. Are you sure you don't want to make love with m-m-me?" she whined like a spoiled brat, nipping his chin. Needing quality time with him to replace the apprehension churning in her gut. "An orgasm will help me forget everything that happened better than lying around resting and thinking." *And worrying. And wondering…*

He blinked those sexy blues like he was having second thoughts. But then, "No," he murmured. But he sounded less sure of himself, like a little more coaxing might push him over the edge.

But Persia honestly didn't have the strength to argue her case. Walker was right. She had been through hell. She blew out a small sigh through pursed lips, not up for sex like she wished she were. She wanted it. Knew his mouth all over her body would help her forget. But what she needed now was the warmth of the massive body wrapped around her. Like a great, big, impenetrable castle wall. A stronghold with hairy arms and legs and muscles that nothing could get past or through. Her private force field.

Tears. Damned, weak, silly, feminine tears flooded her eyes.

Walker rolled onto his side and took her with him. He tucked her under his arm.

She let him become everything. Her rock. Her fortress.

"I couldn't get away," she cried, out of control again. "I… tried. God, I tried!" *Sob. Sob. Sob.* "But I never stood a chance. One minute I was… I was me, damn it! I was strong and invincible! I could fight anything! But the next, he was there, and someone came up behind me, and I was… I was… weak!"

"You, Agent Persia Coltrane, are not weak," Walker growled, his deep voice vibrating soft and low in her ear, "and you're sure as hell not nothing."

She closed her eyes, shocked she'd spoken those pitiful words out loud.

"You think you're the only one who's ever been shanghaied? Guess again, sugar. It was two against one. An ambush. By a fuckin' Navy admiral, a United States officer, you should've been able to trust, for fuck's sake."

Wow. Two fucks in one sentence. Walker's vehemence actually helped. The tension in her shoulders eased.

"And don't forget you were the one who got my sorry ass out of ICC's detention unit. Or that I was the one who got bushwhacked by a female Russian spy with a tranquilizer dart full of fuckin' Special K, and I don't mean the kind that goes *snap, crackle, pop,* either."

He was trying hard to make her laugh. She almost did. Instead, Persia sucked up what was left of her shattered pride, still shaking like a leaf. She forced a swallow, determined to catch her balance. "But I really would like to make love with you." *Someday soon.*

"And I'm dying to be inside you, but what you need most right now is this…" He dipped his head and swallowed her lips. "Just this," he mumbled, licking his way inside her mouth, his slick, sweet tongue sweeping her regrets away, making soft, gentle love to her tonsils. Healing her heart and soul with his breath and his mouth. Somehow, even his love for America seemed wrapped up in this tender, wet kiss. Sex or not, he was still giving her everything he had to give.

Tears welled again, but Persia hung on, squeezed them away, and gave back as good as she was getting. Walker was right. Her cup truly was empty. But this was also making love, just on a more elemental level, where spirits joined and soared and danced and loved without end. Where miracles happened and stayed and happened again. Where a damaged heart could finally… heal.

This feeling of oneness between her and Walker was intimacy in its most spiritual dimension. It came without physical demands or expectations. Without grunts and groans and precautions. Like the waves on an eternal beach, it rolled over her, seduced her with its gentle power of peace and wellness, of being right with the world.

Peckering was dead. She was not. That simple truth spoke volumes.

At last, a full cleansing breath filled her lungs. She sniffed, feeling stronger. Her body didn't have to orgasm to prove she was loved. Walker hadn't made a sexual play yet, just held her, and kissed her, and let her acclimate to her new normal. Yes, she'd been taken down, but he had her back. He always would. This solid wall of male dominance and power was right now, blanketing her with his entire body, with every last piece of his genuine, loving heart, and his all-American soul.

Walker Judge loved her. He'd told her, and now he was showing her in the kindest, sweetest way possible. He was all she needed.

"I love you," she murmured, her eyes closed, yet finally opened. She didn't need to be a one-woman army anymore. Never again. She was part of something bigger now.

She was part of Walker.

# Chapter Forty-Six

It'd take a couple days, maybe a good long sleep, but Walker knew Persia would be back on her feet and fighting the world before they made San Diego Harbor. There was no weakness to the lioness in his arms. Yes, she'd been beaten by a master jackass, but only because she'd been outnumbered. That was simply the law of the jungle. Even a pack of cowardly hyenas could take down a solitary king—or queen—of beasts. But it was Peckering lying on a cold metal slab in Puerta Vallarta's morgue right now. Not her.

Best yet, she'd finally told Walker she loved him. What more did he need?

At the moment, *Persia Smiles* was tracking north along California's southern coast, headed toward San Diego Harbor. They'd left Puerta Vallarta behind late last night. Walker'd told Persia she could have Rodrigo, but he'd already turned Peckering's toady over to the local police. Guess it was illegal to kidnap foreign citizens, even if you just wanted them to walk the plank. Go figure.

Not that she would've done anything to him anyway. But Goff? He was still here, and it'd be interesting to see how Persia handled seeing him.

By the time Walker had returned to port yesterday, Alex, McQueen, and Izza had Ryder out of the water and onto the dock. Someone had called the port authorities. A medic was checking all of them. Well, make that a medic was checking Ryder and Izza. Alex and McQueen were giving orders as usual. Persia had still been asleep, Rodrigo hadn't stirred, and Rover had still been locked below.

The first thing Alex had done when Walker'd tossed him a line, was secure *his yacht* to the well-bumpered dock. Alex had acted as if he were a mere deckhand, then he'd lifted his ruggedized sat phone from his rear pocket and held it out like a trophy. "You finish it?"

Brim had shot back with a surly, "We wouldn't be here if we didn't, would we?"

"Good. We now have all the evidence we need to prove your innocence, Agent Judge."

Walker had glanced at the sat phone in his palm. "Does that mean you recorded everything he said?"

"If he didn't, I sure as hell did," McQueen had groused. "When I get through with you, LT, you're going to be a free man."

Sweetest words ever…

Until Alex had caught sight of Goff, bandaged and cuffed to the aft railing like the dog he was. "He's still alive? Thought you said—"

"Wanted him alive, Boss." That word had rolled easily off Walker's lips.

"He's got nothing," Goff had sputtered. "Just you wait! I'll put all of you in Leavenworth."

"Who shot him?"

"US Army Sergeant Brimley Scott, at your service," Brim had said as he'd grabbed Alex's hand.

"You asshats have nothing on me!" Goff had screamed. "You can't prove anything!"

But Alex had grinned. He'd actually grinned!

By then, Izza was onboard sitting with Persia. But when she'd seen Goff's hands, she'd jumped to her feet and yelled. "That ring! That's the same ring! Crap, it was you!"

He'd turned an icy glare to her. "Stay away from me. You can't have it. It's worth more than all of you put together."

She'd spun on the ball of her foot, her ponytail whipping over her shoulder. "Alex! It was him! He was there!"

"Where?" Alex was on board by then.

"At Walker's trial. The first day. I've seen the video footage. He was in court, and I can prove it!"

"You can't prove anything!" Goff had roared.

"Oh, yeah?" She'd stalked to where he'd crouched, her hands on her hips and her swagger on full-beam. "You and Peckering thought you were clever to sit in on his trial, behind his back where he couldn't see you. But you're dumber than shit, because Hans has a video of Walker's trial. I don't know how he came to have it, but that was you sitting in the last row of the spectator section. And that ring on your finger proves it. You were there!"

"But, but, but…" Goff had sputtered.

By then, Alex had been peering down at the massively ostentatious, bright gold ring that, without words, declared, *"I always wanted to be a real Navy SEAL, but, boo, hoo, I'm a lying pussy!"*

Talk about penis envy.

"Stop! You can't—"

"You son of a bitch!" Alex hauled back and punched Goff square in the face. "Stolen valor will never make you half the man Walker Judge is!"

*Whoa.* Walker'd startled at that blatant praise. "Boss," he'd started to tell him not to hit Goff again. The man had sure looked like he might.

But Alex had hissed, "Shut up, Junior Agent. This bastard's not worth shit. Don't you dare defend him!"

Walker'd wanted to laugh and cry at that outrageous order. He'd been praised and bitched out in the same breath. Made a man feel like he was finally going to be A-Okay. But he couldn't let his boss beat a defenseless prick, err, man. He'd put a hand over Alex's flexed bicep then. Holy shit, this man was made of steel, piss, and vinegar.

"I know that," he'd told his new boss. "but America needs the truth, and to prove our case, we need to turn over a live suspect to someone other than NCIS or any branch of the Navy."

"Already taken care of," McQueen had drawled. "The US Attorney General will be there waiting when we dock. Pretty sure he's bringing a couple Marines with him. Heads are gonna roll, son. Trust me."

But Alex had still been steamed. And God, Walker had wanted to let him beat the shit out of Goff. He'd wanted to do the same, but…

"That's not who we are, Boss. He's the asshole. Not us."

It had still taken a full minute before Alex had cooled down and backed off. Damned if that spit-in-your-eye loyalty hadn't been further confirmation that Walker had chosen well.

For the duration of the short trip to San Diego, Alex had kept Goff sitting on his ass, flex-cuffed to the railing on the far end of the aft deck. He'd only uncuffed the rat bastard twice, once to escort Goff to the head, then when he'd allowed

Goff ten minutes to eat. Not one second more. Then back into flex cuffs Goff went to await judgement day.

If it'd been up to Walker, he would've keelhauled Goff for the duration of the trip home. But common sense and his innate sense of honor demanded he prove to the world and to Alex that, above all, he was everything Goff was not. Honest. A vow-keeper, not a vow-breaker. That he'd only ever supported and defended the Constitution against all enemies, foreign and domestic. That, like Alex Stewart, he'd done the job America had asked of him.

Turned out the Senator and Alex were good for their word. The moment they'd put Puerta Vallarta in the rearview, Senator Sullivan had called the Secretary of Defense and provided all the evidence his and Alex's teams had uncovered. Every last detail. About the bogus trial. The human trafficking. The gangs in Guatemala. Officer Bruno's disappearance. Renzo's suspicious suicide. Persia's abduction. The fact that Goff had also bribed the ICC judge. Hans Koning was the one who'd discovered that. He was another unexpected ally in what had become an all-out battle for Walker's freedom and his life.

The Sec Def had taken it from there. Yesterday's morning news had reported he'd fired his underling, the Secretary of the Navy. Not that the man had known what Peckering and Goff were into, but purely on principal. As the top naval officer, the Secretary of the Navy was responsible for everything that went down on his watch. Turned out, the Sec Def was especially pissed the Navy had been depriving quite a few American sailors of their rights to fair trials. Apparently, Walker Judge wasn't the first accused of crimes he hadn't committed, but the Sec Def was adamant that he would be the last.

As always, America's talking heads were spinning the blatant corruption under Admiral Peckering's command. NCIS, the Naval Criminal Investigative Service, was also under hot and heavy scrutiny, not only by the US Attorney General, but by the very press they'd leaked all their slanderous lies about Walker Judge to. But that was the media for you. Ready to turn on anyone, even their buddies, if it made a buck.

By the time *Persia Smiles* purred into San Diego Harbor, Captain Spenser Cole, the presiding judge over Walker's trial, had been called in to answer to the US Attorney General for his too-close association with Prince Khalid, as well as the US contracts that had come out of the now-suspect program management review years earlier.

McQueen seemed to have enough clout to make heads roll and do it quickly. The Navy prosecutor overseeing Walker's trial, Commander John Cudahy, had failed to show that morning when summoned to the Sec Def's office in the Pentagon. The Coast Guard had already found his body, floating offshore near Chula Vista. There was no evidence of foul play. Investigations were pending.

But Miss Sunday Night Breeze had no trouble making plenty of statements on last night's late-night propaganda show. Where Walker had once made a typical-male error in hooking up with her, Commander John Cudahy had turned his male stupidity into a fine art. He'd proposed to Breeze. She had a ring to prove it. And a prenup! No wonder he'd committed suicide. *Allegedly committed suicide, that is...*

Lieutenant Cameron Kroft, who'd never seen combat and shouldn't have been assigned to defend a Navy SEAL, had been swiftly summoned back from his cushy new assignment in Hawaii. Instead of sipping Mai Tais on a Waikiki beach, he was now headed for Basic Underwater Demolition/SEAL Training Center in Coronado, CA, per Sec Def's direct order. Looked like Kroft was going to learn what being a SEAL really meant. No pre-BUD/S apprenticeship training. No mentorship from any former or current SEALs. And no Admiral flying cover for his sorry ass. Just wham, bam, out of the kiddie-pool and straight into the deep end—with the real sharks.

By all accounts, numerous news reports, and most of all, according to Senator Sullivan's terse conversations with the Sec Def, former USN Lieutenant Walker Judge was well on his way to being a free man. Somehow, the missing Navcompt 3065 leave request had finally been 'officially' located. Lo and behold, it *had* been duly signed and recorded—by Goff— just like Beau Villanueva had said. How about that? The Navy made a big deal of how thoroughly they'd searched for what was now being heralded as proof positive of Peckering's, Goff's, Spenser's, Cudahy's, and Kroft's crimes.

Best news of all? Sec Def had ordered the brand-new Secretary of the Navy to get his house in order, and make damned sure former USN LT Walker Judge got his Trident back.

Overall, Goff's diabolical Black Dragon Syndicate had proven how poorly he'd chosen throughout his naval career. But not Persia. She'd only ever chosen light and life and honor, and those things had come back around to work for her now. For that, Walker was grateful.

But holy shit, it'd been one helluva close call. If he hadn't connected with Izza in Puerta Vallarta when he had… If Alex hadn't been the OCD asshole that he was and stored all those medical supplies on board… If Walker hadn't left his pistol with Persia when Goff ordered him overboard…

Things could've gone so, so wrong. A chill shivered over his shoulders at how much he would've lost if he and Ryder had taken off like he'd planned. Shit. Persia would be dead or whored out by now. Damn Peckering's and Goff's souls to the lowest pits in Hell.

The quiet rap at his door told Walker that Izza was back. That knock was his signal to get moving for the day. He and she had been taking turns staying with Persia. Walker suspected Alex knew he'd spent the night with his agent, but it seemed smart not to rub that fact in his new boss's face.

Easing out from beneath her lush, warm body, Walker showered, dressed, and exited the cabin as quickly and quietly as possible. When he closed the door behind him, she was still on her stomach and asleep. Her glossy black hair draped her pillow, and he could hear her breathing. Good. She needed to stay that way for another day or two.

"How is she?"

Walker turned to find Alex asking, not Izza. *Shit.* "She's having a hard time accepting that Peckering got the drop on her. But she'll be okay."

"Did you tell her about Goff?"

"Not yet."

"More nightmares?"

Ah, so Alex knew about those. Walker nodded, not willing to divulge anything personal about Persia. Those were her stories to tell.

"She decent?"

"She's asleep." Alex could take that however he wanted.

Unexpectedly, he ran a hand over his head and turned to stare off the port side. "I've got sleep-aids and pain pills, but they're just temporary fixes and all that crap comes with side-effects. She doesn't need them."

"Sleep'll do her the most good. She'll snap out of it. Don't worry."

"I'm not worried, I'm pissed. Should've known Peckering had someone watching the marina in Portugal."

"Well, he isn't a step ahead of us now, is he? Neither's Goff."

"So.... What's next?" That was unprecedented, Alex asking Walker for his thoughts on a way forward.

The more he worked with Alex, the more Walker understood the guy. "You tell me. You're the boss of this outfit."

"We still need to know who's buried in Goff's grave. And I need to tell you about Dan Peters and the Black Dragon Syndicate." Alex nodded aft. "Izza fixed breakfast. Let's eat first, then there's someone I want you to meet."

"Out here? On the ocean? What's he going to do, just drop in?"

"Something like that."

Walker joined his boss in the galley.

"For you," Izza said, handing him a mug of coffee. "Didn't know if you liked cream or sugar."

"Black's good. Thanks," Walker said, curling his fingers around the cup.

McQueen and Brimley were engrossed in a discussion about art and painting, of all things. Ryder had recovered from being taken down by Goff. At least, his head had. His pride? Not so much. He lifted a mug to Walker in a silent salute, his dark eyes mellow, yet still sharp.

Alex's sat phone rang. He palmed it out of his pocket, answered it, then handed it to Izza, his brows spiked nearly to his hairline. "It's for you."

"Me?" She took the call. "Hello?" Her eyes turned into puddles of melted fudge. "Aww, Connor…"

Walker had to look away. He didn't care if Connor was the world's biggest sissy. What he had with Izza was what Walker wanted with Persia. Only she needed rest more than she needed him. Yeah, it was only temporary, but how he wanted his woman.

# Chapter Forty-Seven

Turned out Walker didn't have to wait long. A low flying Piper Cub dropped two black chutes into the blue sky over San Diego Harbor. "That who you're expecting?" he asked Alex.

"Prepare for men overboard." Already on his feet, Alex ran to the swim deck shucked off his shirt, prepared to dive in if needed. How about that, not a single tattoo. That surprised Walker. The man was fit. Not heavily muscled, but athletically trim. Tanned. Scarred a little. But solid. A true alpha predator if Walker had ever seen one.

In no time, they hauled two more TEAM agents aboard. One was a mocha-colored behemoth, the other a blond that could only be Connor, the way Izza squealed as she tackled him. "Aw, baby! You're here!"

Her husband was not what Walker expected. Not at all. The guy looked more like a tanned surfer dude who'd just scored the perfect pipeline off Oahu's world-famous North Shore. Like a love-starved sap, he dipped her back in his arm, kissed and groped the hell out of her, right in front of everyone.

"Later, you two," Alex groused as he clasped the other man's hand. "Walker Judge, this is Zack Lennox. Loverboy over there's Connor Maher."

Connor stopped molesting his wife long enough to toss Walker a cocky grin. The guy was Walker's height and just as wide across the shoulders. Bright blue eyes. Perfect white teeth. One of those cover model types. Setting Izza back on her feet, he stuck a hand out. "LT. I've been looking forward to this day. Good to finally meet you."

Felt like freakin' *"Groundhog Day"* all over again. Someone else who'd actually *wanted* to meet him? Walker shook Connor's hand, still getting used to this new, expanded reality. Being welcomed by anyone and everyone was going to take some getting used to.

The man standing with Alex was everything Connor was not. Zack Lennox was built like a tank. Tanned. Shaved head. Black brows and a ton of wrinkles stretched across his forehead when he smiled. Which he was doing now. He'd already climbed out of his wet gear. Down to nothing but red swim trunks, he'd exposed a massive chest, and a tattooed sleeve draped over a shoulder that could've passed for a side of beef. His arms were as thick as tree limbs. Like Ryder, Zack was built heavy and durable. But his skin was lighter than Ryder's. More of cream, than of coffee.

After he donned a white t-shirt he pulled out of his bag, he didn't waste time with a handshake. Instead, he grabbed Walker into one helluva manly bro hug and growled, "Thanks, you son of a bitch. My wife thanks you. My three little girls thank you. God, man… I…"

Walker stilled as the guy who could break him in half choked up. Without thinking, he patted the massive muscles across Zack's back. "It's okay. Really. It's okay."

Zack shoved back and dashed the back of his hand over his eyes. "You don't have a clue what I'm talking about, do you?"

"Umm, no," Walker had to admit. But he wasn't going to argue with *"Mighty Joe Young"* here.

Zack tipped his head back and laughed, but when he lowered his chin, his big brown eyes were luminous with unshed tears. "You did it," he said as he dashed a wrist over his eyes this time, blinking like he knew he was crying, and he didn't care who saw. "You did what Alex and me couldn't. You found them and you ended them. The Black Dragon Syndicate. Do you know how many years we've been hunting those bastards?"

"Seems like forever," Alex said. "Grab a chair. Izza just made breakfast. Dig in."

"Nah, I'm good," Zack muttered. "Want to talk to this guy about the Dragons for a few. Join us?"

"Sure," Alex answered. "Cockpit okay?"

"Hell, yeah," Zack breathed. "Wait. I'll grab a couple drinks. Man, I'm thirsty."

Izza dashed to the table where she'd set up another tasty looking buffet. "Orange juice or water?"

"OJ's good."

A couple dripping bottles sailed end over end in Zack's direction. "Thanks, Izza. We won't be long."

She grinned like the cat that ate the canary. "Take all the time you need."

Walker settled sideways behind the wheel while Alex swiveled the co-pilot seat around to face Zack, who'd made himself comfortable on the bench. He'd already drained one OJ dry.

"Man, that's good," he said as he cast Walker a sideways glance. "I don't know about you, but jumping out of airplanes always scares the crap out of me. Bet you're just like Adam, though. You like skydiving?"

"I like flying, not falling. Adam can keep that shit," Walker muttered. "I take it you guys have both been inside the Dragons? Did you know Goff?"

Alex growled. "Only Peters, the lying bastard."

Zack shook his head. "Never met your CO, but yeah, a few years back, The TEAM tangled with the guy we thought was in charge. Guess Peters wasn't, but we didn't know about Admiral Pickering and Commander Goff then. D.C. Interpol Director Daniel Peters took that detail to his grave, but not before he and his goons got the jump on us in the office one day and…"

Zack seemed to be having trouble speaking, so Walker waited.

"Fucker almost killed us. Me and Mark. David and Harley and—"

"I was out of the office the day Peters brought an army to kill my TEAM," Alex growled.

"He'd already bombed our underground parking garage," Zack said. "Damn near killed Alex. That's the only reason you weren't there when he showed."

Alex nodded. "Yeah, but he didn't anticipate my TEAM."

Zack grunted. "What that smug bastard didn't expect was that you'd lived. Almost lost my job over that op."

"You did what you had to do."

Zack turned to Walker. "I was working a joint op with ATF when I stumbled across a little girl being sold by the Dragons. I couldn't just leave her. She was so cold, barely breathing.

Ended up screwing the op to save her. Pissed Alex off, but only because it put him in the middle of a war with then ATF Director Kevin Carducci. But it also led me to join up with Mei Xing, a mother looking for her kidnapped daughter—"

"The Dragons took her daughter?"

"Yes and no. Mei thought they'd taken LiLi, but Mei was a crazy, mad woman back then. She was running on nothing but fumes, not thinking right. Her boyfriend, LiLi's biological father, was the one who'd kidnapped her. Bastard took her out of the country. But when Mei got wind of a child smuggling ring working inside the District, she jumped to conclusions. Little did we know then, but it turned out her ex came from old money. He'd had her apartment wired, then paid a couple jerks to pass themselves off as phony detectives and cops to respond to her calls for help. When she thought law enforcement failed her, Mei took the law into her own hands and" —he ran a big hand over his bare head— "turned into a walking nightmare."

Alex nodded. "Mei was fierce. She finagled her way into the Bureau, DC Metro's main precinct, the local morgue, Child Services, even Immigration and Customs Enforcement. ICE. That about sums up what was running through her veins back then. Nothing but sheer grit and a helluva lot of ice water. Poor thing thought she was good enough to infiltrate my TEAM."

"Let me guess," Walker drawled. "You shot her down."

"You know it," Zack answered. "He's got the instincts of a stone-cold killer, but the heart of a lion."

Alex's nostrils flared as if he'd smelled something that didn't agree with him.

Walker let the comment slide, but Zack had summed up Alex perfectly.

"Anyway…" Zack lifted his face to the roof. "Boss tasked me to work with Mei. Mei thought I was a joke, a playboy. I thought she was a beast."

"Which she probably was," Walker added. "Quinn Dooley was the same kind of beast when he first approached me about going into Guatemala. Desperate moms and dads are like that."

"Yes, I get that now. But I wasn't a father then. I'd just come home from the sandbox and was working for Alex. After my time in the Corps, I just wanted to live my life, you know what I mean? I had a fast car and a bachelor pad. I thought I had everything. I was living the life. But working with her was like playing with a buzz saw every single day."

Alex grunted. "She was just a mom under stress."

"I understand, but nothing I said or did was right or good or fast enough for her back then. Every word out of her mouth was just plain bitter and nasty. Trust me, my wife's tongue can slice you to ribbons before you know what you did to piss her off, but" —he sucked in a deep breath— "everything changed the morning we infiltrated one of the Dragons' illegal foster homes…"

Walker stilled as Zack stopped talking.

The gleam in his eyes was gone. A full minute passed before he could speak. "The second I picked this one little girl up" —his voice turned low and somber— "the exact damned second I had her little butt sitting on my forearm… Her name was Song, but she smelled so bad, and she was so small and soft. She had cradle cap and lice and thrush, but when she blinked up at me… when I looked down into her pretty brown eyes… When she snuggled under my chin and sighed like she was finally wanted and loved and…"

His big fist came up and thumped the center of his expansive chest. "It got to me, Walker," he growled, his voice tight and his eyes gleaming. "Right here. She was so little and so damned helpless. That place" —the muscles in his thick neck worked as he forced a swallow— "reeked of urine and filth. Nothing was clean. And the bitch showing us her wares—all those babies—was smoking! With those little baby girls still in cribs, that old hag had a cigarette hanging off her nasty lip, and they were breathing her shitty air! And then we… Then I… Shit! I didn't think talking to you was going to be this hard."

Zack's fingers curled into fists. Whatever he needed to say seemed too hard for him to articulate, so Walker said it for him. "Then you knew exactly how Mei felt."

"Yeah, yeah, right. Then I knew nothing else mattered. I… we" —his index finger toggled between Alex and him— "had to get back into that shithouse and save Song and all those other babies. Like I said, nothing about that op went right. I damned near got beat to death, and Mei was insane with worry. But in the end, we saved three hundred and eleven little ones, didn't we, Boss?"

"We did," Alex answered quietly. "Some were straight out of China's orphanages. Others had been kidnapped. It was a human tragedy of epic proportions, right in the middle of Washington, DC."

"But we got Song out of there, by hell," Zack insisted. "Mei and I fostered her until we were able to adopt her. Not long after, Mother found LiLi in Paris. I went over there to bring her home. But man, when I finally had her safe in my car, she was just like her mom. Sharp-tongued and emotionally unstable. So damned demanding." He ran a quick hand over his head again. "And I loved it."

"Women do have a power all their own," Walker murmured, thinking of the dark-haired, strong-willed, and very capable agent he'd fallen in love with.

"They do," Alex sighed. "So, listen up. Walker, you'll team up with Zack and Senior Agent David Tao."

"You want me to work with you?" Walker asked Zack. "But you don't even know me."

Zack grinned. "So? I got a feeling it'll be fun."

"Exactly what do you do?"

Alex turned somber. "We rescue children and women who are either already being trafficked or who are in transit. We pull them out of human trafficker's hands, and, when possible, we end the bastards who captured them, as quietly as possible. David Tao operates The TEAM safe house in Phnom Penh, Cambodia. He's my single point of refuge in a culture that feeds off its young."

"You'll like him," Zack added. "David's a great guy. He's quiet and reserved. A Buddhist. Never gets mad. Could've been a monk, but I swear, the man can hit a gnat's eye at a thousand yards."

Walker doubted that. "And you? What do you do?"

The sparkles in Zack's stare darkened. "I'm the guy who goes into the dying rooms in China's state-run orphanages. I adopt the babies no one else wants. The ones waiting to die. If I can't adopt them, I… I find a way…"

"Jesus," Walker breathed. He'd heard about those wretched rooms. Couldn't imagine the emptiness in a child's soul that made him want to die. "You smuggle them out of the country?"

"Well, yeah. I'm sure as hell not going to leave them."

Walker pursed his lips. Man, these guys were bigger than life. And they had guts.

"I'll be honest, it's damned tough work," Alex said. "It's heartbreaking. Won't be easy."

"Always feels like I'm walking into a concentration camp when I first get there," Zack added.

"Is it legal? You going into China to do that?" Walker asked his boss.

"Hell, no. It's black ops work, and it's dangerous. But there are a lot of good people over there who can't tolerate what goes on with their country's unwanted girls."

"And I've got a few sources who've put their lives on the line for me. They've been telling me I needed more help and" —a big toothy grin split Zack's face— "here you are."

"How can you stand it?"

"What? Saving kids? Babies?" Zack shrugged. "Nothing else I'd rather do."

"But you can't save them all."

Alex growled even as Zack replied, "But I can save some. Like Song. I saved her, didn't I?"

Walker stared into this brash man's dark brown eyes. This was a warrior made of different steel than most. He enjoyed what he did. "So it's just you, me, and David Tao saving the world?"

"Beau Villanueva and Hunter Christian will also join this task force against human trafficking," Alex said. "Smoke Montoya wants in. Cord Shepherd, Seth's brother-in-law, too. Senator Sullivan's offered up Pagan Sinclair. You know him?"

"I do. That'll make seven. Seven against the world."

"Well?" Alex bit out. "Are you in or out?"

"Count me in. I've seen worse odds," Walker breathed without thinking more about challenges or risks. He already knew saving one child was worth everything, even dying for. Didn't know why he'd asked. He'd saved Emily, hadn't he?

"I knew you'd want in," Zack purred. "Until we heard about your case, Alex was thinking of ending The TEAM, weren't you, Boss?"

"My case?" Walker asked.

Alex's gaze dropped to his intertwined fingers. "Yes, you, damn it. The more I dug into your trial, then found out you'd gone to Guatemala alone to rescue Emily Dooley, I knew you'd fit right in. And yes, I've considered changing our mission from working federal contracts to hunting down human-traffickers one hundred percent of the time. But not every agent can handle these situations, and there are plenty of other people who need our unique brand of help." His head came up, his blue eyes lethal. "Like Mei, LiLi, and Song."

"Like Quinn and Emily Dooley," Walker added. "Quinn didn't know who to turn to without getting the media involved."

"What would those folks have done without guys like us to go into Hell and save their kids?" Zack asked quietly. "Their souls?"

"I only need a few good men." Alex sounded like a damned USMC recruiting poster.

But Walker understood the import behind those words. *Save the world.* His line of work. "When do we start?"

"Soon as you get this tugboat back to Florida," Alex groused. "That's where you're headed, isn't it?"

"Yes, but that will take a couple months," Walker answered. "I'll have to take her back through the Canal, and I don't sail alone." Not anymore.

"Then get it done."

Walker took that for permission to select his one-woman crew. "So what else is going on? Why are Lennox and Maher really here?"

"Because…" Alex scrubbed a hand over his face. "Like everyone else in this damned world, Zack and Connor just *had* to meet you."

"And you paid for them to…? Come all this way just to meet… me?"

"Hell, yeah. You're a fuckin' star." Zack leaned over his knees and grinned at Walker. "Welcome to The TEAM, Junior Agent Judge."

He saw that meaty ham-sized set of knuckles coming dead center of his still-healing shoulder. *Ouch.* But did he flinch? Not. One. Bit.

Alex muttered. "You'll do."

"You'll do, too, Boss," Walker replied. "Yeah. You guys will do just fine."

# Chapter Forty-Eight

**Two months later**

With a sigh, Walker settled on the blanket he'd spread under the trees beside Persia's bungalow, the same trees she'd hidden beneath the night he'd come ashore to kiss America goodbye. The night he'd thought he was alone in the world. Everything had changed since then.

Stretching his legs, Walker crossed his ankles, leaned back on his elbows, and breathed. Just breathed. It was a lazy, late summer afternoon. Blue sky stretched forever overhead. A handsome green iguana ambled by, his magnificent tail dragging behind him.

This island was as close to heaven as Walker could get. Straight ahead, his second home, the sea, redolent in all its turquoise majesty, beckoned. To his right, the bungalow that housed the sexy goddess he adored. Walker had a ring in his swim trunks' pocket. If there were a better place in the world to propose, he didn't know it.

Familiar scents of salt and sea rolled ashore with the breakers. The ridge of waving sea oats between him and the shoreline of this tiny island made a decent privacy screen, in case things went the way he hoped.

For now, *his yacht* bobbed calmly at the deep end of Persia's sturdy dock. He meant to buy it when it came up on the next FBI auction. The last two months traveling from California, through the Panama Canal, and onto Florida, had been time well spent. He'd gotten to know Persia better. He'd swum with her every chance he could. They'd played on every shore they'd dropped anchor on, as well as on every flat surface the yacht offered. For the first time in a long damned time, Walker hadn't felt the need to look over his shoulder. Not even once.

But of all the places they'd been, this was the only place to propose.

After off-loading Goff to the local authorities in San Diego, and after answering three days of questions from those same authorities, Walker and Persia had finally been allowed to hoist anchor and sail away. By then, Alex, Zack, Izza, and Connor had flown onto Virginia. Senator Sullivan was back on the Hill. Walker didn't know precisely where Brim and Rover had gone, only that they'd disappeared the same time Alex did.

The Navy scandal was no longer front-page news. Except for an occasional uneducated hater, America and the world had accepted Walker's innocence and moved on. The body lying beneath Goff's headstone? One of California's poor homeless, a middle-aged woman. No name. No birth certificate. No DMV license. No record in any government system. Which made the discovery even sadder.

There was no way to know who'd killed her, but the blunt force trauma to the back of her skull testified her death had been violent. Turned out the local medical examiner had also been one of Goff's buddies, which was why those morgue photos looked authentic. They were. Goff had actually posed for them. But there was no way to prove he'd murdered the woman, and his ME buddy consistently declared he'd only done what Goff had told him to do. That Goff provided the body that went into the casket. Not him.

None of that mattered to the US Attorney General. Goff's ME buddy went down for complicity. He and Goff were now sitting in the Navy brig in Miramar, San Diego, hopefully on their way to Leavenworth.

Walker wished he'd known then, when he'd worked for Goff, what he knew now. He'd give his last dollar for a time machine to go back and prevent Emily's abduction. Problem was, there were so many predators like Goff and his lackeys in the world today. And plenty more children who needed saving.

He glanced up at the sound of Persia's bare feet padding over the sand. She'd brought two frosted bottles of beer, a couple glasses, and she was wearing nothing but the slip of a halter top dress he'd bought her in San Diego. Mint green had never looked so good. This was their coming home celebration, and that dress would look just as good on the sand. Nothing was going to spoil what Walker had planned.

The longnecks made him smile. This would be their first alcoholic drink in months, and that beer was old. She'd bought it months before she'd gone to the Netherlands to bring his ass home. But he'd drink it. Hell, he'd toast to their new life together, even with stale beer.

Tugging her onto his lap when she drew close, he set them on the wooden tray he'd located by the blanket.

Twisting around on his thighs, she tipped forward and set two frosty glasses with the bottles. Her delightful breasts filled the cups of that halter top perfectly. Fully. She was ripe, sensual seduction personified, and her nipples were diamond hard. This woman had proven she could be a handful on the job any day, but she was his handful today.

Just that fast, every muscle in his body turned to steel. His palms settled on her hip, his fingers splayed, already absorbing the seductive sensation of her bare skin under the thin fabric of the dress. He licked his lips, wanting another kiss. Another taste. Another long, drawn-out suckle… But no. Not yet. They had business to discuss. Work first. Play—a lot—later.

"Before we head up to Virginia for work, I'd like to meet your parents," he declared, his voice uncommonly ragged, his throat dry. "Remind me what your dad's name is? I don't think you've ever said."

She hooked one arm around his neck. "I'd love you to meet them, my sister and her family, too. But I'll bet you've probably already heard of Dad. He's Dupree Coltrane."

*Oh. My. Hell.* "As in General Dupree Coltrane? The officer who accompanied Schwarzkopf into Baghdad back in 1990, after the invasion of Kuwait?"

"He was only a colonel then, but yes. That's my dad." She cocked her head, those sultry browns so damned sexy.

A man could fall into those deep, dark pools and never be seen again. It was an effort to pull back far enough from this alluring woman to collect his senses. Her scent enveloped him and her fingertips were fluttering like velvet butterflies over his skin. Everything Persia was turned Walker inside out. He couldn't think!

"Sugar," was all that came to his lips.

"Are you afraid to meet him?" she breathed in that come hither, kiss-me tone she did so well.

*Yes!* "No. Certainly not. I just…" *Damn. I was going to ask you something, wasn't I? Oh, yeah.*

"So you're an Army brat," Walker said once he could speak again. Only that wasn't what he'd wanted to ask, not by a long shot. General Coltrane was her father? *My hell…*

Walker had never once connected her cotton-growing dad with that particular, hard-driving US Army officer. General Dupree Coltrane? *Holy shit!* Being who he was certainly explained Persia's audacious nerve. Her dedication to country. Her tough as hell work ethic, and her innate ability to lead.

"No, I'm *your* brat," she murmured suggestively as she pressed her lips to his chin, then ran the tip of her tongue up his neck to his ear. "Want to do something about it?"

"I do," he purred, slipping his hand beneath the mint icing on tonight's dessert and his fingers into Persia. She was bare to the touch. Slippery. Ready for the real question of the day.

Her lips parted on a heated sigh. The long-ago day when he hadn't been able to perform was a fuzzy memory. He'd proven himself a hundred times since then. Meant to prove how much he loved her again on this very beach. Until the stars came out.

The sensation of her fingertips scraping over his scalp worked shivering magic up his spine. Walker tipped flat to the blanket and took Persia with him. She was right where he wanted her when she landed, straddling his hips. No panties. Just the way he liked her.

Arching his back, he slipped his swim trunks down his hips, then toed them off.

She tipped over him, her long fingers splayed on his pecs, her dark eyes shining on him with sparkling light. The rest of the world disappeared. He was so damned in love.

They were different people now. On the night they'd first met, she'd been running on empty and fighting demons. There'd been sparks in her eyes then, too, but they'd been warning shots. Staunch declarations for him to move on and take off.

He hadn't been in much better condition. Hell, he hadn't been able to make love to her correctly. But now? She owned him, his ass, his yacht, this beach house, and together they were shopping for a stylish home in Falls Church, Virginia. Her nightmares had stopped, and they hadn't had so much as a beer in months. He had his life back, and a career that promised not only out-of-sight benefits, but the satisfaction of knowing he'd make a difference at the end of every day.

When her hair spilled like cool, silky ribbons over his chest and neck, he pulled her in for an urgent kiss. Persia was everything good and sweet and holy in his life. She was perfect. The moment he deepened the kiss, he knew it was time.

But the moment he opened his mouth to ask, she whispered, "Alex and his wife are expecting a baby. Do you like kids?"

That seemed like the perfect segue, so he licked her lips and replied, "Love 'em."

"How many?"

"Ten."

"Ten? Really?"

Walker didn't really want to discuss kids at this moment, but he knew what this line of questioning was about. Persia had grown pensive and quiet their last days aboard the yacht. Knowing she'd almost become part of Goff's harem—or whatever he called his 'girls'—had changed something in her.

She'd been asking different questions since then, questions about the cost of childcare, even Medicare, for hell's sake.

Walker paused in his quest to propose and settled both hands on her hips. She needed to talk and he needed to listen. "Too many?"

"My sister has two boys."

"Are you pregnant?" He wouldn't mind if she was.

Breathing out a long sigh, she leaned into his chest and settled under his chin. "No, but I've never really wanted to be a mom. I had a career, everything I wanted. Until I met you."

He noticed the tense in her verbs. *Had. Wanted.* "Is that a good thing?"

"Yes. Of course. Since I met you, I don't drink anymore. I don't even think about sneaking a flask into my bag, and I sleep better. I'm putting on weight. That's got to stop, but the point—"

"You're healing, sugar. You don't have nightmares anymore, either. And you don't turn the nightlight on when we go to bed." Just saying those four words—*we go to bed*—brought a deep sigh up from Walker's heart. He and Persia shared a bed, and sometimes, they actually slept in it.

"That's because I'm with you."

"And because you know I'll never leave you again. You're stuck with me, woman. From this day forward." *For better or for worse... Until death do us part...* A lump formed in his throat at the unspoken question. Maybe if he just blurted it out...?

"Am I? Because I've always thought I was born for bigger, grander things than just motherhood and being a housewife. If I really meant to get ahead, I knew I had to be the toughest woman in the world. I brought Domingo Zapata down, damn it. I did that."

"Yes, you did." Walker let her own that dubious distinction. Her bringing Zapata down had nearly been the death of her peace of mind, but she didn't need to be reminded of that.

"But now…" Lifting her chin, she stared into his eyes. "Do you know who's tougher than both of us put together?"

Patiently, he settled both palms to the sides of her head, his fingers threaded in her hair. This dark-eyed beauty got him like no one else ever had. "Who, sugar?"

"Quinn Dooley and Alex and Kelsey, and Zack and Mei Lennox, and Mark and Libby Houston, and…" A sigh whooshed out of her. "And all the ordinary parents of the little girls Goff and Peckering were trafficking. All those little kids…" Another sigh. "Plain, everyday moms and dads are tougher than us, Walker."

Damn. She was right. His eyes misted as he stared up at his queen. Whatever Persia wanted, she would have. All she had to do was ask. But first, she had to figure herself out. Children were a lifetime of joy and pain. They deserved to be wanted. Cherished. That meant a man and woman had to make compromises and changes. They had to alter their careers and future plans. Because babies really did change everything.

"You do know I love you," he murmured, pouring his heart out to the only woman he'd ever loved. "And anything you decide is what I'll do."

"And you know I mean what I say."

He smiled. "So what do you say, princess? Want to make babies? Because I will if you will."

Leaning back on her butt, with her knees still snug beside his ribs, she said, "I just know I want… more. I feel like I've had my career ladder up against the wrong tree for a while now. I've done a lot with my life. I have, but I've watched my sister with her little boys, she's got something I don't. Then there's Mark Houston and Libby. She's a doctor and yet, they have five kids! Mark adores those girls. They both have crazy jobs, but they're happy, and somehow, they've made it work. All you have to do is see them together and… Then there's Izza and Connor and… I just don't want to die without really living. Does that make sense?"

"Marry me," Walker breathed. "When the day comes you're sure—"

"I'm already sure," she whimpered, melting onto his chest.

The sweet perfume in her hair messed with his brain. He nearly forgot what he needed to say. "I'm pushing forty," he breathed, wanting her to think long and hard about their age difference before she decided. She hadn't hit thirty yet.

"You're thirty-nine. I read your file, remember?"

"But you're still a kid."

Wrong thing to say. She canted her head, a lethal sparkle in her brown eyes. "Excuse me?"

"I just meant I'm older. Ten years older. I'll be decrepit while you're still ready to dance."

"So? Ten years means you're finally emotionally mature. You're ready to settle down. Besides, I've been missing something in my life, and that something is you, and—oh, damn." Persia rolled to his side, straightened her dress, and covered her bare backside. "We've got company. Get up, honey."

Not the answer Walker expected. He threw out his best two-year-old whine. "But I *was* up." *And you haven't said yes yet.*

She swatted his belly, making him jump. "Trust me, I was up for it, too. Now get moving because we've got company. Looks like Alex brought everyone. Hurry. The TEAM just landed."

"Answer me first. Will you—?"

Persia fell into him, her arm around his neck in a stranglehold as she breathed, "Yes, I'll marry you, but I want kids. Two to start with. A boy and a girl. Okay?"

His chest heaved. "Yes, ma'am. Two to start with, then we'll go from there."

"Now move it. The TEAM's here, and they brought their kids."

Walker lifted his head. This wasn't how he'd wanted his proposal to end, but Persia was right. Alex was already standing on her dock like he owned the place. He was helping a tiny woman and a little girl, both with long dark hair, come off a magnificently huge, pontoon boat. Another man… Was that Zack Lennox? The son of a gun had jumped the boat and was tying mooring lines to the dock's cleats. Looked like he knew what he was doing, too.

By then, a couple more pontoon boats had bumped the dock, and more athletic guys were ashore, mooring their boats. An outboard putted between two pontoon boats, bringing another man and a woman with red hair, along with two red-headed boys, to the party.

All these guys were former military. It showed in the way they held their heads up, their shoulders back. The way they bantered. Each of them had come with a strikingly beautiful woman. And kids. The three little girls with Zack had to be his. The woman, too. Long, sleek black hair, blunt cut and swinging. Had to be Mei. Which made the girls' names LiLi, Song, and MiKi, if Walker remembered right.

Still on his back and out of sight, Walker scrambled into his swim trunks. Persia had already stepped beyond the curtain of stately sea oats and called out, "Hey Boss! What's going on? Did I miss a memo?"

Walker left the blanket where it lay, but ducked into the bungalow with the glasses and beer. He grabbed a shirt and buttoned up, ready to face his new world. Back outside again, he shielded his eyes with one hand to his brow and faced an impressive group of…

Was that Senator Sullivan? Julio Juarez and Meg and… Trevor Duncan? Baffled, and more than a little emotional at the show of force now mixing it up on Persia's beach, Walker ran a hand over his head. They were all here. Once again, they'd come. Alex's TEAM. Persia's friends. His friends. They were all here.

The dark-haired man with the blue-eyed blonde tucked under his arm and five little dark-haired girls lined up behind him like ducklings, had to be Mark Houston. Julio and Meg had just climbed off the third pontoon boat. The giggling little guy they were swinging between them was… Walker's throat tightened. Dominic! He looked so damned good.

A hard knot swelled in Walker's chest. His lungs struggled for a breath he couldn't seem to draw. The last time he'd seen that little boy, Dominic had been in sickbay aboard the *Iwo Jima* and diagnosed with tuberculosis. He'd been near death, not expected to live. But look at the mischievous grin on that little tyke's face now. And he was fat. Chubby!

Persia turned back then, her eyes big and glimmering and tender. Running to Walker, she pressed her body to his side. "We have company, honey."

"I see that," he stammered, his jaw tight to keep his eyes from watering.

"It's about damned time!" Alex boomed. "Welcome home, Walker Judge!"

*Oh, hell. Not that.*

As if they'd been coached, every kid on the beach called out a boisterous chorus of, "Welcome home, Uncle Walker! We missed you!"

A thunderous roar of adults followed. "Welcome home, Lieutenant Judge!"

Jesus. He was an uncle. And he was falling apart.

Walker turned his back on all these people. Not today. Not now.

Persia's arm slipped warm and strong around his waist. "The TEAM's kids call us aunts and uncles," she whispered. "We're family, Walker."

"I can't," he choked. "Man, I… Persia, I just can't."

All he'd lost these last couple years roared over him like wildfire. He'd been running too long, an unwelcome cur in the only land he'd ever loved enough to die for. Made out to be a pariah by the greedy, self-serving press. Unwanted and disbelieved by Americans everywhere. Wrongly accused and condemned. Lied about. Slandered. A man so damned alone, he hadn't realized until now how much he craved being back in the land of the noble free. Of belonging to something bigger and far greater than the Navy. Of being home. Damn it, he missed his mom and dad and Kenny.

A big hand landed in the middle of his back at the same time a crazed, scruffy dog nearly knocked him over. Rover! Brim! "Hey," Walker ground out, his eyes watering plenty now. He dashed the back of his hand over his face, but knew he hadn't done it fast enough to fool Brimley.

"Good to see you again, son." Brim always had a way of getting inside Walker's heart. He'd trimmed his hair and mustache.

Blinking like a damned sissy, Walker looked his friend in the eye. "I still owe you for storing my yacht."

"Friends don't owe friends nuthin'," he growled as he draped an arm around Walker's neck, pulled him out of Persia's arms and into a bro hug that quickly turned fatherly.

Walker couldn't seem to let his buddy go. A stupid sob retched out of his throat. His dad would've loved being here for this reunion. But since he wasn't...

"Shhhhh," Brim breathed into the side of Walker's head. "It's okay. It's all right. Welcome home," said the man who'd probably never heard those words when he'd returned from Vietnam.

"I can't do this," Walker ground out.

"Sure you can. You just turn yourself around, and you tell these nice folks, hey. It'll come natural after that. Seems to me these people came a long way to see you. They care about you. Give it a try. Just say hey. Then thanks. See what happens."

Walker swallowed the hard knot in his throat and nodded. He'd walked into danger, enemy fire, and sheer hell in foreign lands. He'd killed terrorists with his gloved hands. But coming home to America and facing people who were actually glad to see him? Incredibly difficult.

So… with Brim on one side, Persia against his other, Walker turned and faced his new boss and the amazing TEAM Alex had brought with him. And all those kids. Damned if Senator Sullivan hadn't just stepped off the deck of another arriving pontoon boat. He'd brought the three Sin Boys with him. Two of their wives. Smoke Montoya and his wife and kid! Who wasn't here?

Kenny, that was who. Mom and Dad. The people Walker loved the most and the ones he would have gladly died for. The pain of losing them rose sharp and deep, unrecognized until now. He was home, but they weren't here anymore, were they? Once again, the loss of them swamped him. Shit, he had to get a handle on his emotions.

Persia leaned up on tiptoes and planted a warm kiss to his cheek. "This is the more I was talking about. I want a family, Hotrod. I want kids and a home and forever. With you."

Which was precisely what his proposal had been about. Not just him and her. Not just romance and making love. Not just buying a house together or skinny dipping off the side of *Persia Smiles*. But this damned big family. Maybe some were missing, like his folks and Kenny, Ryder and the guys. But a few of the people here had gone to Ireland and Portugal just to be there for him. They'd worked on his behalf before he'd even known they existed. This TEAM, these people, had already signed up to be his family.

And more were on the way judging by the size of the baby bump Alex's wife sported. Man, she was pretty. All these men's wives were, but none were as beautiful as Persia.

Walker turned to her, took hold of her slender hand, and did as Brim suggested. All he said was, "Thanks."

It came out hoarse and raspy, no more than a whisper. But the beach exploded into cheers and squeals and a bustle of activity. The line of fireworks someone had set-up along the shoreline exploded into sparks and whistles, pops, booms, and sizzles overhead. Several kids took off, chasing each other as if they played here all the time.

In the middle of the organized mayhem, Walker dropped to one knee and pressed his lips to Persia's knuckles. Tugging the ring out of his pocket, he slid it onto her finger. "I can't promise you blue skies and easy times, princess," he declared. "Life doesn't work that way. But I can promise I'll love you forever. Will you marry me?"

Her breath caught at the sight of the glittering rock on her finger, then quickly, those deep, dark browns brimmed with tears. "Yes, Hotrod. I'll love you until the day I die. Then…" she breathed. "I'll love you forever after that."

And Persia smiled.

# Epilogue

Peering through the narrow lens of his high-powered scope, Walker zeroed down on the stubby man crossing Tiananmen Square, headed to the Forbidden City in the heart of Beijing, China. Wearing a black woolen overcoat and the same color bowler hat, Mr. Su Chen Fong reminded Walker of Oddjob, Goldfinger's evil assassin and manservant in the 1959 *"James Bond"* novel. Short. Squat. Ugly as the sins he committed upon the bodies of countless, unknown, little girls.

Walker knew a cold-blooded killer when he saw one. Fong walked with his head up and with more attitude and arrogance than Oddjob ever had. Tourists scurried out of his way. Some actually bowed at the man who'd ordered and paid for Emily Dooley's little body. He had yet to acknowledge they breathed the same air. To him, tourists were mere peasants underfoot, while he, an emperor in his own mind, suffered their presence.

Dusk arrived early in autumn. It was nearly time for lowering the Chinese flag. Walker lay beside Persia, his cheek snug against the buttstock of his sniper rifle, his eye never leaving his target. They were hidden from sight, both on their bellies, trapped high within a maze of construction scaffolding overlooking the southern entrance to the Forbidden City. An impressively large photo of Chairman Mao hung there, as if he still guarded the ancient treasure.

Tiananmen Square was oriented north to south, the Forbidden City taking up the northern most end. Mao's impressive picture graced the entrance. The flag-lowering ceremony took place to the immediate south of his picture. Tonight's crowd was thick. The color guard looked as stiff as the ancient Terracotta Warriors. Tourists were plentiful. Security, as well. There was no place on earth more closely watched, patrolled, or guarded by armed and undercover policemen. Which made this operation almost fun.

"He's nearly in position," Persia breathed.

"I'm on him," Walker assured his wife. He'd never had a better spotter. Sharp-eyed and accurate to a fault, he also got to sleep with this one.

After his rowdy welcome home beach party with The TEAM, Walker and Persia had spent a week with her parents in Mississippi, where they'd been married by a Justice of the Peace in Persia's parents' front yard.

After a reception of mega-proportions, they'd then traveled on to Norfolk, Virginia, where they'd visited now four-year-old Emily at her parents' home. Never again would she be the innocent, wide-eyed cherub who'd once believed in *Big Bird*, the Tooth Fairy, and Santa. Poor thing suffered severe separation anxiety from what she'd lived through, along with night terrors, and killer migraines. She'd been clinging to her mom when Quinn's wife Luciana had first opened the door.

Yet when Emily had seen Walker again, she'd smiled shyly. She'd been hiding behind a well-loved fuzzy blanket and sucking her thumb, yet she'd reached for him, then snuggled under his chin. He'd been so damned humbled at the way she'd still trusted him when he'd taken her in his arms. It'd been hard not to cry.

To hide his emotions, Walker had bowed his head and breathed the flowery scent of her shampoo. It hadn't helped that Persia had been teary-eyed and wiping her face as much as Luciana Dooley had been wiping hers. But holding that delicate little-girl body once more, and knowing Emily was home and safe, that two fierce Doberman Pincers and a top-notch security system protected her and her family, made every second of the misery that Peckering and Goff had put him through, worth it. Walker knew he'd do it again. In a heartbeat.

Emily Quinn was the reason he and Persia were where they here today. Justice might be deaf and blind, but Walker wasn't, and neither was Alex. He'd signed off on this op without batting an eye. It was Walker's first TEAM op, his first time inside Communist China, aka the People's Republic of China. But it wouldn't be the last.

Officer Bruno and Renzo had already gotten their comeuppance, albeit not the way Walker would have preferred. They hadn't suffered enough in his book. Senator Sullivan had assured Walker that Goff was about to get his just rewards, a couple former NCIS officers, too. But the buyers of all the other sad little girls would forever stay free, unknown, and untouchable. That just wasn't right. They were the real monsters who powered this modern-day Black Plague, as Alex called human-trafficking. They were the seemingly unstoppable force behind every illicit transaction, every assault and perversion, every sweet child's death. More than anyone else in this disgusting business, they needed to be brought out of the shadows and held accountable.

But not Mr. Su Chen Fong. He'd never once hid his perverse appetite in shadows. Which meant the lucky bastard was finally going to get what he deserved—in public.

"It's definitely Fong," Persia breathed, as her unique rangefinder's optics verified the sixty-eight landmarks of her target's facial geometry. Ember had already matched the man's handwriting against his written purchase orders. Goff's meticulous record-keeping, his way of covering his ass in case his buyers turned remorseful, had provided Fong's location.

"Proof positive?" Walker asked the very capable Mrs. Walker Judge. He loved that she'd taken his name instead of the hyphenated version so popular today.

"Yes, but wait until he stops and bows. That'll be your best angle."

Walker and Persia had observed Fong for days. Every morning, he strolled from his plush apartment a mile from the Square to attend the sunrise and dusk flag ceremonies. Which had made him a very easy and predictable target.

Walker had once told Alex and Zack that he couldn't save every child caught up in human trafficking. But he could prevent this bastard from deflowering the little girl now caged inside his bedroom. If the current schedule held, Zack already had her.

Walker knew everything about Fong. How the children delivered to his residence were never seen again. How many he went through each month. Every year. How he preferred virgins, the younger, the better. But Walker also knew what the kinetic energy from a fifty caliber round did to flesh and bone. He knew how to blend in after a hit. How to fade to black. So did Persia.

"He's almost there," she whispered. "Get ready, honey."

Walker stilled, holding his breath pending his wife's next command. He'd only end Fong once he knew for certain his backstop was clear. Just one person needed to die today.

"Do it," she breathed.

Walker fired, then hurriedly jumped to his knees without watching Fong's demise. In seconds, he'd dismantled his weapon, and slid the pieces into the large, hollow pipe that comprised this section of scaffolding.

"You got him," Persia confirmed the hit.

Walker hadn't needed to look to know that his round struck true. Fong was dead the second he'd unleashed the power behind that fifty-cal round. But they did need to hurry. The rifle pieces wouldn't be found until much later, if ever. By then, Fong's remains would've been cremated, and the Judges would be back in the USA. Better yet, the world would be a tiny bit safer for little girls.

Some woman in the Square below screamed. Someone else yelled. Sirens shrilled outside and within the walls. A weapon fired, probably an overzealous guard taking down some unwitting soul who'd simply been in the wrong place at the wrong time.

"Let's do it," Walker told Persia as she finished breaking down her rangefinder, then plinked its cylindrical pieces into another larger than normal scaffold pipe. Zack had prepared for this day well. But the hotel would soon be swarming with security, as would every other building within miles of the Square. They had to hurry.

Side-by-side, they fast-roped to ground level, then ran down the alley beside the hotel, dodging construction supplies and heavy equipment. Two blocks over, they turned toward the Square. While they ran, Persia removed a violet-fringed coolie hat from her brightly colored shopping bag, placed it on her head, then tied its violet ribbon under her chin. She'd already turned her jacket inside out, converting it from black to bright purple, the American tourist look. He tore his black TEAM polo off, revealing the white t-shirt with a smiling *Mickey Mouse* beneath. His polo went inside the jacket draped over his shoulder. His other arm went around Persia.

Walker's heart-pounding strides matched hers. He swallowed hard at the enormity of the crime he'd just committed. With his new wife, no less. Somehow that ranked right up there with Bonnie and Clyde's crime-spree during the Great Depression. Yet they'd been stone-cold-killers, who murdered innocent people for the thrill of it. Walker had merely taken down a known pedophile no one else could've reached, and Persia hadn't killed anyone. Despite the very real possibility they'd be killed if they were caught, possibly after being tortured, she'd just been his spotter.

They were both running for their lives. But when she laced her fingers with his, her eyes twinkled. She loved what she did for The TEAM and the world, and it showed all over her pretty face. Walker hadn't thought he could fall more in love, but he did, right there, in the middle of Communist China.

He had to admit she was safer working for Alex than she'd ever been with the Bureau or the Agency. He stood rock-solid by his team. He protected them, fought for them, and without a doubt, Alex would die for his TEAM. He might be as rough as a battle-ax at times, and he could certainly be a flaming ass at the drop of a dime, but he'd never send a lone man or woman into a hellhole like Zapata's lair. The TEAM was his family. His friends. They were Walker's now, too.

If Alex had been tasked to bring Domingo Zapata down, he would've sent his entire TEAM to Brazil, not just Persia. He might've caused an international incident doing that, but office scuttlebutt told how Agent Seth McCray's foray into Cuba had already done just that. Then there was the gunfight in Mexico between Mark Houston, Rory Dennison, and some now defunct drug cartel a couple years back. As well as the terse face-off between Alex and some North Korean navy captain, the time Adam crash landed in the Pacific with four of Paul Reagan's much-touted, yet totally bogus, drones. Each one of those operations had created significant international incidents, yet Alex didn't seem to care. He took care of his people, and he was damned proud of it. There was no stopping the guy. He should've been a SEAL.

"On your six," Zack Lennox rasped tersely over Walker's earpiece. "Slow down, guys. We're almost done. Don't blow it now."

Breathing hard, Walker settled into an easy stroll, still holding his wife's hand. "You've got her?" he asked, surprised at Zack's uncharacteristic snark.

Today's plan had been two-pronged. While Zack removed Fong's latest feminine acquisition from his locked apartment, Team Judge terminated the pedophile in public. After which, all TEAM assets were to meet at a previously designated point for extraction. From Beijing, they'd travel into Cambodia. The stealth helo was already on standby for a speedy exfil. All Walker and Persia needed was to get the hell away from Tiananmen Square alive.

"Already handed her over," Zack clipped. "She's been doped, but David's wife will know what to do. Nancy's a doctor. Harry's straight ahead."

"Got him in sight," Persia replied breathily.

"See you at the helo?" Walker asked. That was the plan. Meet up with Zack, David Tao, and the rescued girl. Get the hell out of China.

But Zack didn't answer. When Walker glanced over his shoulder, the big guy was gone.

Walker doubled down on getting Persia safely inside the quaint Chinese rickshaw parked curbside straight ahead. Once aboard, Harry, a spry youngster of fifty-five, steered toward the south entrance to Tiananmen Square, where armed guards now blocked entry. One barked at Harry. Another shoved him back from the gate, his eyes sharp with anger.

Humbly, Harry bowed, turned the rickshaw away then pulled his 'tourists' alongside the southern wall and away from trouble.

Persia let out a soft breath. "So far, so good."

"Don't jinx us. We're not out of this yet," Walker murmured into the side of her head, breathing in the flowery scent of her hair.

"I wonder what's wrong with Zack. He's got the girl."

Walker didn't want to think of all the things that could be wrong. "Don't worry. Zack can take care of himself." But something wasn't right. He could feel it.

Harry set a quick pace to the prestigious Bank of China, a well-known, thirty-story landmark seven miles west of Tiananmen Square. Corporate helos were known to take off from that rooftop daily. It might seem risky flying from a state-owned banking institution in this particular country, but that was the point. To be seen. They just had to get there before the country was locked down. Which meant Harry had better run.

And he did. Because of Zack's humble friend, the rest of the operation went like clockwork. Within minutes, Walker and Persia were at the landing pad, then belted inside the helo. Zack was already seated across from them, quiet and remote, while David Tao sat up front in the co-pilot seat, the girl asleep in his arms.

Only now…

Walker's mouth went dry. This was that deadly pregnant pause that came to every operator in the last seconds of every mission. Just when exfil was imminent and freedom was so close you could smell it… When they weren't safe quite yet, and everything could still go wrong…. When he could lose everything. His wife. His life.

If they were caught now…

If this helo didn't take off exactly as planned…

If they didn't clear Chinese airspace in time…

"Here, Junior Agent," David said as he turned around and laid the unconscious girl Zack had rescued in Walker's lap, interrupting his brain-numbing anxiety. "You earned this. Please keep her warm."

The helo lifted, and automatically, Walker's hands closed around the tiny dark-haired girl wrapped inside the plush gray blanket. She was so fragile, dressed like a fairy in soft green silk. Obviously Chinese, her long straight hair had been braided and flopped over one shoulder. Her thick black lashes rested on plump, rosy cheeks like velvet butterfly wings. She smelled of baby powder, which only added another layer of perversion to Fong's sticky sins.

"She's so quiet," Persia's voice breathed over Walker's earphones. "Is she okay, Zack? What's wrong? You're just as quiet."

He took too long answering.

Walker's head came up. "Did he hurt her?" snapped out of him. "That's it, isn't it? Did he already—?" He couldn't speak the ugly word.

There *were* tears in the big man's eyes. Zack choked. He looked away, cleared his throat, and shook his head. But he finally whispered, "No, Walk. Not that. There were two girls in his cage. This one was alive. I had to…" He faltered. "I had to leave the other one."

"Shit," Walker hissed, his heart shredded at such awful news. After all they'd done, they'd still arrived too late. One dead child was one too many.

Rage filled his All-American soul. "How do you stand it? How the fuck can you keep coming back to this… this… country?" The precise curse for the vile practice of virgin sacrifice in this part of the world escaped him. How could adult males ever believe it was acceptable to hurt children?!

Persia's hand settled warm on his shoulder. "It's the way of the world, Walk," she said calmly. "Pedophilia has been around as long as murder. Fong didn't create it. He's just one of the many who practice it. A wise man once told me I wasn't Joan of Arc and I wasn't Jesus Christ."

He didn't have a clue what she was talking about. It was too hard to swallow or think.

Yet she kept going. "It's taken me a long time to puzzle it out, and Doc Fitz is a good one to talk with if you need to. But the thing is, we're not here to save the world. That's not our job. But we are here to grow and learn and become who we choose to become. That's our primary mission in life. We get to choose, Walk. Light over darkness. Goodness over evil. The point is who we are at the end of every day. Did we do our best? Did we do any good? Were we kind and loving and thoughtful? Did we save each other?"

"But there are so many kids out there—" The thought of what Fong had done to the other girl was unbearable.

"We can't save them all. Get used to it," Zack growled. "Sure wish we could. Wish I were Jesus Christ. Hell, I wish Persia was Joan of Arc!"

"But I'm not," she said firmly. "And we're here to save as many of these little ones as we can. That's your job from now on, and I'll always be here with you guys. Anytime. Anywhere."

The helo banked westward. They were well over the city, but not out of Chinese airspace. Zack had turned to the window, maybe thinking of his girls and his wife. Still hurt and still as angry as Walker. But just like Walker, going to strap on and perform this same type of operation again tomorrow and the next day and the next. For as long as he could.

Freeing one arm, Walker drew Persia inside this precious bubble of life. His heart was back on track and his goal was once more crystal clear. "You mean everything to me, I hope you know that."

She leaned into Walker, her dark brown eyes focused on the sleeping princess in his arms. "I do. Isn't she beautiful? Makes you want a baby, huh?"

He smiled at the way her female mind worked these days. Persia was definitely baby hungry. Slipping his headset off so no one would hear, he leaned into her ear and said, "Not exactly, but it does make me want to make you."

That earned him one of her heart-melting smiles. "You're incorrigible, Hotrod."

And just like the first time he'd met Persia, Walker was once again Hotrod and the Princess. Yeah. He could do it. He could spend the rest of his life saving princesses. Maybe a few princes. A few queens. He'd save as many trafficked victims as he could. One at a time.

That was what SEALs did. They never slowed down, never backed down, or gave in. They geared up, showed up, and gave their all. Sometimes their lives.

Always their hearts.

# *The End*

***Thank you for reading Walker's story!***

You are the key to this book's success

Please tell other readers why you liked WALKER by leaving an honest review at the retail site where you purchased it.

Recommend it to your friends. Lend it. Most of all, enjoy it!

# Other Irish Winters' best-selling books/series

## *In the Company of Snipers*

*Alex*
*Mark*
*Zack*
*Harley*
*Connor*
*Rory*
*Taylor*
*Gabe*
*Maverick*
*Cassidy*
*Adam*
*Lee*
*Ky*
*Hunter*
*Eric*
*Jake*
*Seth*
*Beau*
*Renner*
*Beckam*
*Christmas Hearts*

***Coming soon:***
*Jamison*

## *Deuces Wild*
*King of Hearts*
*Joker Joker*
*One-Eyed Jack*
*Ace*

## *Hearts and Ashes*
*Smoke*
*Ash*

## *SOBs Novels*
*Angel*
*Assassin*
*Vaquero*

***Coming soon:***
*Kruze Sinclair's story*

The best way to keep up with my new releases, giveaways, and actionable intel is to sign up for my spam-free newsletter at IrishWinters.com.

Keep reading for another tasty tidbit!

# Preview of Vaquero

## An SOBs Novel, #3

**JULIO JUAREZ**, currently attached to an elite, former military group of covert presidential watchdogs, watched and waited in the trees. He wouldn't move until Pagan Sinclair lifted the woman he loved, Julio's sister, into his arms and carried her into her poor excuse of a house. It had taken Pagan nearly two years to track Paloma down. They had a lot of catching up to do.

The hut she called home was insufficient by United States standards, but she was happy here. She'd made a life for herself in this humble Mexican village. Better yet, the people accepted her. Julio'd checked. Everyone thought highly of her. They might not be rich or famous, but it was obvious they considered her part of their *familia*. That was all Julio wanted for his baby sister, that she finally had what she'd been searching for.

Whether Pagan actually stayed in this part of Mexico for long remained to be seen. Julio suspected not. The Sinclair Boys all had bigger-than-life, winner-takes-all personas. He and his brothers, Chance and Kruze were meant for better things than the simple, unobtrusive, backward ways of village life. Pagan was one of those Chris Kyle types, a former Navy

SEAL still out to save the world. He'd been born for more than happily-ever-after in a wooden hut. That'd never be enough for him.

But the Sin Boys were not Julio's problem, and he'd interfered in his sister's life enough. "What do you say, *amigo*?" he asked the sniper fidgeting at his side. "Are we done here?"

"Yeah. He's got what he's always wanted. Let's move." Kruze grunted as his fingertips toyed with the cigarette he had yet to light. Whether they realized it or not, snipers who smoked had a death wish. If tobacco didn't kill them, their target would once he or she caught a whiff off that cancer stick. Kruze was in desperate need of a nicotine fix. It was time to move before Pagan realized he'd been followed.

Julio faced west. The Pacific lay beyond the sandy, grass-covered berm, so close he could smell the salt in the water and the seaweed on shore.

Paloma had chosen her hideaway well. Southeast of the Baja Peninsula and north of Guadalajara, she could've lived out the rest of her days here if she wanted. Maybe she would, but Julio doubted that also.

Now that Pagan had come for her, it was easier to leave. Julio had a date with the ocean. One he couldn't break. That was where he was headed. To the Pacific and his dead wife, Bianca.

"Where to?" he asked his *compadre*.

Kruze hooked a thumb over one shoulder. "Back to Sonora." Which meant he'd soon cross the border from Sonora into Tucson, where he'd catch a ride home to Montana.

Julio had never understood this recalcitrant Sinclair brother. Of the three, Kruze was the tight-lipped one, caught forever between Chance, his domineering older brother, and Pagan, the razor-sharp baby of the three. Surrounded by a good strong family, Kruze still didn't seem to appreciate the richness of having two brothers who loved him the way Chance and Pagan did. If anything, Julio got the impression Kruze avoided his brothers, which was just plain sad. *Familia* meant everything to Julio. He'd give his soul to have his back.

But that day was gone. During the past two years, Julio had lost everything. With a sigh, he offered his hand. "Then this is adios, *amigo*."

Kruze squeezed harder than Julio expected. But no problem. Everything with Kruze seemed to be a contest of wills or strengths. As if he needed to prove he was tougher, he stared Julio down and held on for a fraction of a second too long.

Wincing, Julio let his friend think he'd won. What did it matter? In the end, they were all losers.

"I'll see you around, won't I?" Kruze asked, suddenly more perceptive than Julio had given him credit for.

Playing along, he lifted his shoulders. "Of course. Why wouldn't you?"

"Hell, I don't know," Kruze muttered, as he let go and ran his fingers over his head. "Just thought maybe you were tired or something. Maybe sick and tired. Like me."

"We are all sick and tired, my friend." Wasn't that the truth? "But there's someone else I need to visit before I leave. Be at peace, brother." Then he lied and said, "If you need me, call. I will always come."

Kruze's head nod said he believed his friend. "Later then," he said, as he faded into the fronds and tall grasses that grew along this stretch of the beach.

Breathing a sigh he hadn't realized he'd been holding, Julio set a steady pace away from Paloma and toward the pounding surf. This stretch of the Pacific wasn't the exact location he'd planned on, but it was the same ocean Bianca had once sought out, and that was good enough.

He ran his palms over the tips of thigh-high grasses that clung to the sandy shoreline, letting them tickle what was left of the shredded husband and father in him. Which wasn't much. But Bianca would've loved this beach and this view. So would Tomas. Which was why Julio was here.

The tide was in. The tremendously huge rollers pounded the surf, demanding to be heard perhaps even miles away. Anyone might slip and fall to their death. It was possible, especially if they were foolish enough to be caught on those massive rock fingers that broke through the sand and reached for the ocean. That took the beating the surf dished out. That waited for him.

Gulls hovered overhead, caught in the brisk breeze like living kites. They squawked. Their silvery gray wings flapped. They screeched and they called. And once again, Julio heard Bianca's sweet siren call in the wind.

*'Come with me,'* she begged again. Just like she'd begged that last day.

Yes. This stretch of the Pacific would work just fine. He would leave the earth here. He could float away and finally be done with the lies all survivors told their well-meaning friends and neighbors. Because, no. He was not okay, and he would never be okay again. The pain had to stop. This was the only way.

The greatest regret Julio carried was that he hadn't gone with Bianca that day eighteen months ago. Her depression had grown more stifling over the three months since she'd been found. But sweet battered Tomas had cried non-stop the night before. It wasn't until early morning that he'd finally fallen asleep from exhaustion. Their son hadn't been right since Julio rescued them from Domingo Zapata's hellish, Brazilian home. But worse, Julio hadn't understood how Bianca could want to run away to the beach when her only child needed her so desperately.

So he'd held Tomas, while Bianca left the two of them behind. She'd always told him that sitting near the ocean gave her hope. Like a fool, he'd believed her. But hope was not what she'd gone to find that day. Only relief from the demons Zapata's cruelty had embedded deep in her soul. Only the final peace of never having to wake again.

Ironically, a SEAL had pulled her lifeless body out of the ocean just off Coronado that morning. A SEAL like Julio could've been, had Zapata not broken his life and ripped his family away. This guy had simply been swimming with his girlfriend when he'd spotted Bianca. But he'd never resuscitated her. Hadn't even tried. There was no need. No reason. You can't bring a woman who'd slashed her forearms from wrists to elbows back to life.

Bianca finally had what she'd wanted. A way out.

As for poor sweet Tomas? Julio swiped at the bitterness stinging the corners of his eyes. He hadn't been able to save his son, either. The two people in the world he treasured most were gone. In the end, Zapata had taken everything. Even Tomas' will to live.

The breeze off the ocean was stiff once Julio crested the berm, and at last, the dazzling Pacific stretched wide and long, deep and turquoise-blue ahead of him. He could almost feel its tender, cold embrace wrapping around him. Holding him down. His greatest fear at this pivotal point in time was that he'd struggle when the final moment came. That his body's natural instinct to survive would kick in and sabotage everything. That he'd be forced to live without Bianca and Tomas.

Like his wife, Julio needed the pain to end. His soul begged for relief. Julio steeled his courage. It must not fail in this, his final endeavor.

An old man tottered along the shore at Julio's left while a black dog scampered into the waves, chasing sandpipers or fish. Julio no longer cared what the man saw or who the dog belonged with. He truly cared about so few things these days. Now that Paloma was in Pagan's good hands, he had one less reason to worry or live.

With one hand, he tugged his shirt over his head, tossed it to the sand, and began jogging along the shore. That way the old man and the dog wouldn't think it suspicious when he dove into the surf. They might think he was crazy. They might try to rescue him. But by then, Julio's powerful strokes would've taken him beyond their reach. He was an excellent swimmer. Every SEAL, even the ones who rang out, knew how to swim. He'd give it his best until he tired, then he'd roll onto his back and float. He'd close his eyes and pray, until the Pacific took him under the way it had taken Bianca.

He was deep in the shallows when a buzz in his rear pocket told him he had an incoming call. Julio's heart kicked an odd beat and a half. He stopped short of the beckoning waves. "No," he told himself with conviction. "It's too late. I'm not answering."

But yes. His dutiful fingers had already maneuvered the cell into his palm, and…

*Okay, fine. One last call. This won't take long.*

"Hello?" he asked, as he turned aside from the breeze to better hear his caller.

"McQueen here. Got a minute?" Sullivan asked, as in Senator McQueen Sullivan, the force behind the darkest black ops team in the United States. Sullivan was a devil in his own right.

Julio let his gaze scan the distant western horizon where Bianca waited and whispered, *'Come with me. I'm waiting.'* "Actually, sir, I'm in the middle of something important. Can I call you back?"

"No," McQueen bit out, his cheery Texas twang gone, and his I-am-the-boss, do-you-want-a-piece-of-me persona radiating loud, clear, and nasty over the connection.

Automatically, Julio snapped to attention. His shoulders squared. His gut sucked in like it had been trained to. His brain cleared enough that his mouth replied, "Yes, sir. What can I do for you?"

"I've got trouble in Brazil. A former Army corporal. Duncan's his name. Runs an orphanage. Claims he and his kids need immediate evac. Didn't ask why, because I don't care when kids are involved. Can you do it or not?" Sullivan might make it sound like a question, but Julio knew an order when he heard one.

"But sir, isn't that *Dia de Muertos* territory?"

Like the *Sin Boys*, the *Dia de Muertos* were another of McQueen's deep, dark, black ops teams. He managed several. The Sinclairs handled terrorist troubles in the Middle East. The *Lone Wolves,* a covert team of former Army Rangers known to frequent the inner workings of Russia and China, operated out of central Wyoming. *The Panthers*, an elusive group of former CIA agents, worked deep in the Everglades, as well as both Atlantic and Gulf sides of the Florida panhandle. Former FBI agents, who'd seen too much and felt like they'd done too little, comprised The *Night Shadows.* They resolved American terrorist issues in general, from sea to shining sea.

But the grief caused by South American despots and tyrants, belonged to the deadly *Dia de Muertos,* headquartered out of New Mexico. Comprised of an elite team of three former USA border guards, they were the ones who should handle this assignment. Not a guy on his way to meet his dead wife, who even now called to him with a hushed but persuasive, nearly irresistible, *'Come, Julio. Please, come to me. Join me. I've missed you.'*

"No go, Juarez," McQueen replied tersely. "Lost two of those agents last night. Firefight outside of Tegucigalpa, Honduras. I'm in trouble. I need you."

Julio's heart sank at the thought of his brothers' deaths. "Which agents, sir?"

"Diego and Seb. Santiago's bringing their bodies home today. They'll be at Dover before nightfall, and I'll meet them there. Can you do it or not, damn it? This is urgent. I can't wait."

This was another unexpected blow. A loss for the world, not just the States. Julio had known Diego Cortez and Sebastian Torres from his Navy days. They hadn't rung out, and had gone on to become decorated SEALs. Diego signed up to work for Sullivan as team leader of the ruthless *Dia de*

*Muertos.* "But I work directly for the President, sir. Have you cleared it with—"

"Yes, Goddamnit. President Adams is on board. Did you hear what I said? Kids are involved. Orphans, damn it. The world's lost enough of its next generation. Are you with me or not?"

Julio cast one last longing look toward the ocean.

"Talk to me, Juarez. Someone's got to replace Diego. I need an answer, ASAP."

"You want me to lead *Dia de Muertos*?" *Unbelievable.* "Now?" *When I have nothing to live for?* "Why me?"

"Yes, now, damn it. Because more than any man on this team, I trust you. Sign up with me once and for all. Be the leader I know you are. Say yes."

Julio could actually hear McQueen's fingertips drumming his desk over the line.

"No," he replied evenly. He didn't want anything but out of the highly secret, super-covert world. Not only no, but Hell no. He'd lost too much already. He was done with too much death and not enough family.

Only now that he thought about it... Kids were involved? Orphans? Innocents like Tomas?

Julio glanced one last time at the Pacific with its cold, endless embrace. Bianca wasn't really out there, was she? The only part left of the beautiful body he'd had cremated, according to her last wishes, were ashes. Even those he'd let loose on the outgoing tide of a different shore of this same ocean. The mighty Pacific had done what it did best. It'd diluted her earthly remains and dispersed what was left, so far and so wide not a trace could ever be found.

The voice he'd thought he'd heard wasn't hers, either. It was just the wind moaning over the waves, luring his broken heart with the only thing it had to offer. Cold and final death. Like Bianca's. Like Tomas'. That was all. In her passive-aggressive way, she'd reached behind her and she'd taken the tiny boy Julio still loved with her.

*Dulce Madre de Dios!* This was a hard decision. Stay and die? Leave the only family he had left behind? Paloma and Pagan. The men who called him brother. Chance and Kruze Sinclair. McQueen Sullivan. Rick Santiago. Or live, when he couldn't seem to find any reason to. Rescue other poor, defenseless children. Find a way to breathe around the hole in his heart.

Julio cast a lingering glance over his shoulder, back to where Paloma's humble little home stood beyond the sandy berm and those gently waving grasses. Back to where she and Pagan were no doubt happily getting busy. Back to where another life might just be starting, if Pagan finally had his way. Julio hoped he did. The man wanted a family more than any man Julio had ever known. Except for him. Only Julio wanted his family back.

But that wasn't going to happen, was it? He'd lost the right to ever be called lover again.

Husband.

Daddy.

Then Sullivan made it worse. "It's Oz, Goddamn it. Oz is hunting Duncan and those kids while we're wasting time talking. You go in now, you secure Duncan and his orphans. Then you wipe Oz's ugly ass off the face of the earth once and for all. You hear me? With extreme prejudice, by hell."

*Oz.*

With that one word, the Earth stopped spinning. The tumultuous waves of the great Pacific ceased crashing. Even the seagulls overhead held their peace. All creation sucked in a combined breath, waiting on Julio's answer.

He'd frozen, but not in terror. Julio wasn't afraid, not of Oz, nicknamed after the *'great and terrible'* deceiver from the movie, *"Wizard of Oz"*. Oz, as in Orlando Zapata, the sadistic baby brother of Domingo Zapata, the diabolical spawn from Hell who'd kidnapped and tormented Bianca and Tomas until they'd broke.

If anyone needed to die, it was Oz. Domingo Zapata, too. But, for the moment, he was untouchable, locked away in a top-secret private facility north of Deadhorse, Alaska, alongside the former governor of Oregon, Mick Tennyson. It had taken every last shred of Julio's restraint not to kill Zapata back then. It would've been easy, and he would have done it. No one would have blamed him.

But the memory of his son had stopped him from exacting righteous judgment on Domingo. Pure, sweet Tomas hadn't asked for the life sentence he'd been given. Neither he nor his father could've foreseen the trials he'd had to endure. Julio refused to add the burden of a revenge killing on that small soul's shoulders. He'd strived to be an honorable father. Had even accompanied Zapata the day he'd been locked forever away.

A man could die in there. Julio hoped Domingo would. Then, and only then, could the need to strangle Zapata with his bare hands until his ugly face turned red, then blue, fade away. Julio's fingers clenched tight at the thought of that bastard's black eyes rolling back in his head when he gasped his last wicked breath.

It was hard to breathe. Even now, Domingo Zapata was still killing him.

"I'll do it," Julio blurted before he gave himself more time to think.

"Well, good," McQueen replied, as if he'd known what Julio's answer would be all along. "Check your email. I sent an encrypted file with what details I know now. You'll fly out of Houston. Be there by seven tomorrow morning. Locate and hook-up with former US Army Corporal Duncan as soon as you can. I'll send coordinates where to find him."

"Sir, may I ask how Duncan knew to call you?"

"He didn't. Duncan sent word to an Army Ranger I know. Asked for help. Said Oz is after his kids. Don't know how many. Only know Oz is behind the disappearance of hundreds of adults and children in Minas Gerais, Brazil. He forces them to work his mines. Kills those who refuse. He's a bastard. Keep your sat phone charged. I'll forward more info as I dig it up. Be safe."

The connection ended. Julio sucked in a lungful of the contrary winds blowing off the Pacific. Swallowing hard, he pocketed his cell. Bianca would have to wait.

# About the Author

Irish Winters…

…is a best-selling author who, when she isn't writing, dabbles in poetry, grandchildren, and rarely (as in extremely rarely) the kitchen. More prone to be outdoors than in, she grew up the quintessential tomboy on a dairy farm in rural Wisconsin, spent her teen years in the Pacific Northwest, but calls the Wasatch Mountains of Northern Utah, home. For now.

She believes in making every day count for something, and follows the wise admonition of her mother to: *"Look out the window and see something!"*

Connect with Irish online:
On Facebook: https:/www.facebook.com/author.irishwinters
On Twitter: https://twitter.com/irishwinters1
Or at http://www. IrishWinters.com